Harkers

Harkers

Karen,
Just a little something
I dreamed up along
the way.
     Love,
       Dad. *6/03/03*

Ed Matthews

Copyright © 2003 by Ed Matthews.

Cover design by Kevin Eichner.

Library of Congress Number: 2003092532

ISBN : Softcover 1-4010-8787-6

All rights reserved. No part of this book may be reproduced or transmitted in any form or by any means, electronic or mechanical, including photocopying, recording, or by any information storage and retrieval system, without permission in writing from the copyright owner.

This is a work of fiction. Names, characters, places and incidents either are the product of the author's imagination or are used fictitiously, and any resemblance to any actual persons, living or dead, events, or locales is entirely coincidental.

This book was printed in the United States of America.
To order additional copies of this book, contact:
Xlibris Corporation
1-888-795-4274
www.Xlibris.com
Orders@Xlibris.com
17435

Prologue

Jack O'Brennan felt good about his station in life, and why shouldn't he? The rough waters he'd passed over had come close to overturning him, but those days were clearly behind him, though that transformation didn't happen overnight.

He sipped morning coffee as meandering thoughts transported him back eight years in time. During this moment of reflection, the memory of his wife Mary caused him to shudder. Her sudden death was the darkest day of his life. His world had turned over and he with it. The blush of a once happy life had faded, then disappeared.

The months and years folded in an uncontrolled slide under the thinly disguised emotional chasm called depression The subtle deterioration of a once robust man was now underway.

According to Webster, depression is a pychoneurotic disorder marked especially by sadness, inactivity, difficulty in thinking and concentration, a significant hopelessness and sometimes suicidal tendencies.

The pieces weren't fallling together like he planned; something had gone wrong. His disciplined, well-ordered life had crossed a fault line to embrace an existence full of anger. Trying to make his own rules while unsuccessfully attempting to pull himself out of the state of hopelessness only caused him to dig a deeper hole that relentlessly strangled him.

The resiliency he once relied on had now vanished. Too proud to seek psychological attention, he continually told himself everything would pass, but didn't see the holding pattern he was in. He would muddle through this maze of confusion that had taken him prisoner with smoke and mirrors if need be, yet time he realized had done little to alter his condition.

Reaching for his coffee, Jack glanced at the patio clock that read 4:15. He reminded himself his best thinking was done at this time of the day. He found it an interval to rework his thinking of yesterday and take stock of what lay ahead of him for the day.

He felt his mind shifting gears back three years to when the ringing phone roused him out of the ongoing funk that had enveloped him for such a long period he couldn't remember.

The solicited call from a stranger in Bell Hills, Tennessee, brought with it an unusual request. He had been asked to assign a reason for a 33 year old death. The appeal had given him pause to think about tomorrow.

The facts screamed at him. He had been going through the motions long enough. Becoming an embarrassment to himself and undoubtedly to those who knew him was obvious as handwriting on the wall. The nagging doubts wouldn't go away. Did he possess the courage to stir old juices so finely honed in the art of searching out secrets. A one-time sensible man, Jack told himself the time was right to talk with his circle of friends.

O'Brennan laughed and spoke out loud as he mentally began to replay the events that started with the Bell Hills call. "Wow, that was something!"

1

The phone call started it off.

"Jack O'Brennan."

"I'd like you to investigate a death that occurred in 1953."

"Fifty-three!" Said an amazed O'Brennan. "Who is this?"

"Mr. O'Brennan, I'm Jimmy Cousins from Bell Hills, Tennessee, a suburb of Knoxville. I'd like you to investigate a murder, or I should say, what I think was a murder."

The Sunday call surprised him because he seldom received ringups on that day. To have someone request an investigation of a thirty-three year old death had an unsettling effect and he could feel his large-framed body begin to perspire.

"Normally, I don't take investigations along those lines. My work tends to be very routine. Have you talked with the city police?"

"Well . . . that's where I have a problem. The police told me they wouldn't reopen a case that old without some strong evidence."

O'Brennan felt a flicker of interest as he asked, "What's the story on this death?"

"A fellow high school classmate was found dead in Bridgeton. It happened on July 17, 1953 Unofficial reports indicate his assailant was unknown. I'd like you to follow up on this."

"Why me?" Asked a puzzled O'Brennan.

"I work for the Knoxville Telephone Company and have access to the Bridgeton yellow pages, saw your ad, and it just struck a note to call."

"That's interesting. You chose me for no particular reason, is that right? "

"Put that way, I have to agree. I'm calling for some friends who are looking to hire someone; why not you? We're visiting Bridgeton the third week in September to watch the Tennessee Vols play Bridgeton University," Cousins added proudly. "Using Bridgeton as home base, we plan on visiting DC, Williamsburg and Norfolk. We thought you could look into the matter, and meet with us when we come to town."

"This is highly unusual. How about getting back to me tomorrow evening? I'll give you an answer then."

"Okay. We hope you will seriously consider taking on this case. Your fees, regardless of what they are, will pose no problem."

I wonder if I'm ready for a murder case, O'Brennan thought as he walked to the patio at the rear of his house.

A learned man might call it a psychotic disorder marked by sadness; another might call it a non-productive scheme called depression. Whatever the diagnosis, Jack O'Brennan, recently retired from the Bridgeton Police Department, had it.

Looking at life's horizon, this unhappy man saw not one shred of evidence indicating improvement was around the corner. O'Brennan's bland lifestyle created a monotony that constantly clouded his existence.

He got up in the morning, went to bed at night, with little happening in between. Jack blindly plodded along a tightly laced routine going nowhere.

This Sunday was a classic case in point. At six o'clock, he'd throw two pork chops on the grill, bake a potato in the microwave and open a bottle of pickled beets. That was his Sunday supper, in fact, that was supper every Sunday night. After dinner and clean up, O'Brennan retired to his bedroom to watch an evening of television. He'd watch the remainder of *60 Minutes*, followed by his favorite show, *Murder, She Wrote*. O'Brennan would then watch the nine o'clock movie and call it a night.

Monday would bring more of the same. Up by six, he'd have his daily coffee, oatmeal, and rye toast. By eight, he would have read the morning *Citizen Tribune*, then head down the hill to meet a circle of friends at Inlet Park.

They'd shoot the breeze, then leave for work. After the Group, as they off-handedly called themselves, left, O'Brennan would cross the street and climb to his third floor detective agency office over *O'Hearn's* Bar. He sat by the hour looking at the marina through the office window. The few cases that came his way offered nothing exciting or different. His business career was as listless as his personal lifestyle.

Life had become a blur since his wife passed away five years earlier. O'Brennan missed Mary's companionship more than the intimate moments they at one time savored. He was overwhelmed by this strange phenomenon called loneliness and felt the need to cry out for help; but who was out there to listen?

Sue, his eldest daughter, had moved to Atlanta and was busy raising her own family. Allison, his middle daughter, had recently married and was now living the very proper life of a Bostonian. Karen, his unmarried twenty-three year old was living the life of Riley as an assistant in sales for the Seattle Seahawks. He loved them and felt they had a corresponding affection for him, but they were there and he was in Bridgetown.

O'Brennan had no interests, nothing to keep him busy. Subconsciously, he thought about an article he'd read some time back. Its thesis centered on rational people who when emotionally pressed, consider suicide.

His life, dismal as it seemed, was worthy of something more than the ultimate act of suicide. What? O'Brennan didn't know, but he immediately dismissed the idea as an ill-advised, scary whim.

He had to get his life in order, whatever that meant. Maybe he'd take-up a hobby. At one time he'd been a terrific golfer, so why not get back to the game he once loved? An excellent idea he thought; one he'd think about tomorrow.

He felt like a drowning man reaching for a lifeline, and maybe the call from Tennessee would point him in a new direction. He'd think about its possibilities along with his golf game in the morning.

2

The early morning sun washed over Jack O'Brennan as he walked down the Ford-Ashland hill, a sense of urgency in his stride. Last night's call had rejuvenated the old juices', stirred the desire to work another murder case. He might be working again, and that was good, on a thirty-three year old murder, not so good! He'd kick it around with the Group and see what they thought.

When Jack arrived, he found all four members of the Group, Karl Eichner, John Lloyd, Cal Redout and Red Ted, already seated on a park bench overlooking the Bridgeton Inlet. The meeting place, better known as the Bench, was the scene of some furious discussions.

Karl was a pot-bellied German whom Jack had met in the Navy. He took up bartending after his discharge in 1954 and started as a shot-and-beer man. He enrolled in bartending school on the GI Bill and soon landed a job at the *Ritz Plaza*, Bridgeton's most luxurious hostelry and watering hole. As the supervisor of the Ritz Bar operation, he started work at ten in the morning. Seldom a weekday went by that he didn't occupy the Bench by eight-thirty.

John Lloyd served in the Army during the Korean War. Returning to Bridgeton after his service stint, he attended the Police Academy with Jack O'Brennan. They became the closest of friends with the friendship carrying over to their families.

John's police career began with traffic control. Somewhat of a character, he carried a touch of show business in his blood.

While directing traffic, he waved, bowed, saluted, and generally entertained both motorists and pedestrians alike. To supplement his income, he took a part-time job as a security guard at the Onslow Auditorium. The Auditorium, commonly called the Aud, was the home of the Bridgeton Baysiders, the NBA's most formidable challengers to the powerful Boston Celtics.

Cal Redout was the resident scholar of the Group. An undergraduate at William and Mary, he ventured north to Baltimore where he attended John Hopkins Medical School. Redout completed his medical training by taking his residency in General Medicine. Returning to Bridgeton, he entered private practice, but soon the bubble of success burst when his wife died from Lou Gehrig's disease. Her demise had been slow and painful over a two-year period. Cal had made a choice; first things first. He devoted his waking hours to her and in the interim, lost his practice.

Part of the personal friendship between John Lloyd, O'Brennan and Cal Redout was a genuine attraction stemming from each having lost their wives. The underlying bond and understanding had sustained each of them. They saw in each other the loneliness they continually felt themselves. The void left by the loss of their spouses could not be filled, but when they were together, they felt less alone.

Red Ted was the outsider of the Group. He didn't fit the mold created by the others. One day he just happened onto the special gathering. Although much younger, no questions were asked of him, no answers were offered. He wore clean, but rumpled clothes and his closely cropped red hair, although clean, knew not a comb.

Red never talked during his first weeks at the Bench. Slowly emerging from his withdrawn personality, he displayed a negative attitude accompanied by a wild and shiftless view of life.

The Group saw a sensitive and caring side in Red that he unsuccessfully tried to hide. He had numerous shortcomings which the Group overlooked, and Red was soon granted entry into the membership. Although he fitted in well, what continually puzzled the Group was his apparent lack of visible income.

The Bench overlooked the panoramic view of the Inlet, which was the centerpiece of the city's attractive downtown and geographically located near the river. Across the water, the city marina passively waited for non-existent, Monday morning traffic. The majestic outline of the Regency Arms Hotel with its domed restaurant stretched for a city block. Police headquarters and the cornerstone of the Inlet, The Ritz Plaza, faced the Group from across the sparkling water. The *Ritz*, its limestone block structure serving as a backdrop, was lavishly adorned with orange and brown awnings, and was considered the jewel of this magnificent setting. Looking from the Bench to the far left stood the stately figure of the city's guardian of the news, *THE CITIZEN TRIBUNE*.

Between these imposing structures, office and apartment buildings fronted Gloucester Avenue. The scene portrayed the image of a football gridiron in a horse-shoe shaped stadium.

"By the way, I received an interesting call last night. A guy from Knoxville, Tennessee, wants me to do some investigative work. Kind of unusual getting a call from out of state. He wants me to investigate a murder. What little business I have is pretty well cut and dried and why would I want to get tied down to something I don't even care about? Oh, occasionally I get city contracts, but they're few and far between." O'Brennan sighed, "What I need is time for myself."

A curious look settled on John Lloyd's face. "Jack, let's reduce this little dialog down to its simplest form. Cut the idle chatter and tell us about the case."

After meeting him for the first time, Jack felt he had known Lloyd for a lifetime. John was extremely outgoing, the extrovert of any gathering, most assuredly of the Group.

"I don't know much about it. This fellow said he wanted me to investigate some guy's death who was a high school classmate of his. He seems to think the kid was murdered."

"Has he talked to the police?" Karl Eichner asked, the question crowding his eyes.

"No, and this is the screwy part, Karl, he was killed in 1953."

"Fifty-three!" Eichner said.

"That's right, thirty-three years ago. He was a sailor stationed at the Naval Hospital."

"What else is there?" Karl asked.

"That's all I have now, but I should know more tonight," O'Brennan replied with a sweep of his hand.

"This is an intriguing story and will give you a chance to put a little zip in your life," Cal Redout said. "Why don't you give it a shot?"

"Everything is intriguing to you, Cal, but I may take your advice and do that very thing," replied a smiling O'Brennan.

"You'd be facing overwhelming odds, but I don't see any down side to this," John offered, "but this is the best news I've heard from you in a long spell."

"I don't know, John, I'm no spring chicken."

"Step into my office. You may be over the hill, but you still have certain strengths."

"Could you expand on that?"

"You're a hell of a detective and we could help you. Just say the words and it's a done deal," John said.

"A little of that may be true, but the thing is, what if we don't find anything?"

"Are you that serious about success?" John wrinkled his nose.

"Let me be the judge of that."

Not deterred, a determined John Lloyd continued. "Well, I think you should give it a rip."

That concluded the Freddie Gill discussion and the Monday morning roundtable finished the session with talk of the upcoming Harbor Days.

O'Brennan left the Group with an, "I'll see you later" wave.

3

Jack spent an uneventful day waiting for the evening call from Tennessee with no golf game.

"Mr. O'Brennan, this is Jimmy Cousins. Have you arrived at a decision?" Jimmy Cousins said loftily.

A high-speed character with an annoying voice, O'Brennan thought.

"Yes, Mr. Cousins, I have. I'll take a preliminary look into the matter. There are two directions we can go. If my initial investigation doesn't look promising, it wouldn't make much sense for me to continue, and I'm certain you agree. However, if leads show early, I will continue with the case. Either way, it'll be your decision. Give me a couple of days and I'll be in a better position to provide some background on where we go from there. My rate is $50 per hour, plus expenses."

"Good on both counts," countered Cousins.

"I'll need some preliminary information."

"Well, yes, that I can give you. His name was Frederick Michael Gill, USN, 422 69 10. His rate was Hospital Corpsman third class, stationed at the Bridgeton Naval Hospital and died July 17, 1953. Freddie lived at 132 East Avenue, Bell Hills, Tennessee. He lost his parents when he was a kid and was raised by an old maid aunt."

"What about his personality? A thumbnail sketch will do. Good guy, bad guy, a little bit funny, you catch my drift?" O'Brennan said.

"He had some history. I remember Freddie as a bad boy, not

a real troublemaker, but constantly in one scrape after another. A follower of sorts, definitely not a leader. Its been said Freddie was always on the periphery of trouble."

"What did his classmates think of him?"

"He was an unpopular sort and we thought him obnoxious."

"Why, after so many years have you become so interested in this Freddie Gill's death that you'd attempt to hire a detective you know nothing about?"

"My closest friends and I attended our high school class reunion last Saturday night. The program started with the class observing a moment of silence in memory of our deceased classmates. It was only natural to think back to those we lost along the way. The truth be told, while playing golf yesterday, we got talking about Freddie and decided it would be interesting to find out more about his death."

"What do you expect me to accomplish?"

"Not to put too fine a point on it, but things like what really happened? What he was involved in? That's the type of question we have. Everyone has secrets and we're just curious to what Freddie's were. As far as I'm concerned, whatever you find about Freddie will not be good. That you can bet your last dollar on."

My life is full of contradictions, Jack thought. I sit around regretting not having a quality case to work on and when the opportunity rolls around, I have second thoughts about whether it's right for me.

"One last thought, Mr. Cousins, please send me all the information you can get your hands on. A photo would be most helpful."

"I'll get all I can on Freddie, and send it out tomorrow. As I mentioned last night, we're coming to Bridgeton in September to see the game. We're even bringing our wives, so we'll be on our best behavior, if you know what I mean." Cousins' laugh sounded unpleasant.

Beautifully presented, O'Brennan thought with distaste, a marked smirk on his lips. Jack knew exactly what he meant. This Cousins and his redneck buddies gave every indication of being a little on the soiled side themselves.

"We're only doing this for the hell of it. From the way I'm talking, you probably think I know something, but that's not the case. We're flat curious about Freddie and we're willing to pay whatever you charge us."

There's something wrong with this picture flashed through O'Brennan's mind. In other words, you don't give a damn about Freddie Gill, or his memory, Jack thought as he returned to his conversation with Cousins.

"Okay, Mr. Cousins, I'll see what I can do. Please give me both your home and business numbers. I'll need a couple of days, so plan on hearing from me Thursday evening. Based on what I come up with, we go from there."

After hanging up, Jack attempted to organize his thoughts. Maybe Gill had been a bad boy, but he didn't have any great admiration for this Cousins or his buddies either. There was something gritty about their request and he was certain they were flying under anything but true colors. What they were O'Brennan didn't know, but like everything else in his business all things came to ground. That was the problem Jack had with his profession, many of his clients were in need of a little class themselves.

4

On a bright Tuesday morning, Jack O'Brennan walked into police headquarters dressed in his uniform of the day. His natty attire consisted of tan chino slacks, a blue-button down, short-sleeved shirt and cordovan penny loafers. He liked the dress of his college days and saw no need to change. After retiring as Chief of Detectives, O'Brennan joined a unique cadre of retirees who had been retained by the department as part-time detectives.

In the early sixties, Bridgeton initiated a program which complimented their investigative ability. After four months, unsolved cases were turned over to the retired detectives on a contract basis. Many of these cases were solved because of the sheer resolve they brought to the case. To be needed was a gratifying plus for the retired men. They also provided a useful service to the community, which was more important than the money they earned. Early on in the program, the city realized the cost-effect ratio was exceptional. There was little doubt the city was gaining far more than what was paid out.

After two hours at the computer, Jack walked to the Bench for his daily rendezvous with the Group.

"Here comes Bridgeton's favorite son. What did you decide?" Karl asked.

"I decided to take the case. There's not much to it, but it should keep me busy for a couple of days. In fact, I've already started."

"Don't keep us in suspense. What's the story?" questioned a rumpled Red Ted; "You planning on keeping it a secret, or something?"

17

"What is it with you, Red?" O'Brennan asked.

"Jack, you'll have to excuse old Red this morning. He's having one of those monthly things and he's just been impossible. Even Karl is acting up a tad, must be the company he keeps," John Lloyd said as he first looked at an unhappy redhead who had the look of a wheat field in a wind storm.

O'Brennan looked at the smiling face of an immaculately dressed bartender and laughed, "I see the whole contingent is here today. You must be interested in what this old-timer has up his sleeve."

"Okay, you've made your point; we're curious as hell. Let's get on with it and quit beating around the bush," Cal answered, somewhat berating O'Brennan.

"His name was Freddie Gill and he worked in the pharmacy over at the Naval Hospital. This guy was killed on July 17, 1953, and was found in an alley off a place called Cayuga Street. Seventy-two Cayuga to be exact. He had the usual things in his pocket: comb, wallet with no bills, small change, keys to a locker, and a shot glass."

"A shot glass!" exclaimed an interested John Lloyd.

"That's what I said, John, a shot glass. By the way, where is Cayuga Street?" O'Brennan asked.

"Cayuga Street was in Harkers and that's no more. You forgot didn't you?" John good-naturedly nodded at his longtime friend.

"You're right, John, I did forget. I must be losing it." Jack's comment brought smiles from all except Red.

"Don't be too hard on yourself, Jack; it isn't a perfect world, you know."

"Thank you for that," Mr. Lloyd, "I find your words most comforting."

"So this guy died, or was killed in a place that was ripped down in the early sixties," Cal pointed across the Inlet as he spoke. "The Government Center is where Harkers used to be."

When a position opened in the Medical Examiners Office, Cal Redout jumped at the opportunity. Without a pathological background, he attacked the new discipline with a furor that amazed his colleagues. He soon became an authority in the field, eventually working his way to Chief of Pathology for the city. His ascent to chief had been as much a tribute to his tenacity, as his native intelligence.

"Why would a guy carry a shot glass with him?" Cal shook his head, "It just doesn't make sense."

Bridgeton's chief pathologist had stumped the Group with the shot glass question, a question he himself could not answer.

"Jack, you know Al Simons, don't you?" Karl asked.

"Yeah, he owns the *Eagle* on Niagara across from the shipyard," Jack countered.

"Why don't you go see him? Al's a retired corpsman and I believe he did a tour of duty at the hospital. He might have been stationed there about the same time as this Gill. Regardless, he may be able to help you."

"That's exactly what I'm going to do, have a little chat with Simons." With that, O'Brennan walked off, not bothering a goodbye.

Redout's eyes followed O'Brennan as he headed home, then Cal sighed and turned to his colleagues.

"Sadly, since Mary died, I've observed little discernable change in our friend's disposition. But this morning for the first time in years I sensed a glimmer of excitement in him. Am I imagining what I thought I saw and heard?"

"You're not alone, Cal. I got the same impression." John Lloyd turned to Karl.

Karl nodded. "I agree. Cal may be on to something."

"You guys never ask what I think, but I'm going to tell you anyway," Red offered. "Jack needs something we can't give him. He needs a woman more than this stupid Gill case. Don't get me wrong." Red ran a hand through his ruffled hair while shaking his head. "I'm not talking about him jumping in the sack with just anyone."

"Who do you have in mind?" John asked.

Red opened his hands in a "I don't know" gesture.

Cal studied Red with interest, trying to assess what he was

observing in this wind-blown wanderer that he failed to see before. Maybe he inadvertently displayed a flash of sensitivity that he'd tried so hard in the past to conceal.

Niagara ran parallel to the Rappahannock River and east of the inlet area, or as the locals called it, the U. Driving east on Niagara, O'Brennan turned left and parked his Blazer in front of a sign indicating, *Eagle* Parking Only. The *Eagle* was located across from the shipyard entrance and had served as a watering hole for generations of shipyard personnel.

"Jack O'Brennan, seeing you is like a step back in time. How are you? It's been years since I've seen the likes of you. What have you been doing with yourself?" Simons asked.

O'Brennan reached across the bar to shake hands with a substantial figure by most standards. A giant of a man. Although the same six-three as O'Brennan, the likeness ended there. Jack, a trim two-hundred, appeared dwarfed by this bald hulk who weighed in at a full blown three-hundred pounds.

"Al Simons, you can't believe how good it is to see you. Draw me a beer and we'll talk a spell."

The conversation carried on for many enjoyable minutes until Al said, "I haven't seen much of you since you've been off the force."

"No, you haven't. After Mary passed away, it wasn't the easiest of times for me. As a matter of fact, it's been a living hell. I spent too many hours downtown at *O'Hearn's*. Like they say, time heals all wounds, but I don't believe that anymore than I believe in the tooth fairy. My wounds aren't totally mended, but I'm getting on with my life."

Simons stoically listened. "Jack, the old-fashioned habit of love is hard to forget, but what you said is good to hear."

"My only problem is I don't seem to fit anymore. I'm not part of anyone's lifestyle, and it feels like I'm an outsider looking in. Enough about me. I started a case this morning that's kind of strange. A sailor was killed in 1953 and I'm investigating it."

"That's thirty-three years ago!" An amazed Al Simons answered.

"So I've been told. You sound just like John Lloyd."
Simons opened his hands to O'Brennan and shrugged.

"Well, that's what I keep hearing this morning."

Simons turned his index finger in a circle signaling O'Brennan to keep going.

"This guy Freddie Gill was a corpsman who worked at the Naval Hospital pharmacy." O'Brennan's line of concentration appeared to momentarily drift away. "Al, you were stationed at the hospital about that time?"

Al nodded.

"Any chance you might have known him?"

"No, Jack, sorry. Early in 1952 I got transferred to FMF duty down at Camp Lejeune. As far as this Gill character goes, he must have come to Bridgeton after I left for the Marines."

"Oh well, nothing ventured, nothing gained. He was found in an alley off Cayuga in the old Harkers, and had been hit on the head with a blunt instrument. He'd been cleaned out, no money in his billfold, no watch or ring. All he had on him was some loose change, a comb, keys to his locker and a shot glass. It appeared to be robbery, but maybe some window dressing to make it look that way. Al, that's just a guess, . . . I really don't know."

"A shot glass!" returned Simons.

"This time you sound like Cal Redout, but why would he carry a shot glass around?" Jack asked.

"I honestly don't know." The burly barkeep absently picked up a shot glass and turned it over in his enormous hands while giving O'Brennan a meaningless shrug. "Jack, in my business, patrons rip them off all the time. About the only thing I can think of is he stole it that night."

"So it would appear." O'Brennan thought for a moment, then continued. "Maybe that is a logical answer, but it still seems odd. Thanks, Al, I have to run, but I'll be in touch."

An hour later, Jack walked into a cluttered mess of a place called the Medical Examiners Office.

"Find out anything?" Cal asked as he looked up from his desk.

"Not much. Can you get me the autopsy report on Gill?"

"That I can do. See what happens when you know well-connected people in lofty positions?" Jack's doctor friend smiled.

Cal walked over to the computer and began punching the keyboard until the terminal was filled with technical information. Scanning the screen, Cal said, "Nothing much here. The apparent cause of death was a bashing to the head. There is one thing that might interest you. He had a tattoo on his left upper arm that was C shaped. Size wise, it was the size of a quarter, and was done in a vivid green, monochrome if you like. Sounds like a wacko to me, Redout said. He waited for a reply but none came. Very strange he thought as O'Brennan left his office without a word.

Could there be a connection between the C and Gill's death? Jack thought as he left the morgue office.

O'Brennan spent the rest of the afternoon looking up information about Harkers. He wasted hours finding out nothing, but consoled himself knowing this mundane work was part of his chosen profession. Tuesday had proven to be another illuminating day in the life of the self-effacing detective. He had ventured but not gained.

5

After reviewing the meager information he gathered Tuesday, Jack turned to the Group. "It appears I need to find out more about Harkers. Where can I get the real scoop on that place?"

"If I recall, *The Citizen Tribune* featured the demolition of Harkers. I'm pretty vague on this, but I think it was written up in the Sunday supplement. The story was an historical overview of Harkers. Can't remember when the feature came out, but I'd say it was probably around sixty-three or sixty-four," John Lloyd said. "Any of you guys remember?"

The other men shook their heads, registering a silent no.

"If they had torn Harkers down in the early sixties, wouldn't they have written about it at the same time? That would have been big news," Red said.

"Just stay out of this, Red, you know nothing about Harkers. You were still in diapers when it came down," Lloyd said, prodding the redheaded drifter.

Red rolled his eyes skyward in an unapproving manner. "Don't treat me like a dumb cluck; I'm not you know."

Lloyd merely shrugged.

Red liked playing the nonconformist of the Group and patterned his remarks to elicit such negative reactions from them. It was all a game he loved to play, and he relished every minute of it.

After his discharge, Red had returned to Bridgeton, where he stayed for only a short period before drifting off. Three years later he returned to stay, and made Gloucester Avenue, the street that ran around the Bridgeton Inlet, his stomping grounds.

At this point, Karl chose to enter the action. "Red, you remind me of a joke some wild salesman told last night. In fact, he drew a crowd with all his nonsense." Karl had the best of all worlds. His job provided him with a high profile and excellent pay. The opportunity to meet and talk with some of Bridgeton's most noted visitors was an added plus. A love for coastal waters prompted Karl to buy a home on the water. He moved to Scots Harbor, a small fishing village located on Chesapeake Bay, twenty some miles east of Bridgeton. He and his wife, Phyllis, raised three children and were currently enjoying the twilight of his working career.

"Give it a rest, will you, Karl? Who wants to hear a stupid joke this early in the morning," Red said.

"We're listening, Karl. I'm sure Red will enjoy your story," Cal said as he winking at the smiling bartender.

Karl laughed, then started. "A little Jewish woman calling Mount Sinai Hospital said, 'Hello, darling, I'd like to talk with the person who gives the information regarding your patients. I want to know if the patient is getting better, doing like expected or is getting worse.'

The voice on the other end of the line said, 'What is the patient's name and room number?'

She said, "Yes, darling, she's Sarah Finkel in room 302.'

He said, 'Oh, yes. Mrs. Finkel is doing very well. In fact, she's had two full meals, her blood pressure is fine, and her blood work just came back as normal. She's going to be taken off the heart monitor in a couple of hours, and if she continues this improvement, Dr. Cohen is going to send her home Tuesday at twelve O'clock.

The woman said, 'Thank God! That's wonderful. Oh, that's fantastic, darling! . . . That's wonderful news.'

The man on the phone said, 'From your enthusiasm, I take it you must be a close family member or a very close friend.'

She said, 'I'm Sarah Finkel in 302. Cohen, my doctor, doesn't tell me squat.'

All politely laughed except Red who generated little more than a groan.

"Karl, that was probably the worst joke I've ever heard," Red said. The others probably agreed with him but remained silent.

There wasn't much left to talk about, and shortly the Group drifted away.

Jack headed for the Tribune building. As much as he liked his friends, he had other things to do and listening to those blowhards was not for him this morning. He made copies of the feature on Harkers and realized Red was right. The article had been written when Harkers was under the wrecking ball.

O'Brennan crossed Glouster Avenue to *O'Hearn's* Grill. He knew the story would come to life by the hand of one Patrick Terrance O'Hearn.

Jack found O'Hearn busy setting up the bar for the midday traffic. Every time he entered the dimly lit restaurant of polished stained wood, thoughts of how *O'Hearn's* could have been used as the prototype for the TV show, *Cheers* came to mind. O'Hearn subscribed to the fact his restaurant's charm was a sterile one. He never allowed a pool table, computer game, juke box, or shuffleboard near the threshold of his front door. He claimed they contaminated a drinking and eating establishment such as his.

"How about a cup of coffee?" Jack asked as he slipped up on a bar stool.

"Here you are, Jack," O'Hearn said as he placed the coffee in front of him. A raw-boned face with bronzed skin drawn tight gazed at his longtime friend. He knew Jack was looking for something, because Jack displayed curious eyes and had once mentioned, 'The eyes always tell the story'. "What can I do for you?"

"Pat, you can begin by telling me about Harkers."
"What do you want to know?"
"What was it like?"

O'Hearn closed his eyes as he retreated into the past, and began his litany with a shrug.

"Harkers was like any navy town, never intended for the

faint hearted, and much like Scollay Square in Boston or East Main Street in Norfolk. The major difference was Harkers had two main drags, Cayuga and Seneca Streets. They ran from Niagara Avenue to the river with side streets running between them and on each side of them."

"See if I have this right. Harkers ran east and west between Georgetown and the river. First the Inlet, the park, then Harkers. On the other side was the Naval Base, then came the shipyard."

"That's right; remember, Gloucester stopped at Niagara. That's about the only thing that hasn't changed over there."

"That helps with the logistics, Pat; now can you tell me about the place itself. I've been in navy towns, but never this one. When I joined the force, they were tearing the joint down, so I'm at a disadvantage."

"Let me think." O'Hearn looked out the window and smiled. A pause followed, then Pat started. "It was a big patchwork of sleaze. Harkers was a place of disordered lifestyles where people made their own rules." O'Hearn waved his hand with authority at the Government Center.

"When the sailor went into Harkers, he had three choices: drink beer, drink beer, and lastly, drink beer. The bars came in all sizes, smells and appearances, but with one longstanding tradition of fieldstriping the sailors of their last dollar. Greed is an unseen virus that starts in the soul and works outward." O'Hearn sighed and again looked out the window where the cesspool called Harkers formerly existed.

"Is that wizardry of words from an old Irish proverb?" O'Brennan asked.

O'Hearn smiled. "No, my friend, I think I made it up, but I'm not certain."

"Tell me more."

"Harkers met all the sailors needs; from booze to women, it was all there. Bars catered to a special clientele. Sailors from each ship and shore unit hung out in their own bar. It was important to start and finish a night of drinking on secure ground. In between came the rip and the bang.

"Decay never sleeps, nor did Harkers. The devil was always at work down there and the fleet was his oyster. There were tattoo parlors, uniform shops, movie theaters, and the ever present burlesque house. Burlesque was around long before X-rated movies went public. Back then, if you wanted to see some flesh, that's where you went."

"What about the women of Harkers?" Jack asked.

O'Hearn shook his head in amazement. "Women! Jack, tons and tons of them were around. There were bar flies who hung around the same bar night after night. They looked like they had their clothes sprayed on and needless to say, they were available. Then there were the street-walkers, not many mind you, but they were out there. I heard about call girls being obtainable, but why a call girl would hang around down there is a mystery to me, but whatever. This I know for a fact, there's many a middle-aged American male who got deflowered down at Inlet Park. The girls would pick them up, take them to the park and ply their trade on an old park bench. A tough way to get introduced to the ways of the flesh, but what the hell, any port in a storm."

This came as no great surprise and Jack got Pat's drift. He had a much clearer picture of Harkers now. Somewhere during the investigation, Pat's information would help.

"There's another thing I should mention; there were some good people down there, but the lion's share were the devil's own kind. But you know, Jack, there was a certain hard to define quality about the place.

After leaving *O'Hearn's*, Jack was convinced all roads led to Harkers. It was time to regroup and put his thoughts in order. He climbed two flights of stairs above *O'Hearn's* and entered his postage stamp sized office. The window in back of his desk faced the Inlet and much of the U. Jack loved the sight, especially when it rained. He'd sit by the hour watching the rain drops creating circular patterns on the calm water. That wouldn't be the case today, for Bridgeton was in its annual battle with the dog days of August.

Absently, he opened the letter from Knoxville which had come in the morning mail. It produced some extraneous information about Freddie Gill, along with a newspaper photo. Now he could get serious. He again read the *Citizen Tribune* feature story on the demise of Harkers. O'Brennan jotted down bits and pieces he could find on the people mentioned from the district. The name Duke Frontier, an old-time tattoo artist seemed to leap from the page. Checking through the yellow pages, he found Frontier's name and address. His tattoo shop was the only parlor in town still operating.

6

After lunch, O'Brennan drove out Niagara Avenue toward the shipyard. Strange, he thought, seems most of the Freddie Gill investigation has led him to this street. In the feature, the skin artist had expounded on the art of tattooing while discussing his experiences in Harkers from 1932 to when they started knocking it down in 1961. With some luck, this old geezer could shed some light on the tattoo. Maybe he put the green C on Freddie Gill.

Jack cautiously entered the tattoo shop, almost afraid of what he'd find. The interior looked like a forgotten museum. The waiting room, such as it was, reflected the art form practiced by Duke Frontier over a fifty-plus-year career. Tattoo designs covered one wall of the fifteen-by-fifteen front room, while calendars, hats, a ball glove and mementos of the past, too numerous to mention, filled another. The back wall was reserved for framed pictures of celebrities. It appeared Frontier had colored the skin of more than a few notables.

Seating himself in one of the straight-backed oak chairs, Jack continued to peruse the room. Minutes passed before a little old man, his once young body beginning to wilt with age, shuffled out of the shadowed backroom moving with care. Frontier looked to be in his mid-eighties. Bald and shriveled like a prune, he approached Jack.

"Yes sir, matey, what will it be today?"

"I gather you're Duke Frontier."

"Sure am, partner." His voice crackled like dried out leather.

"My name's Jack O'Brennan. I'm a private investigator who . . ."

His face displayed disgust as he locked gazes with O'Brennan. "I don't talk to dicks," he barked like a marine drill sergeant as he hunched his shoulders as if to say, get lost.

This old duck is tougher than day old tripe, Jack thought as he appealed to the little skin artist. "This is different. Please hear me out. I'm working on a case that occurred some thirty-three years ago. I just finished reading a news clipping on the demolition of Harker, that one over there!" Jack pointed to an aging copy pinned to the wall.

"That article called you the Dean, the 'Master of Tattoos' in Harkers."

"Yeah, that's right," Duke replied, warming to the subject. He enthusiastically continued, "Had a shop in Harkers for thirty years. Still been there if the bastards hadn't ripped the damn place down."

"I'm investigating the death of a sailor who was killed in 1953, and found in an alley off Cayuga Street. A friend told me, 'if there's anyone left in the city who's an authority on Harkers, it's Duke Frontier'."

"He's got that right. Know all about the place." The wrinkled little man gave Jack a thorough once-over, then asked, "What did you say your name was?"

"O'Brennan, Jack O'Brennan. I'd like to ask you about . . ." he stopped short. "What the hell, you've probably forgotten. I talked to several old-timers and they can't remember squat!" A tale out of school never hurt anyone, especially when you were trying to puff up a tough old bird like Frontier.

Duke's vanity was showing. Bristling outwardly, he answered, "I never forget anything about Harkers! Not by a long shot." Frontier looked like he was about to explode. "My memory is sharp as a tack, and don't you forget it, sonny boy!"

"I hope you're right, my friend. The dead sailor I'm talking about had a tattoo that was kind of unusual. One might call it an oddity of sorts. There may be a possibility you put it on him."

"Sonny, I've done more tattoos than you got hair on your head," Duke gloated. "That's all I done all my life. Done thousands and thousands of 'em. So put some faith in this old boy. I'll tell you one thing, if I did it, I'll remember."

Jack got serious with the old gent. "This tattoo was C shaped and about the size of a quarter. It was done in green ink on the upper left arm, near the shoulder." Showing Duke a photo of Freddie, Jack continued, "This fellow had that green C on his left arm. Do you remember him?"

Squinting at the picture, Duke frantically shook his head. "No, I don't remember this guy!"

"He probably didn't come to your shop," Jack displayed disappointment in his voice, "but would you look again?"

"Now wait a minute! You young fellows are in too big a hurry. I said I didn't remember this guy," Duke said, pointing to the picture. "The face, I mean. I don't look at faces, never did; but I can remember the bodies and the tattoos I put on them"

Jack's face lit up, "How about the green C?"

"That I remember. The fella came into the shop and showed me a card with a green capital C he had drawn. Sure, I remember the green C."

"How did you put it on"

"What do you mean, how did I put it on? I put it on free hand, you numbskull; it's the only way I know. I'm a damned good artist if you ask me." With a sweep of his hand, he pointed at the wall, "See all them designs on the wall, I put 'em on all kinds 'ah people. And I did all of them free hand, you big stoop."

"That's good to hear. That takes care of Gill, now . . ."

"Hey, slow down!" Duke interrupted, "I ain't finished yet. It was a funny thing," Duke rubbed his bald head. "Within the next couple of weeks, I drew two more. That's kinda' odd wouldn't you say?"

"Two more! Yes, I agree, that was very odd."

"Yeah, two others, but they weren't C's."

"What do you mean they weren't C's?"

"Like I told you, they just weren't C's. You young'uns don't listen so good, do ya'?" He paused, appearing to snarl, then continued, "Oh hell, they could have been C's, I guess. There is one thing I do know, they each had a different direction for the opening."

"By the opening, do you mean how it faced?"

"Yeah, that's just what I mean. They were all drawn in the same place and I put one on a woman. When you do a single, it's seldom done in green."

"By a single, you mean one color?" Jack asked.

Frontier nodded yes "When you ask a question," he shook his head, "you don't know the right words to use to ask. A single color like I'm talkin' about is called a monocrom. I don't remember who got what, but I'm sure those three all got C's put on them. You said the dead guy had the regular C; well the other two were turned around."

"Inverted?"

"I don't know anything about inverted. The only thing I know is the son of a bitch was turned around . . . you understand that?" The little weasel appeared to bark as he pointed a bent finger at Jack.

"Yeah, Duke, I understand," Jack laughed as he looked at the furious little man.

Disregarding Jack's laugh, Frontier continued. "The third C had its opening at the bottom."

"Did they ever return?" Jack asked.

"No, never did. A lot of times, I'll give somebody a tattoo and later on, they'll want something else done to it. Something more fancy, but no, not in this case."

"Let's go over this one more time. Gill, we'll call him one, had a regular C, two had the opening facing left, and three had the opening facing down. Is that correct?"

"That's it! Just the way I put 'em on."

Jack stood up, shook hands with the little man and said, "Thanks, Duke, I really appreciate your help."

"You're welcome, big man. You know, you're a pretty good guy for a dick."

Jack laughed, "And you're a pretty nice guy yourself for being such a hard-ass."

Delight showed on the old-timer's weathered face for the first time. He had let go of his hard look and replaced it with a hearty, contagious laugh that came from the pit of his stomach. It was a laugh Jack never expected from this scruffy stump of a man.

There was no doubt about it, Jack thought, this rascal has an incisive mind as sharp as a razor. Jack liked Duke a lot. They looked at each other, a period of silence followed; then Jack waved goodbye and left. It was one of those special moments.

Driving back to Ford Ashland, Jack pondered a question he couldn't shake. Why in hell do you meet people you truly enjoy when they or you are old, and there's so little time left to enjoy them?"

As he drove around the U, O'Brennan stopped at headquarters and walked downstairs to the property room of Charlie Winder, a grizzled old-time desk sergeant who had weeks to go on a forty-year stint with the Bridgeton Police. When Charlie returned from the Pacific in 1945, he joined the police department. As an adult, police work was the only job he ever had other than fighting Japs.

"Hello short-timer, how ya' doing?"

"Jack O'Brennan, my favorite detective. It's nice to see you; come in and have a cup of coffee."

Charlie drew coffee from the percolator, then returned to his desk. Placing the cup in front of Jack, he grinned, "Damn, you look great! Will I look as good after I retire?" he asked kiddingly.

"Charlie, when you look in the mirror to shave in the morning, your reflection will overwhelm you."

"I hope you're right, but I have no idea what you mean, sure sounds good though." Charlie laughed, then quickly turned serious." Jack, this beat-up old fuzz-man has been down here since Hitler was a corporal, and I can always tell when guys need something. Now, my friend, what can I do for you?"

O'Brennan sheepishly began, "Yes, I did come down here to get something." He recited the facts as best he could on the Gill case, and Freddie's subsequent death on Cayuga Street. "One of the items found on his person was a shot glass and that's what I need. Can you let me take it for a couple of days?"

"O'Brennan, you know better than to even ask such a question. How am I going to do that?"

"Charlie, you yourself know you're a short-timer and there'll be no records, nothing showing. We both know that stuff back there," Jack waved to the rear, "is just collecting dust. It might help me."

"How is it going to help?" Charlie asked.

"I was afraid you'd ask that question." O'Brennan laughed, then continued, "I honestly don't know, but what the hell Charlie, lighten up. We're only passing through once and what real difference will it make? I'm in a jam, please help me."

Charlie nodded. "I've been there myself."

"Well, how about it?"

Charlie played with his half full cup, then said, "What are friends for? All right, Jack, let me see what I can find back there. It will take me some time to dig it out, so come back later in the afternoon, say around four."

Returning home, Jack decided a walk around the quiet neighborhood might be in order. Walking through the beautifully sculptured tree-lined streets constantly amazed him. The gas-fed street lights, barely recognizable in daylight, still added an undefined charm to the area.

The Hill at one time had been home for the Bridgeton elite, but the post World War II era had brought change to the area.

The old money moved from Ford Ashland to newly created suburbs west of the city. These fresh new neighborhoods would better accommodate the egocentric drives of the rich new arrivals. The Ford Ashland left behind by this mass exodus provided young middle-class couples the opportunity to purchase homes at highly devalued prices. Many homes were of the Federalist Period, reflecting such distinctive characteristics as keystone window lentels with recessed arches.

Each building appeared to have differently shaded brick. All the homes had a common denominator in that their frontage was fifteen feet wide. Why would the rich build homes so cramped and narrow with each house touching the building next to it? Jack inquired around the neighborhood and finally came up with an answer that satisfied him. The wealthy families of Bridgeton built these homes for their domestics. They themselves lived in mansions at the crest of the hill.

Walking around the area's colonial bricked sidewalks, Jack's thoughts drifted to C's. He mentally arranged and rearranged the C's until he came up with what could be a *Shamrock*. There was no stem, but never the less, the possibility of a *Shamrock* existed.

7

Thursday morning is Thursday morning, whether it be Bridgeton, Buffalo or Boston. The meeting in the park had an added dimension this sun-struck morning.

There appeared to be urgency in the Group's questions about the Gill case. Jack talked about his visit to Frontier's tattoo shop and the tattooed C's on three different people. He told of arranging the three C's in the shape of a *Shamrock*, then asked John if there was anything in Harkers that had a *Shamrock* associated with it.

"Yeah, the *Shamrock* Bar. Never hung out there, but I know it was a busy place with a lot of activity. Why don't you ask Al Simons. I'm sure he can fill you in on the operation."

"That's a good thought," Jack said as he glanced at his watch. It was early, but he was certain Simons would be serving his early morning regulars. After several minutes of small talk, Jack headed for the *Eagle*.

"You back so soon?" Al asked with a broad grin.

"When you were stationed at the Naval Hospital, did you ever go to Harkers?"

Simons nodded happily. "All the time."

"Did you ever go to the *Shamrock* Bar?"

"Sure did. It was the corpsmen's hangout and a hell of a place it was."

"Can you give me some background on it?" Jack placed his elbows on the bar, folded his hands and closed his eyes as if praying at an altar."

"The *Shamrock* was located on Cayuga Street and it was really big. Probably the largest bar in Harkers and that's saying a lot. The bar was circular, maybe thirty feet across. I'm not sure how many people it could handle, but a good guess is forty to fifty. There was a massive dance floor in the rear, with booths on both sides and in back. They were the high variety, you know what I'm talking about. You could find them in any port" Jack nodded his understanding.

"Anyway, it was dark back there. The only lights showing were pin-up lamps screwed against the wall of each booth. On pay day and a couple of days after, the 'Rock' did a land office business. Naturally, as the money ran out, business dropped off." There was a pause, then Simon continued, "When the destroyer fleet pulled in, they'd be loaded. Especially, if they'd been to sea for a long time. Now you know yourself, when a sailor comes in from sea, he spends money in a hurry, just throws it away." Jack laughed, because he knew exactly what Al was talking about.

"Harkers existed for the sailor, as did the *Shamrock*. If you've been in one *Shamrock*, you've been in all of them," Simons said with a wave of the hand. "Bar flies, prostitutes and hustlers, all looking to roll the first likely prospect that came their way. It was a tough place with a carnival atmosphere, but my friend, did we have some time there!"

"You told me what I needed to know; got to shove off."

There were no farewells between the men. Jack's brain was miles ahead of his body. From the *Eagle*, he half ran, half walked to Duke Frontier's tattoo shop, not a hundred yards away. Entering Duke's work place, O'Brennan called out, "Duke, are you in there? It's O'Brennan."

Duke shuffled into the waiting room, appearing much shorter than his actual height. "I know who you are, big man. Like I told you before, got a memory sharp as a tack."

Reaching into his pocket, Jack pulled out a three by five index card. "Yes, you have a damn fine memory and I need to hear more of it. Yesterday, you remembered the three C's you tattooed many years ago. Your memory is very important, I might add." Pointing to the card in his left hand, O'Brennan added, "If you arrange the C's in this pattern, they look like a *Shamrock*, do you agree with that?"

"Agree."

"I have a problem with what I just showed you, there's no stem. You know what? I've never seen a *Shamrock* without a stem and Ill bet you haven't either. Did you ever do a stem?" Jack turned the card over which displayed the outline of a stem. "Something like this, if you know what I mean."

"Got ya'. No I haven't and yes, that I did. "Duke's answer momentarily stumped O'Brennan. "One just like that except the bottom turned right and was shaded in with the same green I used on the C's."

"Thank you my friend," Jack said as he slipped a twenty into the old guy's shirt pocket. That's just what I needed to hear. The next time I come to see you, we won't talk business, we'll just lie to each other until we can't stand it."

A broad smile shown on Duke's face. O'Brennan knew he had pleased the old-timer with his last remark and had also pleased himself.

"Keep in touch, Big Man," Duke said to the departing O'Brennan.

Returning to his Ford Ashland home, Jack reviewed the case. He surmised four people were tied together in this *Shamrock* thing, whatever that was. He had three leaves and a stem, one part tattooed on each partner. He knew Freddie Gill had a leaf, the woman had one, and there were two others. One with the third leaf, and one with the stem."

Picking up the phone, he realized his excitement was the real thing. He didn't feel depressed, nor did he feel sorry for himself. He liked the new Jack O'Brennan and was acting like he did when Mary was with him, and that was good.

Jack called John Lloyd at the Onslow Auditorium. The security job provided John with more than extra income. It afforded him the opportunity to see great sporting events and meet many famous athletes.

He needed professional advice, and Lloyd was his man. "John, this is Jack, I need your help. I went back to Frontier's place this morning and he told me he drew a stem on a sailor. I now have four people with tattoos, Freddie, a woman, and two others. Tell me, old toothless wonder, how do I go about checking this woman out? With your endless wealth of information, you should be able to help me."

"Let me tell you, ragpicker, I probably have more teeth in my head than you do! Getting back to your question, this thought came to me earlier. Do you remember how the Salvation Army workers used to canvas the bars? We called them the tambourine shakers. On pay day they'd cruise the bars looking for donations. Even though they were a pain, the servicemen would give them money. Their efforts were well worth the sacrifice of some loose change."

"Get to the point," Jack said.

"There was a good-looking woman who daily made the rounds. She was gorgeous to be exact. Well, that lady is still in town. She's in charge of the Bridgeton Salvation Army unit. I can't remember her name, but I can find it out for you."

"Sounds good, but how do you know about this lady and her role in Harkers?"

"A year ago, I was at a human-development meeting at church, and the lady who's in charge of the Salvation Army was mentioned. Seems she started her career working the streets of Harkers."

I'm impressed. I didn't know you were a churchgoer. John, you never cease to amaze me."

"What do you think I am, a heathen like you?" Lloyd's retaliation amused O'Brennan. "Well, enough of this nonsense. See what you can find out. I'll be waiting for your call."

"Where are you?"

"I'm home. Catch you later."

With diligence and good luck, John Lloyd moved up the promotion ladder until becoming Security Chief of the Aud. After twenty-five years of service with the Bridgeton Police, twenty of which were spent in the detective bureau, he retired.

John's return call sent O'Brennan to the Salvation Army headquarters on the double. After a brief wait, Jack was seated in front of an exceedingly attractive woman in her mid-fifties. Her erect posture gave hint to her pride in wearing the uniform. Lloyd was right, she had to have been gorgeous then and she hadn't lost a step since.

"Mrs. Hope Langly?" Jack asked.

"Yes, what can I do for you?" Langly displayed a straight-toothed smile.

"My name is Jack O'Brennan. I'm a private investigator currently working on a very old case, thirty-three years old to be exact. While discussing the case with a colleague, your name came up. He mentioned you once worked the Harkers area, and also mentioned you've become a moving force in helping the area's less fortunate."

Jack found himself unable to look away from her beauty.

"Yes, Mr. O'Brennan, I was very familiar with Harkers. I worked there for a number of years before it was torn down. That's where I started by the way."

She momentarily drifted off to another time. Mrs. Langly noticed her visitor watching her. "Even I permit myself to dream a little."

O'Brennan's reddened face caused her to laugh.

Jack pulled Gill's picture out of his wallet and laid it on the desk. "Do you remember this man? I've been told he was a Harkers regular."

A glimmer of recognition shone in her eyes while viewing Freddie's picture. It was obvious she knew him, or knew about him. After a pause, she pointed to the picture. "We all live with memories, and he is included in mine. Certainly, I remember this young man from the Harker days. As a matter of fact, he was found dead down in Harkers. I'd say in the early 50's. How close am I?"

"You're right on the money. I'm investigating his death, which could very well be a homicide. Can you remember anything about him that might help?"

"Why are you investigating his death now? Isn't it a bit late?"

"It's never too late to catch a killer, Mrs. Langly."

Maybe a tad melodramatic, but nevertheless true, Jack thought.

She appeared to appraise O'Brennan as she leaned her slender body back into her chair. "Yes, I agree. Freddie was a nice young man, as was his girl friend. I'd often see them sitting in a back booth at the *Shamrock*, just talking. Sometimes there'd be another fellow with them, but more often than not, it was just Freddie and his girl. They didn't seem to fit in with the rest of the crowd. It was as if they were sitting on the outside, window-shopping. I suppose I'd have to call them misfits."

"What do you mean, they didn't fit in?" Jack asked as his curiosity began to build.

"For one thing, they always had money and gave freely. Their manners, general behavior, you know, were a cut above the others. The one thing that got my attention was their graveness. It was if they had the weight of the world on their shoulders."

"Very interesting," Jack said, as he stared into alert brown eyes.

Pointing to the picture, Mrs. Langly added, "I know this lad was shore-based because he was always around. I became acquainted with his girl the first summer she lived in Harkers. She attended Hood College in Frederick, Maryland, and would be around Harkers from about the first of June to mid-September."

"What did she do during that period?" Jack asked with his eyes glued to the stately woman in front of him.

Mrs Langly briefly tilted her head to the side. "She had the best gimmick of anyone in Harkers. She sold magazine subscriptions at the fleet landing. I think half the fleet bought from her, hoping the opportunity to climb in bed with her would be part of the package." She noticed O'Brennan's uneasy look. "You may think me somewhat crass, but I've stated the facts as candidly as I can. My life's work exposes me to the real world with all its scabs and sores. So at times my tongue leads me to say rather irregular words that conflict with my religious work." She shrugged her shoulders and smiled.

"By the way, she didn't appear to be that kind of a girl. At the time, I knew her as Sally Ralston, but I know her now as Sally Ralston Hunter. She married a David Hunter and together, they ran an import-export business, coupled with a local wholesale operation. Her . . ."

O'Brennan interrupted, "Are they still in business?"

"Her husband died several years ago, but Sally still lives in the city and runs the business alone. She's a very active woman, into all types of social activities and the benefactress of numerous charitable organizations. Sally is a wonderful person, and incidentally, she's on our local Salvation Army Advisory Board."

Jack thought as he asked, "Do you ever speak with her now?"

Langly touched the lapel of her well-tailored suit. "All the time. I'd say we have become good friends over the years."

"I know this is an imposition on you, and for that I apologize, but would it be possible for you to arrange for me to see her? A woman as busy as you suggest she is may not have time for a simple investigator like me."

"No one is simple when I'm involved. After all, Mr. O'Brennan, I'm here to help people and that includes you." She laughed a glorious laugh and reached for the phone. "I'd be pleased to help."

Mrs. Langly's soft admonishment sat well with O'Brennan.

"Sally, this is Hope Langly. Just fine . . . I have a gentleman in my office, a Mr. Jack O'Brennan and I'm calling for him as a favor. He is a private investigator looking into the death of Freddie Gill. Would it be possible for you to meet with him?" Mrs. Langly pushed a strand of hair from her forehead as she listened.

She looked to O'Brennan. "Was there anything in particular you are interested in?"

"Nothing special, just general information about his time in Bridgeton," Jack said.

Langly returned to her business on the phone. "Just general information about his tour in Bridgeton."

She listened for a brief moment then asked O'Brennan, "Would Monday morning at ten o'clock be convenient?" Jack nodded.

"Yes, Sally, ten will be fine. Many thanks, and remember, we have an advisory meeting next Wednesday evening."

"There you are, Mr O'Brennan, you can meet her at her warehouse on Churchill Street."

"Thank you very much for your kind help. Good morning to you and have a pleasant day."

"And have a pleasant day yourself, Mr. O'Brennan."

Jack's euphoria continued as he drove to the *Red Rooster* on Niagara Avenue. The meeting with Mrs. Langly had gone well. He now had two names and half the *Shamrock*. He still had to find the other leaf and stem, and this is where his snitch might help.

Walking into the *Red Rooster* was always an experience. Whatever you wanted could be acquired here. The spectrum ranged from getting drunk to buying dope. Between these happy little ventures, one could get laid, fight, or meet some of Bridgeton's most unsavory characters.

The bar was gloomy, dark, musty, smoky, and down right dirty. Billy Olsen, Jack's favorite informant was nowhere to be seen. Although in his early seventies, Olsen never worked a day in his life, and wasn't about to start. He was an old-time hustler and former boozer who quit the jug some twenty years earlier.

The police occasionally used him as a contact to the underworld, and in that position Billy commanded a lofty and somewhat secure position in that he was trusted by both sides. Jack once asked him why he hung out at the Rooster, even though he had quit drinking. His answer was typically Billy Olsen. "He hung out here because this is where the action is."

"I'm looking for Billy Olsen, don't see him around." Jack spoke to a beefy-looking thug with a stomach rolled over his belt serving as bartender. Writing a short note on the back of his business card, he handed the card and a fin to the back-bar crud. "Make sure he gets this, will you?"

The fat pig looked at O'Brennan with a cruel smirk. "Yeah, when he comes in." The answer came in a gin-scorched voice. His tight-lipped reply convinced O'Brennan fatty was a lousy human being.

8

Jack reviewed his Thursday travels with the Group, talking at length about his conversation with Mrs Langly and his meeting with Mrs Hunter next week. Interest was intense and O'Brennan thought that a good omen. He planned putting the Group to work shortly, and willing workers were always the best kind. The name Sally Ralston Hunter was known by all members of the Group, except Jack He thought it strange that even crazy Red Ted would know of her. All agreed she had done some remarkably good deeds for Bridgeton.

For now, Jack chose to reserve judgement on this new player in the game and strangely felt she wasn't all she was cracked up to be. Even Hope Langly's sterling comments hadn't completely convinced him of her impeccable character. There was an embedded feeling in the pit of his stomach that wouldn't go away. This pretty lady was involved; that he was certain of.

The discussion was getting too serious for Karl, so he changed the subject. "I heard a good story over at the Ritz Want to hear it?"

"You might as well tell it and get the stupid thing over with," responded an indifferent Red Ted.

Red joined the Navy during the nation's Viet Nam venture, and it was in Nam where he found his place in the sun. After boot camp, he attended Hospital Corps School in Portsmouth, Virginia. The school trained medics for the navy hospitals, surface ships and shore installations. Navy Corpsmen also served with the Marines, and in this capacity, Red found his niche. A person with no parents or family, He had developed an attitude problem early on. To call him a misanthrope was inaccurate. He just didn't give a damn about himself or anyone else.

"Jack, the other day I told you about Red having this monthly thing. Well guess what, he still has it." The Group laughed at John's comment.

"Go ahead, Karl, we're interested. Like John said, old Red hasn't been himself lately," Cal said in an amused tone.

The noted pathologist's approval was sufficient for Karl. Undaunted by Red's biting comment, Karl launched into his story. "This woman went to the doctor for her annual physical. After finishing, the doctor said, 'Grace, for a sixty-year-old woman, you have the breasts of a twenty-year old, and I'd like to write you up in a medical journal'. That evening as the woman was getting ready for bed, she stood naked in front of the mirror admiring her breasts. Sitting in bed, her husband asked her what she was doing. Grace spoke up. 'I'll have you know my doctor told me I had the breasts of a twenty-year old and wants to write me up in a medical journal'. Oh yeah, did he mention anything about your sixty-year old ass? Her husband asked in a smart-alecky manner. 'No', she replied, 'your name didn't come up in the conversation'." All of the Group howled except Red.

"Red. Didn't you find that amusing?" John asked.

Red helplessly shook his head. "Lloyd, my tolerance for nonsense is quickly eroding away with old age."

"You can't stop the clock of time," Lloyd said.

"That is the most insipid statement I've ever heard," the redheaded drifter said.

"That's very nice wordology you used, Red, but I'll bet you can't top Karl's story, "John countered.

"No I can't, John, nor do I plan to try."

"Karl, I thought they didn't talk that way in the Ritz," John said.

"John, they talk as bad in the Ritz as they do out at the *Red Rooster*," Karl replied with a shrug.

When one talks about somebody sitting in the catbird seat,

John Lloyd was your man. He knew all the players; gregarious in nature, he knew everyone.

"Damn, I almost forgot, Billy Olsen stopped by earlier, and left a message. He wants to see you at the Rooster this morning."

"John, did he mention a time?"

"He did. Ten o'clock."

Driving to the *Red Rooster* gave Jack time to reflect on the case. The investigation was slowly falling into place, and he felt Sally Ralston Hunter would eventually be the key to this puzzle. So far, she appeared squeaky clean, but that didn't mean a damn thing. Maybe Billy Olsen could shed more light on this lady.

Looking around as he entered the saloon, Jack observed the same tired faces at the bar that he'd seen on his last visit to the joint. The ever-present smell of sweaty bodies filled his nostrils and hung low like early-morning fog on a spring morning.

Billy sat majestically at a table near the shuffleboard, working on the morning crossword puzzle.

Jack sat down opposite Olsen, waiting for him to acknowledge his presence. Billy knew he was there, but enjoyed making him wait. To Billy, it was like getting the better of the fuzz. Jack knew the game, so he patiently waited, showing no sign of being annoyed.

"Hi Jack. Let's eat."

Jack took the suggestion to heart. "That sounds good. I'm having a great day and I'll even pop for breakfast."

"That's no big deal, you always buy me breakfast." The *Red Rooster* like many old saloons, had excellent food. Bridgeton's elite never dined here, but the quality of the food had a widespread reputation. The dining room with its clean and airy atmosphere was a far cry from the dingy bar next door.

The waitress brought their orders on medium-sized meat platters, adorned with an anchor and Bridgeton Naval Base, Bridgeton, Virginia printed in the center. Lumberjack portions of fried ham, golden-brown homefries, and three perfectly cooked, sunny-side eggs provided a challenge to the long-time adversaries. Anxious to get on with it, Jack began to prod Billy.

"Let's get down to business. I need your help, and . . ."

"Now look it, I got nothing to say 'til we finish eatin'," Billy snarled.

O'Brennan was totally irritated as he rushed through breakfast He didn't have all day to sit at the Rooster and Olsen knew it. Billy never missed a beat and knew exactly what he was doing. What the hell, he'll get his someday Jack thought as he watched Billy finish his breakfast.

After the last bite was eaten, Billy demanded, "Put up your money."

"I'll go for fifty and that's it! You tell me whether we can deal or not," Jack snapped. "What's your pleasure?"

"Speak to me," Billy said with a full-blown smile.

O'Brennan reviewed the Freddie Gill story in detail, not leaving out the smallest particle of information.

"What do ya' want to know? I know a number of things."

"What I'm looking for is the fellow with the other C and the guy with the stem."

Billy rolled his eyes skyward. "Ya' don't want much for fifty dollars, do ya'?"

O'Brennan pulled out Freddie's picture and placed it in front of Billy. "Know him?" He asked sharply.

A quick glance brought an immediate response from the little stoolie. "Yeah, I know all about this guy. In fact, I may know more than I want to tell you for a lousy fifty bucks."

"That's it, Billy, no more than fifty," Jack admonished.

Olsen laughed. He had got to O'Brennan again. "Deal, I'll have to get back to you."

"When?"

"Ah, . . . tonight. Yeah, tonight! Come around 'bout ten and I'll have somethin' for ya'."

Because he was in the neighborhood, Jack stopped at the *Eagle* to ask Al about the shot glass he'd picked up from Charlie's property room. He was puzzled by its appearance because he couldn't recall ever seeing one like it.

"You back again?" Simons greeted O'Brennan with a wave. "Time went on and I never saw you, then all of a sudden, I see you more than I see my wife. What can I do for you?"

"This." Jack placed the shot glass on the bar and turned it in his fingers. "When I was in here before, I mentioned something about a shot glass this sailor was carrying when he was killed. You seemed to think it was no big deal that people steal them all the time, and very possibly he had stolen it earlier in the evening. Any thoughts on that?

"This is the glass they found on Gill and it's different than the others." Jack slid the glass over to Simons. He smiled while picking it up.

Simons reached to the back bar and picked up a similar looking glass, then placed it next to the one Jack had just given him. Simons appeared to be digging out memories from earlier days as he absently dried a glass, still looking at the two short glasses. "I'm amazed at how quickly we forget, but I may have something for you. This scam is older than the hills and I know navy corpsmen used it at one time. Don't know if it's still SOP, but here's how it used to go."

"What do you have up your sleeve?" Jack asked.

Simons held his hand up as if to say, "just hold on".

"To maintain a certain reserve of blood, sailors were continually brought in for the donor program. Corpsmen would draw a pint of blood, then give the donor a chit to get a double shot of whiskey at the pharmacy. The sailor would go to the pharmacy, present the chit, sign the log, then drink his shot at the counter. Now is the time for the scam to begin.

"The pharmacy corpsman would use a double-shot glass with an extra thick bottom," Simons pointed to the glass Jack had put on the bar. "You can see how the bottom of the glass you brought in is thicker than the regular one. Actually, your glass would hold a single shot. After the corpsman used a bottle, he then tucked away one under the counter. Now remember, the log indicated two bottles had been distributed. It was damn near fool proof."

A customer banged his empty glass on the bar. "Excuse me Jack, got to go make a buck."

Simons quickly returned. "Here, let me show you. Now watch, I'm going to fill a single shot glass." After filling the single with water, he poured its contents into the double, the liquid climbed to the brim.

"Presto! The sailor drinks what he thinks is a double but is really a single, and you're in business. By rights, that double should be half full, but as you can see, it's full to the top. That my friend, is the way it's done. What I've accomplished is nothing short of magic. I've given you a double, you sign for it, drink it with no questions asked. What the hell, you'll drink paint thinner at this stage. You've given a pint of blood, walked away with a shot in you and I have one under the counter. I know this doesn't help much, but it may apply to what you're looking for."

O'Brennan stood up preparing to leave.

"Jack, one moment. Take this from your friendly bartender. I have a gut feeling this Gill character is interrelated with something more than whisky."

"I have to run, Al, but I appreciate your help with the shot glass. And what you said about Gill is probably closer to the mark than I realize."

Jack returned to his Ford Ashland home and worked chores he had neglected since the case began. He mowed his mini-sized lawn, washed the Blazer and the house windows. That was enough for the day. What he left undone would be waiting another day. He read for awhile, took a nap, and finally heard the grandfather clock strike nine. After a quick shower and change of clothes, he left for his meeting with Billy.

Nothing had changed at the Rooster since morning except the bar's clients. Billy in his usual spot appeared to be the resident guru of the establishment. His table next to the shuffleboard afforded him a clear view of all that went down in the *Red Rooster*.

Billy followed Jack's every move as the big man eased into a chair opposite him.

"What did you come up with?" O'Brennan asked.

"Let's see your money first." Fifty dollars changed hands under the table. "The guy with the *Shamrock* leaf is a Fritz Hansen. He was stationed on a can over at the base. They went out on maneuvers, but Bridgeton was their home base. The can stayed in port more than it was in the stream. This Hansen was a hospitalman, first-class when he got out."

"How did he get to be an HM1 in four years?"

"The word is, he's really smart, and corpsman tests are nothing more than book studying, they say."

"Where is he now? What does he do? How did you find out so much in such a short time?" Jack asked impatiently.

"One question at a time, my boy. He lives at 32 Gates Avenue, down in Craddock."

"Virginia?"

"The very same. Craddock was taken over by the city of Portsmouth years ago." Billy shrugged as he eyed O'Brennan.

"You mean it was annexed," O'Brennan corrected the little stoolie.

"I'm saying it was taken over, annexed, whatever you want to call it. Why do you use these big words on me, you big jerk?"

Jack laughed, "Annexed isn't a big word, Billy."

"Well, it is to me."

"Enough said, what does he do?"

A dark look crossed Billy's face. "Jack, Hansen is a big-time operator in the underworld and I'm not going to say another word."

"What are you driving at? You haven't given me much, so far," Jack said.

"Do I have to draw you a picture? I told you everything I know, and that's as much as yer gettin'. The name of the game is to keep breathin', and I wan'ah do that more than help you."

His sentence just hung there and Jack understood why Billy was troubled.

"You're scared to death, aren't you?"

"You've got that right! I'm bummed out, man. I think I asked too many questions. This guy Hansen is a big leaguer, a flame-thrower. He's dangerous and got a bunch of palookas sitting around looking for trouble. I wish the hell you hadn't come here, because I'm not used to foolin' with tough guys like him. What I heard about Hansen makes me feel like I'd been run through a cotton gin. I'm in a different league than this Hansen. Now, I'm warning ya', if I was you, I'd watch my ass. You may have a little problem with this guy, and I'm not happy with the direction you're taking me."

"Billy, there's no such thing as a little anything."

This guy's a mean one. The word has it, with a snap of the finger, he can send a person away. Anybody crosses him ends up in the bay wearing funny looking shoes."

"Thanks, Billy, I'll follow your advice to the letter. I'm sorry I can't give you more help, but I think you should keep a low profile."

Billy shrugged and smiled. "So what are you sayin'?"

"Nothing changes, everything changes." Billy looked puzzled. O'Brennan's eyes drilled into the little informer. "There is no way around this. You see Hansen as a bad dream, but even nightmares go away. Remember one thing; this problem will also pass."

Billy looked puzzled as Jack stood up to leave.

There was little doubt Billy Olsen was pressed against the wall of desperation. He had added a new dimension to the game that needed to be checked out. O'Brennan decided a drive to Craddock was in order.

On his return to Ford Ashland, Jack decided that drive to check this Hansen out should be taken in the morning.

9

The wind blew through Jack's auburn hair on his drive to Portsmouth. He loved driving along the shore of Chesapeake Bay. The water on his left, patches of sea oats here, little sand dunes there. Occasionally an abandoned boat skeleton popped into view along the roadside that appeared as if by design.

There was nothing better than driving his red and white '57 Chevy convertible around the countryside on a glorious Saturday morning. Even at eight, the sun was high enough to signal another great but torrid day was in the works. The salty air, the top down on a vintage car, a magnificient sunrise, money in his pocket, good health, his life was picking up.

Until recently, the days and weeks had melted together into an umbrella of gray, but the Gill case appeared to be what the doctor ordered. As if by magic, his depression and loneliness lifted, and he felt great. Well, not great but better.

His thoughts drifted to earlier days in Bridgeton and his life with Mary. He marveled at a professional career that had propelled him from a rookie cop to Chief of Detectives. His retirement brought with it a detective agency that allowed him to dabble in his chosen profession, yet not be consumed by it. The agency had helped, but recently, he had felt himself coming unglued. The one big minus was not having Mary. Her absence created a void he felt could never be filled.

As he drove, suspicion began penetrating his every thought. All the moves he'd made on the case proved to be the right ones. Each turn had provided a stepping stone to a new clue. This case was becoming too easy; nothing in his detective past had been so simple. He knew that sometimes one has to pay a pound of flesh for success. Would this be true in the Gill case?

Billy's limited information about Fritz Hansen added a menacing new dimension to the investigation. With it, came a king-sized dose of anxiety. Not the best of worlds for a man who seldom carried a gun.

Driving through Portsmouth brought back memories of his Navy days. Jack had been stationed on a ship berthed at the Naval Base. He and a friend began riding city buses, hoping to find a quiet place away from the hubbub and glitter of the downtown strip. The Craddock Extension proved to be the answer to their quest. At the end of the run, they entered the small suburb community of Craddock. The village could have been the subject of a Norman Rockwell painting. Its tree-lined square proclaimed a message to all who passed through 'This is America as it was and is'. The *Park Theater* and the next-door drug store stood across from the square. *McWilliams* bar, a thriving business in the community was at a right angle from the movie house. Jack and his buddy frequented Craddock for the remainder of their Portsmouth stay. They never mentioned this secret little haven to their shipmates, and soon blended in nicely with the numerous retired and career navy personnel of the community.

Pulling into Craddock Square, Jack surmised that nothing had changed, but that wasn't the case. The theater and drug store had succumbed to a pizza shop and laundromat. Unlike the rest of downtown, the corner bar had missed the shift in time. Entering *McWilliams*, Jack found the bar as cool, dark, and comfortable as he remembered it from the fifties.

O'Brennan immediately spotted Kenny Ross, a former detective colleague, who like Jack, had taken early retirement. He happened onto the *McWilliams* bar, liked what he saw and bought it on the spot. Ross stared briefly at O'Brennan, then said, "You just made my day, boss. Jack O'Brennan, it's great to see you." The two friends talked to each other as if time had not passed between them.

Surrounded by highly polished wood, Jack felt like he was standing in a forest, then he looked up. Shiny walnut beams with white ceiling covering between them caught his eye.

"Kenny, this is terrific and really hasn't changed from what I remember back in the early fifties."

"This is the first time you've been down here since I bought it, right?"

"Yeah."

"Well, I can't believe my luck. By my own definition, I have it made. You know, I have such a great thing going, I have to pinch myself to remind me this is really happening."

"That's good to hear," Jack said

"Most of the Portsmouth detectives hang out here. The retired ones come in during the day, while the working ones straggle in during off-hours. Sailors are in and out all day long, depending on their duty hours. We have a lunch business Monday through Friday and Saturday is our big day.

"Today, we'll serve a light buffet out there," Ross pointed to the dining room, "and we get a hell of a crowd. You can't believe how well it functions. The reason I think it works is the little twist I put on it. Actually, this was Grace's idea but I'm going to take credit for it." Kenny's laugh brought back fond memories of the old squad back at Bridgeton and how much Jack missed the life. "What has come about is the guys who come in Saturday morning bring their wives. They'll come in at ten-thirty, eleven o'clock and they all mingle. Of course the women know each other and tend to be together, and the guys talk shop and drink beer.

"They eat with their wives, then go home. The guys have a nice morning and have their women with them. They're not going home all juiced-up; instead, everyone's happy and we're making money to boot. We're open Sunday but don't serve food. As soon as we clean up on Saturday, Grace and I hightail it for the Outer Banks and spend the rest of the weekend out there. It's amazing Jack. Grace and I always got on pretty good, but now working together, our marriage is terrific. It's everything I ever wanted."

Kenny knew at a glance that Jack was hurt by the comments

he'd made about the morning crowd and his relations with Grace, and felt a twinge of pity for his long-time friend.

"Damned I'm sorry I ran my mouth off. I can sense the great loss you still have with Mary gone and all." Regret shown in his eyes. "Jack, you have a quality about you that people like. Things have a way of working out when we least expect them to. Hang in there, pal."

O'Brennan felt uneasy. "That's all right, Kenny. Until recently, I've been going through the motions, but of late things have picked up. It's times like this that really bother me, but I'm not down here to tell you my troubles. I need your help. What do you know about a Fritz Hansen?"

"Whoa," Ross said. O'Brennan could feel his warning system going off. A look of concern, something akin to fear crossed Kenny's face. It continued as Jack reviewed the case, sharing his previous conversations with Hope Langly, Duke Frontier and Billy Olsen. "What do you think?"

With a serious tone in his voice, Kenny suggested they move to the end of the bar where privacy was assured. He carefully thought out his words. "Jack, you've always had a lot of class, popular, better-looking, smarter, a cut above us other detectives. You had it all. Use your smarts, and leave this alone. Do what you have to do, but stay away from this Hansen! He's bad news, believe me."

"Kenny, I probably have enough to satisfy those guys in Tennessee who hired me; but it's something I must finish. I just can't drop it. You appreciate what I'm saying, I know you do. I can't let go of it."

"Jack, you're just not big enough this time. I don't think any one person is. No reflection on you, hell, you're the best, but this guy is dynamite, a black-belt bottom-dweller. This is no idle warning, but Jack, the army of darkness lives in Hansen's camp. You must understand one thing. If you continue with this investigation, your life won't be worth a plug nickel."

Jack ignored Kenny's words "Do you know someone who could help me; possibly give me information on this Hansen, some inside scoop?"

"Yes, I do, but I'm not sure I want to give you any names. I'd hate myself if your death came early because of something I gave you."

"Kenny, you know I'll get it one way or another, no matter how long it takes. If you can save an old friend some time, I'd appreciate it."

"I have a hellava thing going here for myself and I don't want to jeopardize it in any way. There might be some one here willing to help you."

"Anyone particular?"

"I suggest you talk with Nick Steinman. He's a good one, a top-notch detective who can be trusted. I'm sure Hansen has a conduit in the force, but it's not Nick; you can go to the bank on that one." Gesturing toward the growing crowd with an open hand, Kenny added, "The people who come in here are good guys. In thirty minutes this place will be buzzing with locals, and you can find out anything you want." Ross looked away when he spoke. "But, and I use the word advisedly, tread softly. I'm taking a hands-off position on this baby. I have to live with this Hansen and he casts a mean shadow. I hope you understand where I'm . . ." His sentence drifted away.

"Absolutely. I'd do the same thing if I were in your shoes," Jack answered sincerely.

Just as Kenny predicted, the bar began to fill and Jack felt saddened as he watched the friendly banter going on between the men and women. It was times like this Jack hated most. Kenny waved over Nick Steinman, a tall thin man pushing forty with a weathered face. Patting Jack on the shoulder, he said, "Nick, I want you meet an old friend, Jack O'Brennan. We date back a long time; I worked for this character when he was Chief-of Detectives in Bridgeton. He needs some answers and I'd appreciate any help you can give him."

Steinman shook hands with O'Brennan in a hurried manner.

Jack again went through the Freddie Gill story, prodding Steinman for information relating to Fritz Hansen.

With a hardened look, Nick began. "You know, greed is an

important commodity to possess if you are driven by the need to accumulate money. I've been keeping an eye on this Hansen for the better part of ten years and can't put a finger on him. Can't do a damn thing about him. I know what he's about, know his operation, or at least I think I do, but it ends there." Steinman laughed. "He's just a local boy who made good. The truth of the matter is I'd like to repay him in aces for all the hurt he has put on people. I want to get close enough to smell his breath, then rip his heart out, but . . ."

People seeking revenge should dig two graves, O'Brennan thought.

"Can you tell me what he's about?"

"Yes, that I can do." Steinman's eyes honed in on O'Brennan like they were equipped with lasers. "I know he's connected and am certain he's the main man between Miami and New York."

His eyes flashed a fleeting sign of caution.

"Drugs?" Jack whispered.

Steinman nodded as other detectives drifted over to where he and O'Brennan were sitting. The discussion continued to centered around Fritz Hansen. All agreed he didn't get where he was by being an altar boy and shouldn't be taken lightly. They felt he was dealing in something big, the something being drugs. That was all they had going for them, pure conjecture. Nick promised to put together a package on Hansen by Wednesday. Both agreed to meet at *McWilliams* that evening. The cards had been dealt, and O'Brennan now understood Billy's reluctance to say more.

As he left *McWilliams*, he could hear the laughter and well-being sweeping the neighborhood bar. Men my age should have a woman around them to enjoy the good end of life, but sad to say, I'm not part of that life back there.

10

On his return drive to Bridgeton, O'Brennan pulled off into a turn-off and left his Blazer for an empty beach. He sat in a stoic position with his head bowed and replayed glimpses of the happy crowd at *McWilliams*. How Mary would have loved that gathering, he thought. He never left her memory, but was it enough to sustain him.

Thoughts of Kenny Ross's admonition about staying away from Fritz Hansen returned. Jack was not intimidated by the thought of crossing paths with this downstate heavyweight, but if a confrontation were to occur, he should choose the battle site carefully if at all possible.

A sudden shiver passing over him caused Jack to look up. He observed two ships in the distance heading toward Norfolk. A grim honesty dawned on him. Unlike me, they know where they're going. I'm like a fragile rowboat sailing in a hostile sea masquerading as something I'm not.

Then the melody of the wind and water lapping at the beach joined in concert with the salt air to snap him back.

I have so little time left, he thought, there has to be something or someone out there that can help me over these rough waters.

"When does your new life begin. It starts with your next breath," he asked and answered aloud. O'Brennan walked to his car and listlessly headed toward Bridgeton.

Arriving home in the early afternoon, O'Brennan tried settling into a mystery he'd been reading. Why was he reading a make-believe detective story when he had a real live one going in the

Freddie Gill case? He asked himself. There was but one thing to do. He'd spend the rest of the weekend at the cottage.

He packed an overnight bag and headed for the bay. Driving out Niagara Avenue, he was suddenly overwhelmed by the stark reality of it all. He was desperately lonely and working the case was providing some relief, but the fact remained, his was a shallow life and it had never been more evident than at *McWilliams* that morning. He lacked the companionship people his age should be experiencing. Maybe a day at the cottage would pick him up.

The cottage had been in the family since the twenties. When he and Mary had taken ownership in the earlier sixties, the fashionable thing to do was to modernize the bayside properties. The quaint cottages were turned into year-round homes, a far cry from what Jack thought a cottage should be.

Constructed of concrete block to combat the occasional hurricanes that passed the way of Sands Beach, the cottage wore a corral-colored coat of stucco with Carolina-blue shutters accenting the windows. A front porch stretching the entire width of the structure added to its appealing appearance.

Jack's place overlooked Sands Beach, nine miles north of Scots Harbor. Most of the cottages fronting the beach had been refurbished into gleaming buildings of glass and aluminum that resulted in not much more than fancy property. Jack and Mary had been swept up by a similar mania but faced one important obstacle; there wasn't sufficient money to follow suit. Instead, they painstakingly fashioned the old four-bedroom cottage into a home with personality rather than a house lacking dignity. A structure no skilled carpenter could duplicate, so, the cottage remained.

To call the furnishings found throughout the one-story dwelling stark would be inaccurate, but calling them an eclectic collection of odd parts put together with loving care closer to the fact.

O'Brennan continued east until he reached Sands Beach, a mile-long area that was structure free on the ocean side of the road. The one exception, *Sands Beach Restaurant* nobly rested on a knoll at the head of the crescent.

During his happier days, Jack regularly went there for dinner with Mary, but hadn't been back since her death.

Parking the Blazer in the driveway, he hurriedly entered the cottage and threw on a pair of faded swim trunks. Grabbing a cold beer, he sat on the front porch viewing the scene before him. The cottage is the right place at the right time, he thought.

A commanding view of Sands Beach could be observed from where he sat. White sand was everywhere. Bordering the beach was an elevated macadam walkway, four feet above the sand with a grass belt running between the walkway and road. Cottages lined up like soldiers faced the beach from the road's leeward side. To his extreme left, he could observe huge sand dunes that appeared to guard the beach from the North. Though similar in size to the ones at Provincetown and Kitty Hawk, they never became a tourist attraction, and for that, the Sands Beach community applauded.

Mary and Jack treated the cottage as a retreat from the rigors of the city. Over the years, he was always puzzled by the fact his neighbors spent more of their beach time trying to outdo the people along the strip than enjoying themselves. They'd return to the city dog tired rather than renewed for another week. It didn't make sense. Why should he kill himself for that rat race?

Jack crossed the road, and settled on a bench close to the water. Around five-thirty, the sun started its daily descent into the cloudless sky. The beach started to clear as one group after another picked up and headed home. He felt alone until an old friend sat down next to him.

"Jack, when did you get in? Didn't see you earlier in the day."

"Just got here, Charlie. I've been working on a new case and needed to relax. The damned thing is getting to me, so here I am."

Charlie waved in the direction of the kids playing on the beach. "Jack, did we ever have a school boy innocence like those kids out there?"

"Charlie, even old gas bags like us had some degree of innocence; although I hardly remember it."

"Yes, I guess you're right."

A retired teacher from Roanoke, Charlie was the dean of scavengers who daily patrolled the beach. Considered the character of Sands Beach, he walked away from city life and moved to the beach as a permanent resident.

"Have you made your afternoon run?" Jack asked.

"Yeah, just finished. I must have picked up eight dollars or so, and I consider that a fine day." He systematically roamed the beach with a hand metal detector and a small wire sand scoop. Each evening, he'd find lost articles such as watches, keys, rings, along with the usual change lost by the sunbathers. He placed all the newfound articles on a collection board nailed to the wall of his front porch.

For years, Jack observed Charlie in his dogged search of the beach. He walked back and forth from wateredge to walkway with an intensity that Jack admired. He would occasionally stop to scoop up an item found by his detector. Like a good farmer, when it was time to make hay, he made hay and instinctively knew where the heavy yields would be.

From the front porch, Jack enjoyed watching Charlie scour the beach. He faithfully searched the sand and had reduced his hobby to a science. The young people with their hyper activity were more productive. They produced most of the lost change while their elders tended to lose personal items.

Charlie was no fool. He saved the loose pocket change in a five-gallon glass jug, and at the end of season, he easily accumulated enough change to pay the annual property tax on his cottage.

"What you and I do is not so different. In fact, very similar."

"How so, Charlie?"

"How many cases have had you stymied? I'm sure you retrace your footsteps looking for clues missed during your first pass through. What do you find? More clues. Can you imagine the amount of money people lose on the beach that will just disappear in the sand? That money will lose itself in the depths of nowhere. The same must be true in your business. Am I right, my friend?"

Jack nodded yes, barely moving a muscle as he gazed at the water. Finally, he spoke. "It's so peaceful out there now," he gestured toward the water, "yet before long we'll be talking about how wild it is." Charlie nodded in agreement.

Charlie didn't speak for several minutes "No matter how many times you look, more things are found. They're out there, coins, clues, whatever. They're waiting to be found and many escape us." Charlie paused, then continued. "It's like life, old boy. Some try to bury their past; some succeed, but only from others, not themselves." Charlie sighed. "Nothing goes away. Like I said, I bet it's also true in your line of work."

"That was some charge of philosophy you just laid on me," Jack said. "Would you screen the beach if you didn't make money off it?"

"Certainly! It's great exercise and keeps me on the beach, and that my friend, is a life I love. I must admit, the tax-free money doesn't hurt me one bit. Do you know what's more important than the money, it's something else. I don't profess to be a big benefactor to the area, but over the years, my family and I have taken much from here. We owe the beach a lot! Why not give something back to it? Why not keep it clean? Sands Beach is a nice place for people to come and enjoy themselves. Why not be the keeper of lost and found? I can't tell you how many people have been grateful that I provide this service. I never understood how I felt about this beach until I got older. It's not much, but I'm pleased to return the favor."

"You have a wonderful gift for distilling matters to bare bones," Jack said.

Charlie didn't reply.

A sea gull gracefully floated by, circling; it landed in front of the longtime friends. The sleek bird speared a piece of refuge and effortlessly glided off into the steamy evening air.

"By the time I see you tomorrow, those gulls will have pretty well picked the beach clean," Charlie observed.

"Yes, I suppose you're right, but a friend once remarked that a sea gull was nothing more than a flying rat."

"I suspect he's right," Charlie said, "but those flying rats sure do a lot of good by picking up the garbage. And you know what, they sound like crows but possess much more dignity." A happy laugh followed.

The sun was beginning to set as Charlie excused himself to leave for his cottage. Jack was alone with his thoughts as his friend disappeared into his cottage. What a remarkably nice man. Wouldn't it be grand if every person had Charlie's attitude?

O'Brennan stared unseeing at the water, then realized he was not alone on the beach. Soon, two young boys trudged along heading for the sand dunes. Those were the glory days of my youth, Jack thought as he followed their journey to what appeared to be a predetermined spot where they launched a multi-colored kite into the evening air spotted with white puffy clouds. The kite effortlessly darted around, bobbing and weaving; its performance similar to the artistry of a middle weight boxing champion. It rode invisible air currents like the sea gulls watching over the sandy beach.

Without warning, the kite embarked on a death rendering nose dive and crashed to the beach. Several minutes later, carrying the shattered kite, the boys passed Jack on their return home.

"What happened to the kite?" Jack asked with interest.

Looking at the battered kite, the elder of the two replied, "Just came down. It's pretty well banged up, wouldn't you say?"

"Can you fix it?"

The kid looked O'Brennan in the eye. "Yeah, it's fixable. I'm sure it won't be much of a problem. We'll have it flying tomorrow night."

"What caused it to drop like that?"

"It got caught in a down draught. You never know, one minute you expect it to fly forever; the next minute, bang, along comes a current and down it goes."

"You had it up there pretty high," Jack said.

"Sure did. Thought we'd have to pull it down before dark." The boy looked thoughtfully at the kite. "It sure is beat up. I guess Dad was right; nothing lasts forever. That's what it's like flying kites. You think you have everything going for you, and all of a sudden, they come crashing down. It happens all the time. Whatever caused it to crash, you never see coming."

With that, the boys left, waving goodbye with their heads, leaving Jack to marvel at their youthful enthusiasm

I like that, O'Brennan thought. I hope they stay that way. Those kids weren't the first to carry on like that. He smiled as he remembered back to his youth. The end of a near-perfect day he thought.

Jack sat on the front porch drinking a freshly perked cup of coffee observing the first light of morning invade Sands Beach. Dense August fog that had risen before the sun obscured his view of the water and brought with it unique silence penetrated only by the occasional piercing sound of a foghorn.

O'Brennan allowed his memory to drift back to earlier days spent on this same porch with Mary. They spent more mornings then he cared to count sitting side by side holding hands. Few words were needed because this simple gesture of love for each other carried with it its own sweet language. The feel of her hand constantly evoked a different sensation each time they touched. Oh how he missed her with every passing day.

Looking to his left, Jack could see through the relentless gray the vague outline of what appeared to be a man slowly heading his way. Minutes later, the figure spotted Jack on the porch.

Waving, he said, "Nice morning, isn't it?"

"I really can't tell, but I hope you're right," O'Brennan answered

"Oh yes, I can tell, I feel it," replied the jogger as his stocky frame melted into the gray morning fog.

Jack pondered the man's reply. How do we know those things in life? We can't go through life feeling things. Yet, so many jobs, including mine, demand decisions based on one's feelings. Then he asked himself: Who am I to question feelings? Much of a detective's arsenal is based on intuition and feeling.

To hell with intuition and feeling. He was here to relax, to get his mind off the case. Jack opened the Sunday *Citizen Tribune* to the sports page which he found to be the only positive news in the paper. An avid sports fan, he was pleased his beloved Bridgeton Gulls won again last night. O'Brennan read with interest that Eddie Feller, the Gulls noted first baseman was being inducted into the Cooperstown Baseball Hall of Fame that afternoon. A week from Monday had been designated as "Eddie Feller Day" at Gull Stadium. Senator Andrew Kenmore of Virginia, would unveil a plaque honoring the Hall of Famer. Might be a good way to spend a blue Monday afternoon. See you at the ball park, Mr. Eddie Feller, O'Brennan thought.

Sunday morning brought out the runners. The casual joggers moved on the macadam while the serious competitors did their road work on the sand. Many were preparing for upcoming road races. The Falmouth race on Cape Cod started the series in August, followed by the Scots Harbor Road Race in September. The short races in the East culminated in October with the Georgetown 10K.

O'Brennan started to read the file he'd picked up Friday afternoon from the paper on Sally Ralston Hunter. It provided background material about Sally's marriage, business activities and her social life in Bridgeton. Included in the file was a brief biography of her late husband, David Hunter.

Sally was energetic, no question about it, and threw herself full-force into any new venture she encountered. What caught Jack's eye was how she continued to actively participate in old activities. She was a former president of the prestigious Woman's Union, chaired the local cancer drive and contributed many hours to the Red Cross Donor Program. Sally also found time for the Bridgeton Episcopal Church, still a member and former president of the exclusive Fox Hills Country Club and past chairwoman of the annual LGPA golf tournament. She also played an active role on the Mayor's Committee on the Arts and served on the Salvation Army Advisory Board, a fact Jack had learned from Mrs. Langly. The crowning touch to her achievements was the fact she single-handedly ran R and H Imports, Exports, Inc.

After graduating from Hood College in 1955, the file showed no activities until 1960 when she resurfaced. Once Sally settled in Bridgeton, she immediately made her presence felt.

Interesting! Jack thought. What was she doing over that five year period? Her Bridgton career stopped in 1955, however she re-entered the scene five years later. That fact deserved his attention later on.

In a whirlwind affair, she married a David Hunter from the affluent and influential Hunter family of Smithbury. The community was located some twenty miles west of Bridgeton in the rolling foothills of the Piedmont Plateau and was considered the Mecca of the Eastern horse world.

The Hunter family, long entrenched in Smithbury's horse set, annually hosted the Saxon Hunt, one of the oldest in the country. The hallmark of this great social function was its strict adherence to a sense of the past. It was into this social backdrop that Sally had so readily settled.

The storybook courtship between Sally and David culminated in an October wedding that proved to be the peninsula's social event of the year.

At the time, David Hunter, age thirty-nine, had been considered a most eligible bachelor. Sally, on the other hand, was an unknown, which to some, made her unsuitable for the refined Hunter family.

Together they formed R and H Incorporated, more as a lark than out of necessity. The company became an immediate success, and over the next fifteen years, the couple struck a most gracious and dashing figure on Virginia's eastern shores. Suddenly, like a bolt out of the blue, Hunter was stricken with cancer. With his passing, Sally was left with a thriving business and extraordinary wealth

Jack contemplated what tomorrow's meeting with Sally Ralston Hunter would bring. He'd start the week on firmer ground if he handled the ten-o'clock meeting correctly His thoughts started to snowball and bump into each other, a fact that annoyed him. Try as he might, O'Brennan's thoughts seemed disjointed and made little sense as he tried to design a format for the crucial interview. There was a time when such a meeting wouldn't have been a problem, but that was then and this was now. He'd fly blind and hope for the best. Sunday's outing at the beach provided Jack with renewed energy for the upcoming week. Returning to Ford Ashland, O'Brennan felt a foreboding sensation sweep over him about the morning meeting.

11

I'm entering uncharted waters, O'Brennan thought as he parked in the lot adjacent to Sally's Churchill Street warehouse. Entering the office of the converted neighborhood theater through a side door, he was directed by a no-nonsense secretary to Hunter's upstairs office.

Mrs. Hunter stood as Jack entered the lavishly furnished corporate headquarters. She observed him closely while extending her hand across an oversized, cherry desk.

"Good morning, Mr. O'Brennan, please be seated. I'm Sally Ralston Hunter, but call me Sally. This is a new experience for me." She looked at O'Brennan in a girlish way. "Being interviewed by a detective, that is. How may I help you?" She smiled a nice smile, then followed with a stare that made O'Brennan feel comfortable.

O'Brennan slowly seated himself, taking in the beauty of this striking woman. She was tall, but not thin. Her navy linen suit suggested a business woman first, last and always. Her bobbed hair, a beautiful blend of gray and brown, reflected the style of the glorious fifties. Sally presented a picture of a cool, efficient woman as fresh as a gentle spring rain. Jack thought Sally was beautiful, and for some unknown reason, liked her.

"Sally, I'm the private investigator Mrs. Langley called about last week and I appreciate your providing me this time in your busy schedule. As you probably know, I'm working for a client hoping to determine the cause of Freddie Gill's death." Jack observed no reaction from Sally. "Gill was found dead in an alley off Cayuga Street in Harkers, and his death occurred July 17, 1953. Well, there is no need to go over that, is there? You're already familiar with this information."

"What are you driving at?"

"Although my question may sound impertinent, it's not meant to be. Could you tell me what you remember of Freddie Gill?"

With a knowing look, Sally reached for a cigarette. Lighting it from a silver lighter she looked at Jack with dark eyes and appeared to be buying time. She inhaled and her words snapped out like a rifle shot. "Yes, Mr. O'Brennan, sadly, I do remember the incident. In fact, I was with Freddie earlier that evening." Jack hung on to her every word.

"Was that at the *Shamrock*?"

"Yes, it was," she replied with a charming smile. "That's where we used to hang out."

How in the world does he know that? What else does he know? Don't rattle because you're smarter than he, so don't tip your hand, she thought as she stubbed her cigarette out.

"Mrs. Hunter, do you recall what happened that evening?"

Her eyes filled with sadness. "If I remember correctly, we were together for a while, then I returned to my room . . . . I think around ten."

"I noticed from the autopsy report, Freddie had a tattoo on his left shoulder." O'Brennan sought to detect a nuance in her voice that would lead him elsewhere.

"Mr. O'Brennan, when Harkers was at its peak, there were four or five tattoo parlors open for business. Sailors do get tattoos you know," Sally said casually but with firmness.

"Most sailors don't have green C's tattooed on them. Well, actually, I know of another sailor who has one, Fritz Hansen. Know him?"

Sally displayed no anxious moments over Jack's remarks. She looked annoyed with him, but that was it. O'Brennan had incorrectly reasoned that this meeting would be easy, but Sally was not as she appeared. He could sense she was harder than he originally thought.

"Mr. O'Brennan, I ran with Freddie and Fritz, I'll grant you that. As far as Freddie's death, I had nothing to do with it, trust me on that. We were close, but not that close. There are certain things that occurred in my life that are best forgotten, and the mistakes I made will be with me for the rest of my life. You might say, Freddie and Fritz are unpleasing memories I'd like to forget. Even you must agree, our past isn't always what we'd like it to be. Isn't that true of most people?" Sally's smile was both glorious and mischievous.

O'Brennan closed his mouth so as not to say something dumb. After a pause, he explained in a matter of fact tone where the case stood. As he viewed this real looker, O'Brennan instinctively knew the interview was not working out.

"Is there anything you can tell me about Freddie that might help?" He pushed the sentence out casually, but felt uncertainty crowding his voice.

A slack look skirting boredom graced her face as she replied, "Freddie died thirty-some years ago and I can't waste time on him now. I'm no Agatha Christie and must get on with my life." Staring directly into O'Brennan's face, she extended her hands out, palms up. "I honestly don't know what you want from me, but believe me, I have nothing to hide." A dark look swept her eyes, "Mr. O'Brennan, this is as uncomfortable for me as I'm sure it is for you. For the last time, I had nothing to do with Freddie Gill's death!" The tilt of Sally's head indicated her annoyance.

Her sharp words rang with a biting honesty. Rising from her chair, she added in a courtly tone, "Now, Mr. O'Brennan, if you will excuse me; I have numerous appointments this morning." With the inflection in her voice turning dry, she extended her hand to Jack. He numbly shook it as if it were a fragile piece of china.

O'Brennan had incorrectly reasoned the meeting would go well, but left with an empty feeling, hardly believing he had let the interview slip away. He'd handled it like a rookie, no, worse that that. Like a ten-year old. "You horse's ass," O'Brennan shouted at himself. She summarily dismissed me and I'm amazed at how she skirted around my questions. Granted, she answered what I asked and knew exactly what the replies should be, but that doesn't make it easier to accept. Thoughts of his encounter wouldn't go away.

Sally's cut from a different mold, and is more than she appears to be, he thought.

Again, speaking to himself, he said, "Jack O'Brennan, you don't wear indignation very well." Where do you go from here? I know where, he thought. He jumped into the Blazer and drove to the *Eagle* He climbed on a stool at the end of the bar and began replaying his earlier meeting with Sally. Her carefully orchestrated charade, and it was just that, eliminated any edge he hoped to achieve.

He studied rising bubbles in his glass. They had a calming effect that worked more quickly than whiskey. The cold beer tasted too good for so early in the morning. Something he promised himself not to get in the habit of doing.

Al Simons shuffled down to the end of the bar where O'Brennan was sitting. Wiping his hands on a white apron draped around his waist, he said, "You look like you're in the market for a friend. Are you all right?"

"Okay, I guess. Just started the week in a real lousy way, a way I'm not proud of."

Al looked at the half empty glass and nodded sagely "If you mean that, old friend, you're right. A damn lousy way to start a day, even if it does mean business for the *Eagle*."

"Enough said on that subject." Al sat down next to Jack and said, "The other day we talked about that shot glass business. After you left, I began thinking about the whiskey scam. Hear me out and see if this makes sense. I know I mentioned this earlier, but let me review it again."

Al reviewed the pharmacy whiskey scam in detail. "Are you with me?"

Jack nodded. "How many times do we have to go over it?"

"Give yourself a break and listen to this. I checked around and found 800 pints of blood were processed a week. Navy regs said a donor was entitled to a double shot. With that in mind, think about the fake bottom shot glass and look what you get. Eight hundred servicemen give blood a week, that means the same number of shots could be ripped off. My friend, that translates into twenty-seven, twenty-eight quarts of whiskey a week."

O'Brennan picked up on Simon's every word and saw the direction he was taking him.

"Freddie Gill was sneaking whiskey out of the hospital and selling it in Harkers. I've heard he sold it at three dollars a bottle or eighty to ninety dollars a week! That's a hell of a deal for everyone concerned. As a third-class, his navy pay was around $120 a month. You can see we're talking real big money."

"You're right, Al, it all makes sense. I like what you just told me. I'm out of here!" Jack's mind was churning as he rose to leave, shoving the remains of his beer in Al's direction, he added, "Don't need this anymore. It's back to the chase. Thanks!"

"Where are you going?" You just got here."

"To fill in some of the missing blanks."

O'Brennan traveled up Niagara to Gloucester, then around to police headquarters. In most communities, large or small, you travel uptown, or downtown, depending on where you started from. This was not the case in Bridgeton where you went around town.

O'Brennan walked downstairs to the property room and Charlie Winder.

Charlie greeted his friend. "Jack O'Brennan, how about some coffee."

"Not today, Charlie, but thanks. I'm back to pick your brain again."

"Shoot."

"When Harkers was running full bore in the fifties, how much prostitution was going on?"

"You know how that goes, where there's guys on the make, there're women to take care of their needs. There were the traditional bar flies who were all over Harkers like a blanket. But what the hell, any service town has 'em. Harkers had few streetwalkers, never understood it, but there are a lot of things that pass me by. Contacts were pretty much made in the bars. If you ever noticed, and I'm sure you have, the bars always had high booths in the back., It was possible to get done whatever crossed your mind if you climbed into a booth. You know what I mean?"

"Charlie, that doesn't help much. I told you about the case I started last week where a young woman was involved. The feeling here is she was dirty. My problem is I have nothing to back it up. It's my intuition working overtime; thought whoring might be it." Shaking his head, Jack continued, "Just can't imagine she was into back-booth action, just doesn't fit. Speaking of fit, try this one on for size. It's a known fact that officers needed action like everybody else. They couldn't come down to Harkers, so what about call girls? Any around back then?"

"Bull's eye, my man. There were several groups working the area. Damn, I can't think of it. Just a minute, I'll find out"

He dialed a number, waited, then began to talk. "George, this is Charlie Winder down at headquarters What was the name of the escort service Jeanette Purchase ran in the fifties? . . . Greenbriar Escort Service, that's the one. I'll be talking to you later, thanks again."

Charlie looked at Jack with a mile-wide toothy smile. "Jeanette and I go back a long way. Would you like to meet her?"

"Certainly."

"We may catch her at the restaurant this afternoon."

"Sounds good to me."

Charlie dialed another number. "Yes, I'd like to speak to Jeanette please . . . thanks" Minutes passed "Jeanette, Charlie Winder . . . just fine, and you? That's good. Look, an old detective buddy dropped by. He's a private eye working a case you might be able to add some light to. Any chance you'd talk to him? . . . Excellent, we'll be over around six."

"You're in the ballpark," Charlie said with a smile.

Plans were made for Charlie to be picked up at four. Before leaving, Jack asked, "What's this restaurant she runs?"

"The *Red Leather* on Hampton Street is no rinky-dink place. It's a classy joint with classy prices and a classy clientele, so look your best."

Jack spent much of the afternoon stripping paint from an old rocker; a hobby he enjoyed over the years. While working, he listened to *WBRI*, Bridgeton's most popular AM station. They played the *Music of Your Life*, much of which was pop tunes from the late forties, fifties and sixties. Many of the songs brought back pleasant memories from his earlier days. When his children were teenagers, they continually questioned why he played that old-fashioned music. Once his eldest daughter Sue, asked him, "What's so important about playing those old songs?"

He recalled explaining to her, those songs bring back the good old care-free days of my youth. He knew his reply didn't impress her; nor did Les and Larry Elgart. Her idea of good music was the Beach Boys.

Working in the small barn behind his house provided a quiet setting for Jack to review the case. The information he acquired at *McWilliams* indicated Fritz Hansen was a king-pin in the East Coast drug traffic. Hansen probably got his start in Harkers, but how about Sally Ralston? Where did she fit in? Freddie was selling stolen whiskey, Hansen dope, but what was Sally selling? How about flesh? Yes, that was a strong possibility. With her looks, it was very possible!

He pictured Jeanette Purchase who ran the call-girl Greenbrier Escort Service as fat, with dyed red hair, coarse, gruff, a real sweetheart. Well, he'd know soon enough.

His thoughts turned to Danny Tremonte, the *Citizen-Tribune's* police reporter. He authored a column on the Bridgeton police scene and he owed Jack. Maybe he could slip something into his column about the case. This might get somebody's attention.

12

O'Brennan drove Charlie to *O'Hearn's* for a couple of drinks. O'Brennan needed to find out more about this lady of the night he was about to meet.

"Tell me some more about this Jeanette Purchase."

"When Jeanette cut loose the escort service, she didn't know what to do with herself."

"Charlie, why would she give up something as lucrative and successful as the service?"

"When Harkers was demolished in the early sixties, she threw in the towel. Said the business would never be the same."

"Was she making a lot of money?"

"Money, would you go for tons of it? I'll bet she's worth millions and most of it came from wise investments in real estate. Jeanette always kept a low profile when she operated the escort service, so it was easy for her to slip into a new business venture.

"She bought an old supermarket on Hampton Avenue and totally refurbished it. Jeanette opened it as a posh eatery and called it the *Red Leather*. The restaurant was class, she was class and so were the high-class people with their high-class bucks. She immediately turned her restaurant into a first-string operation, and when you meet her, you'll understand why it is so successful."

O'Hearn checked to see if drinks were needed, then continued about his business.

"You know, Jack, I think the restaurant was her entry to a different life. It provided her with a legitimacy she desperately sought, and has done nicely with it since it opened. Have you ever been there?"

"Yes, but I never thought much about it other than the high prices. Years ago, I took Mary there for our anniversary. Charlie, I damn near died when I got the bill. Needless to say, I never went back. Getting back to this Purchase woman, what's she like?"

"Wait till you see this chicken She's probably in her mid-fifties and a great looker. She's not beautiful, but she sure is pretty. Jeanette has a great personality and she's smarter than hell! Tell ya' another thing about her, she's tough and kind of a hard-ass if you ask me. There's one thing I do know about her, she can be trusted. There's no middle ground with Jeanette. If she likes you, she'll go to the wall with you. Like I told you before, we go back a long way. I met her when I was a patrolman. I needed $2000 for the down payment on a house; the same one I have today, as a matter of fact. I didn't have it; the banks wouldn't loan it to me, so she floated me the money. When you talk about quality people, she's the best."

"That's not how I pictured her. I imagined she'd be more or less tough and kind of gross."

"What do you mean by more or less?"

Jack shook his head, "Charlie, I honestly don't know what I mean. Come on, let's go meet this chicken you've been telling me about."

After entering the *Red Leather*, Jack immediately knew who Jeanette Purchase was. He had made a special effort to look sharp. Although wearing casual attire, he felt neat and wanted to look good with no loose ends showing. Hell, he thought, I'm thinking like a school boy on his first date.

Jeanette stood by the cash register looking sleek and trim with the satiny look of money. What Charlie had said about her being nice looking was no exaggeration. Maybe she wasn't beautiful to Charlie, but she was gorgeous to O'Brennan.

Dressed in a red knit dress with matching red heels, she was the youngest looking mid-fifties lady he'd ever seen. He was taken by her height. She appeared just under six foot and had a terrific figure to compliment her size. Her striking shape, graying brown hair, relatively unlined face and fleeting smile combined for a striking appearance. His heart seemed to jump out of his chest as he looked at the lady in red.

After the introductions, the three entered the near-empty taproom where they made small talk until the drinks were served. Seated between Charlie and Jack, Jeanette turned to O'Brennan and coyly said, "Do you know you have a policeman's eyes?" O'Brennan merely shrugged, not knowing what else to do. "Tell me, Jack O'Brennan, who are you and what are you all about?" The little wrinkles around her eyes she so vainly tried to hide with make-up were the only flaws in an otherwise unblemished appearance.

Is this one a little weird or what? Jack asked himself. The whole situation was making him nervous. What did Charlie get him into?

"To be honest, I'm about to faint from your question." Jeanette and Charlie laughed and Jack wasn't sure what they were laughing at.

Jack talked about his background as a policeman, his detective work with the force, his private-eye practice and the Freddie Gill case in that order. He vaguely outlined what he knew, touching on Gill's activities in Harkers and his association with Hansen and Sally Ralston.

"I'll give it to you straight. At this point, I'm against the wall. I don't know where to go and thought you could possibly help."

The beautiful glistening eyes that earlier greeted O'Brennan had now turned to slits of hazel. "What makes you think Sally worked for me?"

"Jeanette, any detective, good or bad, will make calculated guesses. The less there is to work on, the more we make. I'm guessing she was selling her wares. Now, how many alternatives did she have? I met Sally this morning and one classy lady she is. It's my guess she didn't get that way overnight, no, because she has always been sharp and on top of her life. If she were to go into this questionable trade, what direction would her instincts take her? Certainly not in a back booth of the *Shamrock*, or on a bench in Inlet Park. What was her remaining alternative? I believe an escort service would be in order."

Jeanette barely smiled at Jack.

He appeared not to be distracted. "Charlie told me back in the fifties there were four or five escort services in town. All but yours had a questionable reputation. So, here I am talking to the lone lady in town who ran an impeccably clean operation. That's my calculated guess and that's how I arrived at it."

Flashing a smile as he looked at Jeanette, O'Brennan asked, "Can you help me?"

Jeanette pointed at Jack and said, "How tall are you?"

This woman is some piece of work, he thought while replying, "I'm six-three. Why do you ask?"

"Just curious. I like to know as much as I can about the people I talk to." The sparkle returned to the beautiful hazel eyes, glistening as they looked at Jack.

Never in his life had anyone looked at him that way, and she seemed to touch his innermost feelings. He felt embarrassed, faint and on the verge of wetting his pants. Long forgotten sensations from the past resurfaced.

Just tell yourself this isn't happening, Jack told himself.

Jeanette reached across the bar and covered his folded hands. She looked searchingly at him and spoke, "If you want my help, you will have to tell all, Jack O'Brennan. Please don't beat around the bush. Can you do that?"

"Yes," O'Brennan said gravely. "I know Sally was hanging around with several sailors. She traveled with Freddie Gill who apparently was stealing whiskey from the Naval Hospital pharmacy and selling it to bars on Cayuga Street. I'm talking about substantial figures probably approaching eighty dollars a week, and that may be a conservative guess. This computes out to around $350 a month, plus $120 from the Navy That was a considerable amount in 1953."

"Excuse me, Jack," Jeanette motioned to the bartender for refills. "Please continue."

The apparent grace and finesse this lady possessed overwhelmed Jack. She was in a league of her own.

"Fritz Hansen, the second character, was on a tin can and every indicator points to him as a drug dealer. I don't know much about him at this time, but by Wednesday, the picture should be clearer. We have this woman, Sally Ralston hanging around with these rascals. I know she was selling magazines at the fleet landing, and that in itself would make her good money. Everybody figured they'd end up sleeping with her if they bought a magazine subscription. The apparent open invitation to bed was nothing more than a ruse on her part. She might have led those sailors to that conclusion, but apparently it didn't work that way."

The dinner crowd was beginning to overflow into the bar, and the surrounding chatter caused Jeanette to display growing signs of annoyance. "Let's go to the office," she suggested as she picked up her drink and headed for the backroom. Jeanette led the way to a modestly furnished office that quietly stated a woman worked here. "This is heavy material for those curious ears at the bar," she added. Her smile was enough to melt an iceberg. "I keep interrupting you, and for that, I'm sorry. Please continue."

Charlie laughed and took a sip of beer. He appeared to be enjoying himself as Jack glanced in his direction. The details of the case made for interesting listening and the interplay between Jeanette and Jack provided a refreshing addition to his prim, somber life.

O'Brennan, as if on cue continued "So, she hung around Gill and occasionally with Hansen. Sally was in and out like the sun. She'd be seen at six then again at eleven or twelve, but never in between. This I'm betting on; one person was stealing whiskey, one was selling dope and the third was Sally. What's a girl to do? Maybe, she was selling herself."

A pause, accompanied by a expressionless stare, caused Jeanette to momentarily look away. O'Brennan attempted to read her reaction, but dismissed such thoughts as she turned back to offer another warm, pleasing smile.

He continued "I checked around and found she wasn't

walking the streets. She wasn't hustling in bars, so, what was she doing? Reports indicate she made her headquarters in a back booth of the *Shamrock*, but never attempted to hustle the patrons. In fact, she barely talked to them. Both Charlie and I agree she was in some kind of high-class hustle, but that's pure speculation."

"But it would help if you could find out something about her," Jeanette added. "Jack O'Brennan, I do believe you want me to do your investigative work for you." Her smile appeared sweet but hard.

Jack thought about the direction Jeanette had just taken the conversation.

"My friend, Charlie, the beach man mentioned if you keep going back, more clues will turn up. I'll go back and work harder. Something will come up and it will come without you," Jack said as he glared at Jeanette. Why was he so upset with this woman? She had said not one word to provoke such feelings, then why was he feeling emotionally stressed?

"What is it you have to know about Sally Ralston?" Jeanette asked.

O'Brennan could sense he was losing control. "It's pretty apparent you knew what you wanted when you were selling her body around Bridgeton."

She winced at his words. "No, you're wrong, Jack! What you just said was cruel and uncalled for, and there's no need to talk that way," a shaken Jeanette Purchase whispered.

O'Brennan's face reddened. "You're right of course, Ms. Purchase. I'm sorry I spoke to you in that tone, and I'm disappointed in myself for having made such pointless comment."

O'Brennan pushed his chair back and rose in one effortless motion.

"Come on, Charlie, let's get out of here. This was an ill-advised trip."

He gestured for Charlie to follow as he started toward the door.

"You have no right to leave!" shouted Jeanette as she glared at him. He turned to answer, but thought better of it. She raced around the desk and in one swift motion grabbed O'Brennan's arm. She was one powerful woman and her strength surprised him. "No one has ever walked out on me, and you aren't going to be the first."

O'Brennan never professed to understand women, and five years without Mary hadn't helped. "If you have something to say, just get on with it," Jack said, as he shot a reproving glance that served its purpose.

Charlie sat in the awkward silence that followed the crisp exchange of words, not believing his ears. He questioned why O'Brennan had spoken so harshly. He had known Jack for years and had never seen this ugly side. He didn't have a sexist bone in his body. No, there's something else I'm missing, he thought.

"Sally worked for me three summers during that early fifties period. Did you mention when she graduated?" Jeanette asked.

"She graduated in 1955," O'Brennan snarled.

"In that case, she worked from 1952 through 1954."

"When would she have worked for you? What time of the year, I mean?"

"She worked June through August and sometimes a couple of weeks into September. She also worked some holidays, mainly Thanksgiving and Christmas. Sometimes she came down on weekends."

"How good was she?"

"She was the crown jewel of the service. The best I had. Sally was a vivacious young lady and smart too, no, make that cunning. She had repeat calls like you wouldn't believe and commanded the top dollar. Sally . . ."

O'Brennan interrupted, "What would the top dollar be?"

"In her case, around forty. This was when most girls working Cayuga Street were getting five dollars for a short-timer."

O'Brennan hated the way Jeanette so openly talked about such a thing.

"What was so unique about her? Did you get any feelings about her? Like her, didn't like her, that sort of thing."

"I didn't trust her. Don't get me wrong, she was making a lot of money for me as well as plenty for herself. I would have hired the devil if I could have made money off him."

O'Brennan nodded then invited her to continue.

"I say this advisedly; she was always looking for a hustle; greener pastures if you will."

"Why would she be looking for greener pastures if she was doing so well with you?"

"Let me give you an example" Jeanette looked over at O'Brennan with less piercing eyes. She appeared to be mellowing and eager to talk, while Jack remained stone-faced. "Have you ever been in a crowd with someone who constantly looked at you and everyone else in the room? Every time you look their way, they're looking at you. Sally was like that. She looked at people almost as if she were checking their underwear size." Charlie laughed, but neither Jeanette nor Jack thought it funny. "She had an uncanny ability for making people feel uneasy around her. She critiqued everyone she met, but I'm certain you've seen such behavior."

"Why would that bother you?" A puzzled O'Brennan asked.

"Anyone I've ever known who was like Sally turned out to be a sneak. I'm sure she was moonlighting on the side." Jeanette paused, seemingly to collect her thoughts, then continued her appraisal of Sally. "She'd have an appointment with a client, a week later, she'd meet him on the side, then pocket the money from the subsequent meeting."

"Sally must have had something very special. She obviously had a lot of plusses."

"She was beautiful and some of my clients told me she was an ace in bed. She wore a provocative look, not really sexy, but sensuous. Her personality was tops and she really knew how to hook a guy. I agree, she really was something!"

"What kind of men used your services?"

"I had quality clients. That's one reason why we never had problems with the police. My operation spelled CLASS! I had quality women and I knew how to function without being noticed. We were an out-of-sight, out-of-mind operation."

"Would someone like me use your service?" O'Brennan asked, trying to get a handle on the story Jeanette told about herself and her girls.

"No, I don't believe so," Jeanette quickly responded.

"Are you saying I wasn't good enough for your girls?" he snapped.

"I answered a question you shouldn't have asked," Jeanette crisply responded.

He did not reply, but offered a hard look, then motioned with a slight hand gesture for her to continue.

Guardedly, she started, "We had an extraordinarily large clientele made up mostly of Naval officers and other military brass. There were captains, commanders and a preferred list of admirals. There also was the Washington outlet. The DC group had the best of all worlds. They'd slip out of town, drive down here, meet their date at any number of casual places, then shoot back to the city. It took a few short hours, so no one was ever the wiser."

"What types are you talking about?"

"I'm talking senators, congressmen and administrative assistants. I suppose you might call them power brokers."

"That's kind of scary, wouldn't you say?" O'Brennan asked.

Jeanette shrugged indifferently. "Yes, I suppose it could have been, but even in the fifties, there was a tremendous bureaucracy in Washington. The capital was lucrative and did well by us."

Charlie sat listening to their conversation and observed two strong personalities who apparently didn't like each other. But Charlie saw something else. They were searching for something missing in their lives.

Now they were both on the attack and appeared to relish hurting each other. But Charlie saw something else. Charlie took a sip of beer. Sitting back, it came to him. These poor souls are desperately lonely. Lonely or not, he wondered if they'd ever get together without this undercurrent of hostility.

"As you talk, I keep thinking about blackmail. Wasn't there a temptation for a woman to blackmail a client; enter into a little backdoor free enterprise?"

"No, I protected against that. We forewarned clients that under no circumstances would we tolerate even the slightest inference of blackmail. They were to report any irregular requests immediately to a supervisor or me."

"This may sound dumb, but why would you have a supervisor?" O'Brennan. asked.

"This was no mom and pop operation I had. How many girls do you think I had working for me?" The start of a smile began to cross her face.

He shrugged as he looked this beauty over.

"How about twenty-five"

O'Brennan shook his head. "In my fondest dreams, I couldn't imagine such an organization. That's a lot!"

Jeanette readily agreed. "Yes it was. I intimidated the girls, and this threat created an obstacle to their aspirations."

"Was Sally capable of such a maneuver?"

"The view from here is Sally was capable of anything. She worshipped the almighty dollar and worked like a money-making machine for it. Sally was very aloof and extremely secretive. She was a living paradox; on one hand sweet and personable, while on the other, hard, cold and calculating. And I'm certain of this; she had a long line of indiscretions."

Jack stared at this lovely creature across from him, amazed at the harsh indictment she saddled Sally with. "Do you ever see her?"

She gave Jack a blank look. "Does it matter?"

"If you you were in my position, wouldn't you ask the same question?"

"Yes, I suppose I would." Her sparkling eyes flickered like a candle in the wind. "She now is the epitome of a well-bred woman. You can catch her name in the social column a couple of times a week. She appears to do a lot of good deeds throughout the city, but no, I never talk to her, or for that matter, any of my former girls. It's best left that way." Jeanette finished as if she had terminated the interview.

Quickly standing, Jeanette spoke to Jack. "I believe, Mr. O'Brennan, our discussion has ended."

Her last words left nothing for O'Brennan to debate. He did manage to call back, "Ha!"

On the way to Jack's car, Charlie eyes displayed the look of an executioner about to trip the gallows door at a hanging. He turned his fury on O'Brennan, "You really don't get it, do you, O'Brennan? You couldn't leave well enough alone, no, you had to attack her where it hurt. You used to be a damn decent guy, but look at you now. You just treated one fine lady as if she were a nothing. She's got more class than you'll ever have! You're worthless, and for that I pity you."

Jack grunted. He was on a case, not out looking for a woman or popularity vote. "She was the one who came after me. Granted, I said some things that were uncalled for, but I apologized for them. Now you tell me I'm worthless for talking back to her."

"Jack, she didn't come after you, and you know it. Do you think you're the first guy to lose a wife? You treat all women like dirt since Mary died. Even the Group makes fun of you. They say Jack O'Brennan needs a piece of ass to get his head straight. Maybe he'll quit feeling sorry for himself after he gets the pressure off his back."

"They can shove it!" Jack raised his hands in a hopeless gesture, feeling the first surge of indignation at Charlie's words.

"Tomorrow, I'm returning to the *Red Leather* and apologize for ever taking you over there. I'm sorry she ever met you." Charlie's ice-like look said it all.

Jack stammered a few words, but Charlie wouldn't listen. He was mad and felt sorely betrayed by an old buddy. It was evident Jack had lost a friend and made a mortal enemy of a woman he greatly admired.

Jack O'Brennan thought out loud as he maneuvered through the light evening traffic on his return to Ford Ashland.

"I've never mistreated a woman in my life and here I just bad-mouthed a lady I don't even know. I know she provoked some of the disagreement, but I'll be damned if I understand my actions of the last hour. I should go back and tell her how sorry I am, but I guess it's too late to recant such a stupid error."

He sighed. "This has not been a good day."

13

"Danny Tremonte, please . . . yes, this is Jack O'Brennan. I'm at home so have him call me when he gets back."

Fifteen minutes later, the *Citizen Tribune* crime reporter returned Jack's call. "Danny, I need your help and in return, I may have a blockbuster story for you. Where are you now? Fine, I'll meet you at the city marina in an hour."

O'Brennan found Danny on a park bench studying the yachts in the marina. Idle chatter continued for a brief time before Danny said, "I have to take off in a couple of minutes. There's a big shot in town that I have to interview. What's this hot shot story you have? Writers in cities like Bridgeton don't come up with many blockbuster stories like you mentioned."

"This could give you a new lease on life." Jack gave Tremonte some background on the Gill case, focusing on his death. He mentioned the shot glass scam, Gill's two friends, and their tattooed *Shamrock* leaves. He needed to cultivate Danny's interest so he'd write the story. "I need to get this story out to the public; see if it rattles some cages. Do you catch my drift?"

Danny sounded unsure, "I feel uncomfortable doing a story that's so vague. It doesn't seem to wash if you ask me."

Jack sensed his apprehension. "Danny, I have a gut feeling about this one" Jack extended his arms in a sweeping motion.

"Give me something solid," Tremonte said"

"I've been in this business a long time and like I said earlier, it feels right. Somewhere down the line, this could work out very nicely for you. I'll give you the exclusive on the whole story if you help me. It would have to be off the record to start, but when it comes out, you'll have the story of your very young career. There's nothing out there that says I'm right, but I can smell it."

"All because of some half-assed feeling?" Danny shook his head in a skeptical manner.

"All because of some half-assed feeling, but I'm certain of this one."

"What can you give me now?"

"Prostitution, stealing whiskey and drug peddling, how's that for openers?"

"In the fifties?"

"Yes, drugs were around, somewhat a closet thing, but they were there, nevertheless. Tie that in with stealing, debauchery and one dead sailor; what more could you ask for? That gives you one hell of a story."

"How would you want me to approach it?" Danny asked, warming to the idea.

"I'd like to help write the story."

"No way, nobody writes my stories."

"I don't mean write it personally. I'll give you an outline including particulars I'd like in the first article. I know this is pretty one-sided, but you'll have to trust me."

"I have to be careful. I've got to go on facts, and can't monkey with mere speculation. I could lose a career tampering with something I'm not certain of," Danny said.

"Yes, and you could also get yourself a big name along the way," O'Brennan pointed out.

"Jack, I've got to think about this one."

"I'll give you a call later in the afternoon," O'Brennan said

Returning home, Jack settled in for an afternoon's work on the rocker he'd been working on. His mind soon drifted to the case. As far as he was concerned, there were four people involved: Freddie Gill was dead, Sally was involved right up to her pretty ears, Hansen looked suspicious and what about the fourth person?

He probably was the brains of the operation. Would he eventually show? Only time would tell.

O'Brennan rubbed yesterday's scene with Jeanette around in his head. If he could only bury his head in sand, maybe the memory would go away. Maybe working on this chair will do the trick, he reasoned.

But it didn't work that way. He worked on refinishing until he couldn't stand it any longer. The decision was difficult, but right or wrong, he'd follow it up. Returning to the house, Jack dialed the *Red Leather*. He nervously waited for the call to be answered.

"*Red Leather.*"

"Jeanette Purchase please." Several minutes passed before Jeanette answered.

"This is Jeanette Purchase."

"Jeanette, this is Jack O'Brennan."

The gulp of air indicated her surprise at hearing Jack's voice "Oh dear! . . . Does this have something to do with last night? Wasn't it clear I didn't want to hear from you again? Ever!"

"You sound angry."

"You can bet on it," Jeanette said in a shrill voice.

"I can't blame you. I'm calling to apologize for my bad behavior yesterday."

"Fine. You apologized and I accept. May I hang up now?"

"Please wait. We can't leave it at that."

"Leave it at that? There is nothing to leave. There never was anything in the first place," annoyance flooding her voice.

As O'Brennan listened to her lightning-like reply, he thought her voice had a regal air even on the phone. "You scared me yesterday."

Jeanette laughed. "You're wasting my time being humble, so don't patronize me. I scared you, that's a good one! A real classic. How ridiculous can you get?"

"It's true, you most certainly did," Jack responded with an embarrassed but sincere voice.

"Now, how did I do that to a big tough detective like the fabled Jack O'Brennan?"

"You don't have to be a rocket scientist to figure that out. Your class and beauty got the better of me. My wife Mary was kind of plain and was married to just as plain a guy. When simple men like me are around stylish, elegant women like you, they say stupid things and act dumb. You can't imagine what a severe problem it creates for them. In my case, I was intimidated by your style; your obvious poise."

"That's a nice way of putting it, but that's nonsense. Can't you come up with a better reason for your irrational behavior?"

"No, it's not nonsense. When Charlie called to set up our meeting, I pictured you totally differently than you are."

"And how was that?"

"I imagined you as short and fat with dyed red hair. Figured you had blotchy skin and looked like a garbage can," Jack ignored her laugh, "and saw you as the foul talking ex-madam portrayed in the movies. Obviously, you didn't fit that image."

"You had no right to attack me and treat me like something I'm not."

"I admit I made a bad mistake. I also know I acted like a horse's ass and that I'm sorry for. This is the toughest thing I've ever done in my life and believe me, I'm dying inside. Charlie read me the riot act last night about how I treated you, and there's truth in what he said." He paused, then added . . ."I've never felt so lousy about anything in my life, and I'm at a loss to make amends."

"I accept your apology. I'm not a difficult person, Mr. O'Brennan, and I also feel somewhat responsible for what turned out to be a very strange evening. Charlie has a habit of trying to find a suitable gentleman for me, and it would appear he has a paternal interest in my welfare. When he brought you over to the restaurant yesterday, I figured he had lined up another candidate for me to check out. It appears we both overreacted, so, I also am sorry for our major disagreement."

Excitement suddenly grabbed him. "All's forgiven then, but there is a simple request I'd like to make. Tomorrow evening, I'm driving my old convertible down to Portsmouth on a little business.

I have to pick up some information about the case and wondered if you'd ride down with me."

"That is out of the question."

"I hate being alone and I'm amazed how much I seem to be doing that very thing of late."

"Be that as it may, but what you suggest is impossible."

"My problem is, I'm young at heart but old of body. I just thought it would be nice to talk to a woman instead of the bunch of guys I hang around with."

His pathetic voice and the uncertain way he handled himself appealed to her sympathetic nature. We live and learn she thought and I'll probably be sorry for this, but why not. "Yes, I will ride down to Portsmouth with you."

"That's terrific! I'll pick you up at the restaurant, say four in the afternoon."

"Very well, I'll see you then."

Jack's frame of mind did a one-eighty as excitement washed over him. He never thought tomorrow's arrangement possible. He could hardly believe an old turkey like him would end up with a classy lady like Jeanette; even if it were only a one-night stand. Wow! What would Mary think? He hoped she'd be smiling too. His thoughts turned to the Group and he questioned whether he should have asked one of them. To hell with that bunch, he thought; he could drive them around anytime.

After supper, Jack washed and polished the '57 Chevy. The cream colored canvas and matching trim accented its bright red color. He pretended to be cleaning it for himself, but he knew better. He was polishing it to impress Jeanette.

Later, he began an outline for Danny's column. At that moment it dawned on him he'd forgotten to call the columnist. He dialed Danny and got him on the third ring.

"Danny Tremonte."

"Danny, this is Jack. I forgot to call you this afternoon, and regrettably, it completely slipped my mind. What did you come up with?"

"Maybe because I'm an optimist, I'll help you out. Get the outline material over here tonight and I'll put it in the Thursday column. Can't promise much until I see what you've given me."

"Thanks Danny, I'll be over shortly."

For over an hour he pondered what to write. The information he typed included: PI contacted by a mid-west party requesting that a sailor's death be investigated. He had to be careful because Danny would delete anything that wasn't solid.

When Jack felt comfortable with what had been written, he drove over to Tremonte's apartment. Small talk was out tonight because he needed to be rested and sharp for tomorrow. I have a long drive to DC in the morning and have to pick Jeanette up for the Porstmouth jaunt. Regardless of what you choose to call it; you have a date with a beautiful lady tomorrow evening, he told himself. Thoughts of this mysterious lady swept through him as he headed for Ford Ashland and rest.

14

Jack's thoughts drifted to Bud Henry, the FBI agent he was meeting at the George Washington Mansion in Mt Vernon. Their friendship had extended over many years and this would probably be their last chance to work together. Hitting the George Washington Memorial Parkway, Jack was astonished by the early morning traffic. Bridgeton traffic at times was unbearable, but this was ridiculous.

Meeting the soon-to-retire agent in the mansion parking lot puzzled O'Brennan. He knew Henry was full of cloak and dagger shenanigans, and passed it off as just another of Bud's little quirks. After several minutes of gossip, Jack commented, "Bud, our station in life is not commensurate with meeting in a parking lot." Bud merely shrugged and motioned O'Brennan to begin. O'Brennan returned Bud's shrug and started his story. He brought into play the background of the case and why he had called, also adding his suspicions about the three others involved with Freddie Gill.

Henry looked grave as he began his litany "For what's it's worth, this Hansen has a shadowy past and I dread the day when you have to face him. I'm sure you're aware of that, but I must remind you this has to be off the record. Hansen lives in Portsmouth, but that you already know. He joined the Navy in Frostburg, Maryland, his hometown; following which he went through boot camp at Bainbridge. From there Hansen attended Hospital Corps School in Portsmouth. During that period, he got into a couple of scrapes with the police, but nothing major." Henry laughed, "He did get into a fight that damn near turned into a riot and got a drunk and disorderly charge out of it, but he wasn't alone. Compared to the rest of the fleet, it was no big deal.

"After graduating number one in his class, he was sent next door for duty at the Naval Hospital. Eventually, he received orders to a destroyer out of Bridgeton. Hansen had a four-o record aboard ship, but had questionable ties in Harkers during that period. He did have one suspicious incident while attached to the ship. They found drugs in the Black Gang and tried to tie him to their sales, but with no luck. Word had it he was peddling, but nothing ever came of it. After two years on the can, he returned to Portsmouth to finish out his hitch."

"And after his discharge?"

"The interesting part is he stayed in the area. Hansen made first class in four years of navy life which shows he was a real brain. He didn't have much of a high school record, but colleges were following a rolling admissions policy at the time. He enrolled at Old Dominion in Norfolk and majored in finance, with a minor in marketing. Going to school under the GI Bill didn't leave much to live on. What the hell, we both went under the same program. By the time tuition was paid, it was tough surviving. What did we get, $110 a month; that would make anyone sweat but not Hansen. He always had money to burn and spent it like it was going out of style. That's when the Bureau began tracking him."

"What were they tracking him for?"

Bud gave O'Brennan what looked like a smile. "Do you remember the Joe McCarthy days? McCarthy had accused everyone of coddling Communists, including colleges. It was a bunch of nonsense, but never the less, several agencies began looking at some of these schools."

"Yes, I remember. It never hit us at Elon, but some of big universities were nervous," Jack added.

"About 1957, McCarthy died but by then, civil liberties had taken a horrendous battering. Our friend would never have been noticed if not for the Red Scare. Hansen stood out to the practiced observer; not for Communist inclinations mind you, but because he was running with some pretty tough characters in Norfolk. He eventually formed an unholy alliance with that element and has gone his merry way ever since. During his second year at Old Dominion, there were several key hits in the Tidewater area. The Norfolk Police felt Hansen was responsible, but again, they had nothing to hang their hat on. In 1959, he finished school with top honors, and the police agencies down there can attest to how smart he is."

"Did they ever bring him in for questioning?"

"Never did. There's every indication that Hansen is currently the whole enchilada in the area. He's the man, no doubt in my mind. He runs a quality operation, is honest to a fault, and is extremely fair in pricing. He is loyal to his customers, and has built up substantial support in the drug world and so it goes."

"The operation you just described sounds like it had the *Good Housekeeping Seal of Approval* on it," Jack said.

Bud laughed, "You are very quick and still do funny things with words. Getting back to Hansen, the henchmen around him are mean, tough, and one might call them his support staff. Hope chest puritans they're not. This guy has a pipeline to the police and another thing; dealing with this slime will be like opening a jewel case and finding a turd in it."

"Last Saturday, I paid a visit to Portsmouth to see an old friend about Hansen I didn't get much, but I should know more later."

"Your friend is Kenny Ross who owns *McWilliams* on the square in Craddock. As a matter of fact, you have an appointment tonight to meet a detective at Ross' bar; a guy named Nick Steinman to be exact. I assume all of the above is correct."

"How in hell do you know what I'm doing tonight?"

"Jack, it's what I do. Fritz Hansen has a pipeline down there and so do we. It's that simple. That's the price we pay for doing business. A tradeoff if you will."

"If you already know all this, why have you left me out in the cold? This stinks and you know it! If you weren't my friend I'd call you stonehearted," said an embittered O'Brennan.

"Just hold on. You're getting too worked up, so let's backtrack and unravel some of this. I've been watching this guy for a long time and so have the Norfolk Police. In fact, several other agencies are hustling after him as well. It appears we may never get this bird for drug dealing, but let me blow this by you and see if it makes any sense."

Knowing there was more to come, Jack seemed to calm down.

"Do you remember hearing about the Al Capone case in the 1930's? The authorities could never convict him of racketeering, but the Feds eventually came through the back door and hit him for tax evasion. After hearing about your visit to Craddock, we're taking a new posture on Hansen. We came up with 'an around about way' that may help all concerned parties."

"I don't catch your direction with this, 'around about way'," Jack said.

"Maybe Hansen's achilles is much like Capone's. They never did get Capone for racketeering, and to put the worse face on it, I doubt we'll ever get Hansen for drug dealing. Possibly, his weak spot may be his past, not the present."

"What are you driving at?"

Henry appeared to mull his thoughts around before he spoke. "We'd like you to cooperate with us. We scratch your back, you scratch ours. Is that too much to ask?"

That's the first shoe dropping one hears about, O'Brennan thought. "Bud, I have reservations about your proposal because I know how you people run your business. If you come in, you'll have a division of agents all over Tidewater and Bridgeton before the blink of the eye. I also know you can and will do just that! If you were to get into this investigation, you'd break your own rules and that would be that. I wouldn't have a thing to say and you know it. Why don't you stay out of this maneuver before you mess everything up. One last thing, I'm being paid to investigate and you're taking the bread right out of my mouth."

"Now calm down, Jack, there is one thing you must understand. This is official. The assistant director sent this down; if you agree to cooperate, here's what we'll do. You'll run your own show with no changes, that's a given, and we'll stay out of your way. All we want is to be kept abreast of where you are in the case. Whatever you need is yours, but there is one stipulation. Any . . ."

Jack interrupted, "There is always one stipulation, isn't there, Bud?"

"I've noted your concern." Bud's subtle smile only served to further infuriate O'Brennan. Realizing this, Henry smoothly continued. "No, it's nothing like that. Any communication you make with the Bureau goes through me. Now that isn't bad, is it?"

"I don't like it! Is this why we're in the parking lot? Realistically, I don't have much choice, do I?"

Henry said yes with a nod, then began to laugh. "Jack, I'm afraid you're trying to be a general with a private's mentality. Keep this; because you'll need it," Bud said as he handed Jack a business card. "You'll find my unlisted number on the back. We'll be meeting occasionally at different times and places, of course."

"Of course," O'Brennan replied with a snort.

Ignoring his remark, Bud cautioned, "Keep this in mind. We knew about your trip to Craddock and so does Fritz Hansen. That you can count on!"

"You sure know how to make a person feel good," Jack responded with a slight smile escaping an otherwise serious face. "In other words, don't call me, I'll call you, or is it the other way around. I never did get those two right."

Driving back to Bridgeton, O'Brennan found himself in a monumental snit. He had let the Bureau in and this annoyed him, better yet, infuriated was the better word. What alternative did he have? He felt used and betrayed, by whom he didn't know. From here on, he'd be snooping around with Big Brother looking over his shoulder. Did Bud think he was dumb enough to believe he'd be left alone? There was only one solution and that was to keep as far away from the Feds as humanly possible.

Walking into the kitchen, he grabbed a can of beer and retreated to the patio He was furious at himself, so much so that he had driven back from Mt Vernon with the air-conditioning off. A case of self-denial on his part, or just plain dumbness, he thought

What would Mary think about the case? She'd probably tell him to forget it and give it to the FBI with a ribbon tied around it. But Mary was no more, and sitting in a rocker waiting for divine guidance was not the answer. He'd soon have to make a decision whether to continue or not, and it would have to be his choice and his alone.

O'Brennan looked around the patio recalling how much Mary had enjoyed decorating it. The casual room had been her labor of love and he felt saddened she had not lived to enjoy it. His mind turned to tonight's meeting in Craddock, a most delicate one for certain. Knowing about Hansen's eyes and ears made him more apprehensive than usual. The other point of view was different. He hadn't been out with a woman since Mary died, and now he'd invited Jeanette to take along. With the new lady in his life, he'd have to be more careful than usual. I must be getting soft, he thought.

15

O'Brennan gradually arrived at a game plan for the evening He'd pick up Jeanette and treat the rest of the night as a social event. If information came his way, fine; if not, that was fine too. What the hell, nothing ventured, nothing gained, he thought while dressing for his night out.

Attired in charcoal worsted slacks, a powder-blue blazer and white button-down shirt, Jack felt comfortable. Appraising himself while looking into the mirror; he felt and looked sharp, well, as fit as an old guy could appear. His feelings caused him to smile.

Slipping into recently polished cordovan loafers, he was ready to go. He started for the door, stopped, then returned to the bedroom. Seldom did he travel armed, but tonight would be the exception. Jack withdrew a thirty-eight revolver from the top drawer. He had to face the dreary reality that he was walking into the badman's lair and the thought wasn't appealing.

He experienced a brief mental silence, much like that of a writer's block. His eyes misted as he looked into the past. Mary's image and her sweet voice from yesteryear flooded O'Brennan's thoughts. The long and short of it is, I'm in a holding pattern trying to find my way. Mary, the only person I ever wanted was you. I got my wish, but the fact has finally hit home that you are no longer with me, but you'll always be in my thoughts.

O'Brennan thought about his upcoming night with Jeanette on his drive to the *Red Leather*. To hell with worrying about how the evening will go; it will be great. He hoped he wouldn't jeopardize the evening by acting like a jerk. "Don't think another thing about it, just be yourself," Jack spoke out loud. Jeanette was his first date since Mary passed away and that sobering thought followed him to the restaurant.

While O'Brennan was en route to the *Red Leather*, Jeanette faced similar second thoughts about her evening with O'Brennan. This man had a wisp of appeal she couldn't place, so why attempt to unravel the mystery of Jack O'Brennan, she thought. Throughout most of her adult life, her instincts had not betrayed her and she felt there was no need to change course at this late date.

Driving into the parking lot of the restaurant, O'Brennan felt a knot rise in his stomach. It was the same old feeling he felt before a football game. It was terrible until the first hit; then your instincts took over and the pre-game jitters disappeared. He assumed the same would occur this evening.

Jeanette came out of her office dressed every inch the business woman. She wore green heels, a green-striped seersucker suit and a basic white blouse with collar folded over the jacket lapels. A string of simple white beads around her slender neck only served to enhance her beauty. She dramatically displayed her nearly six-foot stature with a soft, sophisticated look.

"Hi!" She said with a mischievous sparkle in her eyes.

Good grief, the smile, the eyes, she is too much. "Hi yourself," he replied. "It's obvious green is your color, you look fantastic!"

"Why thank you," Jeanette returned a half-embarrassed smile.

O'Brennan felt stupid. Of all the classy replies he could have made, out comes dumb. He silently reprimanded himself, "You're so stupid I can't believe it."

She turned to Jack as they neared his convertible. "You said you had an old convertible; and here I was thinking of a junker like Columbo drives, not something so elegant as this."

"Thanks, I'm very proud of it. I don't usually keep it this clean, but I wanted it to look good for this evening." There you go again, Jack thought. I knew I had a blind spot, but I didn't think it was around women. You're shooting yourself in the foot with that dumb mouth of yours.

O'Brennan stepped back as he opened the door for Jeanette She in turn neatly pivoted on her left foot, thus placing herself in a face to face position with her date. Jeanette brought her open hand up against O'Brennan's left cheek in a sweeping motion. The sound of the slap echoed across the parking lot as he jumped back, too late to miss the power of the savage blow. The impact of the blow left a white appearing imprint on his cheek and a stunned look on his tanned face.

"What in hell did you do that for," he yelled.

"That was for Monday night, you turkey!"

O'Brennan was more shocked than hurt by the surprise slap, but observed her satisfied smile and instantly knew something special was about to happen between them. He rubbed the side of his face and said, "You're right, I deserved that." Extending his hand, he asked, "Friends?"

"Friends!" Her face sparkled "Yes, Jack O'Brennan, we are going to be friends."

He didn't know why, but for some reason, he believed what she said. Inviting her into the car with his long arms extended, he stepped back in an exaggerated posture from the door.

Jeanette laughed as she entered the convertible. Looking over at Jack, she smiled, "Don't worry, I'll never do that again, count on it."

They rode several minutes before Jeanette broke the silence. She wanted to know more about this bull-headed man she barely knew.

Jack obliged. "I'd call my life pretty nondescript. After the service, I attended Elon College in North Carolina on the GI Bill. Following graduation, I joined the Bridgeton Police Force, met my wife, settled down, had three daughters and eventually bought a house in Ford Ashland. That's about it."

"That's a pretty classy neighborhood for a young cop's salary."

"Not back then. The wealthy families started dying out or moving to the suburbs. They even moved as far away as Smithbury. It's the old story; when one goes, they all go. What they left wasn't in disrepair, it just hadn't been kept up to the customary standards of old days. Like a lot of other young couples, Mary and I literally mortgaged our lives away and like the others, resurrected the houses. What you now see is a showcase because of the efforts of the people living there today."

"I agree with you about the Hill, it's beautiful."

"Five years ago, Mary just up and died. We always met at Maxwell's for lunch on Thursdays. She didn't show and that was strange because she was always very punctual. I called, but no one answered. I hurried home and found her lying on the floor in the front entryway. She was dressed up ready to go downtown to meet me. It was a massive heart attack that took her.

"I retired from the force and just stumbled around for some time. The girls helped, but they had their own lives. I started the PI agency and picked myself up as best I could. I've recovered from the shock, but the hurt is still there. I'm better than I was, but I'm still not right. That's about it; that's my story, chapter and verse. Do you have one for me?"

"Mine's somewhat different. I was born and raised in Charlottesville. My dad was a geology professor at the University of Virginia, or as we call it UVa. I went to Mary Washington College as a math major with every intention of becoming a teacher. When the Korean War broke out, my high school sweetheart joined the Marines. Nick was headstrong and although I tried to talk him out of it, he wouldn't listen. We became engaged during his last leave; after which he shipped out to Korea. I had just finished my junior year when word came that he'd been killed in action on some stupid hill I can't even remember. I felt swallowed up in a dark hole as large as the bay. My well-ordered life was in shambles and I gave up."

"Not a pretty picture," Jack said.

"No, it wasn't. I quit school and came to Bridgeton. The sound of trumpets were missing when I entered our fair city." Jeanette laughed, then continued, "Kind of dumb on my part, but here I was in Bridgeton looking for a job. I found work as a secretary at the shipyard and that's when my life changed. I think it was at that time I realized I had a considerable amount of resiliency."

"How so, how did your life change?" Jack asked with interest.

"I began hanging around Harkers, it was that simple. Harkers at dark was really something back then. Every night was New Years Eve. The sidewalks were packed with servicemen, civilians and girls my age. Everyone was looking for fun-fun that would make them forget the harsh reality of being in a war none of us understood. Harkers was a circus, a parade, a carnival all rolled up into one big splash." She paused, then continued, "You're probably asking yourself how I got into the business. Well, I never did. I never sold myself in my life, nor would I ever consider it."

"How did you get started if you never hooked?"

"I got to know some of the girls who were running around Harkers. They were doing some tricking, mostly on a semi-pro basis and were practically giving it away. As a lark, I organized the girls. I'd go in a bar and hustle around for them. I think many of the sailors wanted me but I wasn't about to let that happen. They ended up with my girls, and it worked too. I got them off the street and into clean sheets. From then on, my friends started making some real money, and I made a couple of bucks myself. I guess you could call me a classy pimp."

Amused at her disclosure, Jack said, "You've got that right."

"Over a period of time, I became so involved that I realized the American Dream; I had become a success. When Harkers slowed down, there was no future in what I was doing. With my contacts, the next progression was into the call-girl business. My operation was clean, well, clean as soliciting can be and it paid well. When Harkers was wiped out, I closed shop because the business would never be the same. My clients weren't that involved with Harkers, but I was. When it went, so did I. I know this is out of character, but I bought the restaurant in 1965 and I've been clean ever since. The restaurant has been kind to me and there you are, my life's story."

Small talk finished the drive to Craddock.

McWilliams was quiet with only a handful of patrons as they sat at the bar near the front window overlooking the square.

The neighborhood bar invited seclusion with its amber lights over the high backed side booths. "This mahogany bar is priceless and look at the old brass!" Jeanette said. "I can't believe the foot railings, spittoons and overhead antique lights. It's wonderful."

"It certainly is." Jack swept his hand downward, "The black and white marble floor has been here since day one."

Kenny Ross entered the bar from the backroom. Spotting O'Brennan, he walked up front. After the desultory introductions, Jack asked, "Where's Steinman?"

"Don't ask, Jack, we have to talk. It's important!" Ross' voice sounded gentle and uncertain.

"You can talk in front of Jeanette," Jack assured him.

"The truth is, Nick Steinman is dead."

O'Brennan winced, "He's what!"

"It happened this afternoon. I haven't heard all the details, but later I'll know more. The word is, he was hit," Kenny said, his eyes filling with tears.

"The blue disappeared from our sky, to be replaced by dark clouds," O'Brennan said softly while lifting his hands in frustration. "I was to meet him here tonight."

He's so hurt and vulnerable I can't stand it, Jeanette thought. Few men pass our way both steel tough and gentle in the same breath. Dreams are made of such men and Jack O'Brennan is one.

At that moment she realized he was the man she'd been waiting for all her life. This couldn't have happened overnight, or had it? Regardless, she had set her cap.

"I know. Remember, I was in on the conversation."

"Jeanette, excuse me for a minute. Kenny, will you stay with her?" As he walked to an empty booth, Jack took out a notebook. Sitting down, he began to write. Minutes later, he called Kenny over.

A swollen torrent of words raged through Jack's lips, "Kenny, will you do me a favor? It's that important. I want you to call this number tonight without fail. You'll be talking to a Sally Hunter who lives in Bridgeton at the Regency Arms Apartments. You know the complex."

"Yes, Jack, I remember."

"Be certain to reach her tonight. It's critical, so stay with it. She may not come in until late, but she has to be contacted tonight," Kenny nodded. Turning the paper over, Jack said, "Here's the message. I want you to read it as written, then hang up immediately."

"I'll do exactly what you want," Kenny said quietly.

Extending his hand to Kenny, Jack said, "I'm sorry about Steinman. I know he was your friend and he seemed like a peach of a guy. If there's anything I can do, let me know."

Kenny smiled, then lowered his head with a heavy heart.

"We'll be heading back now, but I'll contact you in a day or so." With good-byes said, he and Jeanette left.

The Chevy gobbled up the miles heading north but silence between them remained until they approached the Hampton Roads Bridge Tunnel. Jeanette said in a voice starting to waver, "We don't have to stop at Williamsburg. I understand how difficult the evening has been, and there will be other nights."

"Thanks, but no, it will help me forget about Steinman."

Leaving route 64, Jack took the Williamsburg exit and parked in back of the restored town. Neither walking the streets of colonial village nor the lovely dinner at the *Chistina Campbell Tavern* could lift the shroud of gloom that had settled on the couple. At the *Red Leather*, they stared at each other for what seemed like minutes. Finally, Jack apologized for the evening.

"How could you have possibly known this would happen?" Jeanette softly said. "I feel badly about Steinman and I'm sorry about the disappointing evening it's been for you. But if it helps, you've treated me like a lady, and I shall remember this evening with very special feelings."

Jeanette tried but failed to control her emotions. Impulsively, she reached out to the man who suddenly loomed much larger than his six-three and held him close for a passing moment.

"Thank you for that," a stunned O'Brennan whispered.

Her eyes flashed a fleeting something he couldn't place. "You really are something, you know."

"Do you realize what you're saying?"

Jeanette's eyes filled with tears as she said, "Please call me."

"I plan to do just that."

Before Jack could answer, she was heading toward the *Red Leather*, never once turning to look back at O'Brennan.

16

The very nature of the business demanded her continued presence at the warehouse. She was tied to an enterprise that permitted no lieutenants, no one to entrust a secret to. It would be easier if she had a confidant to share her more intimate thoughts, but that would never be the case.

She'd think about her situation another day, now rest was her top priority. The ringing phone caused Sally Ralston Hunter to jump. Strange she thought, I seldom if ever receive calls at midnight. I wonder who could be calling?

"Hello," she answered.

"Sally Ralston Hunter?" The voice said dryly.

"Speaking."

"I'm an old client of yours. It's important that you understand we're on to you. We know about your ties with Fritz Hansen and what you're involved in. This afternoon, Nick Steinman, a Portsmouth detective was murdered and that, my dear, was the last straw. It's just a matter of time before your organization comes crashing down around you. One last item, Mrs. Hunter, read Danny Tremonte's column in the morning *Citizen Tribune*. It may give your nervous system a little twinge." Sally's lips made a round "O" for the shock she felt.

In Craddock, Kenny Ross hung up before she could reply.

Sally stared at the phone for what seemed like hours before returning it to its brass cradle. A cold veil of terror swept over her shaking body. She debated calling Fritz but decided to wait until reading the morning paper. After a sleepless night, she opened the paper to Tremonte's column with trembling hands.

POLICE BEAT

Danny Tremonte

I occasionally cross paths with some of our city's private investigators. A majority of these men have impeccable records and perform an important service for our community. Over the decades, television has portrayed the PI as a whiskey-drinking, gun-toting womanizer, who always solves the case. Not so. PI's will tell you this is a misnomer and their success rate isn't different than that of the police, maybe even less. Most don't carry guns, and when indulging, usually drink beer as opposed to whiskey. Most are happily married and don't chase around. Much of their time is spent doing monotonous tasks so mundane they go unnoticed by the general public.

As a change of pace, I plan to follow the case of one of our city's most successful PIs. This particular case should be of special interest to my readers who remember Harkers in the forties and fifties.

A week ago, a PI friend was contacted by a mid-western party asking him to investigate the 1953 death of a sailor found murdered in a Cayuga Street alley. This is a unique case, and what makes it so? Harkers and the immediate area has long since fallen to the wreckers' ball and are currently occupied by the Government Center, Onslow Auditorium and the city marina. The unnamed detective has determined that the victim had three close friends at the time of his murder. He and his friends, two men and a woman had tattoos on their left shoulder. The green colored tattoos were in the shape of a *Shamrock* leaf. One of the above had the stem of a *Shamrock* tattooed on his arm.

My PI friend believes he will shortly identify two of the missing links to this intriguing story. He further indicated that one of the victim's three friends is responsible for the murder.

A feeling of foreboding settled in on Sally. The call and article had reduced her to a walking basket case and it was time to call Fritz.

"I received a call last night and they know everything," whined Sally. "Fritz, we are at risk."

After a short silence, he replied, "Now slow down, Sally, what's this all about?"

"I got a call from Portsmouth. No, from the area . . . I don't know where it came from!" said a confused and agitated Sally.

"What did they say? What was the call about?"

"He said they were coming down on us; that they had our number," Sally answered.

"What do you mean, coming down on us?"

"He said they were on to us. That the organization would crash. He mentioned how a Portsmouth detective had been killed yesterday, but I can't remember his name,. The man who called said they didn't like that, and for me to read the Police Beat Column in the morning paper."

"They didn't like that. Sally, what was he talking about?'

"That's what he said. Maybe he was referring to the dead detective."

"Forget the detective. What was in the column?"

"Tremonte mentioned a case some PI is working on here in Bridgeton. The detective also alluded to our *Shamrock* tattoos and how he plans to identify us."

"Did he mention Freddie's name in the article?" Fritz asked.

"No," replied Sally.

"Let me guess. I'll bet this is the work of a guy named Jack O'Brennan; ever hear of him?"

"Yes, he came to the office Monday morning, but I didn't give him anything, not a thing! How do you know about O'Brennan?"

"It's my business to know about guys like O'Brennan," Hansen said.

"Between the call last night and the newspaper column this morning, I've been dying a slow death."

"Don't worry, sweets. I'll check around. And remember one thing, they can't touch us with a ten-foot pole. They don't know a thing! If anything comes up, you can reach me tomorrow. We'll finish this another time."

"What are the chances of seeing you today? I can't stand much more of this."

"I'm busy today."

A bitter Sally again spoke. "This isn't a social call, and I don't care how busy you are. I'm coming down to Craddock to see you and it's going to be today. It's that important! There are strange forces out there and someone is doing things I don't understand," Sally frantically insisted.

"Do I have a choice?" Fritz asked.

"None whatsoever."

Recognizing her hysteria, Fritz agreed. "All right, we'll meet at five this afternoon, but get a grip on yourself before then."

"Where?"

"Under the clock tower where we always meet." Fritz hung up, leaving Sally looking at a lifeless phone for the second time in a ten-hour period.

After finishing with Sally, Fritz dialed area code 202, followed by an unlisted DC number. This call couldn't wait. A no nonsense voice answered.

"Yes, this is the man from down South. Earlier this morning, I received a call from Bridgeton. She was very upset; said a PI had appeared on the scene. Sally said this PI was checking into the death of a sailor killed in Harkers in the early fifties. The Bridgeton party would not be put off and hysterically forced me to meet her this afternoon. I think some damage control may be in order here."

Fritz waited for the reply, then added, "Yes, I'll take care of that immediately. I have an investigator who occasionally does work for me and he'll rustle up whatever we need."

Hansen again listened to the Washington voice. "I think it's a guy named Jack O'Brennan, but that's only a guess. By tomorrow morning, I'll have the story."

This situation with Sally did not sit well with Fritz Hansen. He lived in the shadows and had continually maintained a low profile for thirty years. He'd know more about her problem this afternoon, but he wasn't about to allow her to ruin a good thing.

O'Brennan expected and was prepared for a barrage of verbal abuse as he approached the Bench in Inlet Park. Cal pointed at him, then opened his hands as if to introduce O'Brennan to the Group. "Look what we have here."

"Good morning, gentlemen Would you explain why you're pointing at me, Cal?" O'Brennan couldn't conceal a smile.

"There is a question that needs answering. Where in hell have you been? Monday, your tongue was hanging down to your knees when you told us about this Gill case you might take on. You get our juices flowing then pull a Mary Poppins and fly off into the blue. Knowing him boys, he probably wants a favor," Cal Redout whined, then followed with the slight show of a smile.

"The curtain is about to rise. Let me give you the background on the whole deal," responded a serious O'Brennan. "I've been doing the preliminaries and that's why I haven't been around."

"No apologies needed!" The cool and unflappable John Lloyd responded with a sneer. "We're thrilled you found a couple minutes to spend with your old buddies."

Childless, John had been devastated by the loss of his wife to cancer ten years earlier. The Group had become his only family. Over the years, John had assumed the role of unofficial spokesman for his friends and in this capacity he admonished O'Brennan with his terse reply.

Ignoring John's brief rebuttal, Jack gave the Group a complete rundown of the case up to and including Tremonte's column in the morning paper.

"I'm putting the squeeze on this Sally Ralston Hunter and want her squirming a little. You must remember, one pebble makes many waves. I need your help and need it today." O'Brennan's request sounded much like a command.

"You know, we've been waiting for him to come down here and request our help. Did he ask for our aid?" Red Ted looked to his buddies for support who emphatically nodded no.

"Have a fit, Red," O'Brennan countered.

The redhead paid little attention to his antagonist. "Now, he comes waltzing down here asking for assistance. The temerity of the man, he needs us today. I don't know, Jack, but I think you're losing your magic edge."

"That's it boys, you've had a good time at old Jack's expense, and if I were in your shoes, I'd join in. You've made your point, so let's get down to brass tacks. I want to put Sally Ralston Hunter under a magnifying glass, and from here on, I'll need all the help you can muster. I want someone to follow this Hunter woman today. I don't know where she's going, but you have to be prepared for anything. She's nervous and unpredictable, and that in itself could be troublesome. If you can help, be prepared for an all-nighter. You obviously have special talents for such a job."

"Like what," Red interrupted.

"I can't recall any offhand, but Red, it sounded like a nice thing to say."

All but Red laughed at Jack's reply.

"And he's a comedian as well," Red countered.

"Getting back to earlier moments, can any of you make it?" Jack pleaded.

"Love to help you, but I have to work. First things first, you know," Karl Eichner replied.

"Thanks Karl, I understand."

John spoke up, "We're closed down at the Aud for a couple of weeks, so I've got nothing better to do. Give me an hour and I'll be ready."

"What the hell; count me in," Red Ted said, the slightest impression of a smile breaking on his freckled face. "Jack, you're like James Bond, nobody does it better." O'Brennan didn't catch Red's drift about 007 but thought it prudent to leave alone.

Cal Redout stood up, "I have the day off, so yes, I can make it. All three of us can go and we'll stick on this Hunter woman like white on rice."

"Can we whittle this down a little? I think two will work but three may be too many," Jack patiently explained.

"Hey, what's the story with this boot camp mentality, . . . you want the best of all worlds. Well, you can't have it that way. We're not fools you know, and we can handle this without a hitch. Take it or leave it; all or nothing." Red's chastising statement may have been the strongest he'd ever made in the company of the Group. John and Cal looked at Red as if seeing him for the first time.

"Red's right! It's all of us or no deal. Rest assured there will be no problem we can't handle. We'll tail this woman like you want us to do, so just let it rest," Cal said emphatically.

Cal's position resolved Jack's numbers dilemma. "Okay, here's the deal. She lives in the Regency Arms Apartment Complex. I want you to go over within the hour and tail her all day if necessary. You may be flying around Lord knows where. I want you to keep a journal of Sally's movements; John will know what I need. That should be no problem with three of you tailing the lady, should it?" Jack gently nudged his newly created three-man posse.

"Make sure you chart her every move regardless of how insignificant it may appear. In the final analysis, I believe she'll attempt to meet this guy Hansen. Here, I have some pictures of Sally."

"Not bad looking," Cal said.

"Try and keep the Doc under control, Red; he sounded like he's all horned up," O'Brennan said good-naturedly.

"He's too old to do her any good." Red's comment caused laughter.

"That's enough out of you, fearless redhead. Here's a picture of Fritz Hansen I copied from the newspaper, though I admit it's somewhat dated. If during your travels she meets with someone other than this Hansen, try and get a good description. How they're dressed, what they look like. By that I mean their size and age, that type of thing. I don't know why I'm telling you this, you'll know what to do." Silence invaded the Group as they digested Jack's instructions. "I've got some things to do and I know you'll be busy, so let's plan on meeting here in the morning. By the way, who's driving?"

Cal spoke up, "I'll drive. Red doesn't have a car and John has that cracker box."

"What do you mean, cracker box?" cried an indignant John Lloyd. "That's a restored MG, a classic!"

"How do you fit three people into that classic?" replied Cal.

"You convinced me, Cal, I didn't want to drive anyway."

"Cal's right, let him drive. Which car are you taking, the Olds or the Packard?"

"Jack, I better take the Olds, the Packard would stand out too much."

"Happy hunting, gentlemen. See you in the morning," Jack said as he got up to leave.

"Hey Jack, you forgot something." O'Brennan turned to once again to face a smiling Red Ted. "In your instructions, you didn't mention what kind of wheels she drives."

"Damn, you're right, I forgot all about it. She drives a new tan Lincoln Town Car. I didn't get the license number, but that shouldn't pose a problem."

After Jack left, Red joked, "Some boss we work for. You'd think he was in love or something."

"That, my boy, you won't have to worry about," Cal said.

"Well, if it ever comes to pass, I'd like to meet the lady who turns his head," Red noted happily.

"Let's get on about our business, and we'll talk about Jack's love life at a later date," Cal said thoughtfully.

"You two go ahead, I'll meet you at the marina," John said.

17

The huge complex of the *Regency Arms* ran a full city block from Covington to Niagara. The Regency Arms, its magnificence prominent throughout the Inlet area, consisted of three components: a large office wing, a massive luxury apartment complex and an elegant hotel.

Cal eased into a parking space on Niagara Avenue across from the giant apartment complex. John Lloyd soon arrived and joined in the small talk between Cal and Red. It was during their discussion that the roof of the dome began to retract for the noon lunch crowd.

"They're getting ready for lunch. Ya' know, that sight still thrills me when I see it. They can open the roof in ten minutes, isn't that something?" Red said.

Just as they were watching the movement of the roof, Sally came out of the apartment entrance and crossed the street at the pedestrian crosswalk. Looking neither right or left, she veered toward Cal's car.

"Oh boy, here she comes," whispered Red. It seemed he could reach out and touch her.

Sally appeared deep in thought as she headed down the pier toward the marina's middle moorings. She stopped in front of a large blue yacht, then disappeared below deck.

Lloyd's eyes followed her to the yacht, "She didn't look at our car when she passed, almost as if she was sleepwalking. I wonder what in hell she's doing in that yacht?" John said from the back seat.

Ten minutes later she left the boat and retraced her steps to the Regency.

"We've got to find out about that yacht, and I'm just the person to make that happen." Red jumped out of the Olds and headed toward the middle moorings.

"You better hurry up, because if she leaves before you get back, you'll be spending your afternoon by yourself, 'cause we're out of here," John called after the fast moving Red.

"Don't worry about old Red. I'm no stranger to sneaking around, and I'll be back before you can wink." Red called over his shoulder as he moved in the direction of the yacht, leaving a meaningless little shrug in his wake.

During three separate tours of Nam, Red garnered the Navy Cross, Silver and Bronze Star, and a Purple Heart with two clusters. He had been an ideal servant of his country, but the one pitfall he encountered on the road to promotion was his propensity for fighting. He thrived on it and was profoundly good with his hands.

Red walked several berths past the blue craft, then returned to the car in a trot.

"Boys, it's going to be a hot one." Red mopped his sweat-covered forehead as he entered Cal's Olds. "That yacht is in slip J-24, and is it big! It's named the NITTANY LION, and it's out of Philadelphia. I mentally checked the possibilities and I'm sure they brought it down the Delaware, then through the Chesapeake and Delaware Canal to the bay."

"Who cares!" John said from the back seat.

"Just wanted to let you know I do have some brains," Red added smugly.

"Red's right, he does have brains we didn't know about. Did you hear him use the word temerity this morning? That's a big one for a drifter, wouldn't you say?" Cal chuckled as he laid his zinger on Red.

"You guys are always kicking Red around, but one day in the near future, I'm going to surprise you. Then, you'll feel real nasty about treating the old boy so badly."

"I suppose you're right, Red. I will say in all fairness, you're a sensible person, well most of the time, that is," Cal said.

"Who tills the fields after the men leave?" Red asked.

"And what does that mean?" Cal looked at Red.

"My dignity has been fractured by your question."

"I need more than a glib answer, Red."

"Will you stop that stuff!" John exploded. "You two are driving me crazy. Doc, you're as bad as he is."

Red laughed, further annoying John.

"Doc," (John only called Cal that when he was irked at him), "can't you see what he's doing with us? You just said he was a sensible person most of the time, and he just made some half-witted statement to throw us off balance."

"Here comes Sally's car now," Red said. "Jack didn't mention anything about smoked windows."

As the tan Lincoln exited the underground garage, the sun's glare on the windshield made it impossible to see in. The Lincoln turned left on Niagara and headed toward the shipyard. Cal started the car and carefully eased into traffic, following the tan vehicle at a discreet distance.

"Should we continue to follow? We don't know if it's her or not," asked a concerned Red.

"Suppose it isn't?"

"Suppose it is," countered John.

"You just answered the question of the morning," Cal said as he continued trailing the Lincoln.

Following at a discreet distance, they tracked the Lincoln east until it turned into the *Southam Discount Plaza*. The car stopped and a short fat man bounced out. His bald head glistened in the sun while walking toward the liquor store. He opened the door and went in; it was that simple. They had jeopardized the investigation by following the wrong person.

"The world has turned over on us," Cal said. "It looks like we completely misjudged the situation."

"Now, we're in a jam! Jack'll boil us in oil when he hears about this beauty," a concerned John Lloyd offered.

"You know, it's Jack's fault for not giving us a license number; if we had that, we wouldn't be in this fix," Red added.

"We have to get crackin', because it's too late to worry about it now," Cal said as he quickly crossed onto Niagara and headed back toward the Inlet.

"Pullover by that phone booth," John said. Quickly darting to the phone, he opened the directory, checked a number, then dialed.

"What does he have up his sleeve?" Cal asked.

"How would I know, we're not joined at the hip, you know," Red said.

"Security please," seconds pass, "who's this? . . . Let me speak to Sammy." Valuable minutes passed as John worked himself into a first-class lather. "Sammy, where have you been? This is John Lloyd. I need a favor and don't spare the horses. Will you check and see if Sally Hunter's Lincoln is in the garage? . . . Yeah, I'll wait." Again valuable time slipped by. . . ."Do you have a number for the car? . . . Yeah, thanks, Sammy. Don't mention this to anyone. I'll buy you the biggest drink in town the next time we meet." John turned and beat a hasty retreat to Cal's car.

"What didya' find out? asked Red.

"She's still there. Got the plate number too." Ten minutes later they had re-established their position across from the Regency.

"The race belongs to the swift," Red said triumphantly, "we're still in business."

"That's gratifying to know unless of course she took off after John's call," replied Cal.

Around noon, Sally exited the garage and turned right on Gloucester. Over the next hour she made several stops at downtown stores. Then she headed east out Niagara until she crossed the Rappahanock Bridge and headed south.

"I'll bet she's heading for Portmouth," Red offered.

"I don't think so," countered Cal. "Tell you what, wild one. A case of beer says you're wrong. She won't even go through the tunnel."

"You're on."

The trio followed Sally as she crossed the York River bridge at Fostertown and turned left on 64 South. Driving at a moderate speed, she turned off at the Williamsburg exit.

"I wonder what she's going to do in Williamsburg?" John asked.

Sally parked in a lot adjacent to the restored colonial capital and leisurely strolled to the Merchants Square which was located at the end of Duke of Glouchester Street. The square, situated across the street from William and Mary College contained a cluster of exclusive shops. She stopped in front of a classy woman's store, window shopped for a moment, then entered.

Red took a seat in the outdoor patio opposite the store Sally recently entered. He hoped Sally's visit would be a lengthy one. He liked the atmosphere of the pedestrian mall with tourists casually walking by. This was fun. He was playing detective, sitting in the sun drinking beer and generally feeling good about himself. He should enjoy it, he thought, because his lifestyle would dramatically change during the next few weeks. This was his last hurrah, so why not enjoy it?

Cal stayed in the air-conditioned car while John walked past the woman's dress shop to the campus across the street. He strategically located himself under a tree with the Merchants Square in full view.

Thirty minutes later, Sally returned to her car carrying a large garment bag. Depositing her purchase in the trunk, she soon headed south. After driving several miles, Sally turned off at the Busch Garden exit.

She parked the car and once again returned to the trunk where she changed her high heels for white canvas sneakers. Paying her admission fee, Sally headed for the 'Merrie Olde England' section of the park. Nervously walking to the clock tower, Sally sat down on an unoccupied bench. Several minutes later, Fritz Hansen approached and took a seat next to her.

"Hello Sally, you look worried."

His presence evoked a certain uneasiness she never felt

before. "I have every reason to be, Fritz, it's not working out the way we planned."

"So tell me what's troubling you?"

"You know very well what's troubling me. Like I told you earlier, I received a call out of the blue and I'm not happy with the direction it is taking me."

"What did this guy say?"

"Why do I have to keep repeating what he said?"

"Just tell me and don't be smart about it" he snapped.

"He said they were going to bring us down and told me to read Tremonte's column in the morning paper." Reaching into her purse, Sally handed Fritz the article.

After reading Tremonte's column, Fritz said, "Ah, that's pure nonsense! This is nothing more than filler for this article. Everything's going to be fine, so don't worry about garbage like this."

"I don't care what you call garbage, somebody knows something and we're going to get squeezed. I'll tell you right now, I'm not taking the fall for this mess. You always alluded to Freddie's death as untimely, well, we know it was timely and we know why. If he hadn't tried ripping you off, he'd be alive today. Since we're talking about Freddie, I'll tell you something else, Fritz Hansen. I cannot believe you'd do such a senseless thing as kill him for two hundred dollars!"

"Sally, that's ancient history. I've told you this before; two hundred dollars was a lot of money back then, but more importantly; he was stealing from us. That's what Freddie Gill was all about and that was his undoing."

"I'll not take the rap for this. You know I had nothing to do with Freddie's death," Sally sputtered, "and that's that!"

"Like hell it is. You're up to your pretty little neck in this; you self-centered little bitch and don't forget it!" Excitement rose in Fritz's voice.

"But I didn't . . ." Sally began to cry but never finished her answer because Fritz cut her off with a harsh rebuke.

"Stop that! Crying won't help at this stage of the game. Let me remind you what you're into. You can't walk away from this, certainly not after thirty years. Now, missy, you keep this in mind and damn it, look at me when I'm talking to you!" As Sally turned to look at Fritz, their eyes locked.

"Let me put it another way. If you start talking to anyone, you're out of here." The tone of his voice stiffened. "You'll be with Freddie and you two can rehash old times, laugh and shoot the breeze about how great the fifties were." Placing his hand on Sally's shoulder, he said, "You need a vacation . . . a week or so off. Go to some classy resort and meet some new people, just get away."

"You know I can't do that. The way my operation is structured, I have to do all the packing and I'd miss my shipments," Sally said as she wiped away her tears.

"There's a way around that. All you have to do is call each of your special accounts and tell them you're doubling their phone orders for the next week. Say you'll be out of town for a week or so, then indicate you'll charge them for the first half and catch them later."

Her eyes clouded over with a question. "What if they don't pay? I'll be out a fortune and still owe you."

"Trust me, Sally, there will be no problem. The gentlemen I employ are very adept in the area of account receivable. Tomorrow is Friday, so you'll have plenty of time to handle the problem." Fritz stood, "Now dry those tears because no one will bother you. When this storm blows over, we'll get a big laugh out of the shower that came with it."

"I don't know, Fritz, I'm scared," replied a frightened Sally. "When this O'Brennan visited me Monday morning, I didn't say a word, but he worried me with what he said."

"How so?"

"He said Freddie had a green C shaped tattoo."

"How would he know that?"

"He said it was in the autopsy report, and he also mentioned that he knew of another sailor who had one. Said his name was Fritz Hansen."

"What else did he say?"

"Nothing else."

Maybe Sally did have cause to be alarmed. O'Brennan's name is popping-up too much to be a coincidence. It's imperative I show a cool side to Sally or she'll come apart at the seams, Fritz thought.

"Don't worry, Sally, all this will blow over and you'll soon be back to your old self. Do you have any questions?"

"No, I guess not."

"Later, when you're better prepared to evaluate what happened, you'll see that I'm right. I'll talk to you later and make sure to give me a call about your plans before you leave."

Sally sat staring into space for many minutes after Fritz departed. She appeared to be wishing a bad situation away, but soon headed north to Bridgeton, closely followed by three men in an Oldsmobile.

Once back in Portsmouth, Fritz called the familiar 202 area code. "Yes, I'm calling from the South. I met with our friend earlier in the afternoon and she's terribly upset. She appears to be out of control and that disturbs me. I doubt whether this problem will go away."

Time passed as Fritz listened to the reply, "No I wouldn't say that, but she is seriously frightened. I think she'll need watching."

Fritz listened intently and finally replied after several minutes. "She mentioned the telephone call and the column in the morning paper . . . Yeah, I have it here."

Fritz read Tremonte's article to the opposite party. "At that point, she kinda' busted up. Said she wasn't taking the fall for Gill's problem, accident if you will. Sally mentioned what a nice thing she had going and how she wasn't getting involved any deeper." Fritz paused to listen. "Hell yes, we both agree she's involved, there's no doubt about it." Fritz listened for several minutes, then answered, "There's one thing that came up this afternoon that definitely is going to bear watching. Sally mentioned that this O'Brennan knows about Freddie's and my tattoo, but that's all."

Fritz spent more time listening which made him increasingly uneasy. He hated telephones and this conversation was taking too long.

"I don't know much about this O'Brennan character, but like I told you earlier, he's being checked out and I'll have information on him by morning."

The question from Washington was brief and caused Hansen to shake his head. "No, I don't know if he's still alive, but I should know that by tomorrow. I told Andy, he's my investigator, to check any tattoo artists in Bridgeton, so that end is covered. We'll soon know how deep this O'Brennan's water runs. I'll be talking to you and I agree she's on the edge."

Hanging up, Fritz thought, days like this I wish I hadn't got out of bed.

18

Friday morning, the trio ran through the previous day's travels with Sally, along with John's written report of their surveillance activities.

"What were your observations, anything unusual?" Jack asked.

"As a matter of fact there was. She acted like Christmas was around the corner. After she came out of the complex at noon, she must have hit five or six stores downtown before she left the U. She bought something in every store and didn't appear to be one bit troubled or rushed, I'll say that for her," Lloyd said.

"John's right. She looked like she didn't have a worry in the world," Red said with a flourish. "When I was sitting across the way in Merchants Square, she . . ."

"What do you mean across the way?" Jack interrupted with grimace.

"I was sitting in an outdoor patio across from the fancy store Sally went in," Red replied.

"And the bastard was drinking beer while I'm across the street sweating away. Is it all right to drink on the job?" John cheerfully asked the rhetorical question.

"All you can get your hands on," replied a smiling O'Brennan.

"Then she left the village and drove out to the Busch Gardens. She entered the park and sat in the 'Olde England' section waiting for Fritz. He eventually showed and did most of the talking," John said.

"Anything unusual happen?" Jack asked.

"Nothing really until she began crying, then I thought it was all over. About that time, Fritz started getting after her and she turned the tears off in a hurry. I wonder what he said to get such a reaction?" John said.

"You're right, John. Did you notice how animated Fritz got? It was like he was peeling her ass out," responded Red.

"Red, did Fritz touch her, grab hold of her?" Jack asked.

"Just before Fritz left, he put his hand on her shoulder, somewhat in a forgiving manner."

After that, no one said a word for several minutes. It was as if the Group had been rendered speechless by an invisible force.

Jack interrupted the icy silence by saying, "I think she's beginning to unravel a little. Hear me out on this and tell me what you think. Karl, you're it! If you were hiding some hidden secret from your deep past, and out of the blue you get a call reminding you about it, what would you do? How would you react?"

"Depends on what I was hiding. Something minor, I probably could care less. On the other hand something bad, that's different; I'd probably be scared to death. If I got this call you're talking about and Tremonte's column is mentioned, I'd say, what's happening?"

"You still haven't told me what you'd do."

"Jack, I'd be nervous as hell, really upset. If I had something to hide and some unknown person comes out of the woodwork and reminds me of it; especially some thirty years back; yeah, I'd be upset and have every reason to be."

"Karl's right. People understand what they want to and it would appear she sees danger in this situation. Like the example you just used, she probably wants to react, but against what and whom, she probably doesn't know," Cal added.

"It never occurred to me that Hansen would enter the scene so quickly. Now we have a new twist to the situation, and I don't have to tell you, with him in the picture there's an element of danger in our little game. But like they say in the movies, danger is our game. Why not stir the pot a little and let her stew in her own juices for awhile?" Jack suggested.

"Sounds like a good idea, but what can we do?" It was obvious John couldn't wait to dig in.

"I think we should attack her soft underbelly, play on her emotions," O'Brennan said.

The Group pensively kicked around ideas on how to rattle Sally, trying to create a scheme that would agitate and promote her collapse. Jack finally broke the silence.

"Did you ever drive down a road and come to a detour? Let's say you're redirected around a bridge under repair. This happened to me so I know it's possible. I had to turn left at a detour out by Smithbury. Driving down the alternate route, I got thinking about a case I was working. I was so deep in thought, I continued past the turn off back to the main road. Moments later, I thought maybe I had driven by the sign but continued down the road. I asked myself did I drive by that sign and almost immediately began having second thoughts about missing the turn. Did I imagine it, or was it real? Continuing to drive, I eventually realized that I had indeed missed the turn."

"How do you work your experience in with Sally?" Cal questioned O'Brennan.

"Because of that detour, I was rerouted. What I perceived as true was false and visa-versa. Why couldn't we do something to Sally that would be similar to my experience. Send her on a detour and get her head swimming. By sending her in the wrong direction, she may not miss the turn, but we could redirect her every breath and control her destiny from now on. Do you follow me?"

John nodded. "I like it. Nothing's impossible, but how can we detour her enough to screw her up more than she is already?" John asked.

"I honestly don't know," O'Brennan said with a shake of his head.

Karl Eichner was the quiet one who rarely entered into the heavy conversations of the Group. A love for coastal waters prompted him to buy a home on the water. He moved to Scots Harbor, a small fishing village located on Chesapeake Bay, twenty some miles east of Bridgeton. He and his wife, Phyllis raised three children and were currently enjoying the twilight of his working career.

But today was different and he excitedly raised his hand, "I've got something."

"Hey Karl, you're not in school, put your hand down," Red said proudly.

"Go ahead, Karl. Red seldom hears what anyone has to say, so don't listen to that silly twit," Jack countered.

"We give her a call when we know she won't be in the office. Make believe it's this Hansen. We leave a message stating he has to meet her tomorrow morning."

"If we were to make such a call, she'd recognize the voice as not being Hansen. We don't know his voice but she does. If she isn't there, she'd have an answering service, same problem," Jack said.

"How about this," interjected Red. "Call the warehouse when we know she isn't there and ask for Sally. Leave a message when we know the secretary is in. When we . . ."

"Suppose Sally gets the message and calls Hansen. There goes your scheme," interrupted John Lloyd.

"John, let me finish. When we leave the message, we mention that Hansen will be out of town for the remainder of the day and overnight," added a smiling Red Ted.

"That sounds about as good as we can do," Jack said.

"I hate to admit this, but you, my boy, are beginning to exhibit signs of superior intelligence," Cal nodded at a grinning Red.

"What's the message?" Jack asked, looking inquisitively at Karl.

"Like Red said, just say Fritz called and he'd be away the rest of the day and evening. He'd see her tomorrow morning at Scots Harbor. She's to go to *Sonny's* Restaurant and sit on the patio. He'll meet her at ten."

"That's pretty good, Karl. Tell us more about this *Sonny's*," John encouraged.

"You all know I live in Scots Harbor. At this time of the year, the village is really busy. There's a lot going on with tourists running around all over the place. Tomorrow is special." Karl paused, pointing his finger at nothing in particular, then continued. "And to add to the congestion we're having the annual flea market in the municipal parking lot. It'll be held Saturday and Sunday and the place will be jammed. Based on her mental state, we know she'll go flying down to *Sonny's*."

"Let's assume she goes flying down there as you so quaintly put it, what do we do then?" Cal asked.

"Karl, explain the physical layout at Scots Harbor. You still haven't told us about this *Sonny's*," Red questioned.

"There is a giant parking lot downtown that runs from the street to the edge of the water. From the lot, a long fishing pier runs into the Chesapeake. As you enter the lot from the street, *Sonny's* is on the left. It's big, but the major feature of the restaurant is its massive outdoor patio. That damn thing will probably seat two hundred people and is decorated in a nautical theme. It's a very popular place and there's one thing for certain, you can't miss it with the blue and white awning over the patio."

"Where does Sally fit into this?" Jack asked.

"There's no parking in the lot this weekend because it will be full of stands. As a matter of fact, they're even putting vendors on the pier. Why not have her go to *Sonny's*, sit on the patio and go from there?"

"If you have such large crowds, how do you get her placed on the patio?" Asked a concerned Cal Redout.

"That's the least of our problems. Sonny and I are good friends. I occasionally bartend for him when he's in a pinch, so I'm sure he'll help us out. Why not show Sally's picture to Sonny? That way he can arrange for her to be seated where we want her."

Jack stood up and began to pace. Finally he asked, "Where do we have her placed so she can be observed. We want to be close but not overdo it."

"Near the edge of the patio. That way she can be watched from the lot. Let her sit there for as long as she's going to wait;

which will probably be close to an hour. After the hour, chances are she'll split. As she's getting ready to leave, have a floral arrangement delivered to her with some kind of message; and see how she reacts. How does that sound?" Karl sat back, very pleased with his proposal.

"That sounds good, Karl. What kind of message do we want to give her?" O'Brennan asked.

Karl frowned. "I'm missing something, but what, I can't say."

"It will probably come to you when we don't need it," the negative Red was back.

By now, the Group had totally immersed themselves in the investigation. Eager as they were to contribute, the message proved more difficult to formulate than did the plot, to harass Sally. After considerable effort, Jack jotted down the finished message.

When Freddie passed on, we never sent him flowers. Since you're here this morning, we're giving them to you, and are certain you'll know what to do with them. There is one last thing, Sally. When you look at all those faces in the parking lot; bet you can't tell who sent this message."

"Has a nice ring to it," Cal said.

"How do we handle the floral arrangement?" John asked.

"I'll take care of that," Karl answered.

"Who will you get to deliver it?" Jack asked.

"I'll also take care of that," smiled Karl. "I'll have my neighbor do it. Jimmy's a wild one and will go for anything."

"That's terrific. Let's check this out one last time. Karl is going to make the seating arrangements with Sonny, get the flowers and have his neighbor deliver them along with the message." Jack ticked off the list of duties as he looked at the smiling bartender. "You're going to be very busy, Karl.

"No problem," said the rotund bartender.

"I have the duty tomorrow, so I can't help out," said a discouraged Medical Examiner, "but I will make the call to the warehouse."

"How about old Red and John?" Lloyd asked. "We want a piece of the action, right Red?" Red nodded in agreement.

"John, I want you and Red to go out on your own and find out anything you can about Sally. We really need to know more about her operation and you're just the two to get those details. See you Monday, no, better yet, come over to the house Sunday morning about eight. I'll make breakfast and we'll see what we've accomplished."

"John, they've turned a blind eye to us," Red said.

John comforted Red: "That's the way life is."

Cal laughed. "Red, that's a clinical term that doesn't apply to this situation. Let's face it, you have a flair for nosing around. I'm banking on you to come up with the scoop of the day."

"One last thing, Jack. I'll try and save a parking spot for you opposite the parking lot; so be alert when you come into the harbor area in the morning."

"Thanks, Karl. Well boys, I've got to get with it; got things to do and that other good stuff. We have Sally going now and I think we're in business. The rest of this case should be downhill from here."

"That's it!" John said as O'Brennan stood to go. "How about damage control?"

"What do you mean?"

"Jack, suppose Sally does something unexpected after she receives the flowers. And what happens to the note after that?"

Each conspirator drifted off to silently ponder John's "what if."

"In that case," Cal said, "there isn't much we can do."

"I think it's ridiculously simple; we just punt." Red once again full of himself grinned at the Group.

"It works for me," Jack said he departed, slowly followed by the Group. As they left, Cal observed, "I hope he's right, but my mother said it best with an old cliche, 'There's many a slip between the cup and the lip'."

19

O'Brennan called out as he entered the waiting room of the Niagara Avenue tattoo shop, "Duke Frontier, you in here?"

From the back room came, "Who's out there?"

"It's Jack O'Brennan. Are you decent?"

"Not in seventy years," Duke shuffled out, squinting as he entered the sunlit waiting room. "Hello there, big man, how ya' doin' today?"

"Good, Duke. I'm trying to regroup and come up with some new ideas."

"Before you start, I got somethin' for ya'. A fella' came in here yesterday afternoon and was askin' 'bout you."

"Do you know who he was? What did he ask about me?"

"Now hold it, young fella'. Like I say, this bird comes in yesterday and says he'll make it worth my while if I give him some information."

"What information?" O'Brennan could feel his tension growing as he waited for Duke's story.

"He wanted to know if I ever put any *Shamrock* leafs on anyone. He also wanted to know if a guy named O'Brennan had been in here."

"What did you tell him?" Jack nervously asked.

"Told him I had put thousands of tattoos on people, but I couldn't remember what they were."

"Why did you told him that?"

"'Cause I liked you better than him. Ya' know I got a memory sharp as a tack, but I played dumb like I didn't know nothin'." The old guy laughed and shook his head.

"What did you say about me?"

"Told him that you had come in and I give him the same story 'bout not rememberin'. I talked some crazy stuff to him, I did."

"Then what happened?"

"I think he felt sorry fer me, because he just shook his head and said, 'old-timer, you've had the meat'."

"What did he do then?"

"Give me twenty bucks and left. I have something that can help 'ya. I've been thinkin' about them tattoos and I remember the girl, kinda' remember the guy that was killed. The third guy, I don't remember so good. Big man, that was a long time ago, but the fourth jasper rings a bell. He was odd," Duke paused, then continued, "yeah, he was an odd son of a bitch. Can you believe it; he didn't like hurt."

"He didn't like hurt." Duke's reply puzzled Jack.

"Yeah, he wanted this tattoo, wanted it bad, but he wanted a novocaine shot."

"A novocaine shot?" Jack again appeared bewildered. "It's my understanding when you get a tattoo, you pay a little price in pain."

"Yeah, you're right, but sometimes I gave a shot, even back then. Sometimes women want a shot with their tattoos. Now the bird I'm talking about wanted a shot, and raised hell until I gave him one."

"How do you know his tattoo was related to the other *Shamrock* leaves?"

Duke looked at Jack with a scrambled gaze. Jack caught on immediately. "Connected."

The little guy nodded his understanding. "He's the guy that had the stem and I'll bet you he's part of the *Shamrock* thing you keep talking about."

"What about this guy?" Jack asked, feeling his excitement rising to fever pitch.

"I can remember him pretty good. He was about two hundred pounds, almost as big as you and in his early twenties. He had sandy-brown hair, freckles all over the place, a good-looking rascal. Ah . . . it was like his fingernails was polished. Not really polished, mind you, just real clean. A hell'va lot cleaner than the average guy comes in here. I get some pretty crusty people, but not this guy, he was a first-stringer."

"So he was tall and good sized. How did he speak?" Duke looked puzzled. "You know, how did he talk?"

"Oh, I don't know. What'ya mean, how'd he talk?"

"Did he have a Southern accent?"

"No, he wasn't Southern, he sounded like ah . . . I'll tell ya' who he sounded like, President Kennedy. Yeah, that's who. He talked kind'a funny like Kennedy." Jack looked at Duke with a questioning glance. "Well, Kennedy talked funny to me. I don't care if he sounded funny to anyone else or not."

"You know, Duke, you're a piece of work." Jack laughed as he continued to question Duke. "Did he have a New England accent? That's what I meant."

"Yeah, I guess. He talked like Kennedy! I don't know about the New England thing. Listen, you big bastard, he talked like Kennedy and I'm not going to say it again.

"Okay, Duke, he talked like Kennedy." Jack laughed again. "Do you have anything else?"

"Nope."

"Are you mad at me?"

"Nope."

"Are you going to be around for awhile?"

"Yeah, I'll be here. Where in hell am I goin'?"

Jack hurried to police headquarters filled with a surge of excitement. After entering Charlie Winder's property domain, he wondered how Charlie would react when he walked in.

"Good morning, Jack. How's the case coming? Make any progress?"

"Just fine, Charlie."

"Heard you took Jeanette for a ride the other night."

"You don't miss much, do you? The last time I saw you, you were madder than hell at me."

"That was the other day, now that you're back together, everything's just fine."

Jack let that pass. "Jeanette told me you're always trying to fix her up. Is that right?"

"On occasion I've tried, but you know she's fussier than hell! You came here for information and I took you over there. That's all there was to it. Innocent on all charges," Charlie said with a broad-faced grin.

"I need the New England dialect tape and a cassette player."

After returning to the tattoo shop, Jack set up the cassette player. "Duke, this is a tape of different accents found in New England. It's arranged by states, then broken down into regions. After I play this through, we can go back to any region you want." Jack turned the machine off after playing the tape, "Duke, did you hear anything close to what I'm looking for?"

"I don't think so. That Boston one sounded close, but I don't know."

Jack reran the sound from Maine. After the cassette ran out, Duke asked to hear it again. After the tape finished, Duke excitedly called out, "That's it, I'm sure."

"Duke, thanks. I appreciate what you've done, and remember, if you come up with anything else, give me a call. You have my number." Jack laid two twenties on the counter. "Again, my friend, thank you. You take care and I'll be around to see you soon."

After returning the tapes to property, Jack again headed toward the shipyard. Pulling into the *Eagle* parking lot, Jack felt terrific. He had done a massive stroke of business and it was still morning. The pungent smell of stale smoke, rancid beer and sweat hit O'Brennan as he entered the bar. "Al, how in hell do you stand the smell? It should knock you over.'"

"You just came in from the fresh air. Stay around for awhile and you'll get used to it. How's the case coming?"

"I'm really not going any place with it, but I do have some

pictures you can look at." Jack pushed the pictures over to Al. "They hung around the *Shamrock*." O'Brennan pointed at the pictures and said, "You were stationed at the hospital back then, can you identify them?"

"Give me a look," scanning the pictures, Al offered, "yeah, I remember them. This guy," pointing to Freddie Gill's picture, "worked in the pharmacy."

"That's the sailor who was killed. You're on the right track," Jack quickly responded.

"The girl I've seen, but where, I don't know. This other guy hung around with the dead sailor, but wasn't a regular, "Al said.

"Didn't she hang around the *Shamrock* with these two?" Jack pointed at the pictures of Gill and Hansen.

"You're right, Jack, that's where it was! You know, that was an odd deal. They used to sit in a back booth and were they thick. She was good-looking, I'll give her that. There was another guy who would come in occasionally and sit with them."

"Was he about six-two, sharp dresser, brown hair, freckles and good-looking?"

"You've got it! That's the guy."

"Anything else about him?" Jack asked anxiously.

"I don't know . . . that was a long time . . . now wait," Al said thoughtfully. "The other day I was listening to a radio commentator and he was talking about left-handed people. He said they were disadvantaged because the system was against them. This guy . . ."

"What does left-handed have to do with this Gill thing?" Jack interrupted Al impatiently.

"Just listen. This guy told about how car shifts were on the wrong side; how scissors were designed for right handers; and golf courses the same. He mentioned other examples, but the jist of his commentary was left-handers got the shaft. I never thought much about it before. The . . ."

O'Brennan again interrupted Al. "Will you get on with it? You're driving me crazy with this left-handed nonsense. I haven't got all day!"

"Getting back to what I was talking about, the outfit that sat in back," pointing to the pictures, Simons continued, "they occasionally played darts. Jack, nobody played darts back then, yet they played by the hour. You could count on them playing when this brown-haired guy came in. The fourth guy I'm talking about was left-handed. I don't know why, but I remember he was a portsider."

Jack got up to leave, "Ah, what the hell, give me a draught. I might as well sit here and enjoy myself." Over the next half hour, Al and Jack rehashed old times.

"Simons, I've got to run. I should be going home, but guess what, I'm going out and make a date for myself. If I'm going to drink beer today, it'll be with someone prettier than you."

The *Red Leather* was quiet when Jack walked in, but soon the lunch crowd would fill the restaurant.

"Hello again, what brings you to a place like this on a lovely Friday? You should be out enjoying the sun. If I could get away, I certainly wouldn't be sitting around an old bar like this. Jeanette smiled as she waived her hand at the mahogany strip.

"It's good to see you again and this is hardly an old bar, is it?"

"That was just a figure of speech." Once again the brilliant smile.

"I stopped in to ask you something," Jack paused, "I have to take a little trip tomorrow, and I wonder . . ."

Jeanette cut in. "You're always taking little trips, aren't you? I suppose you're going to ask if I'd like to go along." Her brilliant smile went to magnificent.

"That's the reason I'm here."

"I'd love to. Tell me more."

"I can't tell you the whole story, just that we're going to a flea market at Scots Harbor in the morning. Ever been to one?"

"Never in my life. What time does this flea adventure begin?"

"The sale begins at nine, but I'll pick you up at your place, say six-thirty. We'll stop for breakfast along the way."

"My place, huh? Sounds good to me. Do you know where I live?" O'Brennan shook his head.

"It's 166 Saxon Drive. Now you know where I live."

O'Brennan smiled. We're practically neighbors. I live on Kent Street which is two streets up from you."

"What should I wear?"

"It's going to be hot tomorrow, so dress casually. You'll know what to wear better than I. We'll be doing a lot of walking, so wear sneakers. Scots Harbor is somewhat of a tourist trap, but it's a quaint little village, and I'm certain you'll have an enjoyable day. I'll see you in the morning."

This man has been popping in and out of my life a lot since I met him, Jeanette thought as O'Brennan left the *Red Leather*.

Driving back to Ford Ashland, Jack thought about this newfound relationship with Jeanette. Here is a woman who at one time ran a string of prostitutes, though she doesn't come off that way. Very much to the contrary, she acts like a lady, dresses like one and is very classy. We're like two ships passing in the dark, so why think about it?

20

Jeanette stretched and inhaled the crisp and clean-smelling morning air. What a wonderful day, she thought. I can even make myself forget how the rising sun will bring a blanket of torrid humid air with it. She felt like a little girl waiting for the bus on the first day of school. Excited to be going, yet apprehensive about what the day would bring.

O'Brennan pulled up in front of Jeanette's house, half expecting her to make a grand entrance. Instead, he found her sitting on the front steps, dressed in white shorts, sneakers and a blue and white jersey. A picture no artist could capture on canvas. The sight captivated him.

She appeared to be deep in thought as he called out, "Good morning, you have a nautical look to you."

"Hi, I'm delighted to see you. Guess I was having a little daydream. It's going to be a lovely day, isn't it?"

"It most certainly is," Jack said as he leaned across the front seat to open the door. "How come you're sitting on the steps?"

"I come out here every morning . . . well, almost every morning. I spent much of my working hours getting to bed late, getting up late and generally missing the better part of the day. Of late, my life-style has changed and it's early to bed and early to rise for Jeanette. My day starts at five-thirty and by six, I'm out here watching the neighborhood come to life."

"I'm a morning person too. When Mary died, I asked the department to swing me. Guess I wanted to get away from my former early routine. When I retired, I returned to an early morning wakeup. I putter around the house, then meet with a bunch of friends at Inlet Park."

"Are they retired like you?"

"No. They all work except Red. Karl Eichner lives in Scots Harbor and you'll meet him and his wife this morning. He's been the head bartender at the Ritz Plaza for a long time and always comes in at eight to be with the Group."

"What do you do down there?" Jeanette asked

"We just sit around and lie to each other. The snack truck even stops for us, so over the years, our meeting has become a coffee break and gossip session all turned into one.

"John Lloyd is another guy who regularly comes over. He's now head of security at the Aud, but formerly worked with me as a detective on the force.

"Then there's Cal Redout, he's Bridgeton's Chief Pathologist and I'd have to call him the resident genius of the Group."

They sat talking until Jack pulled away from the curb to head downtown.

"And finally there's Red Ted, God love him. He's kind of a dropout, but one terrific guy. Red doesn't work, but he can't be blamed for that. He wanders around all day drinking beer; probably too much for his own good, but he doesn't bother anyone. Red knows everything that's going on in and around the U. Odd thing about Red, he carries around more money than the rest of us put together."

"Where does he get all this money, if he doesn't work?" asked Jeanette.

"We think he inherited some serious money along the way. He's not a doper, so where he gets his money is no concern to us. Red was over in Nam and had one bad time after another." Jack laughed, "I have to admit he gets a little goofy and over the edge at times, but I'm sure you'll like him. Enough about the Group, do you want to stop for breakfast?"

"It's a little early for me, but do as you wish."

"Tell you what; we can stop at the *Village Squire* in Spenser and eat on the patio. There's a nice fishing community in back of the restaurant and maybe we'll see some fishing boats come through the channel that leads to the river. I think Spenser is the nicest village in the entire area and I'm certain you'll agree."

Heading out the peninsula, they could feel the heat rising to welcome them. "Look at the haze out there. When the sun breaks through, it's going to be a blinger," Jack said.

"It's driving me crazy waiting to hear what you have planned for Sally this morning," Jeanette said.

"We're going out to the Scots Harbor flea market and run what we call a detour on Sally." O'Brennan ran through everything that had transpired since their trip to Portsmouth and how he hoped to manipulate Sally. "You know, Jeanette, detectives don't tell all to any Tom, Dick or Harry unless they trust them, and it's obvious I indeed trust you."

"I'm flattered, Mr. Detective, and your trust is well placed." Jeanette again flashed her dazzling smile.

"Last night I met you for only the third time and here I am telling you the whole ball of wax. If you ever leak this, I swear I'll rip your heart out."

"What Charlie Winder told you is the truth. I'm tight-lipped and what's to be gained by going against a trust. I don't understand this investigation, but I'm quite taken by it."

O'Brennan continued explaining his plans for dealing with Sally. "I had a great stroke of luck yesterday and hit on some good leads. Today, we hope to get a major reaction from Sally once she gets the flowers."

"What do you think your chances of succeeding are?'

"Well, this venture isn't one-dimensional. By that I mean there are various steps in this detour fighting to go wrong. Will it work? I have no idea, but it's probably like this," He turned his hand up and down.

"There's something that's been puzzling me, O'Brennan. You talk about detouring Sally, knowing full well she worked for me, correct?" O'Brennan nodded in agreement. "If she sees me, won't that compromise your plan?"

"That will be no problem. We're going to orchestrate this little plot so she'll never notice us. I'm sure you have big lens sunglasses that women carry with them." Jeanette reached into her oversized handbag and put on glasses much like the ones Jack described.

"Like these?"

"The very same. But you don't have a hat, do you?" Jack smiled as he looked at Jeanette.

"I'm not wearing a hat!" She protested.

"My dear, this morning you are." Jack reached to the back seat and brought out a wide-brimmed straw hat. "Here, try this on; it's one of my daughters."

"Okay, I'll wear it, but under protest." Jeanette's laugh provoked a smile from Jack.

"Remember, you're involved in a surveillance, not a beauty contest. Though I will concede you look good enough to enter one".

"You say the nicest things," Jeanette said as she playfully punched him on the arm.

"You're going to look like all the rest of these middle aged honeys down here. When I get you slicked up, nobody will know you."

"Where is Sally going to be?"

"Sally will be placed on the patio at a restaurant called *Sonny's*, which overlooks the bay and is adjacent to the parking lot. She'll be seated at a table very close to the lot, and from the time she gets there until she leaves, we'll be out of the picture."

"What will we do at the flea market?"

"First, we'll go out on the pier, then do the lot away from *Sonny's*. It's a great pier and there'll be more displays than you can imagine. Don't worry, we'll have a great time."

"Will there be things I can buy?"

"Lady, you don't have enough money with you to buy the junk you'll see today."

"If I run out, can I get some from you?" again the infectious laugh.

"Karl's neighbor is giving Sally the flowers when she's ready to leave. After she's gone, we'll walk around and you can buy anything your heart desires. I want today to be something special and hopefully, it will be an event you'll remember for a long time."

This time there was no playful punch on the arm, just a, "I really believe you mean that, O'Brennan." He nodded in agreement, but found himself wishing he hadn't made such a sentimental statement.

"Here's Spenser now. You'll find it a fishing village in the purest sense of the word. Probably a hundred families live here, most of whom are involved in the fishing industry."

"I love the way they bricked the sidewalks and put trees along the curbs. The old gas street lights are marvelous, much like what we have on the Hill." Jack marveled at her girlish enthusiasm. "There's nothing better than being around water with its boats and little harbors. I haven't really experienced such a setting as this, but I do believe that's going to change. I'm sick and tired of running the restaurant and continually chasing the almighty dollar. After experiencing this," Jeanette swept her hand around, "I may sell it for a place on the water."

After ordering, Jeanette got up and walked along the edge of the patio. She spent many minutes looking at the inlet and channel that flowed past her. Returning to the table, she spoke to Jack. "From here you can see the cove and the fishing shacks in back. If you look to the left," Jeanette said with a sweeping motion of her hand, "you can see where the entrance to the channel meets the river. I noticed the restaurant is for sale and this may be a once in a lifetime opportunity for me. Like I just mentioned, I'm getting sick of the *Leather* and may just buy this place". While Jeanette thoughtfully viewed the water scene around them, Jack's thoughts centered on how remarkably pretty she was.

"A boat is coming in now." Jeanette excitedly stood up and pointed at a low-slung fishing boat loaded with nets and white buckets barely easing under the bridge on its way to the cove. It appeared the boat's design was meant to accommodate the low clearance of the bridge rather the other way around.

Maybe twenty feet long, the craft looked like a rust bucket

with splashes of red-lead painted here and there strategically placed to battle the inevitable rust that attacks all seagoing vessels. Not upscale by any means, it gave the appearance of being seaworthy and properly maintained.

A lone fisherman wearing a black baseball cap with a red B was obviously a card-carrying citizen of the Red Sox nation steered from the rear. Attired in the traditional version of what hardworking men of the sea wear; he was dressed in yellow rain jacket, matching bib overalls and Wellington boots.

As the boat passed by the deck, he smiled and waved at Jeanette who happily returned his salute.

She laughed while resuming her breakfast. "Wasn't that wonderful?" O'Brennan smiled in agreement.

Throughout breakfast, Jeanette discussed the potential of a waterside eatery. She talked with conviction and eagerness about running an eatery for the average person.

"Yes, that would be the avenue for me to pursue A place where they could enjoy the best food in the area at a modest price."

Jack passed her idle talk off as just that, idle talk, but he did marvel at her unflappable enthusiasm. He had no way of knowing what a critical role the restaurant would play in concluding the Freddie Gill case.

"There is one thing I must tell you, but please don't laugh," Jeanette said.

"I wouldn't do that."

"When you hear it, you just might. This is the first time I've ever been down this way. I've never been here in Spencer, nor in Scots Harbor for that matter," she admitted. "When one talks about a sheltered life, they must be referring to me."

O'Brennan laughed.

"See, you're making fun of me."

"No, not really. It's just that to have lived in Bridgeton for many years and not have been down here is wild. We better not waste any time getting to the metropolis of Scots Harbor, because you may want to buy the entire village before the day is done."

Jeanette laughed and linked her arm into Jack's elbow as they headed for the Blazer.

At the moment Jack turned the corner in Scots Harbor, a car pulled out from a parking space opposite *Sonny's*. The driver waved as he left, providing Jack with an exceptional view of the flea market.

"We were lucky to get this spot," Jeanette said.

"There was no luck involved. That was Karl Eichner, and he probably parked here last night."

"What do we do now?"

"We do what most detectives spend their life doing, we sit and wait for Sally to come."

"Look out there!" Jeanette excitedly pointed toward the selling stalls that clogged the parking lot. "Here it is eight-thirty and people have their stands set up ready for business. I've never seen so much stuff in my life."

"The stuff you're seeing is the tip of the iceberg and runs all the way to the end of the pier."

"When did they get here?"

"They've probably been here since dawn. I see there's something else you don't know about flea markets. This is a business for the people out there. The free-enterprise system is alive and well, and that's why they're up so early. They want to make a buck."

"How long does the event run?"

"Every market is different, but this one opens at nine and probably shuts down at five."

"I can't believe the number of people flowing in. They look like they're dressed incognito."

Jack laughed. "They not dressed for summer, it's the flea market they're dressed for. They could care less what they look like because they're on vacation. Ah, the hell with waiting for Sally, let's walk out to the pier and meet Phyllis."

By the time they walked to the pier, Jeanette was awestruck by the sheer number of exhibitors. Phyllis Eichner stood by the pier admission booth watching Jack walk up with this mystery woman. He then introduced her to Jeanette.

"Karl took care of placing your friend on the patio. He gave me the A-ok sign and these are his exact word. 'Everything is go and she has taken the bait,' You men and your lingo. At times, I hardly understand a word you're talking about. You know what I mean, don't you, Jeanette?"

"I know exactly what you're saying, Phyllis." Jeanette's laugh caused Phyllis to follow suit and it appeared a new friendship was about to blossom.

"Are you two coming over after you finish here?" Phyllis asked.

"Karl didn't mention anything about it."

"Well, the horse's ass was supposed to! I told him this morning to invite you over."

"Phyllis, we didn't speak this morning. He gave me a wave as he was pulling away from the parking space he saved for us, that's all."

"Well, he's still a horse's ass at times." Phyllis' laughter prompted a similar response from Jeanette, and with it, the budding relationship continued.

"In that case, come over because we're having a cookout."

"We'll be there."

Sally sat watching the people scurrying around the vending stands like ants at a picnic. The midnight call followed by Tremonte's article had started the erosion of her confidence. Her talks with Fritz had not helped and she was frightened.

Odd that she would think of it, but she felt like Adlai Stevenson after General Eisenhower had defeated him for president. Stevenson had uttered the famous phrase, 'it hurts too much to laugh and I'm too old to cry'. I feel like crying now because Fritz isn't going to show up, Sally thought as she prepared to leave.

From the far side of the flea market, the threesome observed Sally sitting on the patio. Her ten o'clock meeting long since passed with no Fritz. It was after eleven and she appeared to become more confused as the minutes ticked by. Calling the waitress over, Sally appeared to ask for the check. Shortly after paying, she stood up to leave when an older man approached her. He handed Sally a bouquet of flowers after which a brief discussion followed.

Her look of shock was total after reading the message accompanying the flowers. Sally appeared stunned as she turned and started toward the exit. She shifted her feet helplessly and suddenly started to crumble into the flower man.

"Oh boy, she's fainted." Earlier, Jack had talked about a major reaction, and now he had one. A crowd slowly gathered to view this meticulously dressed woman who had fainted dead away. Almost instantaneously, the local ambulance crew administered first aid and soon had her standing. Eventually, Sally was led away from the restaurant in a very shaky condition.

Tears came to Jeanette's eyes as she began to speak. "What you just did to that poor woman was horrible. No person alive deserves that kind of treatment."

What you think about what happened to Sally doesn't matter to me. She deserved more than she got, Jack thought.

"Let me tell you about this little honey you want to protect. Do you know what she does for a living?"

"Yes, she runs a wholesale business!"

"What do you think she wholesales?"

"Pottery and items sold in boutiques and gift shops."

"Let me be more explicit about your former colleague. These are the facts or what we believe them to be. She's a major distributor of cocaine in the Middle Atlantic Region. Now what do you think of the delicate Sally Ralston Hunter?"

"I had no idea . . . I can't believe what I'm hearing," said an astonished Jeanette.

"This isn't the good ship Lolly Pop. Why would I lie?"

A catch appeared in her throat. "It's difficult to believe she'd do such a thing. I don't know what to say."

"I know this is a tired old chestnut, but in my business, we do what it takes to win. We may not like it, but when you run into a Sally Hunter, everything is fair. Remember the picture you painted of Sally the other day? You yourself said she was capable of anything. This will provide a very humbling experience for her; I'm sure you agree with me on that."

"I guess you're right. When I first saw her reaction to the note, I felt compelled to fire out at any one close and you happened to be that one. Though I have to admit my words were a shade overstated. But O'Brennan, hearing about what she does for a living is depressing. I guess it takes all kinds, doesn't it?"

"Sadly enough, yes it does. I know the affair on the patio was unpleasant, and I'm not proud of what came to pass, but ugly happenings like that are part of the work I do. Let's forget this little incident with Sally and spend the next couple of hours like we haven't a care in the world. We can't change her past anymore than we can change our own," Jack said as he reached for her hand. The brief exchange of words about Sally had ended.

While Jeanette and Jack shopped, Sally returned to her office where she had a long and emotion-filled discussion with Fritz. Her call stood Fritz's hair on end. The incidents with Sally were getting out of hand. He dialed the familiar 202 area code, followed by the unlisted number. After what seemed an eternity, the ringing stopped.

"This is the Southern guy and we're in the middle of a crisis. Sally just called and she's out of control." Fritz replayed his conversation with Sally, providing a detailed sketch of the Scots Harbor incident. After several agonizing minutes, he said, "I know it. What can I do? She's up there and I'm here in Craddock. She's being pressed and I'm certain O'Brennan is responsible."

Fritz again listened. "That's pretty severe. By Tuesday you say. We've been friends for over thirty years and that'll be awfully tough." Again more discussion came from the other end. Fritz rolled his eyes. "No, I don't have a problem with it, none whatsoever. I'll take care of it."

21

By the end of the afternoon, Jeanette bought enough junk to partially fill the back of the Blazer. Pulling into Karl's driveway, Jeanette started talking about how lovely his house was. It faced the bay with the front lawn running to the edge of the water.

"My word, this is wonderful," Jeanette exclaimed. "It's odd the way he built the house. When you pull into the driveway, you're facing the side of the house and you enter through the back door."

"You won't think it's odd when you taste his food, because Karl may be the best cook in the world." Jack looked at Jeanette and laughed.

"Honestly, you're impossible." Jeanette shook her head in mock disapproval.

Karl came out of the kitchen carrying a large covered pot. "Hello, Jeanette, I'm Karl. You're prettier than Jack described you and he said you were gorgeous."

Jeanette turned a sunset red and mumbled a barely audible, "Hi."

"Come out front you two. Jeanette, you're in for a big treat. Sit down in the shade and grab a beer while I explain what I'm going to do This pit is lined with stone. Earlier, I made a fire of drift wood and let it burn down. I just finished cleaning out the ashes before you came so it's ready to go. The food will cook in the steam created by the juices dropping on the hot stones."

"Karl, your house seems to fit in with those giant trees and I just adore it. It feels like I can reach out and touch the water from here. Do you use the boat much?" Jeanette asked as she pointed to the partyboat tied to the wooden dock.

"All the time. After supper, I'll take you for a ride."

"That would be wonderful," replied Jeanette.

"Jack, what did you think of the little to-do we had this morning? Jimmy's coming over in a couple of minutes, then we'll get the inside story," Karl said.

"Earlier, I told Jeanette we were hoping for a major reaction from Sally. Wow! What a reaction."

Jimmy and his wife crossed the lawn from next door. The little guy jauntily strided along, his face overflowing with a gigantic smile. Karl introduced Jimmy and his wife Marion to his Bridgeton guests. Following the introductions, Marion excused herself, claiming Phyllis needed help. Jeanette rose and followed her into the house.

"She seems like a nice lady," Karl said.

"She is, and do you know what she told me?" Karl merely shrugged.

"She told me she was going to change my life."

"It's about time somebody changed it."

Now it was Jack's turn to shrug. "Yeah, I guess."

"Jimmy, grab a beer and get on about this mornings," Karl said.

"What a morning I had. I'm still excited. That thing at *Sonny's* was really something; the damnedest thing I've ever been involved in. Sally just kinda' wandered in about quarter to ten. Sonny did a terrific job getting her placed at a good table She was having an awful time and believe me, I've never seen a person so upset She sat there chain-smoking and drinking coffee like you wouldn't believe. Ten o'clock and no Fritz. She appeared on the verge of tears and kept getting wilder and wilder. By eleven, she was beside herself and I could feel her tension from across the patio. She called the waitress over, paid the check, then got up to leave.

"I was almost as nervous as she was and honest, I thought I'd have a stroke." Karl and Jack laughed at Jimmy's discomfort. "I wanted to get it right, but she changed all that. Before I realized it, here comes Sally right at me. I walked up to her and said, 'Mrs. Hunter, I'm to deliver these'. I handed her the flowers and she stood there in a confused state. I didn't know what to do, so I turned and started walking away."

Jimmy took a sip of beer and laughed in a nervous way.

"Sally called out, 'Wait a minute'. I didn't know what she had in mind, so I stood there waiting for her to open the envelope. When Sally read the message, she looked scared, upset . . . no, even worse than that, she had a look of horror about her. It was something like you'd see in the movies. She was totally stunned.

"She took a couple of steps and fell, no, she fainted, that's what she did. I caught her as she went down, the flowers going one way, the message the other. I lowered her to the floor and turned her over. Sonny came running over and took charge."

"Damn, that must have been some experience," Jack added.

"It was and do you know what was so odd? Here's a good-looking, expensively dressed woman who had just fainted dead away The people sitting nearby looked away as if to say, 'I don't want to get involved'. I could feel the tension hanging from the ceiling, then confusion took over. I looked on the floor and there was the message. I don't know whether I did right, but I grabbed the damned thing and put it in my pocket, then screwed. It was a spur of the moment reaction, but it didn't make much sense to have evidence around."

"I'm amazed you pulled it off, that was good thinking, Jimmy. Getting that message was important. I kept running schemes through my head on how to get it back but drew a blank. Thanks to you, it's no longer a problem. I figured she'd walk away with the message, and that would be the end of it. That was a tremendous feat and more than we could have hoped for," Jack said with conviction.

"I think that calls for another beer," Karl said as he reached into the cooler.

Marion called from the front door," Karl, it's time to start the bake; you men come in and carry out the food."

"Jeanette, have you ever eaten a shore bake?" Karl asked

"Never."

"This will be unlike anything you've ever had before, and I'm certain you'll like it. I'll explain how to put it together as I go along. When I was stationed at Newport, Rhode Island, I learned how to do bakes. As I mentioned earlier, the stones are already hot, so we're ready to go. I need your help, gentlemen."

They picked up huge clumps of seaweed and carried them to the edge of the bake pit. Karl lined the sides and bottom with seaweed causing great billows of steam to rise to the sky.

"I'm pretty much of a traditionalist when it comes to shore bakes, Jeanette. Everyone layers according to their own tastes' but personally, I think the Rhode Islanders do the best job." Karl placed small salt potatoes and onions in the first drawer, then lowered it to the bottom of the pit.

"How will this food cook in such a short period of time?" Jeanette asked, her interest at a peak.

"You'll see in a minute. I cover each drawer with seaweed and start again. As you can see, these drawers are made of clear pine with small wire mesh on the bottom." In the next drawer, Karl placed small pieces of chicken breasts, sausage and sweet corn. He again followed the same procedure of covering the food with seaweed. The next drawer was filled with soft-shelled crabs, then again topped with seaweed. The last drawer was filled with clams, oysters and small pieces of haddock. Karl then placed the remaining seaweed over the entire bake and covered the pit with a heavy canvas.

"In New England at the shore, they push sand over the canvas to form an airtight compartment. I use these water weights around the edge and they do a pretty good job. "

"Your pit looks something like a pressure cooker, what happens now?"

Karl took a sip of beer. "Jeanette, you're right about the pressure cooker. The juice from the top drops through the lower drawers until it hits the bottom stones. It is then converted to steam and that's when the cycle begins. In an hour, we'll uncover the canvas and eat the food in the top drawer."

An hour later, Karl placed the top drawer on the table, signaling the start of the feast with a sweep of his hand. He announced himself as a man of miracles. "Now we can get serious, so let's get on with the bake."

"Why does he say these things? Marion asked.

"It pumps up his ego, Phyllis explained.

"How do you control him?" Jeanette asked.

"Cut him off." The women's laughter went unnoticed by the hungry men.

The smell of the escaping steam was good enough to eat.

"We have melted butter for the clams, red hot sauce for the oysters and hollandaise sauce for the haddock. There you are folks, dig in." The late afternoon sun splashed down on the bay as the diners helped themselves to the New England Shore Bake served on the Virginia shore of the Chesapeake. Jeanette dug in with an intensity that even amazed her.

"I'm going to take the rest of the drawers out and place them on the table. This is home style, so go after it," Karl said like a proud father.

Phyllis came out of the house carrying a large basket of hush puppies which she placed on the table. Over the next thirty minutes a stillness settled over the backyard caused by the diners' preoccupation with the succulent food.

Jeanette said with a contented sigh, "I've never eaten such food in my life. That was marvelous. I can't imagine going through life and not having eaten such a tasty dinner."

As Jeanette had keenly watched Karl put the bake together, she had begun to formulate a plan. By the time she'd finished eating, her plan was complete.

"Ya' know, Sally . . . ah Jeanette, I mean. Guess I still have this morning on my mind," Karl said.

"Think nothing of it, Karl. After that lovely dinner, you can do no wrong," Jeanette's smile spoke for itself

"The best is yet to come, it's Phyllis' coffee and Sweet Potato-Pecan pie," Karl announced.

The inviting water sparkled from the setting sun's amber rays.

After coffee and a short boat ride, the friends returned to the house where Jack and Jeanette said the customary thank you's and headed for Bridgeton.

Little was said as the Blazer drifted along the moonlit road. Only after parking in front of Jeanette's house did the two begin to talk.

"Let me help you with your new found riches," Jack offered, as he walked around to open the door for Jeanette.

"I don't know where I'll put all this junk, but it was fun buying it." Standing at the door, Jeanette impulsively reached up and hugged Jack; then kissed him on the cheek. He could feel her tears run down the side of his face. Pulling back, she looked at him through glossy, tear-filled eyes.

"O'Brennan, you've given me something very special and today was the nicest day of my life. Thank you and let's do it again." She turned abruptly and closed the door behind her.

Jack returned home very shaken by his last moments with Jeanette. Was their relationship headed toward a romance that might prove difficult to handle? That question would have to be answered at a later date, because O'Brennan was too tired to think.

22

Red's Saturday morning started by walking down Gloucester Street, the radiant sun indicated a brilliant day was in store. He aimlessly wandered along not knowing where to begin. He'd start in *O'Hearn's*.

"Give me a draught, Pat. I need some information about Harkers and you're just the gentleman to help me."

"I've already told O'Brennan everything I know about it. There's nothing I can add that will do you much good. I do know a guy who worked down there for years. If you're looking for a push, he's the one. He knows every twist and turn that ever existed in Harkers. He owns the *Clipper Ship*. Do you know where it is?"

"No, I don't."

"It's way out on St Alfred."

"How do I get there?"

"You get on the subway and go," O'Hearn shook his head.

"I know that; just tell me where to get off," Red said sarcastically.

"Get off at the Circular Hill Station. The Clipper is a real popular neighborhood bar and you can't miss it. He went out there after Harkers was ripped down This guy worked for years at this joint and eventually ended up buying it."

"What's his name?"

"Joe DuPont. You'll like him and if he can help you, I'm sure he will."

Red finished his beer and headed for the subway. The train banged and shuttered on its way toward the west suburbs. He exited at the Circular Hill Station and immediately spotted the *Clipper Ship*.

Entering the nondescript watering hole, he found a comfortable bar that obviously catered to the area residents. He passed a group of early drinkers and settled at the back end of the strip. Ordering a beer, Red smiled; "Hi, are you Joe DuPont?"

"Yeah," came the answer from the gruff owner.

"I'm Red Ted and I'm working a case that involves a sailor who was killed in Harkers. That was in fifty-three, course you know its long since been ripped down. Patrick O'Hearn sent me out here to talk to you; said if you can't help me, there's nobody in the city that can."

Dunlap smiled modestly. "How is that old duck doin'? I like Pat, he's a good man." He fixed Red with a curious look. "What did you say your name was?"

"Red, Red Ted."

"Nice to meet you," his handshake was powerful but short and to the point "Well, Red, if you're a friend of Pat O'Hearn, I'll help you all I can. What do you need to know?"

"You worked at the Clipper down in Harkers."

"Yeah, I worked there from the time I got out of the army in forty-five, until they ripped it down in the early sixties. That was too bad, hated to see it go. What about this sailor?"

"Here's what we know and it isn't much. We have nothing even approaching a clue, but we surmise there were three people who could have killed him. They ran around together and we believe they're somehow tied to this sailor's death. I've got pictures here that probably won't mean much to you, but please look them over."

DuPont reached to the backbar for his glasses.

"Here's a picture of the murdered sailor. The gal still lives in the city and this guy," Red pointed to Fritz Hansen, "lives downstate. The two guys were Navy Corpsman, while the girl hustled magazines down at the fleet landing. They hung out at the *Shamrock* with a fourth person we know little about."

"That cesspool! The *Shamrock* was the armpit of Harkers."

DuPont looked intently at the pictures, "I can remember this guy was a hustler." DuPont pointed to Freddie's picture. "He was trying to sell us whiskey, said he'd give us a hell of a great deal. Later, we found out he was stealing it from the hospital pharmacy. My boss at the Clipper wouldn't touch that juice with a ten-foot pole. The shore patrol, as well as the police hung out at the Clipper, and that was too close to home, if you get my drift? What was this guy's name?" DuPont absently pushed Freddie's picture around in a clockwise circle.

"Freddie Gill," Red answered.

"You know, Red, you could tell he had a dark side to him the first time he came in the joint. This Gill character," DuPont pointed at the picture, "was selling top shelf whiskey for half the wholesale price."

"Did you ever see him with anyone else?" Red asked, warming to the art of questioning.

"Yeah, this Gill character came back with another guy, but not this one," DuPont said as he pointed to Hansen. "This scamp starts by making the same pitch about the whiskey as the dead guy did. He then shifted gears and added a new twist and tried to hustle a whore. He claimed he had a call girl who would service the bar at special rates. Then the son of a bitch said he could get drugs for us. Ya' know back then, I don't even think they called it drugs, narcotics maybe. The boss turned him down of course; wouldn't listen to him."

"Pretty racy." DuPont nodded in agreement.

"Do you remember him?"

Running a hand through his graying hair, DuPont absently looked at Red. "Kind of. He came in early one Saturday morning with this Gill guy. He talked to the boss at the empty end of the bar. The more I think about it . . . yeah, I think I can describe him.

"He was a big guy, maybe six-two, two hundred, brown hair, a sharp dresser. Could he be the same one?"

"He is, he's the one!"

"Can't believe this, but I can remember how he was dressed.

He wore khaki pants, a short-sleeved button-down shirt, and polished penny loafers. He looked like a thinly disguised Ivy-league Harvard type."

"Can you remember anything else about him? The guy I'm talking about was left-handed, do you recall that?" Red persisted.

"No, I can't remember anything about that, but that guy was a dead beat if I ever saw one. Thinking back, there was something strange about him."

"What would that be, Joe?"

"I'd say he was about twenty-one and that's awfully young to be a hustler, but maybe he was beyond his years. Another thing you might be interested in, he smoked cigars."

"A lot of young guys smoked cigars back then."

"Yeah, but do you know what kind he smoked?" DuPont answered his own question. "He smoked those little black ones."

"What do you mean by those little black ones?" Red asked.

"I think you might call them a stoogie; we had them at the bar. They were called DiNapoles and two came in a pack. They were small on one end, big at the other. They're an Italian cigar and not many people smoked them back then; too strong I guess."

"Would you call him a heavy-handed type?"

"Naw, anything but, not that guy. I guess he had what they call on TV boyish good looks. He wanted you to think he was a gentleman, but had a shifty look to him and was a first-class boob if you ask me. Red, that's all I can think of. If I come up with something else, I'll give Pat a call down at his place."

Maybe further discussion with DuPont would provide a window into Gill's ominous past, but Red thought not.

After several beers on the house, Red located the address of Sally's warehouse in the yellow pages and headed downtown. He transferred to the Niagara Limited and got off at the Churchill stop.

Red walked six blocks to 940 Churchill Street. The warehouse was located in an old neighborhood theater with a sign reading *R and H Wholesale* facing the street. Jack hadn't discussed the warehouse's location and Red wondered what else he had failed to mention. Finding the warehouse closed, Red crossed the street to the *Churchill Grill.*

"Hi, do you know if that place across the street will be open today?" Red pointed at the converted theater.

"No way, they're closed on Saturdays," answered the bartender.

"I'd like to talk to someone who works there."

"Why, you lookin' for a job?"

"No. I need to know some things about the business, and I'd like to get it today."

"I don't know anybody who works there, but the fellow who bartends nights used to. He's coming to work at three, and if you wait around, you can talk to him then." Red drank beer for the next two hours until a new bartender came on.

"Tony said you were asking about across the street." The new guy whipped his head in the direction of the warehouse. "Why you interested in that place?"

"I want to find out about the operation."

"You know, I can't say enough bad things about that place; and I can't guarantee anything good about Sally."

"Why would you say that?"

He didn't try to hide his bluntness. "Because that miserable bitch fired me about six months ago. I worked there for fifteen years and was practically the whole operation. Took care of all the shipping and she up and fired me."

"Did she give you a reason?"

"Well, I went out on a weekend bender and missed Monday, a real beauty I must say. When I came back the next day she canned me and didn't ask for explanations. I'd been real good too, hadn't missed any work or been a problem. She threw me out just like that. I think there was more to it than that," he shrugged, "but I don't know what. What are you, a cop or something?"

"No, I'm no cop. I'm helping a PI friend of mine out. Sally's involved in something we'd like to know about, but nothing major, mind you. I really don't know what I'm doing, but I'm nosing around trying to find out what her game is."

"You came to the right guy. I'll tell you whatever you want to know." Red could feel the butterflies tap-dancing in his stomach as he sensed something huge coming his way.

"Could you tell me about the operation?"

"Sure. It's your typical wholesale business; the manufacturer ships to her and she in turn ships to the retailers. We shipped goods to gift shops, garden stores, department stores and those fancy stores they call boutiques. As much as I hate her, I've got to admit she has one hell of a business."

"What kind of goods does she handle?"

"We did a lot with ceramic and pottery items. She bought most of her stuff from the Sharply Pottery down in Williamsburg. Most of her ceramic ware came from the Saber Kilns in town." The bartender paused to rework his memory. "She also received large shipments from Hong Kong."

"Anything unusual about the operation?"

"Not really. I packaged and shipped the orders, and that was about it. A lot of the orders would be ready when I came in."

"You do anything else over there?"

"Certainly did. I used to drill holes in the pottery vases."

"Drill holes?"

"Sure, we had these red pots I'd say were a foot tall. They had little pockets on the side. People plant flowers in the pockets and on top. They look like a hanging basket, except you couldn't hang them."

"Yeah, I know what you mean." Red didn't know what he meant, but it seemed like the right thing to say.

"I drilled three holes on top, so they could be hung; that was my creation. The idea caught on and she stole it from me."

"Did you ever have much trouble with her before she fired you?"

He absently fingered his ear lobe. "Never did . . . except one time she pealed my ass so bad you couldn't believe it."

"What was that about?"

"I was drilling one of those pots and dropped it. It broke in a thousand pieces and did she have a fit!"

"Why would she raise hell about a pot that cost her a couple of pennies?"

"Ya' got me on that one, but she sure went nuts. I can't believe how upset she got."

"So what made the pot so valuable that she would be that mad?"

"I don't know, but I never saw a pot like it before. Funny thing, it had a false bottom."

Red was thrilled and knew he had the answer to a lot of questions. "How big a bottom?"

"Oh, I don't know, not very big.

"How much would it hold?"

"Oh . . . not much."

"How many people worked there?"

"Judy Fuller was the secretary and George Light worked in receiving, and me of course. That was it."

"Let's talk about those pots again. Was there anything different about them?"

"Not really. They all looked the same, well almost the same. Some were kept on a different shelf."

"Why would that be?"

"The ones with the compartment were taller than the others; maybe by an inch or so."

"Did you work a five day week?"

"Yeah, Monday through Friday, seven to four."

"Did you see much of Sally?"

"No, normally she'd come in just before we left."

"Anything unusual about her?"

"What do you mean?"

"I know this may sound stupid, but did she ever do any work in the warehouse?"

"That goes without saying. You can't imagine what an incredible mind-set Sally had about work. She worked harder than I did, and she put up a lot of orders herself."

"How were the pots packaged?"

"We shipped them in cardboard boxes, sixteen on the bottom, the same on top. They were separated by dividers, so they wouldn't break."

"So she did some of the work?"

"She worked like hell, I'll give her that. Sometimes when I came in for work, she'd have everything ready to go."

"Then she always worked at night?"

"You've got it. I used to come over here after work, and if I stayed late, she'd still be there"

"What time would that be?"

"Two, three in the morning I worked here as a part-time bartender. Fortunately, when she fired me, a full-time job opened up here. It's worked out so good for me I'm making more money than I did with Sally. From here, I can still see what's going on over there, and yes, she still works late."

"One last question. Can you tell me who carted the boxes away?"

"Dobbins and Friend Trucking."

"Thanks pal, I may see you again about this matter. I never did get your name. Mine's Red."

"Mine's Phil. There's another thing I should mention before you go. Sally used to have a visitor come around late at night. Not often, mind you, but occasionally somebody would park in the lot next to the warehouse and sneak in."

Red blinked. "Did you ever see his face?"

"No, sorry Red," Phil softly said.

Red waved at Phil as he tossed a twenty on the bar. This had been a productive day, and as he headed back to the U, Red thought he'd done a masterful stroke of sleuthing. There wasn't much to this business if you asked the right questions and used a smidgen of deduction, he thought. Though he did admit to himself that luck had to enter into the fray at some point.

23

O'Brennan scurried around putting together breakfast for his friends. The Group drifted in, helped themselves to coffee and talked about Saturday's events.

"Breakfast is ready, so help yourselves," Jack said as he made his way from the kitchen to the patio with baking powder biscuits. Breakfast consisted of: sausage, Virginia ham, Pennsylvania scrapple, home fries and crispy fried red tomatoes, and fried bananas.

After the hearty breakfast, Jack and Karl reviewed their Saturday experience with Sally at Scots Harbor. Red followed with his findings from his journey to the Circular Hill and Churchill bars. He was pleased with his efforts and let the Group know it. John concluded the discussion by reporting that he had nothing to report. He had started for Portsmouth, but was called back to check on some vandalism at the Aud.

"All right gentlemen, let's review what we have." The next fifteen minutes was consumed by a review of the accumulated facts. "I have some personal opinions on those involved. Starting with Sally, we know she's about ready to be tapped. She's on thin ice and with the trauma suffered yesterday, she can't take much more. Hansen, we don't have much on. And there's the Stem. We're starting to find out a lot about him. Red, what you came up with yesterday was truly remarkable."

"Hell, Jack, I just stumbled onto it," replied a subdued Red Ted.

"It was still excellent work."

"I've thought about this Stem and I believe he's the cog that makes this outfit run," Karl said.

"I agree, Karl. We've been through the Stem a hundred times, but let's do it again. He weighs around two hundred, is six foot plus, has sandy hair, is left-handed and is or was a sharp dresser. He was a master hustler when he was in his early twenties. The Stem smoked little stoogie cigars and very possibly came from Maine. There's something else, but I can't think of it. Someone help me out."

"He doesn't like pain," volunteered Cal.

"We know he has a stem tattooed on his shoulder," added Jack, "so where to from here?"

"After hearing these reports, it would appear we're going along first rate. How about getting back to Tremonte? Have him slip something else into his column," Cal asked.

The Group agreed with Cal. "Red, what would you write? You're currently on a roll," Jack asked.

"Let's say the expanding investigation has gone from the remnants of Harkers, south to Portsmouth and up to our nation's capital."

"We haven't had contacts up there, why would you say that?" Lloyd seriously questioned Red's strategy.

"John, you thought sending flowers to Sally was a good idea, correct?" John nodded in agreement "How about another misdirection? You guys talk about a detour, here's a beauty. We can even mention the Stem, squeeze him a little."

"Red, I don't want that in the article. Let's leave him out of it for the present and make it appear we know nothing of his existence. From what Red came up with, let's assume Hansen is shipping coke to Sally, who in turn is sending it to her special retail outlets. What else would she be doing with the false-bottomed pots? For that matter, she may be shipping all over the East Coast. Let's work on the Stem, but keep it quiet, be cool with him," Jack said.

"What's next?" Cal asked.

"I've got to meet with Bud Henry as soon as possible, maybe he can help"

"Red, you mentioned this trucking company, Dobbin and Friend. If we could get to them, we'd know where this stuff is going. We can conclude legitimate dealers are also buying from Sally. Finding out where she ships would give us a leg up on her distribution pattern. John, how would you approach this?" Jack asked

"Look at it this way; small dealers would buy their seasonal stock in one shot. Their orders would be small to guard against building up too large an inventory. Their repeat orders would also be small and irregular. If we can define who the heavy regular buyers are, we'll have a good idea who's doing coke."

"That's a good assumption. Next question, how do we access this trucking company?"

No one stirred. Finally, Red offered, "I know a girl who works there as a bookkeeper, or at least she used to."

"Are you telling us you had a girlfriend?"

"Naw, Cal, she wasn't really a girlfriend, although I went out with her a lot."

"Red, that's difficult to fathom; pretty hard to believe. We've known you for years, well, you know what I mean?"

"No, Cal, I don't know what you mean."

"We never thought you were funny, or anything like that. But you always gave the impression of not particularly caring for the ladies."

"Cal, you're driving your heel right into my heart. I like the ladies just fine! What are you talking about?"

Cal had Red on the ropes and he wasn't about to let him go "You know exactly what I'm talking about. Where did you get that heel in the heart routine? Getting back to the ladies, we never saw you with a single one. How would we know?"

"I used to be around with one," countered an increasingly annoyed Red.

"All right, tell us about her," continued Cal with the needle.

"I used to go out with her."

"You told us that. How long ago has it been?"

"Five, six years ago."

"You probably don't even know where she lives," Cal continued to irritate Red Ted.

"Well, like I told you, I used to know her."

The Group laughed at Red's discomfort.

"I didn't tell you I had a handle on her."

"You can't imagine what a comfort that is. Did you break up on good terms?"

Red's face reddened as he focused on Cal. "You're pissing me off with all your stupid questions. No, she told me she didn't want to go out with me anymore! Do I have to draw you a picture?" Red displayed a rare emotion that surprised his friends.

"It isn't any of our business, but why would she do that?"

Red put his chin on his chest for a moment, then returned his gaze to his antagonist. "You're right, Cal, it isn't any of your business, but what the hell, it's the story of my life so you might as well hear it. I got drunk and missed a date, made another and missed that one too. The next time I called, she told me that was it. How does that strike you!"

Red's story saddened Cal, but he continued to probe, "You don't drink like that now, do you?"

"No, but I drank like hell back then. She got sick of it and threw me out."

"Is she a nice girl?" continued Cal.

"Betty's a good one, a real lady. She's about my age and was divorced when she was a young. Her old man did about the same stuff I was doing. Betty said she'd be damned if she'd go through that nonsense again, so there you are."

"You know anything about her now?"

"Don't know a thing She's probably married. Is there a point to all this? Obviously there is."

"Why don't you contact her?"

"I don't know, Cal, I just don't know." Red thought for a minute. "Okay, when do you want me to call her?"

"How about now?"

"I can't do it now! What are you talking about?"

"Call her now," Cal ordered.

Red sheepishly headed for the phone in the kitchen without speaking another word.

Silence claimed the patio until Jack said, "You were a little rough on him, Cal."

"Jack, do you want the accounts or not?" O'Brennan merely shrugged.

"Hello Betty, this is Red."

"Red who?" Came the reply.

"Red Ted." The sound of her voice caused the months and years they'd been apart to fold together under the cover of longing.

"I don't know a Red Ted. Why are you calling me?" A catch appeared in her voice.

"I need your help."

"Why would I help you after what you did to me?"

"What did I do to you?"

"You know exactly what you did. You were drunk the last two weeks we went out."

"There's not much I can do about it now."

"You sure can't and neither can I. Red, you're just a wild, not-so young man still growing up."

"A friend once told me the only thing you remember about the past are the good times. Betty, I remember you."

"Red, the music stopped a long time ago."

"Look it, I need your help. Do you still work at Dobbins and Friend?"

"No! I haven't worked there in four years. I'm at Peninsula Cable now."

"I've got to get some information about the trucking company."

"I couldn't do that."

"You don't even work for them now, so what's the big deal?"

"Why do you want to know about them?"

"I'm helping a private investigator who's trying to find out about some goods being shipped out of the city. We have to know, it's that important."

"I don't know, Red"

"How about me coming out to see you?"

"I don't want to see you, nor do I want you out here. As a matter of fact, I'm not going to be home today."

"Couldn't I meet you some place?"

"What's the point. I told you I wasn't going to be here. I'm going down to Harbor Day for the afternoon."

"That's right, I forgot all about it."

"Yes, that I can believe. You probably forgot about it because you were drunk."

"Listen to me, I haven't been drunk since we quit dating. I've got myself squared away and my new friends are directing me toward a better life. Let me tell you about old Red . . . ah, forget it."

"I'm going down with a girl friend."

"If I see you at the festival, will you talk to me?"

"Damn you, Red, you're impossible. You get your foot in the door and you won't accept no. Yes, I suppose so, but don't count on much."

"Then I may see you later. Take care."

Cal continued his onslaught on Red after he returned to the patio. "Well, lover boy, what's the verdict?"

"She's going over to Harbor Day this afternoon and I'm going to meet her."

"I guess that's the best we can do," Jack said. "What do we have to know?"

"Who the big shipments go to," John replied.

"John, do we need addresses?"

"No, I don't think so. We can dig those out of Directory Assistance, but Jack, we do need the name of each store and the city they're located in."

Karl Eichner stirred, "Jack, could there be a sequence in the shipping, some pattern, maybe a tendency? It may help us to know the day of the week, the month, that kind of thing."

"You're right, Karl, but she probably won't be able to come up with that information."

Cal was delighted with the verbal assault he'd laid on Red and couldn't resist giving him one parting shot. "Red, if this Betty is as nice as you say, how'd you let her get away?"

"I was hitting the bottle and that's that! You know it, I know it, everybody knows it." Anger began to rise again in Red's voice. "What do you want from me? It's done and there's not a damned thing I can do about it."

"Well, you have cleaned your act up, I'll give you credit for that. You ought to clean yourself up if you're going to meet the apple of your eye."

"What in hell is the matter with you, Mr. Coroner? You've been on my back all morning and I'm well sick of it. I'm as clean as you are, maybe cleaner, you phony! I shower and shave every morning and that's probably more than you can say!"

Cal laughed at Red's remark, which only served to further exasperate the redhead. "Get a grip on yourself and go home and get some decent clothes on; you look like a ragpicker's dream."

Red displayed a wounded look as he regarded Cal. "Yeah, I guess you're right, Cal, I don't look too good."

"That takes care of you, Red. When you see your beloved this afternoon, we can count on you looking tip-top." Cal responded, pleased with his tossing of Red's ego.

"Cal, when this Gill matter is over, so are we," Red said as he stormed out of the patio.

"After Red departed, Jack addressed his compatriot with a jaundiced eye. "You don't think much of him, do you, Cal? That was a dastardly stunt you pulled on Red. Whatever possessed you to fieldstrip that poor loser the way you did? You could have cut him some slack, but instead, you may well have pushed him over the edge with your little display of arrogance. You had no right to do that." Jack hunched his shoulders as if to say the matter was beyond him.

Cal laughed and looked around the patio. "I don't believe one word of what you just said, and the last thing you should do is worry about Red. A mental midget he is not. Gentlemen, you are witness to the reincarnation of a lost soul and the embodiment of a new Red. I'm convinced he will shower us with an astonishing revelation, and we shall all be appalled at how we misread him."

"Where did you bury your brains? That's lunacy and you know it!" O'Brennan said in a highly agitated voice.

"Take it from your favorite dream-maker, it isn't lunacy. Think back over the last several days and look at all the suggestions he's made. Check out his work yesterday. No, gentlemen, our Red is something very special. We shall see his potential blossom in the near future; and we all shall be a part of that grand awakening. What I did this morning was give him a nudge toward something great. Forgive the old Doc for what he did, but Red has a brilliant quality fighting to get out and it's almost upon us."

"Maybe you're right, Cal, but you certainly had me bent for awhile."

Silence suddenly invaded the patio and continued until Karl spoke up. "Jack, anything you need from me?"

"You have to work, Cal has to work; man; I thought Sunday was supposed to be a day of rest. Guess that leaves the two of us, John. What do you want to do?"

"Let's go down to the *Red Rooster* and twist Billy Olsen around. It's about time we put the squeeze on that rascal."

"Good idea, then we'll go over to Harbor Day. It'll give us a chance to watch pretty boy in action with that honey he used to date." The Group laughed at Jack's rather inept attempt at humor.

After the others left, John lingered on. "Let me help you clean up."

"No thanks, John, I'll take care of it. One of the things that brought me back after I lost Mary was assuming her house duties. It helped me develop a routine that kept me above water. You know what I mean, you had the same problem."

"Yes, I know."

"I didn't want to talk in front of the others, but a lot of things have come our way in a relatively short period of time. We've zeroed in on some people who could prove dangerous. The path the investigation is taking seems too easy, and that I don't like. What do you think?" Jack said with concern in his voice.

"I think you're absolutely on target, and I've been thinking along the same line. Most cases that come this easy have pitfalls along the way. Jack, I think we should keep our eyes and ears open and our guard up."

"How do you see this mess coming down?"

"I agree with your theory of a chain of command. Sally is at the bottom, and foot soldier of the organization. She's making a fortune, but nevertheless, she's an underling. Hansen's her boss and oversees the operation. We're reasonably certain his boss is the top banana. Hansen has more outlets than Sally, and to maintain such a structure, he needs an umbrella. The Stem may be that person, Mr. Big, if you will."

"That's the way I see it. If the Stem is the top dog and has clout, where does that put us? Earlier, we talked about a DC connection. What if there is someone up there in a position of power?"

"I guess it's a possibility, but it sounds far-fetched to me," John said.

"John, if they take an interest in us; they can find out who we are in a hurry. I haven't mentioned this, but I think we got their attention. The last time I talked with Duke, he told me a guy came in his shop and was asking about me."

"I figured it was inevitable, but I'm surprised they're onto us so soon. You're not telling me a damn thing I don't already know. We sit in the park every day as regular as that statue on the lawn," John said.

"We've talked about this before and are old-timers at this game. We know how to take care of ourselves, that we know; but the others can't, and that isn't good."

"I have a feeling there's some heavy stuff coming our way. I don't know what it could be, but it scares me." John's concern touched O'Brennan.

"I agree. If we start chasing someone in DC, he or they may lay a storm on us we can never imagine or prepare for."

"Jack, those novels you read about business and government are for dreamers, we all agree on that. But have you ever questioned how much truth there is to them?"

"Yes, I have. Anybody in our business has to believe some of that make-believe."

"What should we be looking for?"

"John, you're a cop like me. I think we should be guarded about anything that looks different and unusual." O'Brennan smiled at John. "You'll probably ask me 'like what' but I'm clueless. "We know Sally got to Hansen yesterday, who in turn, got to his boss. If the Stem is as tough as we make him out to be, we could run into major league problems down the road."

"Come on, Jack, let's go squeeze Billy and forget about the Stem."

"That sounds pretty good. Between turning Billy upside down and watching Red, the lover boy, this should be an entertaining afternoon."

24

O'Brennan and Lloyd owned the room the minute they entered. Light from neon signs, both old and new created a surreal atmosphere. The wretched occupants in this miserable setting stopped their laughter and stared at the twosome; but soon returned to their drinks with cautious murmurs.

The stench sweep over Lloyd and O'Brennan as they marched into the *Red Rooster*. The oppressive feeling one got upon entering this depraved hole never changed. As an added feature, the afternoon heat compounded the offensiveness of the grimy saloon.

"Home sweet home," John said.

Billy Olsen sat majestically behind the Sunday sports section and sneered through crooked teeth while gesturing for the newcomers to take a seat. "Hi there, detectives, it's nice to see two old friends from high school. What are you doin' down here on a Sunday afternoon, slummin'? Make yourself at home." An unpleasant smile followed.

"Jack, listen to the mouth on him." O'Brennan nodded at Lloyd's observation.

"This isn't a social call. I always thought you were a cut above the rest of the trash around here, Billy, but I'm beginning to have second thoughts," Jack said.

"I'm shocked you'd think so unkindly of me," the little man said.

"And to answer your earlier question, no, Billy, we're not down here slumming. Jack and I needed a little cheering up, so we decided to come down here and ruin your day."

Billy laughed. "Oh yeah, and how do you expect to do that, Mr. Lloyd?"

Lloyd turned to Jack with a shake of the head, "O'Brennan, the world hates a smart-ass and this little guy is sure one."

O'Brennan pulled some folded bills out of his pocket. Taking a fin out, he placed it under an ashtray in the middle of the table. "I have five dollars that says my friend here gets his message across." Extending an open hand toward John, Jack said, "Mr. Lloyd, you're up."

"Remember when I let you off the hook for that burglary a couple of years ago? Well, Mr. O'Brennan and I figure it's about time you fess up, savy? Your bargaining power isn't what it once was."

The obnoxious stoolie neatly folded the paper and placed it on the table, a slight sneer beginning to show. Waving his finger in a beckoning fashion, he replied to Lloyd, "Tell me more, handsome."

Jack laughed at Billy.

"You should be what the smart people call accountable." The sneer grew into a broad, sweeping smile that further infuriated Lloyd.

"You know, Billy, that shit smile of yours isn't doing you any good, is it Jack?"

Jack shook his head with no show of emotion.

"No sir, it isn't bothering me one bit, not a lick. The cutting edge of thrills has ended for you, big shot. If I banged you around as a policeman, you'd bring charges against me, correct?" A tired look beyond his years crossed Billy's face, and for the first time he displayed an attentive eye in John Lloyd's direction. "Now you know what I ain't, and that's a policeman. I'm a retired gentleman. If I should happen to run into you in the alley and make a punchboard out of you, how could you bring charges against a private citizen? O'Brennan, do you have any idea how that could happen?" Another shake of the head from his partner.

"But I haven't done anything!" Replied a flustered Billy Olsen, a pained look settling on his face.

"Ah, now you understand my drift. My friend here, Mr. O'Brennan, is blinder than a bat, aren't you old-timer?"

"Correct, Mr. Lloyd." O'Brennan smiled as he looked in Billy's direction.

"We all have our faults, but I'm not going to put up with yours anymore. We've been feeding you for years and what we want now is called retribution. The last information you gave us was good stuff, I'll grant you that. You told Jack you had to lie low, that Hansen scared you. We can understand that, he scares a lot of people. You're not the first person to be intimidated by Fritz Hansen, nor will you be the last. You're missing the big picture. If he finds you, he'll throw you out in the street with yesterday's garbage. Billy, we have to know more about Freddie Gill and company, and we need it now."

Billy stared hard at Lloyd while sliding back in his chair. "What do you mean by now?"

"Within a day or so. We're going to leave now. As a matter of fact, we're leaving you with no choice, ya' dig?"

"Shall we return to our regularly scheduled Sunday afternoon programming?" Jack said. "Indeed we should," Lloyd replied.

As the partners left the *Red Rooster*, Jack said with a laugh, "You have all the fun."

"The best ten minutes I ever spent," John said.

On his return from Jack's house, Red had purchased a can of spray starch. He set up the ironing board and prepared to tackle a task he'd long since given up on. He painstakingly ironed a blue button-down shirt and tan chino pants, then cleaned and polished his docksiders; the first shoes he'd cleaned since leaving the service. If his buddies wanted him to get with it, he would oblige. Before leaving, he glanced in the mirror and nodded approval at the new look.

Red's walk around the Inlet lasted longer than his usual half hour tour. Every minute added to his anxiety as he shuffled around the festival grounds. The event consisted of a huge flea market, numerous food and beverage stands, kiddie rides and entertainment at each end of the festival grounds. He walked around for the better part of an hour before spotting Betty with her friend.

I had no idea I'd feel this way. Now don't panic, he thought as he started toward Betty.

This was the crunch time they talked about on television. The very sight of her brought back pleasant memories of their past days. Thoughts of turning around and getting out of this mess crossed his Red's mind, but that wasn't the answer. He'd turned his back on similar situations too often before. He forced himself to face the reality of the moment.

Red walked up to Betty blurting out, "Hi."

"Betty, I'll meet you in front of Pier 1, say three o'clock." Betty's friend walked away leaving two lovers from the past looking at each other.

"Red, you do look good, the best I've seen you since we first met, and that was years ago."

"You really look great too" Good grief, he sounded like a ten year old, Red thought. He had to admit she looked as fresh as flowers in spring. There was no smile, but the rest, from her long blonde hair to a freckled complexion was a fond memory of earlier days. This was his old girl and how he wanted to kick himself for ruining their relationship.

"Don't tell me that! I've gained too much weight since the last time you saw me."

"You still look good. Betty, this is a stupid conversation!" Red said.

"Yes, you're right."

"You still look young and that's the important thing." Red found it increasingly difficult to converse with the new Betty.

"We're not young and you know it." Making small talk was difficult for Betty as well. "What are you doing now?"

"Not doing a thing."

"See, you haven't changed. You're like a wind that never stops blowing." They walked to a vacant bench overlooking the marina. "You know, I've had a lot of lonely nights at home since we broke up. I've thought about our situation and came to the conclusion that I never understood you. From the time you came back from Vietnam, you appeared to be on a course of self-destruction. You were an honors student at the University of Virginia and could have made something of your life. I cannot understand that."

"Why would I work?" Red replied defiantly.

"For self-esteem, if nothing else," answered an equally annoyed Betty.

"I don't need self-esteem, do you know what I have? What gives me self-esteem? I'm loaded; got a bunch of money."

"Money isn't everything. Your life is down the toilet and you tell me money is the answer."

"Money makes this motor run. I can do whatever I want, go where I want, I don't, but I can if I want to. I never have to work because I'm rich. You brought up my college background, well my finance degree taught me one thing, and that was how to figure. You always told me what a crime it was that I didn't use my intelligence. You've got it all wrong. I am smart and know how to invest my money. I've done nicely thank you, and that's the name of the game. I'm worth twice what I had when I went out with you, so what are you talking about?"

"See, you're missing the obvious; your whole life is shattered. Nothing has changed about you, not one blasted thing!"

"It's getting better, or at least it appears to be. How quickly we forget; you always did lay these little guilt trips on me. There is one thing you should know, Betty Green, I am going to do something with my life. I'm going to Bridgeton Law School in September."

Red's disclosure so stunned Betty, she felt unable to reply. She quickly changed the subject by asking, "What do you want to know about the trucking company?"

"I'm going to give you a general background of the case we're working on and you judge whether to help or not." Red sketchily reviewed the case from start to yesterday's trip to the warehouse.

"Why the concern?" Betty asked.

"We think the woman who owns R and H Wholesale is dealing drugs. We're looking for a pattern of shipping, the number of boxes and the regularity of shipments she sends out. We need your help on this. Please."

"All right, I'll try. There were a number in Upstate New York. There was one in Syracuse, Abbott Nursery; the Cayuga Garden Supply in Ithaca; Ontario Novelty in Rochester; and Finwell Gardens in Buffalo. In New Jersey there was Coastal Boutique in Atlantic City and Costalls Thrift Shop in Trenton. We did a lot with Jackson and Jackson Department Store in Philadelphia. Let's see, Mountain Florists in State College, Pennsylvania received large numbers, as did Filbert Wholesale in Cumberland, Maryland. Here in Virginia, there was College Side Gallery in Charlottesville and in Carolina, there were two; McGee Florists in Durham and the Triumph Gardens in Chapel Hill. That takes care of the major ones."

"It appears these outlets are located in good sized cities or towns. This information should help out a great deal. Would you like to walk around a bit?"

"I guess we could for a while."

After walking for a short time, Red asked, "How about something to eat?"

"No thanks, but I would like something cold, the sun is so hot." Red stopped at a nearby beer stand. "You told me you weren't drinking like you used to and look at you now. Red, you can't wait to get that beer into you."

"Having a beer is one thing, sitting down and drinking like I used to is another matter."

She closed her eyes as she spoke, "Maybe you're right."

How he missed her softness, along with the calm manner she displayed under stress. Red looked at this quiet beauty and recalled how she closed her eyes when she agreed with him. He handed her a plastic cup of beer, its sides beginning to sweat in the torrid Virginia sun. Red Ted shook off shadows of his past failings with Betty.

He rubbed his chin. "I've missed you, Betty."

Betty hesitated, glancing down, then up, she finally looked at Red, "You haven't missed anyone."

"Yes I have. Not at first mind you, but after I got straightened out, I did."

"Why didn't you call?"

"I was afraid you wouldn't talk to me. The guys helping Jack O'Brennan, he's a detective friend of mine, met at his place this morning. When I told them about you, they raised hell with me and told me to go in and call. Guess that's the only reason I'm here." Red noticed Betty's friend had returned. "Your friend is back. I suppose you have to go, but before you leave, would it be okay to call you?" A note of urgency entered Red's voice.

"Oh, I don't know, Red; getting together again doesn't make sense. Why are you doing this? I've had too much hurt in my life to get beat up again."

"I just want to talk to you. Maybe we could go to a movie?"

"You're asking an unanswerable question. Let me think about it. Goodbye." Betty turned with her friend and started to move away.

The stark reality of Betty's statement hit home. If she walked away now, that would be the end. "Stop! Goodbye is too final. We can't leave each other like this. There has to be a solution, a way around this. You know it and so do I."

After Red's command to stop, Betty turned to face him. From the way he looked at her, she felt she understood him for the first time since they met. "Yes, I know," her voice trailing away to a whisper. Tears now glistened over pretty brown eyes. "Red, I've thought about you a great deal and have missed your little boy ways." The start of a smile settled on her lips. "Maybe, what we had can never be replaced, but pray to God, we can do something together that we can't do separately. Call me soon."

Before he realized it, Betty and her friend were heading across the Inlet grounds. Red stood silently by himself taking one last look at a fast disappearing Betty Green. Suddenly, Red discovered he had no place to go.

Returning home from Harbor Day, O'Brennan tried to put his thoughts in order. Early in his career, he arrested a man for the slaying of two women. When asked the reason for such an assault, the killer calmly replied, 'The little men in my brain were running faster than I could'.

Jack felt the same way; the case appeared to be moving too rapidly for him. Events were forcing him to run faster than his legs could carry him. He had to better control the momentum of the investigation, and he'd start a slow down in the morning.

25

After delivering the latest information to Tremonte, Jack headed north for his meeting with Bud Henry. O'Brennan thought of Jeanette as he drove toward Fredericksburg. He really liked her. Was it infatuation? Probably so, but he was too old to worry about a new woman in his life, or was he?

The two friends met on a hot Monday morning. "Why the subterfuge?" Jack asked.

"Like I told you earlier, we're to meet away from the city. What the hell, the drive didn't hurt you and I needed to get away myself. Let's hear what you've been up to."

Reviewing the case point by point, Jack discussed the Stem for the first time. "We're convinced the fourth party I mentioned at our last meeting is the Stem, and his power base is in Washington. We don't . . ."

Bud stopped Jack with a raised hand. "What makes you think he's in Washington?"

"We're not sure. Bud, to be honest, I'm just guessing. We don't know what he is; politician, businessman, a bureaucrat, or just some guy lurking in the shadows.

"I think the Group is being shadowed. Maybe I'm being paranoid about this, but there was a gray panel truck parked across the street from where we meet in the morning. It was unmarked and I think it was some government agency vehicle."

Bud laughed. "Why you crazy old coot, that's the wildest story I've heard in years. Jack, if I didn't know you better, I'd think you were serious. Do you have anything to support what you just said?"

"It comes with the job. It's the feel, you know what I mean. Tomorrow, I'd like you to tail these guys, check them out. If you won't do it, we'll do it ourselves."

"I can't, Jack, my hands are tied"

"I figured that would be your answer. I know it's not you, Bud, it's that lousy organization you work for. The trouble with your outfit is they want the best of all worlds. Guess what? That isn't going to happen!" A note of anger rose in O'Brennan's voice. "We'll go it alone, that's what we're going to do. I'm not telling you stones from now on. We won't ask for help, nor are we giving you a thing. I won't tolerate being screwed around by your people."

"Now reconsider what you just said. Admittedly, you're in deep water and there could be problems for you later on."

"Problems you say. Bud, we can live with problems. If they're that severe, then we're in a jam. Our friendship is more important than the Gill case. Still friends?"

"Jack, we're still friends. Off the record, I'm getting squeezed by a young, hard-charging boss who's trying to chase me off the scene. He is in effect dogging all the old-timers. I have the title of agent-at-large, but it's a nothing job. It may sound impressive, but believe me it isn't."

"Why are you hopscotching around? First it was Mt Vernon and now here."

"They want us away from the general scene, and they've developed an out of sight, out of mind mentality."

"That's too bad, Bud. There's something other than the Gill case that needs talking about. I need a confidant I can bare my heart to, and I honestly believe you're the man. I'm close to my buddies back home, but they're pretty loose and at times, don't take things too seriously. What I have in mind needs the delicate touch of an outsider whom I can trust.

Bud Henry knew a troubled mind when he saw one. "Jack, come into my office and we'll talk." He motioned to a bench overlooking the water.

After sitting down Bud motioned O'Brennan to begin.

"I've met a woman who has me twisted around."

"Good to hear. Good to hear," Bud repeated. "How long has it been since Mar . . ." He never finished his sentence.

"That's all right, Bud, it's been five years."

"Sorry for that blunder, but what the hell; you know me. Tell me about her."

"She's just an ordinary person I met a week ago while working the Gill case. Funny, on the way up here I got thinking about her. I think it's a case if infatuation," Jack paused, "but I don't know."

Bud looked at his friend and slowly shook his head. "You know, I've always considered myself as having an ear to the ground, in my business, that is. However I'm no 'Dear Abby' and don't know much about this romantic stuff. But you have to tell me more about this woman if I'm to help."

"Very well. Her name is Jeanette Purchase and she owns a classy restaurant in Bridgeton."

O'Brennan sighed and looked forlornly at the water. "She ah . . . ran an escort service when Harkers was at its peak in the fifties."

Henry merely shrugged and waved Jack's disclosure away like it didn't matter, then asked, "Is that a problem?"

"No, it isn't. You've known me long enough to know I don't prejudge people . . . well, maybe at times I do." O'Brennan laughed at his own admission.

"What are you feeling when you're around her?"

"I'm happy when I'm with her, and can't wait to see her again when she's not around. Bud, this is hard to believe but she looks at me like I'm the only man in the world. Almost as if I were Superman." O'Brennan's laughter caused Bud to join in.

"And when she does, her eyes sparkle like she put those drops in them that cause that to happen."

"So, you like her?" O'Brennan nodded yes.

"This isn't any of my business, but have you been intimate with her?"

"She kissed me on the cheek last Saturday night. Hardly

intimate wouldn't you say? Bud, tell me the truth. I know I'm an unlikely candidate for romance, but what do you think? Is what I told you the first of many firsts, or the last of the lasts?"

Several minutes passed while both men studied a gathering of ducks making pattern in the water. Finally, Bud replied, "I think I have the picture. You are not above romance, nor are you too old for it. What I'm going to say is difficult for me, and probably will be for you. Treat your tomorrows like you would have before you met Mary. Do the right thing and let nature take its course."

On his return drive to Bridgeton, Bud's parting words echoed around in his thoughts. It was much easier to talk about doing the right things then to actually do it.

Once home, Jack diligently occupied himself with the mundane task of balancing his checking account. Finally completed, he gratefully headed for the front door when the phone rang.

"Jack O'Brennan."

"Mr. O'Brennan, this is Jimmy Cousins in Bell Hills."

"Yes, sir. Did you get my report?"

"I did, and that's what I'd like to talk about. We've decided to terminate the investigation. With the information you sent us, we have what we want. We are no longer interested in continuing the investigation to its end. You've been very professional and have done an excellent job for us. Please send a bill and it shall promptly be paid."

"I'm surprised you have decided to conclude the investigation at this time, Mr. Cousins. However, you are the client and that is your prerogative. I appreciate the fact you used my services and shall bill you immediately. Thank you and good day."

John Lloyd spryly climbed into Jack's car. "Nice day for a ball game." O'Brennan turned into traffic and headed for Gull Stadium "You know, these young guys don't play ball at the same level of intensity as Eddie Feller did, do they?"

"He's one in a million. They put him in the Hall of Fame, so he had to have something going for him." Then Jack added, "How did things go this morning at the Bench?"

"Red did good yesterday afternoon, and got the old girl friend talking. She came up with eleven or twelve names that spanned from North Carolina to Upstate New York. Probably the next order of business is to track them down, wouldn't you say?"

"I agree, but there's something else that entered the mix. Try this on for size and see what you think. Just before I left to pick you up, I got a call from Jimmy Cousins out in Tennessee. He's the fellow who contacted me about the Gill case. He cancelled out, said they had received my report and felt they had gone as far as they should. He also mentioned the investigation was getting away from their original intent. Cousins told me to send my final bill. You know the striking thing about his call was the comment, 'We'd like to terminate your services'. The word terminate has a final ring to it, wouldn't you say?"

"Yeah, you'd think he'd have said, stop or what have you. Terminate, that's strange, somewhat scary," replied a puzzled John Lloyd.

"I'm going to continue the investigation and go it on my own. We'll plug along and see what comes up. Was Karl there this morning?"

"Yes."

"Did he mention anything about trailing Sally today?"

John nodded, "He said he'd start after he left the Inlet, Red also went along."

"Good old Red, he doesn't miss a beat," Jack said proudly.

"He said he had nothing else to do. Red's a strange one. He's a hell'va guy, but we don't know one blasted thing about him. Don't know where he comes from, where he gets his money; none of the above. He came over to the Inlet six or seven years ago and that's it. I'd like to know more about him, but he's a tough nut to crack," John said.

"I'll agree with you on that one."

"Jack, he appears to be smart, but doesn't show it. Red sure turned over some stones this weekend, so we better give the devil his due. We'll probably never know what he's about."

"Don't make a big thing out of Red. He happened on to us and like it or not, he's ours. He happened on to a scoop about the shipping business, so let's leave it at that. John, I feel like you do, but . . ."

"Yes, I know he's wild and unruly, but you're right about one thing, Jack, he's ours. That's a pretty important possession to have."

On the way to the game, the men talked baseball. "I've been coming to this ball park since I was a kid. Dad used to haul me out here every chance he got. When Bridgeton was in the International League, we'd go Saturday or Sunday; and when the Gulls got into the American League in the sixties, I really got into baseball. Do you come often?" Jack asked

"I'm like the average fan who comes out when they're making their annual drive for the pennant."

Parking across the street from the park, the duo walked with the stream of fans heading for the gates. "Every seat in this old park is a good one. The new parks they've built of late have no dignity or vestiges of the old," Jack observed.

"You know, Jack, this park reminds me of Fenway Park in Boston. It's not as cramped and not nearly as old, but it has that same good feel."

The main ceremony of "Eddie Feller Day" consisted of the presentation of gifts to Feller and his family. The unveiling of the baseball-shaped sign provided a touching conclusion to the brief ceremony. Feller's name and number in the middle of the baseball enshrined him in the fan's hearts forever. The red lettering against the white baseball provided an attractive adornment to the forest green centerfield fence.

The dedication concluded with Virginia's Senior Senator, Andrew Kenmore being led to the mound with Gull and city officials. After a brief congratulatory speech directed to Feller, Kenmore was presented with a ball to throw to the Gull catcher anchored behind home plate. With surprisingly good form, Kenmore wound up and threw the ball over the catcher's head. The crowd roared with laughter, loving the man with the broad grin. The applause swelled as Kenmore, accompanied by his entourage, waved at the crowd.

Jack laughingly said to Lloyd, "You know, I've yet to see a southpaw with much control."

"Yeah, and he talks funny too. Where'd he come from originally?"

"Up North somewhere. From all reports, he has the inside track on his party's nomination, and could just be our next president. I wonder how good he'll be?" Jack questioned.

"He's pretty smooth, but I think he has delusions of grandeur," John replied.

Heading downtown after the game, Jack asked, "Do you have any plans for tonight?"

"No, haven't thought much about it," John replied.

"How about coming over to the house for supper?" Jack asked "I've got a couple of steaks we can grill."

"That's the best offer I've had today."

Entering the kitchen, Jack spotted the crimson envelope on the table." John, what in hell is this? Somebody's been in the house. It was locked when I left and now I find this. How could anyone have got in? Check that back door!"

"It's locked."

"I think someone's in here, or was here." Jack pulled the shades down as John stood helplessly by. Concern covered his face as Jack opened the blush colored envelope.

You are nosing around in matters that don't concern you. We are directing you to immediately curtail your present activities relating to the Freddie Gill case. The Tennessee party initiating this investigation has seen fit to withdraw. To insure your cooperation, special attention will be directed at your circle of friends. Misfortune will befall each of them should you fail to heed our warning. This should serve as an omen of adversity to come. Let this be your guide. Immediate withdrawal from the case will provide you with a continuing prescription for a long and productive life. We have one parting thought for you, Mr. O'Brennan. Check Billy Olsen's inside jacket pocket the next time you see him.

The stillness of the late afternoon settled over the house as John stoically read the computer printed message. Finishing, he returned it to a pale O'Brennan. Lloyd felt weakened by its starkness.

"With that note they have turned this place into a house of terror," Jack said.

"I will say they left a lasting impression," John added.

"That accomplished, I wonder what they have in store for us next?" Jack said.

"You could walk away from this; do what they suggest."

"John, you know better than that."

Still shaken, Jack headed for the front door. Over his shoulder he called, "Come on, we have to go down to the Rooster and warn Billy."

The quiet of the afternoon joined in concert with the oppressive smell of the *Red Rooster* in creating an almost morbid scene. They discovered Billy had left around three after receiving a phone call. The partners vacated the premises and headed down the street to the *Eagle*.

Al Simons placed two draughts in front of the men, and quickly read in their apparent duress the need to be alone.

"John, I can't believe what I just experienced. Such an overt act, in the afternoon, no less. What a brazen thing to do. When I spotted the envelope, I knew somebody had paid me a visit. My first thought was someone I knew dropped that envelope off, but in a split-second, I had the sinking sensation that a stranger had entered the house. It was at that point I knew we were in trouble."

"What did it feel like, emotionally, I mean?"

"I felt violated and could feel paranoia settle in. Then I started thinking somebody was watching." O'Brennan drank from his glass with a still shaking hand.

Simons started down the bar swinging a flyswatter at any fly that settled in his immediate area.

"The thought of being shot entered my mind. It was an eerie feeling knowing that somebody had been there and gone. And then the anger took over; that dark fury one gets when they have been *wronged*. John, the reverie I so longed cherished in my home had been shattered. I had to get out of that house as fast as I could."

Jack withdrew the note from his pocket, again reading it, he dropped it on the bar. "John, I'm scared for our friends, scared for you and sandwiched in between, I'm sure as hell scared for myself. All the stuff that's written about how tough and fearless detectives are, goes out the window when push comes to shove. We've been driven to the wall." O'Brennan helplessly ran a hand over his hair. "I think I'm made of sterner stuff, but it sure doesn't sound it from what I'm hearing myself say. What should we do?"

"We've got to warn the Group about the note. They should know what's in line for them. Why not get them together tonight and go over the incident," John suggested.

"You're right, that's what I'll do. Let's meet at my place about nine. I'll drop you off and call the others."

The men departed the *Eagle*, leaving a puzzled Al Simons polishing beer glasses. After dropping John off, O'Brennan hurried home and canvassed the immediate neighborhood. Most of the men had stayed in to watch the *Eddie Feller Day* ceremonies, followed by the Red Sox game. Not one person could help Jack.

Entering the front door brought a surge of uneasiness sweeping over O'Brennan. He would have to shed, or certainly mask his fears to the others. There probably would be no bodily harm occurring to him in the house, however, he'd have to live with thoughts of the earlier intrusion.

Jack called Paul Amsler at his home. Paul had succeeded O'Brennan as Chief of Detectives and sought council from his old friend on numerous occasions. Amsler had shown an unusual interest in the Gill investigation, and had exhibited consternation about Sally's past and present activities.

Although reluctant to accept the facts revealed about Sally, he recognized Jack's hypothesis as probable. Over the years, Amsler had served on several committees with Sally and found her to be gracious and personable. He knew of Hansen, his reputation having preceded O'Brennan's scenario. The sketchy details about the Stem, although somewhat vague, intrigued him. Like Jack, he believed in the theory of a big shot heading this dangerous circle of friends. Amsler sensed the urgency and alarm in Jack's voice as he reflected on the events of the afternoon.

"Paul, I can't come up with words to match my thoughts and emotions."

"Jack O'Brennan, you watch yourself; this doesn't look good. If you need help, say so; but don't go off half-cocked."

"I need help and I need it tonight. We're old guys trying to get by, and it appears we're not doing a very good job of it."

"You've got to get hold of yourself and settle down. Tell me what you need, and don't short yourself," Amsler said.

"The Group is meeting at my place."

"What time?"

"Nine. I'm going to review today's events and warn them. Oh, I almost forgot, John Lloyd and I went down to the Rooster looking for Billy Olsen. The bartender said he got a call about three and took off. I'm worried about him, Paul."

"I'll notify street patrol to keep an eye out for him. Now, what about tonight?"

"I'm convinced someone will be followed, and that our meeting will be monitored. I'm willing to bet there'll be some curious eyes in the area. Any chance of putting a couple of your men in the vicinity? They'll have to be on foot."

"Yes. I'll have them in the area long before your friends arrive. And yes, they'll be on foot."

"Who are you sending?"

"Let me see who's on duty." Difficult moments pass for

O'Brennan before Amsler gets back to him. "Yes, I'm sure you know these fellows. I'll send Ralph Washington and Dave Sciera. They're young but trustworthy, close-lipped and smart. Are you going to be home the rest of the night?"

"Yes, all night long."

26

The Group settled on Jack's patio as the clock struck nine and darkness filtered down over Ford Ashland. Nursing cans of beer, they appeared puzzled by the sudden call from O'Brennan. They were expecting one thing, not knowing they were getting another. He read the message to himself and carefully started his discourse.

"I've had a tough time getting in touch with you guys, but this is important." Jack reviewed the events of the day, read the warning and expressed concern for Billy. "We have a major crisis on our hands, and have to use every means available to protect ourselves. What they said in the message is absolutely true. They're saying they can do what they want, whenever they want, and how. It was never more evident than when someone entered the house this afternoon." Pointing to the kitchen, Jack continued, "It looks like a veiled threat, but I think not, this is *real!*"

"If this is as real as you portray, how do you plan on approaching this unknown?" Cal asked.

"We all have questions we can't answer and that's one of them. I want to clear the air and get this out in the open. You gentlemen have helped me a great deal on the Gill case, and for that I shall always be indebted to you. Gentlemen, this could be dangerous."

"I going to continue to pursue the investigation and John is with me. The time is fast approaching when we face the cutting edge; for what protracted period, I have no idea." How he hated the word protracted, O'Brennan thought and couldn't imagine why he had used it. "I need to know whether you want to continue. Again, this will be difficult, and keep in mind it doesn't look good for us."

The only sound to fracture the voiceless silence was chairs shuffling on the slate floor. Finally Red spoke.

"You can't imagine what a comfort it is to hear that," Red said. John Lloyd looked at Red and shook his head.

O'Brennan didn't appear to notice the interruption. "It appears we have ruffled some mighty big feathers, so let your conscience be your guide. To borrow a phrase from I don't know where, we are facing a litmus test of character. I don't want to tie a can to you, and if you choose not to continue, I'll understand and we'll still be friends, I would suggest one thing: if you get out, sever all relations with us until this thing blows over. Stay away from the Group, and this will send a signal you're not connected with us anymore. At that point, I think you'll be safe. That's it. That's what I have to offer. I suggest you kick this around for a couple of minutes. When you come up with a decision; it will have to be binding on your part. If you decide to continue, we'll be bonded together from that moment on."

The earlier casual atmosphere evaporated and a stony silence settled in. Each man searched his heart and soul for an answer that would guide him to or from harm's way. A lonely cricket and the sound of a distant automobile floated through the gentle stillness of the night as the Group pondered their fate.

O'Brennan finally shattered the silence with, "Are we ready to go? Let's start with you, Red, you're the youngest, what's your pleasure?"

"What the hell, I got nothing goin'. I've, ah, what are they going to do to me that Charlie couldn't do in Nam? I'm in." Jack had anticipated Red's answer would be in the affirmative.

Karl, what about you?"

"Are we good enough to handle this problem? This scares me, and I don't know what to tell you. I've got a couple of years to retirement, got a wife, a grown family and a great place at the Harbor. I'm not ready for *this*. Ah . . . I feel ashamed and embarrassed at what I'm saying. I've never been involved in such a mess as this. I damned well don't know! Geez, this really bothers me."

"Karl, there's nothing wrong with how you feel and I can't blame you a bit," Jack said trying to help Karl save face. "Just get up and go. Your leaving will indicate that you are no longer a part of this. You departure will have sent them a message that should suffice."

Karl stood up and walked over to Jack. "I'm sorry." He walked around shaking hands with each man, then wheeled around and headed for the kitchen. Turning, he said, "I'll be seeing you, I don't know wh . . ."

"Don't worry about it, we'll get back to you when this blows over. It's going to, believe me."

Karl left the house with his head bowed and appeared wounded by the words he'd delivered to his friends. Karl Eichner had yielded to an unknown adversary.

"Let's have another beer, I need one." O'Brennan left for the refrigerator, returning shortly with four beers.

"Boy, isn't this *something*." Wit was one of Red's strong suits when the pressure was on and his remark brought restrained laughter from the Group, and with the laughter went the tension.

"How about you, Cal, what are your thoughts on this?"

"When I was a kid I had my heart set on being a detective, now that we're in this mess, I'm glad I'm a doctor. I'm somewhat ambivalent about the whole thing. Although I feel pretty much like Red, don't much care one way or the other. Since my wife died, life's been nothing but a pain. This case has been fun, with something to look forward to. In my business, a body is a body is a body. The Gill case has given me a fresh look at life and how exciting it can be. Dangerous, I suppose, but we live with degrees of danger around us.

"On the other side of the coin; I have a close friend at the hospital, Dr Vivian MacGregor. I haven't mentioned this before, but Vivian is becoming more than a friend. Now, we have this severe problem and to be honest, I've had second thoughts about continuing. I know we're a bunch of old romantics, but like Red said, 'to hell with it!' I'm yours for the duration; that you can count on. "Vivian is going to have to wait, but of course, the way my luck is going, she probably could care less. Yes, I'm in, so let's get on with it."

Cal's answer did not surprise Jack, but his revelation about this Dr Vivian MacGregor did.

"I think our darkest hour is yet to come," John said.

"What's happening is almost like an illusion," Red observed.

"An illusion is whatever you want to make of it and the fact is, we're a bunch of well-meaning guys who have been living in a dream sequence. What passed for fun yesterday has today placed us in a corner with jeopardy all around us," Cal said.

"I think we all agree with you on that," John said.

"We're set then. The first order of business is to review today's events. Before I picked John up, I received a call from Cousins in Tennessee. He called off the investigation. Odd, he used the phrase, 'terminate my services'. John and I talked about it earlier and decided terminate sounded too final, or permanent for us."

"What motivated them into such a dramatic decision? Could they have been squeezed along the way?" Cal asked with considerable interest.

"Maybe you're right, Cal; that sounds as likely as anything."

"Jack, why not give them a call right now. Kind of rough them up a little," John suggested.

"Sounds good to me." O'Brennan's voice could be heard from the patio, "Mr. Cousins, this is Jack O'Brennan from Bridgeton. Why did you drop the investigation? One, your group has plenty of money, so my fee posed no financial burden. Two, you told me this was a lark; why isn't it a lark anymore? Tell me, Mr. Cousins, why are you getting out?" Jack listened, nodded, listened some more, then took over the conversation. "Now, you'll have to pardon me for saying this, Mr. Cousins, but you and I know that what you just told me is a crock of you know what. There's another reason and I want to know why," Jack again listened.

"I want you to understand that I have a pretty long arm, and am well connected in police circles. I don't know what you and your buddies are up to in Tennessee, but there are ways of finding out. The only thing I'm asking is what prompted you to drop the investigation? I can make your life real complicated if you don't fess up. It will be between you and me, and what you say stops here." After several minutes Jack said, "Thank you and goodnight."

Lloyd smiled when Jack returned, "Not a bad job of roughing up."

"You talk about a nervous cat, our Mr. Cousins is that. It was like we figured; they got a call last night telling them to bailout, or bad things would happen. They talked it over and decided to split. Can't blame them much."

O'Brennan took a sip of beer and continued. "First of all, we have to define where we go from here. We also have to accept the fact that everyone out there will be sharp and cunning. Red, what do you have for us?"

"Betty came up with a list of twelve businesses that do heavy business with Sally. I have them here." Red placed the list on the coffee table. "Then this morning, Sally met with Hansen next to the bridge in Fostertown. They talked for fifteen minutes or so, then she returned to the warehouse."

Now was the time to conveniently mention Jeanette's appearance with the handsome stranger "Ah . . . Jack, before we picked up Sally, Jeanette entered the Dome with a gray-haired stranger." Red felt guilty telling Jack about Jeanette's noontime appearance. It would do no good to suppress information regardless how insignificant it seemed to him. Jack could not hide the look of disbelief as he listened to Red's account of Jeanette's luncheon date. Surprise caused Jack to shake his head.

The phone rang breaking the hushed silence caused by Red's startling report about Jeanette. Jack left the patio in a rush of silence, leaving behind friends glancing at each other with guarded looks.

"A good sailor sets his own course, but, Red, what you just told Jack didn't help his direction much," Cal said.

27

"O'Brennan, are you still there"

"Yes, Paul, when did they find him? . . . Okay, John and, I will be right over, thanks." Jack returned to the patio and sat with a heavy-hearted weariness. He waved his arm in dismay, "They just found Billy Olsen. He's *dead*."

"What happened to him?" asked Cal.

"I don't know. That was Paul Amsler and he told me they found Billy in a parking lot on Churchill."

"That's down where Sally's warehouse is. What's the number?"

"940 Churchill Street."

"Damn, that's Sally's place. He was killed right at the warehouse. It's across the street from that bar I was in Saturday."

"Red, you'll have to stay away from the scene, but the rest of us can take a look."

Lloyd coughed, then began to speak. "Jack, it was only yesterday when we went down and squeezed that poor little guy. I'm beginning to have second thoughts about an investigation that caused the death of some old boy we all liked. If those guys from Tennessee hadn't called, Billy would be alive this instant. But no, here we are indulging ourselves in a little game of grab-ass, and now the poor guy is dead."

"John, there's nothing I can say."

"I wonder whether the world will be better off if we solve the Gill case. Will Bridgeton gain anything? Will we? People are starting to get hurt and we've been threatened. Everyone involved was doing quite nicely before, now look what's happened. Only the good Lord knows what's on tomorrow's horizon; and maybe Karl had the right solution."

O'Brennan nodded his head in a resigned show of defeat. "I liked Billy too. But I'm not sure we were getting on that well before this case came along. Personally, I'm better off for having met Jeanette even though I have no idea where we're going. Red here is talking to his old girl friend again. Even our eminent coroner friend, has divulged his little secret about a Dr. MacGregor. I don't mean to sound flippant, but John, even you may be better off.

"This case could well provide us with an unknown strength that will guide us in the future, who's to know. I hate the cliche, it goes with the territory, but it does. Lets face it, we've been trained all our adult life to do this job as effectively as possible. We are what we are, for the better or the worse of it We're old guys trying to do good. There are rules to our profession, John Lloyd; and you and I have tried to live by them since we've known each other. What the hell reason is there to change now?"

"Maybe you're right," John responded in a low whisper.

"Let's go over to Churchill Street," Jack said as he headed for the door.

Leaving the house, O'Brennan looked up and down the street. The amber light from colonial-styled street lights shined through the tree-lined street in mottled patterns.

He called to an empty street. "Ralph Washington, Dave Sciera, you out there?" The two detectives appeared from the shadows and walked cautiously up to the Group gathered in front of Jack's house.

"Everything all right?" Washingon asked.

"Ralph, I just talked to your boss and he wants you and Dave over to 940 Churchill Street to help with what he called a murder. An old-timer named Billy Olsen was found dead in the parking lot This old guy was somewhat involved in a case we've been working on, but I'm sure Amsler will appraise you of it. Paul told me it was your case and you're to go over immediately."

Jack Sciera looked at Washington with a grave stare. Catching the exchange of unspoken trepidation between the two men, Jack asked, "Is this your first case?"

Sciera shuffled his feet, looked at Jack and softly replied, "Yes sir, it is."

"I have some words for you before you leave. First, Amsler thinks a lot of you, and secondly, write down everything regardless of how unimportant it seems. You better head over to the site, because your boss is waiting."

From the shadows up the street, two pair of eyes watched the rookie detectives leave The two observers would make the warning Jack received in the afternoon seem very real before the Gill case was finished.

Driving to the warehouse, Jack asked Red, "What's the name of that bar across the street from Sally's warehouse?"

"The *Churchill Grill*. Why?"

"No reason, Red. Just thinking about something."

"Even though he twisted the facts to meet his needs, Billy was a good old guy. He never hurt anyone and he kinda' snuck around the edge of the law. He helped us out, helped himself and even helped the bad guys. I'm going to miss him." John said more to himself than the riders in the car.

The *Red Rooster* will never be the same, that's for certain. Let's face it, he was a self-seeking little man who reached the end of life's journey," responded Jack.

"With some bastard's help," Red stubbornly added.

"I second that, Red," Cal grunted.

O'Brennan introduced a thought that gave the discussion a new direction. "They kill Billy Olsen who had a minor role in this Gill thing, then leave him on the doorstep of one of their own players, why? Anyone have an answer?"

"That's a question we presently can't help you with," John said.

A crowd had gathered across the street from the bar Red visited Saturday. Billy's misfortune had provided them with an opportunity to rubberneck and guzzle beer at an alarming rate. The cordoned off area around the body now afforded Billy the peace and quiet apparently missing in his last hours.

The darkness and quiet of the parking lot washed over the late Billy Olsen as he lay under a gray blanket. Jack's nod triggered Cal to reach down and take hold of Billy's shroud. His head appeared bathed in blood. "Death is so irrevocable, "Cal said as he covered the body. Guilt swept over O'Brennan as Billy's blood-drenched body disappeared under the blanket

"Justice, you are bullshit!" The words sprang from Jack's lips in rapid succession. "I bad-mouthed him and didn't mean it. Is John right? Would the end justify the carnage done here? No person should meet his maker in such a fashion. Whoever did this would make Jack the Ripper look like a choirboy."

"I wonder who killed him?" Cal asked.

"We'll probably never know because he took it to his grave," John said.

"Well, we're certain of one thing; someone helped him to an early grave and he's deader than a doornail," Cal said.

"Jack, this doesn't look good. It appears they're going to follow up on their earlier threat. I thought you and your crew might be touched; but I never dreamed it would extend this far. Gentlemen, you are too vulnerable for your own good." Amsler turned from O'Brennan to again view the blanket-covered Billy Olsen, with a shake of his head. "Apparently, you were right about Hunter. I'll be damned if I understand why Billy was killed in Sally's parking lot."

"How do you know he was killed in the lot?" Jack asked.

"Based on what you told me earlier, I hurried over here as soon as the call came in," Paul Amsler said. "When I got here, a patrolman had just finished checking the body. Jack, Olsen's tongue had been cut out and I don't have to tell you where we found it. Yes, it was inside his jacket pocket."

A sudden roar of laughter from across the street washed over the parking lot.

Amsler looked over his shoulder at the collection of roughnecks, and called to one of the patrolmen standing nearby. "Fred, go over and put the run on those guys. Those drunks don't even have respect for the dead."

"You know Jack, driving over here, I kept thinking about

what you said earlier about Billy, about check the inside coat pocket. Seeing the blood was gruesome enough, but then I looked inside his pocket, and sure enough, the tongue was in there. Jack, they cut the poor bastard's tongue out of his head. Now if they cut it out some other place, and correct me if I'm wrong, Cal; most of his blood would be gone by the time they dumped him here. As you can see, there's blood all over. Naw, they killed him here," replied Amsler with a shrug.

Turning to the ME, Jack offered, "Cal, what Paul said makes sense. Do you agree with him?"

"Yes. I'll do the best I can with this," Cal said as he gestured toward the gray covered body, "but there's no way of knowing until the autopsy is completed."

"Then we assume he was killed here?"

"Jack, I have no way of knowing, but what Paul said is absolutely dead on. If he'd been killed elsewhere, the loss of blood would have been such that there would be little evidence of blood here at the scene. Obviously, it was done here. That's unofficial, of course, but I'm damn near certain of it."

"If that's the case, he had to holler like hell. Paul, have the preliminary reports turned up anything yet?"

"Nothing yet," Paul added.

"Cal, assuming you wanted to kill someone and cut out his tongue in this parking lot without making a scene, how would you do it?"

"Well, what I'd do is, I would," Cal thought briefly, "knock him out with something. After he was unconscious, that's when I'd cut his tongue out. I'd use something sharp like a straight razor, probably in one swipe. That might awaken him unless he received an extraordinarily strong depressant. If I covered his mouth, there'd be little or no noise. He would die almost immediately. I'm sure the autopsy will indicate he'd been bound or tied up and his mouth taped. I assume we'll find considerable blood in the lungs. Probably death was due to drowning in his own blood. Let me hazard a guess as to what happened. We can check it against the autopsy report in the morning."

"We're still playing grab-ass, aren't we, Cal?" John snapped.

Visibly shaken by John's comment, Cal glowered at his friend. "We all know that fear is contagious, and at the moment, we're not on top of our game because of it. We're like the proverbial fish out of water. John, I'm in this mess just like you." Cal's voice picked up intensity as he resumed. "If you find my approach too unconventional, that's your problem. Anyway, I believe they grabbed Billy at another place; then gave him a shot of Sodium Pentobarbital which immediately rendered him unconscious.

"They then moved him here," Cal waved his hand at the parking lot, "and cut out his tongue. There was an immediate rush of blood which was stemmed by some kind of cover over his mouth. He continued to bleed into his lungs and stomach until they uncovered his mouth. Yes, they wanted to kill him, but they wanted this massive show of blood around him as a display of power. I believe that Billy's death was indeed a silent one and he probably never regained consciousness after going out from the shot."

O'Brennan pondered Cal's opinion for a minute, then asked Paul, "How are you going to handle the investigation?"

"Jack, we need to have a quiet conversation," Amsler said as he walked away from the gray blanket, followed by O'Brennan. "As you know, I put Washington and Sciera on it. They'll be in at six to go over the preliminary work-ups. I'd like you to come in at seven and review the case with them from your vantage point. They'll have to know everything."

"Whatever you say. Anything else?"

"There is. They'll go over to the Regency Arms and talk to Sally after finishing with you. From now on, our arrangement will have to be on a need-to-know basis. I'll have to know your every move from now on, because the bad guys are touching too many bases for you. You're going to need help and that's the way it has to be."

"That's fair enough, Paul." Jack wearily exhaled and pointed toward the *Churchill Grill* and its lights that shown like a beacon in the night. "Boys, I need a drink and I need it now. Shall we?" O'Brennan turned and headed for the bar, knowing full-well his friends would follow.

28

The stillness of the hot steamy morning only added to Jack's early day depression. It covered him like the early morning fog that impregnated the city. Soon, it would burn off and another of August's torrid dog days would blanket the city. At six in the morning, Ford Ashland looked like a midnight cemetery scene in a J Arthur Rank movie.

Everything looked gray and even the coffee had a harsh taste. He replayed the events of last night, culminating with several hours of beer drinking in the *Churchill Grill*. The beer had effectively driven John and Cal into a mello glow, thus avoiding a potentially troublesome quarrel.

Walking into headquarters at seven, reminded Jack of his duty days with the department. Now his position was that of a subordinate to two rookie detectives. Washington and Sciera had just completed a preliminary review of the investigation when Jack entered the detective room. Over the next hour and numerous cups of coffee, Jack reconstructed the Gill case in its entirety. He mentioned every phase, every twist, even his meetings with Bud Henry, the FBI agent.

"If I may ask, how are you going to tackle this killing?"

"You sure can. Dave and I are going over and talk with Sally Hunter. From there, we'll pay a visit to the *Red Rooster*. After that, we'll have to play it by ear." Sciera nodded in agreement with Washington.

"You're getting a good start. Remember what I told you last night; make accurate notes and make a lot of them! I have copies of my notes, so you now have everything I have on the case." Jack handed the rookie team a copy. "Paul Amsler probably mentioned this, but let me explain where I'm coming from. He feels this is getting too big, too full blown for me, and he's right of course. As of now, it's your case. I'm still going to work on it, but in an unofficial capacity. It's officially police business and I'm less a player than you men. If you need some help, give me a call. Otherwise, I'll stay out of your hair."

Leaving headquarters, O'Brennan picked Cal up at his house on Glover Street and headed out to Sands Beach. He needed an uneventful afternoon and evening away from the turmoil that had settled down on him and Cal was the ideal person to escape with.

With apprehension consuming them the rookies headed for the Regency Arms apartment complex. "Well, Dave, this is the start of a new career. We've spent a couple of years in the trenches, now we have our gold shields, we're in the big time," Washington said as he pulled the car into the visitors parking area. The two young men trudged into the apartment complex lobby, awed by their assignment. Walking to the main desk, they displayed their shields to the security guard. "Good morning, this is Dave Sciera and I'm Ralph Washington, please ring Mrs. Sally Hunter. There was a problem out by her warehouse last night and we'd like to talk to her."

After numerous rings on the house phone, the security guard looked over his shoulder saying, "I'll try her outside line."

He dialed again and waited. Finally hanging up, he said, "That's very strange, there's still no answer. On the occasions I've called her, she's always been quick to answer; almost like she was waiting for the call."

"How about letting us go up?" Sciera asked.

"No, I really can't do that unless she calls down."

"This isn't official, as yet. Tell you what, we'll be back in thirty minutes. She may be in the bathroom or still sleeping. We should be able to get her then. Come on Ralph, we'll come back later," Sciera said.

Walking across the street to the marina, Ralph looked at his partner "I didn't know how to handle it when the guard said we couldn't go up."

"Guess we still have a lot to learn," replied Sciera.

Returning to the Regency Arms after yacht watching, Sciera and Washington patiently waited while the security guard again tried both lines without success.

"We have to get up there and talk to her, so take us up," Dave Sciera commanded.

"I'll have to check with my boss first. Yes . . . yes I can do that." Second thoughts apparently overruled the guard's first notion of calling a superior.

"I have to make a call." Turning to the phone panel, he again dialed. "Dick, send Charlie up for a minute, I have to run upstairs."

After a short time, the garage attendant replaced the security guard. Riding the elevator, Ralph said to the guard, "This is a beautiful complex."

The guard replied matter of factly. "Yeah, and beautiful prices too. The rent starts at three thousand a month. How's that for beauty?" The men laughed on the way to an earth shattering experience.

Leading the way, the security guard stopped in front of of the corner apartment facing the marina. "If you look out the hall window, you'll have a matchless view of a full blown marina as well as the Rappohanock at its best. I sometimes wonder how so many people can afford the luxury of those boats. Tell you one thing; you'd be amazed at the number of folks who own big yachts and never take them out. They stay aboard several days at a time and never put them in the stream. They must like the activities around the marina and the smell of the water because they never take them out to the river or bay."

Shaking his head, Washington looked at his partner as if to say, "This guy goes on and on, and I wonder if he'll ever shut up."

"Did you ever notice the activities around a marina? No, I

suppose not. You're too busy. Well, I have. You know, I'm a great observer of human nature; people are my business. I spent all my adult life as a social worker dealing with the general public. There are two life styles out there." The prattler pointed toward the marina, "One group is always working on their boat or taking them out. The other does little or nothing. Now that reminds me of . . ."

"Excuse me, Mr . . . ." Sciera interrupted the wistful thinker before he could continue his incessant chatter.

"George France is the name."

How can he spend so much time talking about nothing, Sciera thought "Mr. France, could we get back to Mrs. Hunter's apartment?"

France walked back to Sally's apartment door. "Here we are boys, number 6A. The corner apartments we have here are beauties and run four thousand a month." France rang the buzzer, waited, rang again, and waited with still no answer. He knocked in frustration, then banged on the door, its sturdy oak hardly noticing. France inserted his master key, then looked over his shoulder saying, "It's peculiar she doesn't answer. Maybe she left before I came in at six."

Turning the key, the door opened into a large-sized vestibule. "Please, gentlemen, wait here until I check around." Morning light drifted lazily through rose colored drapes that embellished a picture-perfect living room. "There you are Mrs. Hunter, it appears you're taking a little nap already this morning. No, you probably slept through the night in the chair. There are two officers out here that would like to talk to you about a little problem at your warehouse last night. Mrs. . . . Mrs. . . ." France appeared ready to faint as he returned to the officers in the hallway.

Reaching for an arm to steady him, Sciera asked, "What is it, Mr. France?"

Pointing toward the living room, France blurted out, "She's in there and I think she's dead!" Walking past the distressed guard, the rookies entered the beautifully furnished, colonial-styled living room. Sally Ralston Hunter was seated in a blue wingback chair. Her head tilted forward, half reading glasses riding the tip of her nose. The book she appeared to be reading lay on the floor near her feet.

Washington checked her pulse, then nodded to Sciera, "She's gone, Dave."

The brass reading lamp on the cherry table burned brightly. It's light casting an invitation for Sally to pick up her book and continue reading. The mystery she'd been reading would remain just that.

Beside the lamp lay an open, blue-leather billfold. Its contents untouched, save for the credit card holder. Two items had been removed from the case; a Master Card and a Virginia driver's license. The front of the license displayed a classic picture of Sally that appeared more a portrait than the run-of-the-mill motor vehicle photo. Included with the picture was her address, birth date, and other physical descriptions. At the bottom, Washington observed the words, continue inside.

Knowing nothing should be touched until the Crime Lab finished up, Washington never the less flipped the license open with a match book. At the bottom was the uniform donor document. Continuing his reading; he felt as if traveling in never-never land.

The declaration stated, 'In the hope that I may be able to help others, I hereby make this anatomical gift without cost to my estate, effective upon my death. The words and marks below, indicate my desire, I give:

A. Eyes and any other parts.
X B. Only the following organs: eyes for the purpose: transplantation therapy or education.
C. Limitations: none.

Sally's signature along with two witnesses followed the declaration.

"More complications, Dave. It appears our Mrs. Hunter was an organ donor. She signed to give her eyes upon death. We better check the place out and probably should secure it. What do you think?"

"Yeah, I'll get France to call a patrolman and post him outside, then we can work this out," replied a frowning Dave Sciera.

The silence seemed deafening as Ralph Washington walked around the room in a desultory manner. He, like Dave Sciera was overwhelmed and baffled by the sudden turn of events.

Sciera returned to the living room, "France is outside and we should have a uniform up here soon. I don't like this organ donor business. What the hell, we're knee deep in this mess and I don't know what to do."

"I feel the same way. I'm shaky about reporting this to headquarters," Washington said.

"No need to be, Ralph. Here's the report-in card for deaths," grunted Sciera.

In the thirties, a far-sighted Police Chief organized the department with guide lines for all personnel to follow. Each officer carried a report-in card that indicated correct step-by-step procedures to be used for any given situation. The two-by-three card folded like an accordian. By following the prescribed mentioned steps, each reported incident was funneled to the proper channel. It was to this card Sciera referred. Flipping through the reference, Dave came to the Unattended Death section (Detective Division}, with a call list immediately below it.

1 Medical Examiner
2 Chief of Detectives
3 Crime Lab
4 Photographer
5 Donor Program (Appropriate donor unit when needed)

Washington's call to the ME's office was answered on the third ring. "Bridgeton City Morgue, Charles Wilson speaking."

"Wilson, this is Detective Ralph Washington. I'm calling from the Regency Arms Apartment complex at Niagara and Glouchester. I have an unattended death, a Mrs. Sally Ralston

Hunter in apartment, ah . . . Dave, what's the number? . . . Yeah, we're in apartment 6A."

"Well, you have a problem this morning, because we don't have any examiners. Doc Redout is off today and tomorrow; I think he's out of town. None of the assistants are in. One took an emergency absence, seems there's a death in the family, one's on vacation and the third one is in the hospital with food poisoning. So there you are. I'll send the wagon over, but without an examiner," Wilson cheerfully replied.

"What in hell will we do without an examiner?"

"Don't worry about it, buddy. We'll pack her up and she'll be out of there, no mess, no stress, get it?" The phone clicked, leaving Washington on uneasy ground. He then called the Detective Bureau. "Captain Amsler please." He waited for what seemed an eternity.

"Lieutenant Girard speaking, can I help you?"

"Lieutenant Girard, this is Washington and there is a problem. I'm over at the Regency Arms with Dave Sciera and we have an unattended death, a Mrs. Sally Hunter. There is no one here to authorize a pickup by the morgue. The examiners office is empty and there are no pathologists working today."

"Listen, you idiot. Don't tell me no one's working today," barked Washington's immediate superior.

"Well, there isn't," muttered Washington. "Dr Redout is off and his three assistants aren't in. One's on vacation, another is in the hospital with food poisoning, and the third went home on emergency leave, a death in the family."

"You listen to me, hotdog. It's your ballgame, so call your own shots," Girard gloated. "You young guys are pampered too much. For once in your life, make your own decision. You figured it out!"

"But, Lieutenant, I . . ." Washington was cut off before he could finish.

"Don't give that *but* business, there are two routes you can take: one, you can release the body; two, you can leave it there. If you do number two, you better keep the air-conditioning on full blast. Let me know how things work out!" Girard relished the verbal assault he laid on Washington and ended the conversation with a nasty laugh.

"That bastard didn't help, didn't say what to do. He said we're a bunch of hot dogs and for us to make our own call on this mess." Washington grimaced as he hung up the phone.

As quickly as it had started, it was over. Pictures were taken and the Crime Lab had come and gone. The ambulance recovery team picked up the remains of Sally Hunter, leaving Washington and Sciera standing in an empty room.

Next came the duty resident from the retina bank. Not finding the body, his rage bordered on out of control hysteria. "Where's the body?" screamed the resident.

"The body was picked up by the morgue attendants," Washington anxiously answered.

"Let me see the release form," the irritated resident demanded.

Sciera thrust the paper at the wild-eyed young doctor. Scanning the document, the intern screamed, "Are you Sciera? What authority do you have to release the body without my approval? I have to have them and that means now! I'll have your job for this!"

Sciera's mood changed from cooperative to truculent. "Listen to me you little sawed-off turd." Looking down as he pushed up to the little doctor, Sciera's voice rose. "Shut your mouth or I'll kick you all over the sixth floor. You get out of here right now, or I'll put you in cuffs and haul your sweet little ass down to the city jail. Then I'll charge you with obstruction of justice and that will put you in the Nick for at least six to eight hours. You probably don't know what happens to cute little guys when they end up in the can."

The intern replied in a whisper, his voice shaking with fear, "I'm to harvest eyes from a Mrs. Hunter, what am I to do?"

"If it's eyes you want, the Mrs. Hunter you're looking for is in the morgue. Doc, it was nice talking to you, now be a good boy and run along." Seizing the young doctor's arm, Sciera briskly marched him out of the apartment to the elevator. As he pushed the down button, Sciera snidely remarked, "Ta, ta, little brother."

Sciera returned to the living room with a spring to his step. Washington laughed, "You're a hard, brutal man. How come you did a tap dance on that poor little guy? He was just trying to do his job."

"After what we went through this morning, I was in no mood to listen to that little weasel threaten me with losing my job," Sciera said.

"What was that bit about the *Nick*? I've heard you use it before, but never thought much about it."

"Oh that!" Sciera smiled."I saw an English movie where two guys were talking about being in the *Nick*. It sounded like a slick word to use for jail. I've used it ever since. Let's get the hell out of here. This place reminds me of the bad morning we've had."

The intern from the eye bank transferred his hostility to the attendant at the morgue. "What do you mean, I can't take organs without the ME's approval? Find an examiner stat, and get him down here!" yelled the resident.

"Look, Doc, you follow orders, I follow orders and mine say no organs removed without authorization. It's as simple as that. So you see, my friend, I can't help you."

"You probably won't understand this, but please hear me out. I'm starting my residency in Urology over at Bridgeton next month. My family doesn't have a nickel, and I'm hustling like hell to make ends meet. I'm just finishing up a twenty-four hour shift, and am whipped. I could say the hell with it, but I won't; it wouldn't be the right thing to do. The returns we harvest from this woman could make the difference for someone down the line. It may not be important to you, but it is to me." The young resident concluded in a conciliatory tone.

"I am sensitive to what you are saying, and do appreciate your position. Next week I start at Bridgeton Medical School and like you, my family isn't too well off either. I'm a short-timer at the morgue so I could care less. I also have a sense of moral integrity and as far as I'm concerned, you can take the eyes. What can they do to me?"

Fifteen minutes later, the body of Sally Ralston Hunter lay in the Bridgeton Morgue minus eyes headed for the Bridgeton Retina Bank

29

O'Brennan slowly returned to the living. Shaking his head from a restless night's sleep, he immediately realized this would not be a normal morning or day for that matter. The local news from his bedside radio brought him to full consciousness.

> "Reports indicate that Mrs. Sally Ralston Hunter was found dead in her Regency Arms apartment at Glouchester and Niagara. Death was due to an apparent heart attack. Mrs. Hunter was one of Bridgeton's foremost civic figures. Again, yesterday Sally Ralston Hunter was found dead in her Regency Arms apartment."

The newscast concluded by stating Detectives Washington and Scirea, who discovered the deceased, had nothing to add.

Jack called Cal, "Did you hear the news?"

Cal made no response.

"Sally Hunter is dead and I'm sure she was murdered! What are we going to do?"

"Jack, what are you talking about? What's this about Sally?"

"I heard it over the news. Sally is dead! They say a heart attack took her, but you and I know better. That's not possible!" Again, prolonged silence from Cal.

"Don't you understand? It couldn't have happened You must do an autopsy," Jack frantically demanded.

"Cool down, Jack. Let's think this over."

"What do you mean cool down? Cal, there's no way she could

have died as they say. There have been too many people dying. We know Billy Olsen was murdered and now Sally is dead. You have to get with it and be quick about it," demanded a disgruntled O'Brennan.

"Jack maybe she did die of heart failure, it happens every day. Why not Sally?"

"Don't give me that malarkey, it's not possible and we both know it. I can't live with this decision and neither will you, so get your ass down to the morgue and do what you do best!"

"Jack, get yourself under control. I can't do an autopsy on a death like this without a court order."

"Get down to the morgue in a hurry my friend, because I'll have a court order waiting for you when you get there. You may think you're the only one around this city that turns the wheels of progress, but you're wrong. We'll have an autopsy today and you'll perform it."

"Jack I'll do it, but why me?"

"Cal, you're a close friend and have been involved in this investigation from day one. You must know where I'm coming from. I have to know and you're the one to help me. I have other important calls to make, so I'll see you in thirty minutes."

"Judge Edward Giles please. This is Jack O'Brennan." The call went straight through.

"Jack, how are you? You must want something or you wouldn't be calling, right?" Giles laughed.

"Judge, I'm embarrassed to say you're right. I'm in a jam and need your help."

"Anything's possible, Jack. If I can help, I will," answered the judge.

"We've been investigating a drug ring in the area and we've turned up Sally Hunter as the king-pin. Maybe you already heard the news."

"No, I haven't."

"Sally Hunter has died of a heart attack, or that's the initial report. I don't believe that to be true because I think she was murdered. I need an autopsy and a court order to go along with it. That's where you can help me."

After giving Judge Giles the facts surrounding the investigation, O'Brennan was assured the court order would be issued within the hour.

It had taken Cal a half-hour to get to the morgue. Good to his word, Jack was waiting with an order for an autopsy on Sally.

The door to the morgue examining room no sooner opened than Jack was all over his Coroner friend. "Tell me what you found. What was the cause of death?"

"The indications are old age, whatever that means," Cal said with an unconcerned shrug.

O'Brennan glared at his pathologist friend. "What in hell are you talking about? She was only fifty-five!"

"Jack, no one understands old age. It's not a biological thing. There's nothing immediately obvious when you look at her. Nothing to show she died of anything unusual. People do just die."

"What about this massive heart attack?" Jack's flushed face showed the trace of a sneer as he spoke.

"You heard that on the radio. It's nothing more than hearsay. The woman died and I can't point a finger at one thing that's unusual."

"Dr Calvin Redout!" O'Brennan said emphatically, "she was murdered, probably poisoned. Yeah, that's it, she was poisoned. You stand here and tell me she died of old age, come on, give me a break! Recent events should indicate she died of foul play."

"Mr. Detective, I'm a man of science, not intuition. The public is living with an image created by writers. All the movies, television shows, novels and whatever, portray the medical examiner as a guy who says, 'bring them in, if they're dead, I'll tell you what caused their death'. Well, it doesn't work that way. I can't give you what you want to hear."

"Yes, but . . ."

"But nothing," Cal interrupted, his voice rising. "I'd like nothing better than give you answers that could help, but my hands are tied."

"Cal, don't you honestly suspect she was murdered?"

Cal nodded as he replied, "Yes, that's why I went along with the autopsy. I believe what you're saying is true, but there is no evidence to prove it."

"That's nonsense. There has to be some evidence, something to hang on to."

"I'm sorry, but that's the long and short of it."

"Do you believe she was killed?"

"You just asked me that, but I'll go over it again. Absolutely, but damn it, there's no evidence. How many times do I have to tell you?"

"If it were poison, what would it be?" Jack asked with a suspicious tone.

"It could have been morphine."

"How would it have been administered?"

"Administered! You sound like a professional. It was probably given to her in a drink," Cal replied.

"Is morphine tasteless when mixed with a liquid?"

"It certainly is. She'd never have known it was in her drink."

"How much would have been added?"

After a tired yawn, Cal answered, "Oh, I don't know. Let me think." Cal's thoughts appeared to absently drift away. "Probably over one-hundred milligrams, no, more than that. Let's say one hundred-fifty. If you go to the hospital in pain, they'll give you two milligrams for relief. That medication will blunt your pain for several hours."

Cal walked to the water cooler for a drink.

"There have been instances where patients have been given one-hundred milligrams by mistake, but don't die. They'll have severe problems for awhile, but eventually make it. Much over that is lethal. Jack, I may be sending you the wrong message about this dosage business. In most cases, much less than one hundred milligrams will prove to be lethal."

"The morphine wouldn't alter the taste of a drink?"
"No."
"So you wouldn't need to mask the taste, like in an old-fashioned?"
"No."
"How would the morphine affect her?"
"The victim would stop breathing and go into immediate respiratory paralysis."
"What in hell does that mean?"
"It means her diaphragm and chest muscles wouldn't function properly."
"So she wouldn't be getting air in her lungs."
"Precisely. She'd die of asphyxiation, which is strictly a respiratory affliction and different from a heart attack."

Jack's head was full of question. He was driving Cal crazy, but what was new? "If she were drugged, wouldn't the eyes be constricted?"

"Indeed they would. The pupils would be pin point in size. That's why I'm up against a wall. She didn't have eyes. They had been harvested."

"I don't believe what I'm hearing. You're not making sense," said an incredulous Jack O'Brennan.

"I'm making a lot of sense. Her eyes were taken by the Bridgeton Eye Retina Institute."

"That was an unattended death, correct?"
"Correct," replied the distinguished coroner.
"Organs aren't to be released without an examiner's approval, that I do know. How do you account for this foul-up?"

"It just happened, but we'll find out how; that I can promise," Cal said firmly.

"Would you explain the procedure?" Jack's voice softened considerably.

"The donor would have his license marked as a donor. In this case, the license would also have the address and phone number of the Bridgeton Eye Retina Institute. Whomever investigated the death would alert the Institute about the donor."

"I know that! I was a cop you know. What about the procedure from there?"

"Normally, they'd have a medical student on call. He's paged, given the subject's address, and over he goes to the death site. Thirty seconds later, *bang,* the job is done."

"The medical student does it himself?" Jack sounded surprised as he asked his friend.

"Yes, it's no big deal."

"What's he going to do?"

"Well, basically, there are six muscles . . ."

Jack interrupted Cal before he could finish the sentence. "He's going to take the eyeball?"

"Yes, he'll clip the optic nerve and the ocular muscles that tie the eyeball to the socket and control its movement. Like I said, he snips the muscles and out they come. Thirty seconds on each eye and he's out of there."

"Cal, correct me if I'm wrong." Cal nodded at the wild-eyed detective. "This medical student comes for the eyes, eyes that look like piss holes in the snow, correct?"

"Jack, I like your imagery, but to answer your question, you're right."

"How could the student miss the size of the pupils? Wouldn't he react, make a note of their condition in his report?"

"Well, he may have been so . . ."

"So taken with the task itself," Jack interrupted his doctor friend.

"Exactly. He hasn't had much sleep, probably finishing a twenty-four shift. He wants to get it over with, get out of there."

There was a pause, then Jack said, "After the doc took the eyes, what did he do with them?"

"The eyes were taken to the eye institute where an immediate report was made of their physical characteristics. Those in charge would then dissect the eye, take the retina and harvest the remaining tissue for research."

"How about using the report you just mentioned?"

"No good, Jack. When the optic nerve is cut, that alters the entire scenario."

"What about the rest of the body?"

Cal Redout shrugged. "Any evidence of morphine?" Jack hoped against hope there would be.

"Not in this autopsy. The most striking finding would be fluid in the lungs, or in technical terms, Pulmonary Edema. That is the tip-off for opiate overdose. In this case, there wasn't excessive fluid, certainly not a sufficient amount to point to anything suspicious."

"The aforementioned facts mean nothing is what you're saying. There is no conclusive proof to point a finger at poisoning, am I right?"

"I'll buy that."

"Cal, I just had a thought. Wouldn't her blood indicate opiates were induced into her system?"

"It would. But it will be a day or so before the report comes down. So, for the moment, I have to go on the information I have."

"Based on the information at hand, do you believe she was killed?"

"No question. In my book, she was murdered."

"But without the eyes, there is no indication to what caused her death. With the eyes, there'd be no question."

"No question."

"They alone would be conclusive?"

"At a ninety-nine percent probability."

"Going back to the fluid in the lungs, there wasn't a large amount of fluid to make a decision."

"It's a tough call, that's the reality of it. See, it's easy to misunderstand, many of these things are gray area matters. There is no black or white when you make these decisions. What's pretty? What's loud? Beauty is in the eye of the beholder. What's an excessive amount of fluid? I don't know. My business is not an exact science and we are not magicians. Many decisions are made because we know a lot about a person before their death. Another aid is the circumstances of the death. With luck, we can make a statement about what most likely was the cause."

"We keep circling back, don't we? I'm so furious, I can't

stand it!" growled O'Brennan. "Those dumb rookies have blown this case. It boggles my mind."

"Your sophomoric temper tantrum is not like you, and the way you're acting disturbs me. Jack, you're missing the obvious; this investigation is coming down around your head and its heat is getting you. You're blaming two good cops for an error they made. They were placed into a situation where they received no support. You yourself continually talk about the Bridgeton Police Department and its reputation as one of the finest in the states. You are a major contributor to the same force and you're chewing up two kids. Grow up Jack! It's no more their fault than it is yours, and you know very well the system failed them." Cal's words poured out in a forceful barrage at his old-time friend.

An apologetic look crossed O'Brennan's face. He knew Cal was right, right about everything. This case was eroding away his confidence in himself. Finally, he conceded, "I know I'm overmatched on this one. It seems like a tornado has zeroed in on me. I'm running every which way to get away from it, and I feel like I'm running in place." Jack sighed as he continued, "I feel my incompetence is getting people killed and that I can't abide."

"I understand the frustration you're going through, but you must remember one thing. You have to take care of yourself, get some rest and eat regularly. You can't solve this overnight and remember you're no kid. Do you understand?" O'Brennan nodded his agreement.

As they exited the morgue, they were immediately aware of the oppressive August heat. Heading toward the parking lot, Jack asked Cal, "Are you off today?"

"Yes," Cal said.

"I think I'll take your advice. I'm going home and take it easy. Come on over and have a beer; you're not afraid of drinking in the morning, are you?"

"Hell no, I'd like that. Feel kind of low myself."

"You know, I may drop this case. Who needs the aggravation. That makes more sense than anything I've said lately. I'll go down to the cottage for a couple of weeks and take it easy. Yes sir, that's exactly what I'll do. I'll walk away from this whole ordeal."

30

A blink of the eye and they'd have missed it, but what a blink it was. Cal turned to answer O'Brennan when an extraordinary blast accompanied by a huge ball of orange flame ripped through the parking lot. A rush of searing air, followed by a concussion knocked the two friends to the pavement. Fortunately, they missed the shattered glass and assorted flying objects that sailed over their heads, but the business end of a bumper skittered to rest near the prostrate bodies.

"What in hell was that?" Cal yelled.

"A car blew up and I think it was yours," Jack said wildly.

Brushing themselves off, they observed the burning hulk of twisted steel. Cal looked with disbelief at what was once a fashionable 1936 Packard. The cars surrounding the still-burning Packard were bashed in a similar fashion. A sizeable crowd soon gathered until police controlled their gawking activities.

Tony James from the fire and explosion team walked to where they were standing, the ever-present cigar stub plugged into the corner of his mouth.

"Cal, that Packard of yours just looked through the prism of bad luck. It was the only one in the city that I know of."

"What are your thoughts about this?" Jack asked his long-time associate.

"Won't know what the cause was for several days, but it was probably caused by something from the plastics family."

"It's a good thing we weren't closer when it went off." O'Brennan paused for effect, then continued, "Damn! Someone tried to kill us."

"Jack, you better quit hanging around with the esteemed Medical Examiner. You lose your objectivity when you get this close," James laughed as he deftly moved the cigar to the other corner of his mouth with his tongue.

Jack fought back a smile, "Let's have some plain talk, Tony."

"O'Brennan, you're not much fun lately." Tony shook his head, "No, sir, I don't think that was their intent. They just sent a big time message that's all. I'm sure it was activated by remote."

"They were getting our attention, so to speak," Jack said.

"It appears that way."

"What's the range of the remote?" Jack asked.

"Again, this is only an educated guess, but I'd say in the three, four-hundred yard area. We'll know for sure later."

"Tony, how about having one of your crew check out my Blazer?" Jack asked.

"Getting a little antsy?" Tony laughed before assuring him he would.

"You better believe it. That explosion almost changed our sleeping habits," the PI said with a wide-mouthed smile.

Thirty minutes later, Jack parked the Blazer in the first open spot he found on Kent Drive. He and Cal talked about the explosion and its implication. Their lives had been threatened, certainly tampered with, and this made them understandably uneasy. The bombing was no joke. Tony was right about the explosion being an attention-grabber.

Walking toward the house, Cal first noticed Red Ted sitting on Jack's front steps. It was obvious he'd been drinking; in fact, he was totally smashed. A near empty twelve-pack of beer and empty cans scattered about, attested to that conclusion. In his stupor, the free spirit sat crying openly.

"Red, what are you doing? It isn't noon yet and you're drunker than a skunk," said a concerned O'Brennan.

Cal walked over to pick him up. "In all the days I've known you, I've never seen you like this. What happened?"

Red gestured with a limp wave of the hand and handed Cal a single sheet of paper. After reading the letter, Cal looked at the redhead with astonishment. "You're an enigma, Red Ted, a shiftless piece of dung and this foolish letter proves it."

Red groaned and asked, "What are you talking about?"

"You know damn well what I'm talking about, but let me spell it out. You are a mystery impossible to understand, a living riddle."

"Why would you say that? I'm no riddle, or at least I don't mean to be."

"First of all, why haven't you told us about law school? Bridgeton has one fine law school."

"What's going on here, Cal?"

Cal handed over the letter. "Red has been accepted at Bridgeton Law, but because of some computer error, he's been notified of his rejection."

Concern crowded O'Brennan's face. "Red, is it true you previously were accepted at Bridgeton for the fall semester?"

Red nodded yes, weaving as he tried to remain standing.

The redhead's friends helped him into the house. It was bad enough to be in such rough shape, but the curious eyes in the neighborhood didn't need a show.

"When did you get this letter?" Jack asked, after easing him into a patio chair.

"This morning," Red replied with a defeated tone, "I got the shitty letter." Tears again flooded his face. After some coaching from Jack, he continued "I drank a pint of Southern Comfort at home, then went down to *O'Hearn's*. It was good, terrific as a matter of fact."

Cal placed a bucket next to Red to accommodate any problem he might have in the foreseeable future. "Cal, he looks extremely pale and I'll give you odds he gets rid of all that juice he dumped down before long."

Red fell into a restless sleep, unable to offer additional

information about his cancellation from law school. The conversation about the morning bombing resumed. Struggling to mask his anxiety, Cal took a long drink from his beer. "They've got us, Jack. What do you think we should do?"

"Now hold on, Cal. Yes, I agree we're in a bad way; but I don't think they'll do anything else to you. About the rest of us, we'll get hit sure as hell. With what, I can't imagine."

"Jack, I'm scared and not sure I like this . . . even question whether we'll get through this."

"We'll get through it, don't worry. Just remember, no matter how devious, how cunning your adversary may be; luck enters into situations like this. Put all that money you have buried in the backyard on luck, because that's all we have going for us."

"This luck you talk about better cross our path in a hurry," Cal replied.

The ringing kitchen phone interrupted their discussion. Jack returned with a mystified look, "That was Karl. He's coming right over. Wonder what's going on?"

Red Ted let out a snore that returned the conversation back to his dilemma. "You know, it's hard to believe that a law school, or any other college for that matter would accept a person, then notify him he'd been dropped days before classes were to begin. You must know someone over there who could give you some answers," Jack suggested.

"I do indeed. Eric Reading and I were roommates at William and Mary in our undergraduate days. He's provost at the Law School. Let me give him a call."

Fifteen minutes later, Cal returned with answers neither gentleman could believe. "Jack, Reading is madder than hell. He said the orders came from the top; that Red had been replaced by a kid from Wisconsin with far less credentials. He was incredulous that our Red had been let go." Cal turned to again look at the slumbering redhead, then threw out his hands in a resigned manner. A laugh followed.

"Mr. Red Ted is a far-cry from being the literary midget we thought him to be. Seems he was a smash at Charlottesville and reads like a Who's Who of All-Academics. He graduated in seventy-four from the McIntyre School of Commerce and listen to this! He finished in three years with 153 hours and an accum of three point seventy-seventy out of four. He majored in finance, and garnered academic honors like you wouldn't believe. It appears Red is somewhat of a mental giant."

"Now, let me get serious about our drunken friend. He is conversant in several languages including: Chinese, Russian, Italian, Spanish, Portuguese and Bulgarian. I don't get the Bulgarian bit, but what the hell, why not?" Cal smiled, "Jack, my boy, we have before us, a veritable genius." As if on cue, the veritable genius belched and returned to his snoring.

"Cal, how could we have missed Red's penchant for learning?"

"Secrets are meant to be kept and it's quite apparent Red is very good at doing just that. Jack, we see what we want to see. We see splish and splash, but seldom do we take the time to search out the qualities of a silent gentle man like our inebriated friend here."

"What's going to happen to the poor guy?"

"My friend at Bridgeton is already working on it. Eric said he'd get him placed in another law school. It might be an hour, maybe a week, but he'll be placed before another semester rolls around."

"Good. That's the kind of news I like to hear," Jack said.

He looked at the prostrate Red Ted, then back to Cal. "Cal, we've been friends for a long time, yet today, right now, I feel like we've just met. I'm amazed at myself, but I don't know you. This morning, I saw your prized possession blown away. I know you fussed and fretted over that Packard for years. Now that it's gone in a flash no less, bim, bam, you act like you could care less." With a shake of his finger, Jack added a serious note to the conversation.

"There's a menacing figure out there and this little show of force if you will; is a forewarning of calamity down the road. Are you concerned? No! Here you sit laughing and having the time of your life drinking beer before what you formerly called an acceptable time of the day. Do you know what I think?"

Cal shrugged as if he could care less about Jack's thoughts. A grin introduced what was left of childhood dimples. "You're more concerned about Red's welfare, than you are about your own. Yes, I know what I'm talking about. Any explanation for that?"

"Certainly," Cal said confidently. "Most people including myself go through life striving toward a goal, an achievement, something material. Once you succeed, it's no big deal." Cal appeared to pause to collect his thoughts.

"I bought that Packard twenty-five years ago and never drove it. I worked on it and turned that beautiful machine into a mechanical wonder. I was so consumed by that stupid car, I couldn't bring myself to drive it. Last year, I started driving it at night and on Sunday afternoons.

"Then I started driving that Packard every day. Do you know why? I was sick of it. Don't get me wrong, it was a marvelous machine and I dearly loved to drive it, but that was all. I liked that darn Packard for all the wrong reasons. That's why there are so many divorces today; because people fall in love for the wrong reasons. Maybe, I'm like those people."

"Yes, I agree with you on the divorce thing, but I'm puzzled about the car."

Cal didn't appear to hear O'Brennan's comment but plowed on. "Well, anyway, when I was a kid, I'd see this rich guy drive around in a big, black Packard. Looking back, I wanted to own that Packard more than I wanted to become a doctor. After starting my practice, that same car came up for sale and I bought it. I had finally realized my goal. But something happened to me and it's never been the same. Most things we cherish have grown on us, and it's difficult to let go of them."

Jack sat back and thought about how his friend was going on and on, then realized he was purging himself about the car and everything meaningful in his life. Cal was on a roll and who was he to interrupt.

"In 1948 I got a pair of leather slippers for Christmas. At the time, they were just slippers, nothing more, nothing less. Years later, they started to become worn and beat up, so I went out and bought a new pair. Would you believe it, those new ones are still in the box. I had grown so accustomed to those old slippers, I couldn't bring myself to use the new ones. If anything happens to those old ones, I'll be crushed."

"I know the analogy isn't very good, but that's the way I feel. I'm glad that Packard is gone because now, I don't have to dislike owning it."

"What will you do now, get another classic?"

"Jack, you missed the point. I'm going out this afternoon and buy a new one. To hell with yesterday's masterpieces. Getting back to Red, you earlier mentioned my concern about him. Obviously, I'm more concerned about him than my own personal safety. They're not going to bother me anymore, because I'm too old for them to monkey with. Once was enough for them, don't you think?"

The phone call for Cal left Jack alone staring at the pathetic figure slumped in a near-bye chair. Red sat languishing in a sorry daze, oblivious to the discussion about Cal's Packard. Jack, like Cal, was more concerned about this poor human being than himself."

Cal Redout returned with a smile a mile wide. "We're in business, my boy. That was Eric Reading and sleeping beauty has a date at Charlottesville tomorrow. He's been tentatively accepted to the University of Virginia Law School. How's that for service?"

Jack was amazed. "How did he accomplish that so soon?"

"Earlier, you talked about needing luck in the Gill case; well in Red's situation, that luck came early. A first-year student had been killed in a car accident. They were in the process of reviewing stand-by candidates when Eric called an old friend at Virginia. After reviewing Red's undergraduate credentials, they agreed to accept him. He has a ten o'clock appointment in the morning."

Cal gently shook Red until he awakened. "First things first, my friend. Get on your feet, because you have an important date come morning."

Red stared blankly at Cal through reddened eyes. He was unaware of Cal's drift. What he needed was gallons of coffee, something Cal already knew.

"Let's get up and at 'em," Cal urged. "Law school beckons, and this old doctor friend of yours is taking you to the 'Land of Jefferson' in his new car."

"I don't feel very good."

"I can't imagine why. Come on, you're a little bent, but hardly bowed," Cal said as he winked at Jack.

After a belly full of caffeine, Red came to his senses. It finally dawned on him there was a new lease on his future. He asked in a stunned manner, "How did this happen? This morning, I was out on my ass, now, I'm in one of the finest law schools in the country."

Cal reviewed what Eric Reading had accomplished. O'Brennan rose to answer the front door bell, leaving Cal and Red discussing their upcoming trip to UVa.

Jack returned with a sheepish looking Karl Eichner. They greeted him casually at first, then realized a troubled man had entered their midst.

"Karl, what's wrong?" Cal asked.

Karl's look of disbelief was total. "I've been fired! When I went in to work this morning, there was a note next to the register. It directed me to see the manager as soon as I arrived. He told me I was out as of this morning. Gave me two weeks severance pay and that was it. He said there was nothing he could do, that it came from headquarters. I think he felt badly about it, but that doesn't help. I had a couple of years before retirement, now there is no hope."

"You know the city and have connections all over the place; how can you miss? Something will come up, count on it," Jack said gently.

"Jack, I was making fifty-thousand a year. Who's going to pay me that kind of money?"

O'Brennan whistled, "Good grief! You are hurt!"

"Forget that part, I came here for another reason. Last night was the low point in my life. I've never felt so beaten, so humiliated. Driving home last night to the relative safety of Scots Harbor, I realized what I had done by begging out of the case. I was scared of something out there I couldn't see, but then I realized that you," he paused to wildly wave his hand at his three friends, "were scared too. I walked away from my family, and one of the few things that mean anything to me, your friendship.

"When I got up this morning, I knew what had to be done. If I hadn't lost the job, I'd still be here. I'm back and willing to do whatever needs to be done. As for the job, yes, I feel bad, but to hell with it. I was sick of serving drinks to phony guys spending their last nickel trying to act important. We have a nest egg and I'm sure we'll get by, but there is one thing I'd like to try."

"What's that?" Asked a somewhat renewed Red Ted.

"I'd like to cook. Wouldn't want a restaurant because I'm too old for that responsibility. I want to just plain cook. Hopefully, that chance will come," Karl said.

Jack went to the kitchen for another round of beers. Returning, he proceeded to pass them out. "No thanks, Jack, I think I reached my limit numerous hours ago."

"Good decision, Red." Cal and Jack laughed at the future lawyer.

"Am I missing something?" Karl asked.

"Yes, quite a bit, but what you have to say is more important at the moment."

"Jack, what needed to be said has been said."

"Very well Karl, let me brief you on the events that have swept over us on this black Tuesday." Jack spent the next minutes reviewing the events of the morning.

"All this happened this morning! Wow! Things are certainly picking up," Karl said shaking his head in disbelief. "Where's John? Anything unusual happen to him?"

"No, he went to Norfolk last night to look over a surveillance system. I have no idea when he'll get back," Jack replied.

"Do you have anything planned I can help with?" Karl asked.

"Nothing, Karl. Too much has happened for this old withered

body. We've all taken a hammering and the emotion of it is frightening. I'm going down to the cottage for the rest of the day and regroup. I'll probably sleep over and come back in the morning. Old Jack is going to relax and forget this mess. You fellows should do the same. I'll get in touch with you tomorrow."

They all started to leave when the front door flew open. It was a wild-eyed John Lloyd. His grave look indicated he had been touched by the same hand of terror that had brushed his friends.

"What in hell happened to you?" Jack asked as he led Lloyd to the patio with the rest of the Group following behind. They looked every bit like mourners at a funeral as they trailed out to the patio.

"Jack, it was like Kent Drive revisited. Someone came in the house this morning and thrashed the place."

"Tell us everything and don't leave out one small detail," Jack ordered.

"I tried the front door and found the security lock was in place. The first thing that went through my mind was robbery. I thought the robber might still be in there and I didn't have a gun. The thought came that maybe it was someone I knew, but a friend wouldn't have chained the front door. I went around back and tried the kitchen door and that too was locked from the inside. That's when I started to panic and instinctively knew whatever caused this wasn't good.

"When I looked through the kitchen window, I saw the house had been ransacked. I entered the house by breaking a window. Both upstairs and down were in a shambles. After looking around and getting my head straight, I called the police and my insurance agent."

Lloyd paused to catch his breath. "Jack, now I know how you felt, only mine is worse . . . much worse. The bastards didn't leave one thing untouched. They ruined my house and if what happened is a window to my future, I hate to see what tomorrow brings."

Jack felt badly for John and the Group. It was his fault for getting his friends involved in this mess. Everything that happened in the last few days was because of him, and he attempted to apologize to them.

"Ah, the hell with it. Don't worry about us; we'll all get through this," John said.

"I'm concerned about you, John. Can you emotionally handle what's in front of us?"

John shrugged, then smiled. "After walking around, I could feel rage boiling up inside me. The more I thought about it, the madder I got. Before I came over, I called the Aud and told them to make arrangements to cover for me until further notice. I'm ready to go, day or night. You're going to get the Stem and I personally want a piece of him."

"That answers my question." Jack turned to address Cal. "A few hours ago, I was talking about bailing out of this fiasco, odd how events change one's plans, agree?"

"Agree!" confirmed Cal

"Well, enough about me, John offered. Why the gathering of the clan?"

Jack grimaced as he updated John on the earlier events of the day. Each member interjected bits and pieces to round out the story

"Do you think the Stem commissioned these assaults?" Karl asked.

"I'm sure he did, but we have a patch-work set of clues that are taking us nowhere. Let's meet here at nine in the morning and make a decision about where we're heading, "Jack said. With that, the Group dispersed with Jack heading for his cottage on Sands Beach.

31

Jack's home-away-from-home had always recharged his enthusiasm for the case he was working. Relaxing on the front porch soothed his frayed nerves and brought him closer to an inner peace. The beach was crowded with families giving it their last shot before school opened next week. He loved the beach after Labor Day because of its deserted look and feel, but today, he welcomed its hustle and bustle. It helped to ease his feeling of being isolated and vulnerable.

He had to develop a strategy that would compensate for recent events. O'Brennan tried with difficulty to focus on what to do next, but soon found his mind drifting off in other directions. One moment his thoughts returned to the exploding Packard. Fighting to regain his concentration, his thoughts moved to John's house being ransacked, a house John had kept intact after his wife died.

His next thought flowed to Elon College and Marilyn Lawson, an old girlfriend. Although they had liked each other a great deal, romantically, they suffered through a stormy relationship. Together they mixed together like oil and water, nothing worked. After they chose not to date, they became the best of friends. Strange thing about romance, Jack thought; sometimes the glint and sparkle is like a lighted match held near a can of gas. Without the spark, their relationship was sane, uneventful, but fun. He'd bet she had made someone a terrific wife.

His relationship with Jeanette was very similar to his college experience. The difference being, this relationship felt right, right that is if he took the initiative to make a go of it.

Getting back to Fritz, the trail was as cold as Sands Beach in January. Jack's thoughts then wandered back to Red Ted and how he'd hoodwinked the Group.

Someone with Red's ability should have a fire in his belly. He did however see a flip side to the unhappy wanderer. When Red talked to Betty at Harbor Day, he displayed a reticence tinged with kindness previously unseen. Maybe this jumbled affair would work in Red's favor. Would it work for the others? How about Cal? He was driving Red to Charlottesville tomorrow with a Doctor McGregor, whomever she was.

His thoughts wandered back to the case. There were hidden answers somewhere and Sally had to be the source, no question about it. There was no way he could get into her Regency Arms apartment; that was out. The warehouse was the answer. He'd go over tomorrow night and break in. Nobody would ever know. He was too crafty for that, or was he? This entire plot is crazy, Jack cautioned himself. John Lloyd was the locksmith expert and the one to bring along. He could open anything, official or otherwise.

What did he expect to find? Her books would be on the up and up, showing the figures of a legitimate business and nothing more. The money from the illicit drug traffic was long gone. Now that she was dead, it would probably never be claimed. No, there had to be something else, possibly something personal.

Jack answered himself. Jack, old friend, the old adage of I'd rather be lucky than good better hold true when we visit the warehouse. There are degrees of honesty and breaking and entering isn't one of them. It may seem repugnant, but what the hell, it's the only thing I have going.

While driving through Scots Harbor on his return Bridgeton, Jack thought about poor Karl. He had left the Ford Ashland house a destroyed man on Monday night, too afraid to continue with the case. When he rejoined the Group, it heralded the return of a regenerated man. Turning his back on his friends must have been dreadful for him. He didn't have a job, but he could live with himself.

As O'Brennan entered Bridgeton, he thought out loud, "Damned, I've got to quit listening to the morning news. First Sally's death, and now the *Red Leather*. This is too much!"

The embers of the Hampton Street fire still glowed as Jack eased the Blazer into a space down the street from the restaurant. Only concrete block walls remained of the once fashionable eatery. Firemen continued pouring water on the charred remnants of Jeanette's pride and joy. A midst the usual crew of TV cameras, print media and casual gawkers, Jack spotted Tony James talking to Jeanette. Dressed in the traditional white helmet, black slicker and boots of a firefighter, Tony shook Jack's hand.

"Jack, it's been awhile, actually yesterday to be exact." Tony laughed as he turned to Jeanette. "We worked some pretty tough cases together and go back a long time."

Shuffling his feet as he looked at Jeanette, Jack said: "I'm sorry you lost it."

"It's all right," Jeanette replied somewhat hesitantly. She did love the place, but it wasn't all that earthshaking to her; that she was certain of.

"Jeanette, I'm leaving now, but when I return, we have to talk!" Tony said.

As he walked away, Jack followed "Tony, do you have an idea what caused it?"

"Not yet."

"I've been on an investigation that's taking some peculiar twists, twists you should know about. I'm sure this fire is interrelated to the bombing yesterday. What I have to offer may help you with this," Jack said, gesturing toward the smoldering fire. "Can I see you this afternoon?"

"Absolutely. Let's meet at *O'Hearn's*, say five."

"See you then. Thanks, Tony."

Returning to Jeanette, Jack asked her if she had eaten breakfast. "No I haven't, but I gladly accept what I presume to be an invitation." Jack felt her need to talk as they departed the fire scene.

Settling into a booth at a nearby Howard Johnson, Jack asked,

"Do you feel like talking about the fire?" He waited patiently for a reply he wasn't sure of. She was a far cry from the agitated state he figured she'd be in. If the fire bothered her, it didn't show.

"Sure," she replied. "I received a call just before eight from Jimmy Donegan. He told me about the fire and how the police and fire department had been called. He figured it was too late to save the restaurant, but thought I should be notified."

"Who's Jimmy Donegan?"

"He's an old friend. Jimmy runs the fish market across the street from the restaurant and supplies us with our special cuts. When I arrived, there wasn't much left of the place. It was an inferno, if you know what I mean?"

"Have you done anything about it?"

"Yes. I called my insurance agent, wanted to get them right on it. I surely don't want to lose a nickel if I can help it." Jeanette smiled, then slipped into a hearty laugh.

"You don't seem very busted up about the fire."

"I'm not and yet I am. A lot of quality memories have gone up in smoke. On the other hand, I'm tickled to death it's gone. Don't get me wrong, I had nothing to do with the fire, but I've been sick of the *Red Leather* for some time. Saturday at Scots Harbor, I realized there are wonderful aspects of life I haven't experienced, and I think my future may be on or near the water. Remember the *Village Squire* where we had breakfast Saturday morning?"

Jack nodded How could he forget? How could he forget anything he'd done with this lovely lady?

"Monday, I went down to look it over and decided to buy it. I met with the realtor to put a purchase offer on the place, and hopefully, I'll be hearing if my offer was accepted sometime this afternoon." Her eyes twinkled as she poured herself another cup of tea.

Jack felt elated. At least he had an answer for one mystery that had confronted him. Comes the dawn. The handsome stranger she went to lunch with at the Dome was the realtor.

"Don't you think you might have been a bit impetuous?"

The twinkle was still there, but the answer in her eyes said no. "Impetuous is a word for people who can't afford to take a risk. I'd call my plan well-conceived and it is no risk!"

Jack's eyes lifted to take in this wonder and liked what he saw. She looked like a schoolgirl with her hair back in a mini ponytail. A loose gray sweatshirt and blue jeans added to her casual appearance. All she needed was a pair of saddle shoes to look like a teeny bopper and he told her so. Jeanette laughed, obviously pleased.

"What about the insurance money? Won't that take time to get with the arson and all?"

"Who said anything about arson?" Jeanette asked.

Several minutes were consumed going over the series of events that followed Billy Olsen's death. Jack carefully portrayed the current situation and the danger involved as accurately as possible. With caution, he added, "Anyone remotely involved with the Gill case has been hurt and that includes you." His eyes widened, then he continued, "Nothing has happened to me, and I find that strange, very strange indeed. The tough part is waiting for the hammer to fall. They're probably saving their best for last. I'm counting on one thing. It should be a doozie."

Brazenly, Jeanette answered, "Jack, if you're trying to scare me, you're not. I feel badly about your friends' misfortune, but I'm so full of what's in my future, I refuse to look back."

O'Brennan's frown alerted Jeanette to his innermost feelings. Reaching across the table, she partially covered his large, freckled hands. "Listen to me, Jack O'Brennan." He looked up allowing their eyes to lock on each other. "Last Saturday, you showed me something simple and wonderful that was outside my world. I liked it better than my current lifestyle and have decided to pursue what you and your friends apparently have." Her eyes never strayed or blinked.

"That's why I planned to sell the *Red Leather* and buy the *Village Squire*. Since Saturday, all I have thought about is what I could do with the *Squire* and you won't believe how much potential it has. I've made plans that are so wonderful, I can hardly contain myself. I feel my destiny is in Spenser and that's why I cut a deal to buy it last Monday, at least I think I did."

"Don't you think it's a little late in your career to make an about face and start something new? At this stage of your life, I should think you would like to take it easy," Jack said thoughtfully.

"You've got it wrong, O'Brennan. I'm nothing more than a wide-eyed romantic at heart, and I'm at an age where I need a change from my recent past. I'm going to live each day as if it were my last, and let the tomorrows take care of themselves. I'm learning new things about myself and I like what I see. The twenty-five years at the *Red Leather* have been good, but I'm planning my next twenty-five to be even better. There is one thought I do have, something I'm curious about."

Again she displayed the twinkle in her eyes.

"And what's that?"

"What my life would be like with you in it?"

Jack forged ahead with the conversation, ignoring Jeanette's last remark. He knew he wasn't ready for that one. "Tell me about the new restaurant." His hardened look softened to a smile.

"Over the years, the *Red Leather* catered to the elite, the big money crowd. If I am fortunate enough to own the *Village Squire*, my food will be affordable and taste good enough so my customers will be fighting to come back. No, better than that, it will be excellent, the very best on the bay."

"Sounds great! What will you feature?"

"The best southern pork and beef barbecue you've ever tasted. There is an old retired gentleman out near Sands Beach who cooks for churches, fire departments and legions in the area. I've already talked to him and his barbecue will be featured on Tuesday, Thursday, Saturday and Sunday. The shore bake at Karl's place was wonderful and I'd like to expose the public to it. Now that Karl is out of the Ritz, I'll talk to him about working for me. He can be bakemaster and oversee the bar operation. I can pay him what the *Ritz* did." With a look of urgency, she added, "In fact, I think I shall go down to Scots Harbor and talk to Karl this instant. Would you like to come along? I'll buy you a drink at *Sonny's*."

"I'd like that, but let me drive."

Stopping at *Sonny's* provided them the luxury of more quiet moments to talk. The afternoon proved to be a fun time for the couple who by all appearances were headed down the delicate road of romance. Karl was pleased at the job offer and readily accepted.

Driving toward Bridgeton on their return home, Jeanette could not contain herself. "Stop here in Spenser! I want to visit the *Village Squire* and see if they accepted the purchase offer." After several minutes, Jeanette returned to a waiting O'Brennan in the parking lot.

"I struck a deal and I'm about to embark on the front end of it." Her bubbly spirit indicated the offer had been accepted. The return to Bridgeton was filled with future plans for the restaurant.

After dropping Jeanette off, Jack headed for *O'Hearn's* where Tony James was waiting. Over several beers, Jack reviewed the events since Monday, touching on some fine points, leaving others out. He brought into play each of the Group's misfortune, and the apparent lack of retribution for himself. After more talk, Jack headed home to grab a bite to eat and prepare himself for the evening's trip to the warehouse with John Lloyd.

Wednesday's mail contained the usual trash, with the monthly bills and a letter from the Bridgeton Traders and Trust Bank. The bank indicated that unless a deposit was made in the next five banking days, his savings account would be cancelled due to a zero balance.

Jack was aghast. What in hell were they talking about? He had over $158,000 in that account. Then it hit him; he had been had. They had stolen his life savings. Packards can be replaced, new jobs found, a ransacked house put back in order, a slot filled in law school, a restaurant replaced, but one's life savings, that was an entirely different matter. If Red were around, he could explain the intricacies of lifting a small fortune from a savings account.

Sally's warehouse would have to wait. He was in no mood to embark on such a risky venture tonight

32

Sitting on the patio, Jack O'Brennan found himself enjoying a tranquil mood that had become difficult to find recently. He tried to focus on his personal problems brought about by the forces of dark and evil. But nothing was working. Suddenly, John Lloyd interrupted his thoughts when he busted into the house with a rush. No knock, just a bang and there he was. O'Brennan waved him to a seat.

"Jack, maybe our luck has finally turned; listen to what I have."

"Before you start popping off, read this." Jack thrust the bank statement at his visitor. "It came from the bank in today's mail."

John looked at the statement with interest.

"That's a lot of money to get ripped off in a little over a week," John laughed as he retreated to the kitchen. Quickly returning, he placed a can of beer in front of his worried friend. "You look nervous, old-timer, what's your problem? Got the heebie jeebies?"

"Why would you sport me about losing my life savings?"

"Ah, what's the matter with you? This can be traced; matter of fact, it may help us later on, though I have no idea how. When Red comes back from UVa, you can put him on it. It will take some doing to get it back, but I'm certain Red is the man to fix it. Now forget that bank statement."

"I hope you're right; now what's this about our luck changing? I need something to pick me up."

"Do you remember Phil Linden, the Portsmouth detective?" Jack nodded unhappily. "He called earlier and told me Fritz

Hansen had been killed in an car accident. He was coming home from the office when a drunk hit him. It's hard to believe a kingpin would die that way. Kind of shocking for an underworld figure to die in such an all-American way; to be killed by a drunk."

"That takes us out of the case. Without him, we're nowhere. He sure as hell killed Sally, now a day later, he's dead himself. A drunk driver no less. Has it been confirmed?"

"Yeah, it has," John said.

"Where does that put us?" A dejected O'Brennan asked.

"That's the bad news, now comes the good stuff. Over the years, I've talked about my neighbor, Dave Strombard. He's probably about eighty and has a severe case of rheumatoid arthritis that practically forces him to live in a wheelchair. Well, that's neither here nor there. When he retired, he started watching birds. I have a large Mountain Ash in the backyard that seems to attract every bird in town. Dave was so attracted to the birds, he had a large window put in so it would be easier to observe them."

"What does your friend Dave have to do with the Gill case?" Jack asked sarcastically.

"Now wait a minute! He's an excellent photographer and if a bird comes in back, he has its picture. When he first put the window in, the birds were scared off by his movements. To counter that problem, he had the window replaced with that one-way smoked glass. Now, when a bird flew into the tree, he'd get a picture without the bird noticing.

"Jack, guess what?" John tossed a packet of pictures on the coffee table. "The visitor who did a bad thing to the house Tuesday morning had his picture snapped in the commission of a crime. In other words, he got caught with his hand in the cookie jar."

"That sounds promising," Jack said as he looked through the pictures.

"This guy walked around the house about ten in the morning. Picked the kitchen door and in he went. He came out about thirty minutes later. You'll find a picture showing him coming out of the cellar entrance. That's how the bastard chained both doors."

After studying the series of pictures, Jack looking up and

said, "The pictures are excellent and we should get a make from them. John, they all get tripped up in the end."

"How will we be able to label them?"

"I'll give these pictures to Bud Henry, and he'll come up with a name. This guy is federal something; he has the look." Pointing to a picture, Jack continued, "Look at the buttoned-down appearance, the wing tips, striped tie, short hair, gray suit, oh yea, he's federal all right. Hate this, but I have to talk with Bud." Jack reached for the phone; Henry answered on the second ring.

"Bud, Jack O'Brennan, I'm going to eat crow. It's urgent; I need to see you tonight." Seconds pass. "Where?" More time elapsed. "Right. I'll be up there as soon as I can. Let's say eight-thirty."

Accompanied by John Lloyd, O'Brennan pulled into a stylish looking roadhouse on the edge of Waldorf. After introducing Bud and John, the discussion immediately focused on the Bridgeton events since Sunday.

"You boys have been busy," said an astonished Bud Henry. Drinking tonic water, Jack started his pitch. "I called because you're the only one who can help us. John here ran into some problems and . . . go ahead John, you tell him."

John detailed the trashing of his house, finally handing Bud the pictures Strombard had taken of the intruders.

"Bud, what do you think?" Jack asked.

"I'm sorry I was so slow on the upbeat, but I didn't believe one lick of what you told me. This is an incredible story. Somebody's been raising hell with you, that's for sure." Bud pointed to the pictures on the bar. "He's a fed, I can smell it. There are a million agencies up there, but I'll find him. It may take a day or so, but we'll put a label on this rascal."

"Do you honestly think you can track him, or are you placating me?" asked a frowning O'Brennan.

"Placating, that's a nice word, Jack. Getting back to business, if he's up there, I'll get him. He's probably working under the umbrella of some nondescript private agency When the word comes back, I'll give you a call. For heavens sake, don't do anything foolish between now and when I call." Henry laughed, "Oh, what the hell, I know you will, so why did I bring it up?"

Returning to Bridgeton, Jack talked about the bank statement and how upset he'd been over it.

"When you read the statement, what did you feel like? Inside I mean," John asked his longtime friend.

"I felt like I had a porno movie going on in my belly." The men laughed as O'Brennan continued, "I came home to get something to eat and you know what? I still haven't eaten. I didn't realize how hungry I was until now. Let's go down to Al's."

The *Eagle* was a lonely place at midnight with Al Simons perched on a stool watching the late movie.

"Evening gents, out late tonight?"

"Yeah Al, it was too hot to sleep, so we thought we'd look around for a couple of women our age. Got any around?"

"I can take care of most your needs, Jack, but two old ones," Al shook his head, "can't help you with that one."

"If you can't help us with the ladies, how about something to eat? We haven't eaten all day."

"I'll go back and check, but it will have to be leftovers. If anyone comes in, take care of them."

Al soon returned with heaping portions of leftovers. The gentlemen of the night dug into meatloaf, baked beans, beef stew, potato salad and chili over egg noodles.

"Damn, I didn't realize how hungry I was. Al, that was terrific!" Jack commented as he pushed the plate away.

"I glad you enjoyed it. There's normally more left, but we had a big night. You should come down some Wednesday night and try our buffet. It's not fancy, but it's good down to earth food and we don't charge an arm and a leg for it either."

"I can believe it," John replied.

As the ex-detectives headed for the door, Jack turned to thank his bartender friend. "We appreciate the food. It was excellent."

"You gentlemen be careful out there and don't take any unnecessary chances."

Jack stopped, "What are you talking about? We're going home."

"Jack, I know my business as well as you and John know yours. No one, and I mean no one eats a gigantic meal like you just put away and goes to bed. They may if they're all beered up, but you haven't been drinking, so there you are. Like I said, be careful."

Driving out Niagara Avenue at two-thirty in the morning was a new experience for the ex-cops. "I haven't been up this late since I left the force. Do you want to hear something odd? When you're young, you hate going to bed, and when you get old, you hate not going," John finished his thought with a flourish.

"John, that was very profound, very deep."

"I'd rather call it that delicate balance called maturity," Lloyd replied.

"Oh, is that what it's called?" They both laughed.

"If we don't find something soon, we're at the end of the trail," John observed.

"I'm afraid you're right."

They had the city to themselves as they parked several blocks from the warehouse, then casually strolled to the renovated theater which served as home base for R and H Wholesale Inc. Turning into the darkened parking lot, Jack whispered, "I wonder if they picked Billy Olsen up yet?"

"Jack, you're a brutal man, but to answer your question, I believe they have. I hate this. It could be our ass if we get caught."

"Just open the door and quit screwing around."

The side door opened with a click allowing two lonely figures to disappear into the darkness of the warehouse.

"These penlights aren't worth a lick. I can't see a thing," John Lloyd said.

"Over here, John, and follow the light." O'Brennan aimed the tiny column of light at the stairs. "Remember when we were kids and the movies had the 'follow the dancing-ball songs'?"

"O'Brennan, you're out of your mind," John laughed at his partner.

"Her office is up there," Jack pointed the light at the second floor loft. "Wait till you see this beauty. It was formerly the old projection booth, but you'd never know it now."

"If the office is half as nice as this stairway, I can't wait to see it. The whole stairway and walls are carpeted; wonder if the ceiling is?" John pointed his penlight at the ceiling of the stairwell. "The carpet on the ceiling is more expensive than what I have in the house."

O'Brennan laughed again. "If you think that's plush, check inside."

A landing at the top led to a cherry-paneled door displaying Sally's name engraved on a brass plate. Picking the lock, John opened the door into a large dark office. O'Brennan eliminated the outside world by covering the office's lone window.

Jack hissed, "Let there be light." A twist of a switch and the darkened room immediately turned into a tastefully decorated office. "How do you like the view?"

"Wow! Isn't this something! If this is where rich guys go to work, then I'm all for it," said an awed John Lloyd. "This room must be forty feet long. How wide, fifteen, sixteen feet?"

"I'd say so," Jack replied.

The office area consisted of a huge desk, a large combination TV and VCR set in the corner, and three filing cabinets placed against the back wall. Every piece of furniture was constructed of solid cherry. Ferns and plants abounded throughout the office area.

The living room was lavishly furnished in an expensive colonial motif with the color combinations reflecting the hand of an accomplished decorator.

At the far end, a cherry door hung next to a wall of louver doors. Opening the door on the right, Jack reached for the light switch. With the light came a scene never before seen by the detectives. An amazed John Lloyd said: "Did you ever? I've never seen anything like this in my life."

What so startled them was a bathroom of red and black. The fixtures, all in brilliant red included a heart shaped bathtub. The floor consisted of shiny black tile with thin lines of red grout. Red flecked midnight black wallpaper covered the walls. Bright red towels of all sizes, hung neatly around the room. John shook his head as he pointed to the ceiling. The bathroom overhead was covered with mirrors, reflecting two startled, middle-aged intruders.

"If Mary were alive, she'd consider this place vulgar. I doubt if she'd use it, even if she had to go real bad," Jack said, shaking his head.

"Allison would have thought the same way. It appears our friend Sally had some rather unconventional tastes, far out, deviate if you will."

"You mean kinky," Jack replied with a smile.

"And dicey too. I wonder what other surprises the fair lady has in store for us?" Lloyd said.

"I don't know, but we better start searching this joint. I'll work this end, you start on her office." Looking into the closet next to the bathroom, Jack called out, "If you're bored with indifference, take a look at this!"

John returned to look into the closet. "You've got to be kidding," he said.

Summer suits were perfectly hung on one side, while leather clothing occupied the other. *Leather* vests, skirts, corsets, and other assorted underwear hung as if waiting for their next sexual encounter. Looking into the drawers, Jack found low cut bras, skimpy panties of all styles, garter belts and dozens of neatly folded stockings of various colors.

"The woman was sexy, I'll give her that," John said, as he held up a leather bra and garter belt set. "What about these leather things? I know women wear this stuff, but boy, am I out of touch. The world is passing me by, and I just don't know what's going on. A woman like Sally would drive me crazy."

"Don't feel alone, I'm with you on that one. We stumbled into Sally's game room; that's for sure. Come on, let's take this place apart and get out of here."

The twosome worked quietly for the next thirty minutes, not

talking, just searching. O'Brennan pulled a cord causing a large tapestry to separate revealing an enormous king-sized Murphy bed. He reached up and pulled it down.

"John, this is the biggest bed I've ever seen. I'll bet this was home base for her sexual escapades, You know, if a man started crawling over to visit a lady on the other side, he'd forget what he was going for before getting there."

"You're disgusting."

Lloyd was pleased by Jack's comment and soon returned to the office area to wrap up a fruitless search. He suddenly called out, "Forget about that bed, we're out of here." He beckoned to Jack with a photo album he held in his hand. Opening the book, he pointed to a picture that showed three men and a woman at the beach. Sally Ralston was standing, Freddie Gill kneeling by her right side, Fritz Hansen on her left. Kneeling in front of the threesome was a blonde youth with a Princeton hair cut. On his left shoulder, he displayed what appeared to be a dark stalk. Their arms close together, each of their tattoos combined to form the semblance of a *Shamrock*

"We have just returned from the ashes," John said.

"John, the Stem is no longer a mystery. Do you know who he is?"

"We're in a world of trouble, that's who he is. There's no doubt in my mind about that," Lloyd replied as O'Brennan turned and headed toward the bathroom. "Where are you going?" John whispered after him.

"I've got to take a leak. Want me to take one for you?"

"I don't care if you do, but I better feel better when you get back."

Curiosity finally overtook John. He placed a cassette in the VCR and waited for Jack's return. Distorted images appeared after he turned the machine on. They soon cleared, revealing the late Sally Hunter with the Stem, majestically performing favors for each other that would shock a collection of Porno Aces. Rewinding the cassette, John shook his head, "Would you say she was out of the ordinary? Jack, what a machine! Here's Sally hiding in the crevice of middle age and she's still performing like she was working Cayuga Street."

"I hope pleasant thoughts crossed your mind."

"They did," John replied, "they did."

"Let's grab one of those pictures and get out of here. If we need a legal search, we know where the bodies are buried. I will say one thing for Sally, she raised common sex to an art form," O'Brennan said as he headed for the door.

33

Nine is late to sleep in, but not if you crawled into bed at five in the morning. Over coffee with John, O'Brennan continued to study the picture he had taken from Sally's office. Fiddling with its edges, the picture squirted out of his fingers and landed upside down on the coffee table. A phone number magically appeared.

"I'll bet that's the Stem's number. If we could connect it to him, we'd be in business," Jack said as he reached for the phone. Over the next several hours, they continually dialed the number with no success.

"Jack, why not call the operator? Maybe she can help"

O'Brennan hung up with a shrug, "No luck, it's an unlisted number. We can call all day and never get an answer. He may have a routine, a sequence of rings at a certain time. No, there's no way we could even luck into it. Where do we go from here?"

"What about a court order? Do you have a judge you can hit up? Judge Hayes might do the job, he's not a bad guy."

"No way, John, he's too tough. The only one down there who might help is Ed Giles, and he'd never go for it. We don't have anything concrete, and he'd want something hard and fast. Ed would be sympathetic to our needs, but he'd never come through on this. We have to go another route, but I'll be damned if I know what it would be. How about you, any suggestions?"

"I have a friend who's a top technician at Bridgeton Tel and did our work at the Aud for years. Let me give him a call." After numerous calls, John tracked his telephone friend down. "Art, John Lloyd. I'm working on an investigation and I need your help. Can we meet today? . . . How about my office at the Aud? . . . Three o'clock sounds good."

"Can you trust this guy?" Jack asked.

"Absolutely. Art has been with the company for thirty years and he's the best. If anyone can help, he's our man."

The detectives were sitting around gassing when Sweeney walked into John's office. Thin and short, Lloyd's friend had the shiniest head Jack had ever seen.

"Jack, say hello to Art Sweeney." A nod of his head made a handshake unnecessary. Lloyd started: "We're in the middle of a case and we're at our wits end. Jack, you go ahead and explain our problem."

"Here's the set-up, Art. We've come up with an unlisted number in DC and we need to find out who it's assigned to. Our evidence isn't solid enough to get a court order, and that's our problem. John and I called hundreds of times, but no answer. We figure there's some call sequence, maybe based on the time, but that's conjectural. Is there anyway you can help? You don't know me, but John and I go back a long way."

"No, I don't know you." This guy is a hard one, Jack thought. "I myself go back with John as well, and this sounds a little heavy for me. It's my policy to keep my nose out of other people's business, and this is no exception. If John," gesturing toward Lloyd, "needs something, I'll take a long look at it. Now John's a hell of a guy, but man, I've got thirty years with Bridgeton Tel. I can't mess around and lose my job and pension over something like what you're asking me do, and that's out of the question. You better have something pretty good to convince me."

"By convince, do you mean money?" Asked an annoyed O'Brennan.

"No. You've got it all wrong. There's not enough money out there to do something like this. I don't want to talk about this any more," said an equally annoyed Sweeney.

"No, no, wait! We're at the end of the rope. We have no other place to go. John told me you are the best technician at Bridgeton Tel."

"He's right, I am the best and plan on continuing to be just that. There's one thing you can count on; I'm not getting myself in a sling over an unlisted number," replied the agitated repairman.

"Is an unlisted number that big a deal?"

"Very big, absolutely . . . but there is a fallacy about the system."

"A fallacy about the system?"

"Many people have a erroneous idea about an unlisted number. They believe it's something that's out there, has kind of a nebulous identity. Not so. We have a reference called the Red Book that's made up like a telephone directory. You have a section of names listed alphabetically, a section of phone numbers and finally, a section of addresses. You can cross-reference any one of the three. For every name, for every number, there's an address and that's what we use."

"So that's how it's done," John said.

"If you get a lunatic who calls up and says he's going to kill himself; the police need to know. Almost instantaneously, we know where the person lives and what the name is. That is, gentlemen, if we have the number."

"Do you carry the Red Book with you?"

"No, it's kept in the office downtown where I do all the tracing. I rip it off, but I better have a damn good reason for doing it."

"Is there a way of finding what we're after without using the Red Book?" O'Brennan asked.

"This request of yours has shadowy overtones and I have a problem with your request."

"I don't want to squeeze you, but . . ."

Art interrupted Jack before he could complete the sentence. "How in hell are you going to squeeze me?"

"You're right, I didn't mean to infer I could. But I need to find out about this number. Can you show me how to get the answer I need. First, I don't understand the complexity of the phone system. Oh, I understand people have a number that's not listed in the phone book. What I don't understand is the concept of the unlisted number."

"I can answer that. The individual who acquires an unlisted number is the only one who knows it. They in turn give it out to the people they want calling them."

"How do they get one?" Jack asked.

"You call the phone company and ask for one. They charge you an initial fee, then a monthly rate is tacked on your regular base rate."

"I'd be the only one to know."

"You've got it. Now it's a secret, the utmost secret," Art said.

"Big time?" Jack asked.

"Big time" replied the repairman.

"No questions asked."

"None. Every big shot in the world wants an unlisted number. If you can't provide the secrecy they demand, you've lost the value of your product."

"Art, I can't get a court order unless I come up with stronger evidence than we presently have, but I've already told you that, haven't I? Will you tell me how to get it?"

"You've got to come up with something that's going to satisfy me. As of now, you've failed to do that very thing.

"Let's go back to base one. Why are you going to lose your pension if you tell me how to crack this thing?" Frustration started to show in Jack's voice.

"If I get caught fooling with the system, I've had the course. We take an oath you know."

"With the telephone company?"

"Oh yeah, Secrecy of Communications; most definitely. It's posted on every exchange you've ever seen. You don't monkey with that stuff, believe me."

"Okay, let's do it this way." Jack's lips closed as if in deep thought. "Two people have been killed in the last two days. They cut one poor bastard's tongue out and stuffed it in his pocket. I'm here because Lloyd said you were a good man. Look, I'm on my hands and knees. The unknowns are raising hell with us, and my friends have taken a frightful battering. A young guy named Red Ted who was going to Bridgeton Law was dropped overnight.

Cal Redout, the city's head pathologist had his classic Packard blown up in front of us. Another guy, the head bartender at the Ritz lost his job. The woman who owns the *Red Leather* had her place destroyed by fire. $158,000 was electronically withdrawn from my savings account and John here, had his house completely trashed. We've had two deaths, and all this personal misfortune happened in the last three days. If you want motivation, how about those reasons? What do you want from me, my life's blood?"

"Okay, John; for you I agree to help, but I have reservations about this whole mess. What's the number?"

O'Brennan handed him a piece of paper.

"Now 202 is a nationally planned area and we all know it's the District of Columbia. As an expert with a ton of experience, this may be the way to go. Between you and me, when the company hires a new operator, they run her through some intensive training. She's trained Monday through Friday, eight to five, with an hour for lunch. The trainees are then put to work with several instructors who supervise them. I want to get you piped into one of these rookies. It would behoove you to call early in the morning."

"What to you is early in the morning?"

"The best time to catch a new operator is between eight and ten."

"Suppose that doesn't happen?" Jack asked.

"You've lost nothing. An experienced one will tell you she can't help because it's an unlisted number. You turn around and dial again. Over a period of time, you may hit pay dirt."

"What do I say?"

"Operator, I need assistance. This is where we try and slick this girl. You don't know whether you have an old pro or someone new; there's no set pattern. Incoming calls are flying around, it's very busy in a city like Washington. There's more rookies, no, not more, but enough of them working that you can get lucky. See what I'm saying?"

"So what I'm looking for is luck."

"All you can get your hands on. You may have to do this any number of times. Maybe day in and day out until you hit home. One last thing, you may never hit it."

O'Brennan nodded that he understood Sweeney." Once I have the operator, what do I tell her?"

"Operator, I'm having an awful time. I'm dialing the following number and I can't raise anyone. My friend, Joe Carter lives at such and such a place in Washington and I know this is his number. She'll automatically display that number on her board. If the operator is young and inexperienced, she may say, 'That's not Joe Carter's number, it belongs to so and so on such and such street'. Bingo! You've got her."

After Sweeney left, O'Brennan and John sat around talking.

"You know, your telephone man is a hard case. He jerked me around for all I was worth."

"He was just looking to cover himself. You can't hate him for that."

O'Brennan just shrugged. "I'm going home." He stood up and headed for the door. "There's nothing we can do until morning, so come over about eight and we'll try our luck."

34

Driving down Saxon Drive, Jack's thoughts turned to Jeanette. Since knowing her he'd often wondered about her past after closing the Greenbriar Escort Service; but that wasn't any of his business. If she wanted to tell him she would. It was that simple.

She answered the door after several rings. "Hi, gorgeous," Jack offered.

"I've been trying to get in touch with you all afternoon." Jeanette motioned Jack into the house. "I wanted to see if you'd like to take a trip, a big one."

"Isn't that a coincidence. I came over to see if you'd like to take a little one."

"A little one! Where to?"

"Out to my cottage at Sands Beach."

"When?"

"Right now."

"That sounds wonderful. Give me a minute and I'll be right with you. What time do you plan on returning?"

"I want to sit around and relax for the rest of the day. Let's plan on eating down there and we should be back by eleven."

Driving to Scots Harbor, Jeanette carried on about the free time she had. "I love the leisure hours I have since the *Red Leather* burned. I was always on the go, so busy; now I have time for myself. The restaurant kept me tied down greeting people I didn't much care to see. But that's part of the business, I guess. Well, enough about Jeanette; catch me up on the case."

"We know who the Stem is. He's in Washington and is very big."

"How big is very?"

"This jasper is one of the real power brokers up there. We have to tie some loose ends together, ah . . . which may take a week or so. We've had some luck but need one big break. If it comes, we're in business; without it, we'll never get him. Earlier, you mentioned a trip?"

"We'll talk about that later. I want to sit back and enjoy the drive."

"What's happening with the *Squire*?"

"We're closing Friday."

"How in the world could you wrap up a deal like that so quickly? No one closes a sale that fast."

"When there's no financing involved, it's very easy to accomplish. I pay the owner cash and its mine. I'm shutting it down during the month of September for alterations. Let's enjoy the ride and lovely afternoon and forget the *Squire*."

"Jeanette, it appears there's a lot to talk about later."

"Won't you be surprised, big boy," Jeanette said with a laugh.

They sat on the cottage porch seduced by the gentle murmur of the waves anointing the sandy beach.

"You can't turn your head on a setting like this, "Jeanette said as she gazed at the seascape of Sands Beach.

Later finally came when Jack spoke, "This small talk is driving me crazy. You have to tell me about this trip you've planned."

"Very well. Earlier, I told you about my thoughts for the new restaurant. How I wanted to serve the people wonderful food at a modest price. Originally, I had been thinking in terms of a formal operation much like the *Leather*; but that format is wrong for me at this stage of my life."

"What do you have planned?"

"I have alternate plans, but that's not what's bothering me." Her eyes turned to Jack. "O'Brennan, I'm worried about the case."

"You told me about not being scared of what they'd do to you."

"I'm not. That's not it. I'm worried about you and your friends. This past week hasn't been the easiest of times for you, has it?"

"You're right, but let's get back to the trip."

"All right, if you must. I picked up some literature on New England from a travel agency and was quite taken with an article about the numerous seafood restaurants along the coast. They featured a place outside Gloucester that serves big numbers and is modestly priced. They're so busy, the people stand in line to give their order.

"The menu is listed on a big board in back of the cooking area. During the tourist season, patrons may wait fifteen or twenty minutes to place their `a la carte order. The more I thought about the arrangement, the more it appealed to me. I like the idea of 'Seafood on the Rough', and a New England tradition in the South is a dream come true."

"What's 'Seafood on the Rough'?"

"From what I've read, it originated in the Northeast. The food is grilled, pan fried, broiled or deep fried. I don't know much about it, but when I come back, I will. This, dear man, is a proposition you shouldn't pass up. Would you like to go up with me?"

"You better believe I would!"

"I'm so excited about this trip, I can hardly sleep. I've never been to New England, can you believe that?"

"You'll love it. It's a classic place to visit, especially after Labor Day. Where would we stay?"

"Where ever we wanted to."

"I guess," replied a frowning O'Brennan.

"You haven't been with a woman since you lost Mary, have you?"

Jack absently looked at the long stretch of glistening white sand. "No, no I haven't," he replied softly.

"Don't you think it's about time you came back to the real world?" Jeanette said tenderly.

"What is the real world?" Jack asked.

"I'm trying to find that out myself. All the years I ran the agency and the restaurant, I never slept with a man. Oh . . . I've been with men; you don't get this far along life's way without sleeping with someone. Let me put it this way, I've yet to awaken with a man in my bed.

"The afternoon Charlie Winder brought you to the *Leather*, I knew you were the person to change all that." Jeanette looked at Jack with moistened eyes. "I'm not a starry-eyed youth and neither are you. O'Brennan, we are lonely survivors who aren't getting any younger. The only thing I have is money and that scares me. What good is money if you don't have a companion to enjoy it with? The companion I'm talking about is sitting next to me on this porch."

Her stare made Jack uncomfortable as he looked into hazel eyes that shined in concert with her dazzling smile. Her voice now reduced to a whisper, she continued, "There is one thing you should know Jack O'Brennan, I'm in love with you."

Overwhelmed by her soft words, Jack stared blankly at the sea gulls walking on the wet sand at the water's edge. The silence seemed to last for hours.

"Do you have anything to say?"

Jack shrugged. Almost pleading he said, "I don't know what to say."

"Well, if you don't, there's nothing more to be said."

An awkward silence continued on the return to Bridgeton. Jack felt powerless to make amends. At her home, Jeanette softly closed the car door, not waiting for Jack to open it and walked away into the night.

For weeks she had thought about whether O'Brennan loved her. Jeanette sensed he liked her a great deal, but had never displayed any real affection. Not even a kiss. Now she knew. O'Brennan had answered that question.

35

John arrived about nine in the morning. "Have you started calling yet?"

"I already started and finished. I went through the dialogue Sweeney set up and bang, on the sixth try, I got our answer. It happened just like he said.

"Well?"

"I was prepared for a long ordeal, but it was so simple you wouldn't believe it."

"Did you get the name?" John nervously asked.

O'Brennan quietly stated: "Senator Andrew Kenmore is the Stem."

John Lloyd appeared as shocked as Jack felt.

Minutes without words seemed to drag by before John thoughtfully said: "Where do we go from here?"

"We can point our fingers at him all we want, but there's nothing solid we can hang on him. It looks like the end of the line unless lady luck noses around." Sitting at the kitchen table, each man appeared enveloped in silent thoughts about the future of the case. The sound of the phone ringing brought them back to their senses.

"Jack O'Brennan . . . Yeah, noon! . . . Okay, we'll be up." Moments passed while Jack listened, "I'm bringing John Lloyd with me. He's the guy I brought up to Waldorf." Returning the phone to its cradle, Jack said, "That was Bud Henry. He's identified your housebreaker and his running mate. We're to meet him at noon in Old Town, so let's get crackin'."

The morning proved dark and misty with little relief in sight.

"Looks like hurricane weather," John groaned.

"Yeah, "Jack said absently, "we're in the season, but there's been no report of one."

"All right, out with it, let's have it. What's on your mind? You're acting like a little kid who just had a funky Christmas. Is it Jeanette Purchase?" O'Brennan's expression answered John's question. "Oh oh. You're a big boy trying to finish up the biggest case in your career," John said, throwing his hands up in despair, "and here you are all bent in two over her. You've got to talk with someone, so it might as well be me."

"Jeanette and I went out to Sands Beach yesterday afternoon. She heard about a restaurant in Massachusetts and thinks she can duplicate their operation down here at the *Squire*. Well, she asked me to go up with her to look it over."

"What did you say?"

"I said, yes."

"What's the problem? How come you're so bent in two?"

"I asked her where we would stay and she said, 'anywhere we wanted to'. Then she said: 'You haven't been with a woman since you lost Mary, have you?'. When I told her no; she asked me if it wasn't time I came back to the real world. Do you know what she said then?"

"I can't imagine," groaned an annoyed John Lloyd.

"She said she was in love with me."

"Geez, that's great! Tell me, what was your answer?"

Sheepishly, Jack replied: "I said I didn't know what to say."

"Boy, that's beautiful. Here's a classy lady telling you she's in love with you and you don't know what to say. Do you like her?"

"Yes"

"Are you in love with her?"

"I think so," Jack said softly.

"Then, what's your problem?"

"I keep having thoughts about what she used to do."

"So why are you playing God? You know what they say about

people in glass houses? Jack, we all have windmills to fight, so you're not the lone guy in the crowd. If you like being with her and she makes you happy, what more could you want?" John sputtered.

"It isn't that easy."

"I do believe you have psychological designs bent on self-destruction. Nothing's that easy, you horse's ass, not one damn thing in this world for guys like you and me. She's a beauty and you know it! How many years do you have left? Probably not many, so take it as it comes. Old guys don't get many chances like this, so grab the brass ring."

"You're an outsider looking in and it's easy for you to come up with logical answers that don't apply to you. What you've said is probably true, but I keep thinking about Mary. At times I feel guilty about even dating Jeanette. Do you have an answer for that?"

"No, my friend, I haven't. But there is one hard fact you must face; Mary is dead and isn't coming back. Sometimes our memories lead us in directions that aren't the answer. I don't know whether this will help, but it may. Last week I watched a counselor on CNN talking about how post death trauma survivor's feel about their departed love ones. He mentioned a case very similar to yours. The wife felt guilty about dating years after her husband passed away.

"After several sessions, he advised her to write a letter to her dead husband. She was to explain how much she missed him, and describe her life after his death. He also directed her to mention the new friend, and explain how she had to proceed with her life without him. The counselor instructed the woman to go to her husband's grave and read the letter out loud. She was to then seal it in an envelope and bury it next to his gravestone. He mentioned that others place the letter to their loved one in back of their picture. It appears this mechanism of purging one's feelings of guilt works. Give it a try, what can you lose," John said.

Lloyd studied the countryside as the Blazer sped along. Time passed, then he turned to look at O'Brennan.

"We've been friends too long for me to be mad at you. Maybe I'm a little annoyed, but you know better than to listen to me. Jeanette is from a different cut of cloth than Mary was, but is that all bad? Think about what I said, it might help."

"Maybe," O'Brennan replied. He would keep his own council on John's suggestion and try not to allow guilt to control his thoughts.

The miles whizzed by in dead silence. Jack finally broke the stillness by saying, "John, let's review what we have. We have the beach picture with the Stem's unlisted number on back, what else?"

"There's the video tape of the Stem and Sally."

"Yeah, how could I forget?"

"We can't forget that what we found in her office was obtained by an illegal search. It's still there, but kind of skimpy. However, if need be, a writ will take care of that," John said.

"I agree. Our only route is placing the guy who busted up your place under surveillance. If he doesn't produce, we're screwed. At this point we need a giant infusion of luck."

A large crowd milled around the entrance of the *Fish Market* waiting to be seated. Walking up to the maitre d', Jack said, "I'm to meet Bud Henry, I'm Jack . . ."

"Yes, Mr. O'Brennan," interrupted the tuxedo dressed headwaiter, "please follow me." Jack shook his head at John and followed the tuxedo-clad headwaiter to one of the numerous backrooms.

"Your man has some clout here," John observed.

After a drink and lunch, Bud looked with concern at the Bridgeton detectives. "What can you tell me?"

"Bud, this is big! It's gigantic! The Stem is a very heavy hitter in your city, and this is going to rock the political foundation of this country. We have evidence that appears solid but is thin. It ties the Stem to the Bridgeton people. But there is one minor problem.

"And that is," a smiling Bud Henry said.

"We obtained it illegally. Obviously, you don't want to hear the detail."

Bud raised his hands in mock surrender while pushing back from the table. "Who'd have thought it," added the federal agent.

"Our only remaining chance is to follow John's house trasher. If we can tie him to our earlier problems, maybe we can squeeze him. If not, we're done and will have to back off this."

"Do you have any other ideas?" asked Henry.

"Bud, we're convinced he had accomplices and think they blew up Redout's car. And I should include torching the *Red Leather*. What happened to the others is probably out of their reach. My life savings of $158,000 got hit and as of now, I have zero dollars," Jack raised his hand, making a zero with his thumb and index finger.

"Wow!" Replied an amazed Bud Henry.

"John assures me the money was stolen by means of some electronic wizardry but can be recovered. Hope he's right, otherwise I'm in a big jam. Enough of this chatter, what do you have on the man in the picture?"

"Jack, your intruder proved to be one Scott Davis. Davis was a former agent with the Bureau. He's forty-five, single, a highly decorated Viet Nam vet, and is a graduate of Alfred University in Western New York. He was cut loose from the Bureau in seventy-eight; couldn't come up with the why, but at one time he worked in the Miami office. Some of the agents who knew him claim he's a treacherous bastard, capable of anything. It's rumored he was skipping around the edges of the drug business down there, but that's only hearsay.

"You were right about him having a partner. His name is Jason Fuller, and like Davis, this Fuller character is also an ex-bureau agent. He was let go for some questionable activities, but I couldn't come up with anything else other than he's single and about Davis's age," Bud reported.

"We now have the frame of reference we need. Are they affiliated with any organization?"

"They work for an agency called The Economic Preservation

League. There are hundreds of these outfits based in the immediate DC area. Many are for real and represent legitimate special interest groups. Most are very efficient and co-operative with government agencies. However, some are fronts for someone who doesn't want to be found out."

"What's this outfit in business for?" John asked.

"This Preservation League is something I know nothing about. I'm sure they're window dressing for someone who silently wants to further their interests. Sorry, that's all I have."

"Where can we pick Davis and Fuller up?" O'Brennan asked anxiously.

"The League is located at 378 Lanier Street"

"Bud, that isn't much help."

"Do you know the Adams Morgan area?"

"Vaguely I've heard of it, but that's it. Do you John?"

John shook his head. "Don't know a thing about it."

"The Adams Morgan neighborhood at one time was a classy area. It's gone through several phases of change, from a slum to a drug haven. The beautiful people of Washington are now reclaiming the district. The Preservation League purchased their house for a song back in the sixties. Now, it's worth a fortune and going up every day. That's where you're headed."

"How do we get there?" John asked.

"Figured you'd have a problem with that. I scribbled out directions to help you get there. When you arrive, you'll run into a bunch of converging streets. Where you go from there is a mystery to me."

Parked on Lanier Street an hour later, the ex-cops sat waiting.

"You ever get lonely, John?"

"Yeah, all the time."

"Ever do anything about it?"

"Why certainly. A little nosey aren't you, Jack?" Lloyd added with a smile.

"Naw, it's just hard to sit here in a hot car making small talk." O'Brennan usually felt comfortable with the arduous routine of sitting and waiting, but on this day, he felt consumed by it.

"To answer your question, yes, I do have a friend and we've gone out for three years. She teaches at Southside Junior High and is retiring next year."

"You never mentioned her before."

"Why would I do that?"

"I don't know, just talking gibberish I guess. Here we sit sweltering in the heat waiting for two guys to come out of that brick house; and don't even know if they're in there or not. Since my run-in with Jeanette, my head's running a hundred miles an hour. I don't know what's the matter with me. Boy, is it hot! Wish the hell we could get out and walk around," Jack said.

"Don't think another thing about it, because, my boy, we're in business. Here come our pigeons now. Check the picture Bud gave us."

O'Brennan held up the eight by ten. "It's them all right."

The detectives followed Davis and Fuller acrosstown to the *Realto Theater*. "I thought they were headed for Union Station, instead, they're going into that X-rated movie," said an amazed John Lloyd.

"If they're going in, so are we! You ever been to a porno movie before?" Jack asked with a smile.

"No, never have. What in hell's the matter with you?"

"Let's go," Jack directed, "This should be terrific."

"Terrific? What else but with two titles like, *Have You Done Alice* and *Don't Say It With Words*. Jack, I can't wait to see these beauties." He laughed as he opened the car door and headed for a late afternoon of classic cinema.

"John Lloyd, you see something good in everything."

36

After the movie let out, the twosome followed by the team of Lloyd and O'Brennan headed south. Entering the U area in downtown Bridgeton, Davis and Fuller turned left on Niagara Avenue.

"Looks like they're heading toward the bay," O'Brennan observed. Traveling eastward, the lights of Spenser soon came into view on the still and silent night.

"They've turned left on the other side of the restaurant. Wonder what they have in mind?" Lloyd said.

"There's the *Village Squire* Jeanette just bought. It's the one next to the channel. A lane runs back to a bunch of fishing shacks on the cove. I have no idea why they'd go back there, but we'll find out soon enough," replied a puzzled O'Brennan.

"Let's park on the street and walk across to the restaurant. It's closed, so we'll have the place to ourselves. If they come out in the car, we can see their movement from the outside deck area. The lane is the only exit from back there."

"It's really quiet out here. What time is it?" John asked.

"Close to midnight."

"I love being around the water when it's overcast and smells like rain," John said. "There's hardly a ripple on the surface of the channel. It's so peaceful now, I wonder how long it will stay that way?"

Jack thought out loud, "What in the world are they doing back there?"

"I don't know, but we may be blessed with the stroke of luck we need. Maybe they've put themselves in a corner by driving back there."

"John, don't make fun of me when I mention this, but what if," Jack paused, then continued. "We believe they smoked the *Red Leather*. What if they've come back to torch the *Squire*?"

"A week ago, I'd say that was a pipe dream, but not now, you could be right," John said.

"If I'm right, there's one thing you can count on. We're finally positioned to do some good." O'Brennan shifted his large frame, "Are you carrying?"

Lloyd answered, "No, I don't have a gun, do you? Question answered, one asked."

"No, let's hope we don't need one. It's so quiet out here. There isn't a breath of air moving."

"It's hard to believe the temperature at this time of night. I'll bet it's close to ninety. What was that noise?" John asked.

"Sounded like a splash . . . probably a fish," Jack responded with a shrug.

"Well, they must be hungry because I heard another splash. There's another and another. If fish are making that noise, then they're using paddles. Jack, there are many bad people in this world, and here comes two of Satin's buddies right now," John said.

"The bastards are in a rowboat and heading this way," O'Brennan said as sweat started pouring down his face. Moments sped by in a blur as the dark figures in the rowboat edged their way toward the patio area.

"They're bringing the boat over to the deck. Oh boy! We don't have guns but I'll bet they do. How is this going down?" John asked in a whisper. "We can't do a thing until they make a move. What do you have in mind?"

Lloyd's partner thought for a moment, "I don't know, but let me take the lead. One way or the other, I'll be the fall guy on this maneuver."

"Here they come! Brazen bastards wouldn't you say? They've

come for dinner and the restaurant's closed." Even as the danger mounted, Lloyd could find the balmy side of life.

After tying up, Davis and Fuller climbed out of the boat carrying bulky gym bags. They silently crossed the deck to the restaurant. The intruders appeared to be placing small packages next to the outside wall of the restaurant.

"It looks like they're putting down some kind of charges," whispered an excited Lloyd.

"They're leaving us with a full Monty."

Lloyd looked questionably at O'Brennan who shrugged. "Didn't you see the movie?"

"Jack, you are fast approaching dementation."

"There's no such word," Jack whispered.

"There is now."

With the fleeting moment of jocularity having passed, the immediate situation required more serious thought.

"They're going to burn this . . . they're going to blow the joint up. We have to get them now because if we wait, they're gone and so are we," O'Brennan whispered, his voice rising with the tension of the moment.

"More importantly, with all the charges they brought ashore, they'll blow your girlfriend's restaurant into the bay." John swept his hand toward the water.

O'Brennan whispered to his partner, "Get ready to move. When I say go for it; go for it! And be damn quick about it."

"Go for what?" Anxiety crowded John's voice.

"Just go for it." O'Brennan's nervous reply sounded hollow.

From out of the shadows, came O'Brennan's voice, "Davis and Fuller, stop where you are. Put your hands up this moment. If you even think about getting cute, I'll shoot before you know what happened. All right, John, go for it!" Jack's voice bordered on a piercing screech. Lloyd scrambled toward the two figures with hands raised high in the air. "John, frisk them. If they move a little, shoot a lot and we'll ask questions later."

"After my man has relieved you of your cannons, get face down on the deck in a spread-*Eagle* position."

Lloyd withdrew a pistol from each man's inside jacket pocket.

"What did you find?" Jack called out, tension adding a crack in his voice.

"I got two Smith and Wessons." John retreated to O'Brennan who by now had stepped out of the darkness. He passed Jack a gun and glanced at his longtime friend. Jack shook his head while playfully wiping his brow.

John responded by laughing in a giddy, relieved manner. "Kinda' clears the air a little."

"Go to the phone next to the post office and call the Sheriff's substation. It's at the other end of town, so they should be here quickly." John gave an OK sign as he took off in an old-timers jog; his legs feeling their age and the tensions of the night.

Jack directed a verbal assault in the direction of the spread-*Eagle*d arsonists. "You boys have jerked us around down here for the last time. You must think we're country bumpkins with corn growing out of our ears. Well, guess what? That's not the case. Tell you something else, you're not up in the big city where big brother or somebody's big brother can take care of you. You're down here, man, and we're going to squeeze you until it even hurts us."

O'Brennan walked around to face the dark invaders from the Inlet. They looked at him with brooding, icy stares as he shook his head. "Still not talking. Before we get done, you'll talk; as a matter of fact, you'll sing like the biggest flock of birds you've ever seen."

John returned from his errand, "He's coming right over."

"Who's on duty? Jack asked.

"Jimmy Childs."

"That's terrific He's a good man and will do a good job for us. John, I'll say one thing about our newly acquired friends, they wear many hats."

"You're very intelligent to have observed that."

"I hadn't noticed."

"Mr. O'Brennan, why don't you tell our friends," Lloyd waved at the prone figures, "what is in store for them?"

"An excellent thought. Gentlemen, the first thing Mr. Childs will do is put you in the can. What the hell, you have to sleep somewhere tonight, so why not with us?"

Jimmy Childs walked back to the deck scene wearing a big grin. Smartly saluting O'Brennan with two fingers to the eyebrow, he said, "Good morning, gents. Jack, what ya' got for me? John here," Childs waved in his direction, "said you had some bad boys down here."

Childs looked at O'Brennan with a smile. "Ya' know, Father Flanigan out at Boys Town used to say there was no such thing as a bad boy. Jack, did you ever hear such a thing in your life? It's hard to believe such nice looking lads would try something like this; them being ex-agents and all. They were probably out looking for new blood, that's all. Ya' know, this younger generation ain't never going to make it."

"John, show Jimmy where our friends left their calling cards." Once again turning his attention to the spread-*Eagle*d Davis and Fuller, O'Brennan said, "Boys, you've had the meat."

John soon returned with the deputy in tow "You're right, Jack, these rascals were trying to do something bad to us old boys down here in Spencer." Stepping toward the captives, Child's voice seemed to screech. "You bastards were going to burn this place down, now ain't that the pits." The deputy said incredulously.

"Do you have enough?"

"Jack, do I ever. I'll secure this area and get the lab boys over shortly. We'll run these birds in and put them to bed in the hotel. You all know the hotel I'm talking about, don't you, gentlemen?" Childs said as he directed the suspects to stand.

"When can we talk to them?"

"Anytime after nine. I'll have an interrogation room ready and would I like to be a bug on the wall."

Two exhausted detectives discussed their busy day on the return to Bridgeton. "Do you think they'll crack?" Jack asked.

"Yes, I think so. When I was showing Jimmy the charges, I

got thinking about how to approach Davis and Fuller. When you talk to them in the morning, mention federal charges. If anything is going to bother them; it's the thought of a former FBI agent in a federal prison."

"That's a good thought. I'll have to come up with questions that will threaten them, but honestly, I have no idea what they'll be. Guess I'll have to work it out when I get home. Where did you leave your car?"

"It's at your house, been a long day, hasn't it?" Replied an exhausted John Lloyd.

37

Sitting at his kitchen table, Jack tried without success to design questions that would upset and intimidate Davis and Fuller. His mind was boggled by the events of the last twenty-four hours, and to compound matters, he continued to replay his porch disaster with Jeanette.

Here was possibly his last shot at true love and he'd botched it. He really did love this woman. Although he hadn't known her long, her easy ways had grown on him. His mind flipped to the upcoming interrogation he and John would face, but again his efforts proved fruitless.

Again the thoughts of Jeanette returned. Maybe John was right about the counselor and his advise about the guilt complex.

O'Brennan thought at length about how to approach his guilt feelings involving Jeanette. In the past he'd been able to determine the difference between black and white, but that had passed and all he saw was gray. The sound of the starter's gun went off in his head, compelling him to move to Mary's desk. Withdrawing a single sheet of rose colored stationary from a bottom drawer, Jack returned to the kitchen table, and sat with a heavy-hearted weariness. The clock rushed toward morning as he continued to think until he finally began writing a letter to his long departed wife.

My dearest Mary,

I feel so guilty because I have fallen in love with another woman. Her name is Jeanette Purchase. She understands me and loves me.

It is most difficult to travel life's journey with two loving women. The first nurtured me and made me a better man for her love. A concerned person who raised her three daughters into the caring, affectionate young women they are today. And finally, a partner who provided me with more love than I could ever hope to return.

The second . . . Jeanette is also a loving woman who has helped fill some of the extraordinary loneliness I've felt since your departure. Mary, losing you was devastating, and you shall always be with me, but I must get on with my life, and it appears Jeanette may be the one to fill my waning years with some degree of happiness.

This is the most difficult letter I have ever written. As I sit at the oak table we worked so hard to recondition, I feel so close to you. I know you'll understand and bear with me as I go through this turmoil.

Till we meet again, I remain your loving husband,
Jack

Carefully folding the rose colored sheet, Jack placed it in a matching envelope. Slowly walking to the living room, he dismantled Mary's picture that sat on the fireplace mantel. He placed the letter between her picture and the cardboard backing, then returned it to it's customary position. He studied it for several minutes before returning to the kitchen table. Placing his head in folded arms, he began to cry. Sobs racked every inch of this tired old man.

Finally glancing at the clock, he rose and walked to the sink where he washed his face with cold water. Using a dishtowel to dry his face, Jack knew what he had to do.

If you are in charge of your future, you need to have Jeanette in it, he told himself. He dialed Jeanette's number. Two-thirty in the morning, he must be mad.

"Yes," a sleepy Jeanette Purchase answered.

"Jeanette, this is Jack. I wanted to say . . ." she cut him off before he could finish.

"Don't you ever give up? Are you drunk or something?" she slammed the receiver down.

O'Brennan dialed again, Jeanette's harsh chide still ringing in his ears. The moment the connection opened, Jack started before hearing a word. "Don't you hang up on me this time, or I'll come over and burn your god-damned house down." A half breath, or sob could be heard from the other end. "I'll not make excuses for Sands Beach . . . that would be stupid, and goodness knows I've been that. You probably don't want to see me again and that I won't like, but even without you I'll still live with thoughts of you. There is one thing you should know; I love you very much and am going to miss you." Jack hung up; wanting to hear her reply, yet too afraid of what it would bring.

Returning to the table, he again tried focusing on the upcoming interrogation. Twisted, jumbled thoughts tumbled around his head; there was no hope. The ringing front door bell returned him to his senses. Opening the door, Jack stepped back in amazement at the sight in the entrance.

Jeanette stood with hands on hips, feet spread as if she'd spent an hour dressing. In white sneaks, wool athletic socks and tan Bermuda shorts, she looked like a fifties college girl. She wore a blue button-down shirt under a gray sweatshirt with Elon College embossed on the front. With graying hair in disarray; and a face unadorned with make-up, she still presented a picture of beauty.

"You're not going to miss me, Mr. Jack O'Brennan, that's not going to happen. No sir, I'm going to be around for many years and I plan on having you with me while I live them."

They stood looking at each other, as warm morning air swirled gently through the front door. Jeanette quickly moved to Jack, a loving smile on her face. They held each other, fiercely pressing together.

Jack withdrew from her embrace, "Come in, we have to talk."

"No, my darling, there'll be plenty of time for talk later." A knowing smile from Jeanette signaled the end of the night. "I know you'll be busy tomorrow, but with God's speed, I'll be taking a trip to Cape Ann and I'll have you along. There is one last thing, my love. I need you more than Freddie Gill does, so be careful," Jeanette whispered her support and was gone.

Jeanette's departure signaled the end of a very long and grueling day for Jack. Setting the alarm for an early morning wake-up, he settled into a deep and untroubled sleep, never looking back. There would be no problem with the questions he would ask this morning.

38

"Good morning, men," Jack said with a smile, "you got yourselves in a real sling this time around."

"A big time sling, as a matter of fact," John cheerfully added. "You haven't said a word since we picked you up at the *Squire* last night. Do you have anything for us this morning?"

O'Brennan looked over at his colleague. "It appears our friends here," waving at the suspects, "aren't in the mood, not in the spirit of things."

"Jack, I'm outraged by their behavior," responded a still smiling Lloyd.

"Gents, it appears we have a communication problem. I'm talking, John here is talking, but you aren't. This old-timer," again pointing at John, "is a retired Bridgeton detective who's been around the horn and knows how I operate. We'll set up some ground rules and go from there. It's your turn, John."

"Listen closely, gentlemen; we're not going to do the good cop, bad cop routine. Naw, we have other fish to fry and don't want to waste our time. We're going out and get a cup of coffee; would you like one?" No answer came from the ex-feds. "Gracious, Jack, they're not going to answer us one way or another. Well, let's go out and get some for ourselves."

Standing by the coffee table, John offered, "I doubt if they'll ever loosen up. They'll probably go down for the arson charge and that's it. Do you have any thoughts on how you're going to crack them?"

"I do. It came to me this morning while I was getting ready to come down here."

"Just wanted to show you what a good guy I am," Jack said while setting coffee in front of the prisoners. "John and I have a busy agenda scheduled for the day and spending a whole bunch of time with you irregulars isn't one of them. Correct, Mr. Lloyd?"

Lloyd laughed. "Correct, Mr. O'Brennan. By the way, I like that irregulars bit."

"Here's the scenario, boys. That's another nice word. John, I should use it more often. Do you think our friends know what it means?"

"Why certainly they do, they're college men aren't they?" John Lloyd was in seventh heaven as they prepared to interrogate the buttoned-down thugs. Okay, boys, let's get it on. One, we have you, Scott Davis, for breaking and entering. That's for trashing my house." John glanced at O'Brennan. "That's not worth much right now, but it will be. We don't have anything on the *Red Leather* fire, but I'm sure we'll tie you into that one before we're done. It's just a matter of time before we hang that baby on you. It's your turn, Jack." John opened his hand to O'Brennan.

"You know, I stayed up half the night thinking how to persuade you boys to cooperate. I couldn't come up with a blasted thing. This is hard to believe, but I have something now. It came to me while I was taking a shower this morning." O'Brennan again turned to John Lloyd with a silly smile.

"John, aren't you glad I regularly clean this magnificent body of mine? I know this tale is hard to handle, but please stay with me. I dropped the soap, and when I bent over to pick it up the thought hit me like the fog from the Rappohanock sweeps over Bridgeton in the morning. Oh, sweet bird of youth. Once our friends are in the Slam, they'll give a new meaning to drop the soap."

John Lloyd laughed at his buddy.

"The counts we have on you are chicken feed compared to the hush money you'll get for keeping quiet. Let's say you do ten years; what are you, forty-five, forty-six? You'll get out in your early fifties and you're set for life."

Scott Davis looked at his partner with no reaction. O'Brennan caught the exchange but chose not to mention it.

"See, John, I told you I was on target. Watch how they react when I lay this beauty on them. I'm so proud of myself, I can hardly stand it. I would love to jerk you guys around all morning, but my buddy, John mentioned something about going out for a cold glass of beer. So you see, that glass of beer with sweat running down its side is calling me. Getting back to the business at hand, here's the deal. Remember now, this is a onetime Charlie. I talked to the DA and he'll go along with what I have in mind. Understand, he's not thrilled with my plan, but he'll flow with it."

"Jack, cut the crazy talk and get with it. Put it to these guys and we're out of here."

"John, you're acting like a smart-ass, be gentle with them."

"O'Brennan, you're beginning to sound like Benny Hill."

"Boys, we're going to charge you with attempted arson and get the bail set so high, you'll not believe it." O'Brennan laughed, "High enough to keep you in the Slam for a day or so. In the meantime, we'll come up with enough evidence to tie you to Doc Redout's Packard. You probably remember, that's the one you blew up."

"Anything to say? This interrogation is not working out. Nothing!" Jack said, throwing his hands up in mock exasperation.

"Jack, don't blow your cool and get all nervous on me. If you don't believe me, look at their eyes. You've got them by the short hairs and they know it," Lloyd said cheerfully.

"Maybe you're right. Again facing the prisoners, Jack knew Lloyd was on target and now was the time to finish them off. "We're bouncing around a federal rap and are going to push for the max. You know what that means; federal court, prosecution and the federal big house. Virginia's prisons are no honeymoon, but a federal prison, wow! They reduce you down to having no self-worth and believe me, I can't imagine a former FBI agent taking a shower in a federal jug."

It was Lloyd's turn. "That's it boys, you have ten minutes to make a decision. It better be a beauty, or you'll never enjoy your golden years of retirement. Why don't you boys stick around while we're out having a second cup of coffee?"

Ten minutes later, Jack made his final thrust. "Gents, we have bits and pieces with no foreseeable future, but we're going to change all that. Do you remember the old TV show, *Laugh In*? They used to say, 'it's sock it to me time', well guess what, it's show time! Scott, how about you? You know the avenues of our investigation have been greatly reduced with the deaths of Hunter, Olsen and Hansen. Did you ever see a bird fly on one wing? Of course you haven't and neither have I. That's what we're trying to do; and it's a bitch, isn't it, John?"

"It most certainly is," Lloyd replied.

"Do something good for a change, because you've been living off the misfortunes of others too long. Make your own bed, because it's now or never! What's your pleasure?"

The accused abruptly changed their demeanor, and appeared cornered with eyes displaying defeat. They were ready to throw in the towel and Jack O'Brennan knew it.

Gesturing with his hand, Scott Davis came to life, "If Jay and I decide to . . ."

"Stop it this instant, that tired old bird won't fly," screamed O'Brennan. "If, ifs and buts were candy and nuts, we'd all have a merry Christmas. Strike a deal and make it now, or we're out of here. Let's go, John, It appears we lost."

"Whatever you say."

John left the interrogation room with O'Brennan closely following. From the room came the voice of a desperate man.

"Come back, we'll give you what you want," called Davis.

Returning, Jack whispered to his partner, "Go out and get a court recorder."

With the legal stenographer in place, Jack began. "Boys, let's talk. You can trust us to honor our obligations to you as best we can. Give us the whole scoop and no federal sentence. Anything less, and it's bang!"

The Jack O'Brennan and John Lloyd interrogation was about to begin.

O'Brennan: "We know you're responsible for the attempted torching of the *Village Squire* in Spenser." Davis nodded in agreement.

"Is that a yes?"

"Yes," replied Davis.

Lloyd: "How about Billy Olsen?"

"We weren't involved," Davis said.

"Who killed him?"

"Fritz Hansen."

"How do you know?"

"He told us so"

O'Brennan: "How about Sally Ralston Hunter's death?"

"We weren't involved," Fuller said.

"Who killed her?"

"Fritz Hansen."

"How do you know?"

"He told us so."

Lloyd; "The firing of Karl Eichner at the Ritz Plaza?"

"We weren't involved," Davis said.

O'Brennan: "The breaking and entering of John Lloyd's house?"

"Yes, I did that,"

"And your name?"

"Scott Davis."

Lloyd: "The blowing up of Cal Redout's Packard?"

"Yes, we did that, Davis said.

"Did you torch the *Red Leather*?'"

"Yes, we did that."

O'Brennan: "Red Ted's cancelled admission to Bridgeton Law?"

"We weren't involved," Davis said.

"My savings account eliminated?"

"We weren't involved."

Lloyd: "The final question; who sent the troops? Who are you working for?"

"Charles Allen Bretton gave us the orders," Davis said.

"And who is this Charles Allen Bretton character?"

"He's an administrative assistant in DC."

"Who does he work for?"

"He works for Senator Andrew Kenmore."

Beads of sweat appeared to leap from Lloyd's forehead as he searched Jack's face for support. "Do you have any questions, anything to add?"

"Nothing other than Providence will reward them both," Jack said.

John's grave look said it all. The chase was much better than the victory and its afterglow was quickly fading.

"The District Attorney will be in to take additional statements. John, let's get out of here."

Climbing into the Blazer, Jack offered, "I can't believe Kenmore is the Stem. Let's go over to the *Eagle* and talk this over." John Lloyd nodded his willingness to follow, but didn't believe his partner's premise about the Virginia Senator.

Sitting in front of two untouched draughts, the men stared at them as if they'd been sniffing glue. The hot steamy morning caused tiny beads of condensation to form on the outside of the glasses.

John made a happy laugh. "These beers look like the ones you described at the jail. Good grief, it's hot!" He removed a handkerchief from his hip pocket and mopped his brow.

"Al, why don't you air-condition this toilet? Those ceiling fans aren't getting it done. The heat is making this place smell worse than *Gloria's House of Love* in Panama," Jack said.

Sauntering up in front of Lloyd and O'Brennan, Al said with a smile, "John, your friend appears to be a tad agitated this fine morning."

John laughed at the massive bartender, "Not really, he's just going through withdrawal, and can't quite get a handle on it."

"Withdrawal from what?"

"Case withdrawal, that's what. We finished up the Gill case this morning."

Who's the boss?" Simmons asked.

"We can't say, but it will be out tomorrow."

"What difference does it make? Tell him," Jack said.

"It was our Senator Kenmore; how about that?"

"Won't that turns some heads? Looks like old Jack doesn't want to talk this morning. To hell with it!" Al turned and headed toward the other end of the strip.

Turning on his stool to face John, O'Brennan started, "This business with Kenmore isn't appropriate for his station in life. I feel there is something wrong, and there's nothing we can do about it. I hate to be redundant, but this doesn't smell right."

"Well, old buddy, like they say in the commercials, 'it doesn't get any better than this'." John said with concern creeping into his voice.

"John, I think we're wrong, still short."

"The hay's in the barn, leave it or it will drive you crazy."

"If you think we're a hundred per cent right, I'll shut up."

As Lloyd looked at Jack, serious doubts registered in his eyes.

"You don't, do you?"

"Well, I'm not sure." John's voice displayed a softness Jack had never heard before. "Maybe we better take another look at it. Could we be destroying the next President of the United States?"

"That makes me feel better. I thought it was just me! Mr. Simons, please bring us some more beer. Lloyd here and old Jack are going to finish up some loose ends and we need some sustenance."

Simons placed fresh beers in front of his friends.

"Jack, you're some kind of moody. Following you around must be like riding a roller coaster. You've got more highs and lows than the Blue Ridge Mountains."

"Now I know why I like coming down here." Jack's eyes twinkled.

"And why is that?" The burly bartender asked.

"Because you tell it like it is and that's a tough commodity to come by. I know listening to big mouths like me is part of your business, but I've not been pleasant this morning, and I'm sorry about that. Al, an hour ago, I thought I had all the answers to this Gill case, but now I wonder if I have any."

"You have business to talk over, so call me when you need more sustenance." All three laughed.

"Do we have enough to get an indictment? John, let's put what we have on the table. This is our moment of decision making. Are we right about Kenmore?"

"One, we have Kenmore's picture with the others, the problem is, they're all dead. More importantly, we have his unlisted number," Lloyd said nonchalantly. "We have Davis and Fuller who got orders from this Bretton character. All the bad things that came our way originated with Bretton, agreed?"

"Agreed." Jack signaled for refills as he drained his glass. "But that doesn't tie Kenmore to this Bretton." John appeared ready to answer his friend, but was cut off. "Yes, I know Bretton is Kenmore's chief assistant. If Kenmore did become President, and there's much to indicate he could, Bretton would benefit. He would be in line for a major appointment in the new administration," Jack said.

"I think we've pretty well summed it up."

John made circle designs on the bar with his glass, studying his effort.

"Yes, I know that says it all, but what if he was set up?" Jack asked.

"Here we go again." John threw his hands in the air. "How would someone engineer that?"

"I don't know. I just don't know, but it's a possibility," Jack said.

"So is snow in July," John added cutely.

The two detectives silently pondered what they had just discussed. Ten minutes later, Jack made his final plea. "What do we have on Kenmore that's concrete? We have the picture of them at the beach showing their tattoos. What if they had them put on for the hell of it? Half of Bridgeton probably has a tattoo. Did they get tattooed because they were involved in an evil plot? I don't think so. They got them for any number of reasons that mean nothing to us. So he has a tattoo on his arm, who cares! Granted, Kenmore was the dominant personality of the bunch, but what does that make him?"

"I'll concede that about the Stem, but what about the number on the back of the picture?" Lloyd asked.

"John, do you think you're the only one who can pick a lock? Someone could have got in there before us and written down that telephone number."

What about the video of Sally and Kenmore?"

"What about it? Kenmore dated back with Sally for over thirty years. Maybe they were involved in casual sex with nothing more included. Kenmore wouldn't be the first man to sneak around on his wife. What if he liked crawling in bed with her and rolling around in the sheets? You yourself said she was like a machine."

"I don't know. Davis and Fuller are up to their necks in this; that we're certain of."

"You're right, but what did they do? They admitted doing the legwork for this operation, that's all. They pointed a finger at Bretton; no one else."

"I'll give you that." Lloyd thought for a moment, then replied, "What about Bretton? We know he engineered this plot, that we're sure of."

"Suppose he's setting Kenmore up. What if he's been bought off."

"How is that going to happen?" John asked, all the time shaking his head.

"How about giving him a ton of dough . . . let's say twenty, thirty million. How does that sound?"

"Ah, that won't wash and you know it. What you just said is hypothetical and I don't buy hypothetical!" John said strongly.

"Explain this hypothetical. We know Davis and Fuller are going to prison, everybody knows that. What if there is an unknown out there who is Mr. Big. Bretton goes to jail for complicity in a wrongful act, probably for no more than five years. Who's left to take the fall, why Kenmore of course. How does your beer taste now?" Jack asked.

"Speaking of Davis and Fuller; there's something bothering me about them."

O'Brennan turned his hand in a circle signaling John to continue.

"When you asked them: 'What's your pleasure?', they immediately did an about face. I find myself asking why did they roll over at that instant? Experience tells us most suspects have to be pulled and tugged before they break, but not them."

"John, I appreciate what you're saying is true, but maybe they're not as tough as we figured. Other than that, I have no explanation for their behavior."

"We've done all we can do, so let Bud Henry take care of that end of it," John said.

"I guess you're right, but there's still something about this whole mess I don't like."

"Forget it. When do we go up to DC?" John asked.

"I called Bud before we left the jail and he's to arrange a ten o'clock meeting in the morning with this Bretton character. We'll meet him at the Senate Office Building."

"Who's going up?"

"The whole contingent, everyone who was involved in Freddie's case."

"Everyone?" John said.

"Like I said, everyone. I have to see Tremonte, then take care of some other matters. I'll be in touch later."

Over a hot dog and coke in Inlet Park, O'Brennan detailed to Tremonte the eventual demise of Freddie Gill, Sally Ralston Hunter and Fritz Hansen. He described the havoc brought down on the Group as well as the capture of Davis and Fuller. He pointed blame at a Charles Allen Bretton, Kenmore's chief go-for, and finally declared Senator Kenmore the chief architect of this master scheme.

As Jack concluded, thoughts of an innocent Senator Kenmore continued to haunt him.

39

O'Brennan's entourage swept across the Virginia roads leading to Washington like conquering heroes.

Entering the Senate Office Building, Bud Henry greeted Jack O'Brennan in the lobby Bud appeared loose and light-hearted, as Jack introduced him to the Group.

"Bud, you 're acting fit this fine morning."

"I most certainly am, my dear boy. Jack, I handed in my retirement notice yesterday, so I'll be out in a week. That string-pulling son of a bitch I call a boss couldn't wait to get rid of me; now his chance has finally arrived. This Gill thing is my last hurrah, and I'm thrilled he doesn't know about it. He'll die of apoplexy when he finds out," Bud laughed, then continued. "Let's go up to see the man, no use screwing around down here."

Jack led the Group into Mr. Bretton's office. Seated at a drawer less desk sat a Ms. Edith Drummond.

"I'm Jack O'Brennan and this is Agent Bud Henry, and we have a ten o'clock appointment with Mr. Bretton."

"Who are these people?" Her slim sixty-year-old face pinched up like a prune. She sneered, then continued, "They can't go in; they'll have to wait out here!"

Paying no attention to the secretary, Jack looked around the office. Pictures of Andrew Kenmore looked at them from all angles. The handsome face appeared much the same as the earlier picture Jack carried in his jacket. His face appeared weathered but not worn. Kenmore's facial skin much like Jeanette's showed few wrinkles. Too bad to have it all and lose it over dust you put up your nose, Jack thought.

The posters of Kenmore flashed red and blue on a white background. **Andrew Kenmore For President** was printed at the top of the white cardboard. Under his picture, **Treat Your Tomorrow Differently, Vote For The Man Of The Hour** was prominently printed.

Turning to his friends standing by the outer door, Jack smiled, "Hey gang, you better grab one of those posters because they're going to be a collectors item in the not too distant future."

"What is the meaning of this? Who do you think you're talking to?" The secretary stood, trying to portray the image of a tough-talking public servant.

Jack picked up her nameplate from the desk, briefly looked at it, then dramatically returned it. "Ms. Drummond, I'm talking to a lady out of work. When I get done with you, you won't be able to get a job as an adjunct-secretary for a garbage collector. Now about the meaning of this, there's a boogie man loose in there," Jack pushed his head at the inside office, "and your Mr. Bretton is it."

He waved for his awed friends to follow, then opened the inner office door and walked to the desk of an infuriated administrative assistant.

Bretton dispensed with the desultory handshake and instead yelled out, "Ms. Drummond, call security! Who are these people? How dare you?"

"You don't know the faces, but I'm certain you'll know the names." Jack proceeded to introduce each member of followers, stating each misfortune they had suffered. Bretton's wary look spoke for itself. He had detected danger and immediately withdrew into a protective shell.

Jack turned on his heals, "Red, close that door!" His instruction sounded more like a command than a request. In preparing for this confrontation, he had pictured Charles Allen Bretton as a mousy little man with glasses, but instead found Kenmore's chief assistant to be a massive man who formerly played defensive end with the Forty-Niners. His five-year career ended with a knee injury that removed him from the NFL playing field and sent him to the political arena and this confrontation with Mr. Jack O'Brennan.

"Mr. Bretton, if we need security, it won't be to usher us out of the building. You're not tough enough to handle what I have in store for you."

"You're right about security. I may do it myself and that includes the ladies." Bretton stood up, displaying his massive six-six frame, massive by comparison to O'Brennan's mere six-three tired body. He waved toward the Group with a menacing gesture. With the exception of Bud Henry and John Lloyd, the Group looked with terror at this giant of a man and appeared to close ranks.

"John, do you understand why he's so pissed at us?" Lloyd smiled and extended his hands out in a I don't know why gesture.

O'Brennan turned his complete attention to the big man in front of him. "Before you do that, Mr. Bretton, you should be advised that I talked to Davis and Fuller yesterday morning, who by the way are currently residing in the Lancaster County Jail."

Bretton abruptly sat down, a major crack showing in his brusque demeanor. His detractor turned to again address Lloyd. "John, the eyes never lie do they? He knows that we know."

"Jack, I don't know whether he'll thank the messenger or not after he hears what they told us." John said smugly.

"Mr. Bretton, Davis and Fuller let the cat out of the bag. So you see, everybody in the world knows about the conspiracy, or soon will. The wheels of justice are quickly moving in your direction."

Bretton's tough appearance vanished as O'Brennan continued to speak. "We want your boss in here right now, so be quick about it."

Bretton stammered, "I can't. Not now . . . he's in Lynchburg addressing the state American Legion Convention, and won't be back until late this afternoon."

"No matter, Mr. Bud Henry here, is with the FBI and he'll be handling the first phase of this wrap up." O'Brennan turned to the Group as Bud stepped forward, "Now, my friends, let's get on about our business."

An hour later, the Group stood in front of the Senate building, realizing for the first time that the Freddie Gill case was indeed finished. The Group would be returning to lives dramatically altered by unforgettable events of the Freddie Gill case.

Jack looked first at Danny, then Bud, "One last question; when will you move on Kenmore?"

"We'll pick him up at Dulles and from there, it's routine. Jack, you laid out everything beautifully. The background of your investigation, the statements of Davis and Fuller started the noose, Bretton finished it," Bud said.

"How about you, Danny, what do you have going?"

"We have a special edition out at eleven-thirty, then we'll follow with one in the late afternoon. That second one will cover Bretton's admission." Tremonte looked at his watch. "The first one should be out anytime."

"Eleven-thirty? Come on Cal, Jeanette and I have to catch a twelve-thirty flight out of National; let's get crackin'."

Looking up as she pressed against Jack, Jeanette's eyes sparkled as she said, "Our moment of truth is at hand."

"Jeanette, I have to make a call. I'm going to tell those slims from Bell Hills off."

"We don't have much time, O'Brennan.

"Jeanette, this call can't wait!" His tone frightened her because she'd never seen him or heard him in such an agitated state. His performance in Bretton's office was nothing short of barbaric, and doubts clouded her thoughts as she watched Jack talking on the phone. Was this man, the gentle one she had grown to love, or a savage masquerading as an honorable human being? As he talked, his animated gestures served to further frighten her.

"Mr. Cousins, this is Jack O'Brennan over in Bridgeton. I've returned your check in the mail; figured you yellow-bastards needed it more than yours truly. You and your buddies should sit down and take stock of what you're all about. When you figure it out, you may not like what you see. By the way, the guy you so playfully sought when you were playing this little game of yours is . . . ah, the hell with it. You'll hear about it soon enough. Now, if you'll excuse me, I'm taking my girlfriend on a vacation. By doing that small gesture, I'll be rid of slim like you and your Bell Hills gang."

O'Brennan's broad smile told Jeanette her fears were unwarranted. Looking down, he placed his arms around her and said, "Come on, pretty lady, we have an appointment on the rockbound coast of Cape Ann."

40

Jack talked about the Gill case during much of the eighty-minute flight to Boston; revealing his fears and concerns about the last several weeks. As he talked, the tensions flowed from him, uncovering the gentle man Jeanette first met with Charlie Winder.

The couple appeared very much in love as they departed Flight 546 at the airport. The next forty-five minutes were spent escaping the maze of confusion known as Logan.

Exiting the airport complex, Jack turned right and proceeded north on Route 1A, the coastline highway. There's nothing like my Chevy, but this is fun to drive, he thought as he sent the red LeBaron rental wizzing toward Salem and Marblehead. Each passing mile brought Jack O'Brennan closer to a sexuality that intimidated him.

His thoughts continually returned a man penciled in for the presidency, Andrew Kenmore. Suppose by some twist of fate, he had erred. What if he had targeted the wrong man? Those thoughts persisted as he drove toward Cape Ann.

Fiddling with the radio, Jack found a station that played 'The Music Of Your Life'. Perry Como's *Magic Moments* drifted through the wind-blown convertible as he looked over at Jeanette. She returned his glance with a brilliant smile and seductively placed her hand on his leg. These are the magic moments in a magic time for me, but how in hell am I going to handle someone with such amorous thoughts, he asked himself.

The couple drove through Rockport on their way to the Sand Castle Inn, advertised as an old inn with New England hospitality.

Walking through the old-fashioned lobby, Jack was dismayed to discover the lack of an elevator. They had to walk to the third floor and Jeanette had brought enough luggage for a month's stay. Climbing the stairs, Jack staggered under the load of suitcases.

"Why did you bring so much?"

"You never know what the weather will be like."

Jeanette smiled as she opened the door to the third floor room overlooking Sandy Bay.

After unpacking, the lovers walked out to the sun porch. The gods seemed to be shining on them as they looked down on the rock-covered shoreline. The late afternoon tide crashed and thundered against boulders of every size and shape imaginable. The rolling surf's continued beating on the ragged coast of Cape Ann provided a constant reminder of the unbridled power of the sea. The air seemed filled with the haunting cries of circling sea gulls as the two stood with arms holding each other.

"A gull is a gull, but these Yankee ones are different than their Sands Beach cousins."

"How so?" Jeanette asked.

"They seem more driven, more determined in their frantic search for food. Jeanette, that shoreline is a gift from the deep, just as is our gentle Sands Beach. The problem I have with nature is that on a moment's notice, on a tiny whim, it can snatch its beauty away from us. In most cases, it reworks its grand qualities into something grotesque and ugly." He could feel his attempt at putting off the inevitable slipping away with his talk about the shore. "I think it happens more in Virginia than here in New England. Our beach is so frail and vulnerable, while this one is so formidable and unapproachable." O'Brennan realized this delaying tactic was running out of steam.

The crashing water created tiny fragments of mist that drifted into the air like the fine spray from a shower. Mixed with the golden haze of a late Rockport afternoon, the scene and mood befitted a Winslow Homer seascape. The aroma of salt and dead fish only added to this majestic setting.

A gentle tugging at his waist pulled Jack back from his thoughts of the sea. "It's time, Jack" She radiated a brightness he'd never seen before, "I'm going in and change."

Jack stood looking at the stately coastline for sometime. Finally, he turned with a sigh and walked through the French doors to the bedroom. After stripping down to his shorts, he waited for Jeanette. The seconds seemed like minutes, the minutes dragged like hours before she swept from the bathroom wearing a different outfit.

Jeanette had changed into a red wrap-around skirt, a black three-quarter sleeve blouse and black high heels. She walked to the doorway and gazed at the rocky shore. Turning, she spoke to Jack in a low teasing voice, "Well, O'Brennan, what do you have in mind?" Her smile was dazzling as she reached to loosen her red skirt. The skirt dropped to the floor as she nimbly stepped away; leaving the discarded garment in a rumpled state.

"I guess you're running this show," Jack said as he gazed at Jeanette, now dressed in black. The strip tease continued while she dropped her half-slip to the floor. Jack gulped as she looked at him. Her long legs encased in black stockings, secured at the tops by ribbons of garter leading under black tap pants gave a "Playboy" appearance.

She did an abrupt about face with her back now exposed to Jack. Facing the water, she unbuttoned her blouse and tossed it to the floor. Over her shoulder, she gave O'Brennan a provocative smile and softly said, "You'll remember this evening for the rest of your life." She now turned to face the wall, Jack on her right, the Atlantic on her left. "Don't you have anything to say, my love?"

Jack replied, "What the hell, hop into bed and we'll get this show on the road."

Jeanette emitted a small giggle as she reached down to her black lace panties. With her thumbs she stretched the elastic which allowed them to slide down shapely stockinged legs. Turning her head to look at Jack, she replied, "All in good time, my honey," her smile more radiant than ever.

"Jeanette, you're driving me crazy," groaned an aroused and half-crazed Jack O'Brennan.

The lady in black reached around and released her bra, which in turn dropped to the floor with the other discarded garments. She then turned to face Jack with feet spread apart. It appeared she wasn't wearing enough to flag down a train.

Jack looked at a still standing Jeanette Purchase. Her large proud breasts a tribute to a well-preserved middle aged woman. As she started toward the bed, Jack thought, the only thing she has on is black stockings, a garter belt and a big smile. As Jeanette turned to get in bed, Jack realized true horror for the first time. Jeanette was wearing something else, a green tattooed stem on her left shoulder.

Confused thoughts crashed through his brain similar to a lightning strike racing across a darkened summer sky. Here was the woman he loved wearing a green tattoo. There are two Stems, but he knew that conclusion was impossible. Did she have her own restaurant burned down, and more importantly, did she set Kenmore up? I may have destroyed an innocent man as well as myself, he thought.

Jeanette had heard O'Brennan say many times, 'Watch their eyes, the eyes never lie and tell the whole story'. His eyes told the story of a man confused and stunned by what had just happened.

Finally, O'Brennan blurted out, "You're the Stem. We're going to send the wrong person to jail! And to make matters worse, what is going to happen to us?"

Her euphoria passed and she was now faced with the reality of the damage she had done with her little prank. Without saying a word, Jeanette walked to the bathroom and grabbed a wet face cloth.

Returning to the foot of the bed, she wiped the fake tattoo off and said, "No, Jack O'Brennan, I'm not the stem. And no, Jack O'Brennan, you did not send the wrong man to jail. And no, Jack O'Brennan, nothing is going to happen to us that we can't deal with." With that she climbed in bed with an astonished Jack O'Brennan.

* * *